SEP   2012

Volume Three

SIERRA JENSEN COLLECTION

Open Your Heart

Time Will Tell

Now Picture This

ROBIN JONES GUNN

Multnomah Books

THE SIERRA JENSEN COLLECTION, VOLUME 3
published by Multnomah Books

© 2006 by Robin's Ink, LLC
International Standard Book Number: 978-1-59052-590-6

Cover photo by Steve Gardner, www.shootpw.com

Compilation of:
Open Your Heart
© 1997 by Robin's Ink, LLC
Time Will Tell
© 1998 by Robin's Ink, LLC
Now Picture This
© 1998 by Robin's Ink, LLC

Unless otherwise indicated, Scripture quotations are from:
The Holy Bible, New International Version (NIV)
© 1973, 1984 by International Bible Society,
used by permission of Zondervan Publishing House
The Holy Bible, New King James Version (NKJV)
© 1984 by Thomas Nelson, Inc.
New American Standard Bible®(NASB) © 1960, 1977, 1995
by the Lockman Foundation. Used by permission.

Published in the United States by WaterBrook Multnomah, an imprint
of the Crown Publishing Group, a division of Random House Inc., New York.

MULTNOMAH and its mountain colophon are registered trademarks of Random House Inc.

Printed in the United States of America

For information:
MULTNOMAH BOOKS
12265 ORACLE BOULEVARD, SUITE 200 · COLORADO SPRINGS, CO 80921ʿ

Library of Congress Cataloging-in-Publication Data
Gunn, Robin Jones, 1955-
  The Sierra Jensen Collection Volume 3 / Robin Jones Gunn.
    v. cm.
  Previously published as separate works.
  Contents: Open Your Heart — Time Will Tell Now Picture This.
  ISBN 1-59052-590-6 [1. Interpersonal relations—Fiction. 2. Conduct of life—
Fiction. 3. Christian life—Fiction.] I. Title.
  PZ7.G972Sie 2006
  [Fic]—dc22

                    2006008136

11—10 9 8 7 6

TEEN NOVELS BY ROBIN JONES GUNN

THE SIERRA JENSEN SERIES

Volume 1
Book 1: *Only You, Sierra*
Book 2: *In Your Dreams*
Book 3: *Don't You Wish*

Volume 2
Book 4: *Close Your Eyes*
Book 5: *Without a Doubt*
Book 6: *With This Ring*

Volume 3
Book 7: *Open Your Heart*
Book 8: *Time Will Tell*
Book 9: *Now Picture This*

Volume 4
Book 10: *Hold On Tight*
Book 11: *Closer Than Ever*
Book 12: *Take My Hand*

THE CHRISTY MILLER SERIES

Book Seven

OPEN YOUR
HEART

one

SIERRA'S HEART POUNDED. Her pulse hammered in her ears. Gripping the armrests of her seat, she tried to scream, but no sound emerged.

We're going to crash! This airplane is about to nose-dive into the freezing Atlantic Ocean! We're doomed!

Instead of Sierra's whole life passing before her eyes, only the events of the past few days flashed through her mind. She saw herself at Doug and Tracy's wedding in Southern California. Her sister, Tawni, was catching the bouquet. Her good friend Christy was standing beside Aunt Marti, and all of a sudden they were inviting Sierra to go with the two of them to Switzerland.

Then Sierra saw herself in California, prompting her parents over the phone as they searched her messy room in Portland to find her passport. "Try looking on my desk," she urged them. "Or maybe it's in the bottom dresser drawer."

These suggestions drifted from Sierra as she watched herself boarding a plane early that morning with her passport in hand.

7

Now, here she was, spiraling into the icy blue. Sierra screamed inside her mind.

From far away, a familiar voice called, "Sierra, are you okay?"

She felt a soft touch on her right arm. The voice seemed to come closer. Sierra's eyes fluttered open, and she gasped for breath.

"We're getting ready to land," Christy said from the seat beside Sierra. "Are you okay? You were talking in your sleep."

Sierra blinked at Christy and took in her surroundings. Looking out the window, she could see the bright blue sky. The plane was confident and steady. In the seats beside Sierra, Christy and Marti were calmly preparing for the landing.

"That was an awful nightmare!" Sierra moistened her lips and caught her breath. "I thought we were going to crash." She tried to act as if the idea was funny, but the terror of the dream still loomed over her. The details were too close to reality.

Sierra was actually on a plane headed for Germany. From there, she, Christy, and Marti would take a train into Switzerland. It really had been only a few frenzied days since Sierra had attended Doug and Tracy's wedding in Newport Beach. After the wedding, Sierra had been invited to travel with Christy and Marti at the last minute. Only one part of Sierra's dream wasn't true—the plane showed no signs of spiraling into the Atlantic.

"Do you want a washcloth?" Christy asked. "I took one for you when they came by a little earlier. It's probably cold now."

Sierra opened the cooled cloth and held it over her face, breathing in the faint citrus fragrance. Lifting her long, curly blond hair, she held the washcloth against the back of her neck and looked down at her loose jeans. The mustard stain above her right knee was still there in the shape of an ivy leaf, left over from a deli sandwich she had eaten somewhere above Nova Scotia. When Sierra had tried to open a mustard packet with her teeth, a flying blob had landed on her leg. She rubbed at the stain with the washcloth. It didn't help. The spot would probably be with her for the rest of the trip.

Because Sierra, Christy, and Aunt Marti had left for Europe from Marti's house in Southern California, Sierra hadn't gone home to Portland to pack the right kind of clothes for Switzerland in August. She also hadn't been able to help her frantic parents when they couldn't find her passport. Fortunately, her brother Gavin had located it behind the dresser, and Mr. and Mrs. Jensen had sent it to Sierra through an overnight delivery service. Now Sierra wished she would have had them send a few more things, like a second pair of jeans.

All the planning happened so fast. Sierra's parents had been supportive when she called them and explained the invitation to join Christy and Aunt Marti. The Jensens were flexible, and since Sierra was the fourth of six children, they tended to be fairly relaxed about her adventures. But this time, even Sierra wasn't sure what she had gotten herself into.

Christy pulled her shoulder-length nutmeg hair up in a ponytail holder and crossed her long, slender legs. Sierra noticed that Christy also looked a little uneasy. Maybe she was stiff from sitting on the plane for twelve hours. Or maybe Aunt Marti was getting under Christy's skin the way Marti had already irritated Sierra.

"What time will it be when we land?" Sierra asked, adjusting her seat belt.

"Eight twenty-seven," answered Marti. "Remember, it's morning here. We'll only have an hour to make it through customs, retrieve our luggage, and catch our train to Basel. We need to be quick about this."

Marti meant business—all the time. Sierra wasn't exactly fond of this petite, polished, and pushy woman. Marti had helped Sierra's sister, Tawni, find a modeling job in Southern California, which made Sierra's parents feel more comfortable about Sierra's accepting this last-minute ticket to Europe. From anyone else, such an extravagance might be unusual, but with Aunt Marti, money was only a method to accomplish her goals. And right now, it was Marti's goal to get Christy to Switzerland so she could check out a college where she had been offered a scholarship.

"Here," Marti said, opening her leather purse and handing Sierra and Christy a pack of gum. "Start to clear your ears now. We're beginning to descend."

"I don't need a whole pack," Sierra said. "I only want half a stick."

Irritation showed on Marti's perfectly made-up face. Not a hair was out of place, and her knit pantsuit didn't show one wrinkle. How did she manage to look so good after this long flight?

Christy's clear blue-green eyes shot a message to Sierra to take the gum and hush up about it.

"Maybe I'll keep the rest for later," Sierra added quickly. "Thanks."

She stuck half a stick of the wintergreen-flavored gum into her mouth and pondered the mystery of why she had been invited on this trip. All Sierra could explain to her parents was that Marti had three ticket vouchers. The third was supposed to be for Christy's boyfriend, Todd, but he couldn't take the time off work to come. Christy's best friend, Katie, had broken her foot only a few days before. Marti hadn't even mentioned bringing her husband, Bob, which Sierra thought was strange. And Christy said her mom turned down the opportunity because she didn't know how she would handle such a long flight.

That left Sierra. She didn't mind being last choice, though. She was excited about the chance to do some more traveling.

"Do you feel rested at all?" Christy asked.

"A little. How about you?"

"I slept for about two hours, I think. Remember how hard it was to get over jet lag when we went to England last January?"

"I remember," Sierra said. "They say it's better if you stay awake the whole first day so you'll be able to sleep that night."

"That's exactly what we're going to do," Marti said, her dark eyes checking Sierra's and Christy's seat belts to make sure they were fastened. "We'll take a train directly from the airport to Basel. After we check into the hotel, I've made an appointment for us to meet with the director of the school at two-thirty this afternoon." She chewed her piece of gum demurely.

"That doesn't give us much time," Christy said. "I mean, for any goof-ups."

Marti gave her a long, raised-eyebrow stare. "We aren't planning on having any 'goof-ups.' And do chew your gum with your lips together, dear."

"I'm just saying I've done a little bit of train travel in Europe before and—"

"—and I haven't?" Marti questioned.

"I didn't hear lunch mentioned in the schedule," Sierra jumped in, hoping to lighten the tone. "When do we eat?"

"We'll eat on the train," Marti said firmly. "At least we're in first class this time."

Sierra knew Marti was still miffed that their airplane seats hadn't been first class as she had expected. Marti had angrily confronted the clerk at the check-in desk, but the best the airline could do was guarantee Marti first-class seats on the way home.

"It looks as if it's going to be a nice, clear day," Christy said, nodding at the buildings, the highways, and fields rapidly becoming visible out their window. "It all seems so charming from up here. Really clean and quaint."

"You don't think it's really like that?" Sierra asked.

She noticed the runway coming into view.

"Well, I've never seen Germany or Switzerland. But some parts of France and Spain weren't exactly postcard set-tings."

Just as Christy finished her sentence, the plane's tires bumped gently onto the runway, and the giant aircraft slowed.

Sierra gripped her armrests and clenched her teeth, waiting for the plane to stop. *We didn't crash,* she thought. *We're here! It was only a dumb nightmare I probably got from rushing around to get ready for the trip. Or maybe from the pickles on that deli sandwich.*

"Ready? Don't forget your backpacks," Marti urged.

Sierra and Christy exchanged glances as they undid their seat belts and reached for their packs under the seats in front of them. Sierra couldn't help but wonder if Christy was having the same thought she was: A week with Marti might be harder than they realized.

two

TO MARTI'S DELIGHT, the trip through customs and the baggage claim went off without a hitch. The women boarded the train, found their reserved spots in a first-class compartment, and flopped into the high-backed seats with sighs of relief.

"I think we set a new traveling record," Christy said.

Marti looked pleased. "This proves my point, ladies. As long as we stay together and stay organized, we can stay on schedule."

"I'm starving," Sierra said, sliding her pack onto the overhead shelf. "Anyone else ready to head to the dining car with me?"

"They come to us here in first class," Marti said, settling back into the seat and glancing out the window as the train began to pull out of the station.

Sierra looked at Christy and back at Marti. "Would you mind if I went ahead and got something in the dining car or at the snack bar? I'm seriously starving." The truth was Sierra's stomach had turned into a big, churning bubble.

She wasn't sure if it was the flight or the nerve-wracking nightmare, but she knew a glass of milk would help.

"Oh, go ahead," Marti said. "Both of you. Just stay together and don't talk to strangers. Here's some money."

"Would you like us to bring anything back for you?" Christy asked.

"No, I'll wait. Thank you."

Sliding open the compartment door, Sierra stepped into the narrow hallway with Christy right behind her. They made their way single file toward the dining car. As the train picked up speed, it swayed gently from side to side. They opened the door into the next car and continued their journey until they reached the dining section. Sierra entered first and slid into the upholstered bench seat of the first open table she saw. A white cloth covered the table, and a short vase by the window held a yellow rosebud, which seemed to nod its head at them in greeting.

Christy sat across from Sierra. "How are you doing?" she asked, leaning closer.

"My stomach is a mess," Sierra admitted. "I think I'll be fine once I eat something, though. How are you doing?"

"Pretty good. Has my aunt driven you completely crazy yet?"

"Not yet." Sierra looked above Christy's head as a tall man in a gray sweatshirt approached them. At first, Sierra thought he might be the waiter, but then she realized he was dressed too casually.

To her surprise, he stopped at their table and with a polite nod asked, "*Sprechen Sie Deutsch*?"

Christy shook her head. "We're Americans," she answered.

"Ah!" he said, his gaze on Sierra. "Of course you are. Americans. Very nice."

His accent was charming, his expression gentle. All of a sudden, Sierra felt she really *was* on the other side of the world.

"I think perhaps I have left a parcel on your seat."

Sierra looked down, and there, next to the window, was a small package wrapped with brown paper and tied with string.

"Here it is," she said, handing it to him.

The man touched his heart with his hand. "Thank God. It is my gift for my friends. I am on holiday. And you?"

Christy and Sierra looked at each other. Neither spoke up right away.

"Oh, I am sorry," he said, reading their expressions. "I have interrupted something. I can leave if you would like."

"That's okay," Sierra heard herself say. "We just arrived this morning, and we're not quite adjusted to the time and everything yet." She felt Christy give her a little kick under the table.

The young man looked harmless enough, in Sierra's opinion. His face was long with high cheekbones and a narrow chin. He wore his dark hair smoothed straight back except for a resistant strand that hung like a black crescent moon over his right eye. His eyes were dark but clear and alive—full of intrigue.

"I am called Alexander," he said, extending his hand to Sierra.

She placed her small hand in his and received his firm, decisive shake.

"My name is Sierra."

"Sa-har-a?" he repeated. "Like the desert?"

"No, Sierra. Like the mountains in California."

"You are named for mountains in California?" Alexander asked.

"Sort of. I used to live in the mountains. Now I live in the city—in Portland. That's in Oregon. Do you know where that is?"

"Of course, yes. And you?" he asked, turning to Christy.

Christy hesitated for a moment. "I'm Christy."

"Christy," he repeated. The "r" rolled off his tongue beautifully. "You are also from rainy Portland?" Alexander asked.

"You've definitely heard about Portland," Sierra said.

She smiled at Alexander and then at Christy, hoping her friend would lighten up. But Christy pursed her lips together and looked down at her hands. Sierra wondered if Christy was remembering Aunt Marti's warning about not talking to strangers. But they were in Europe. People were friendly like this on the trains. What could happen to the two of them? Alexander seemed harmless enough to Sierra. Harmless and intriguing.

"Actually, I live in California," Christy said after an uncomfortable pause.

The waiter stepped up to their table and asked in German what they would like.

"Allow me," Alexander said. He spoke in a deep, rumbling tone, first to the waiter, then to Sierra and Christy. "Did you wish to order some breakfast?" Alex asked them.

"We just wanted a sandwich or something," Sierra said. "And some milk."

Alex spoke again to the waiter and then, nodding his head, said, *"Danke."*

Sierra moved closer to the window, making room for Alex to sit down. "Would you like to join us?"

"If this would be all right with both, then yes." Alex sat down next to Sierra.

She noticed his gray sweatshirt was made from a heavy woven fabric. It didn't look like the thick cotton knits available in the States.

"Are you from around here?" Sierra asked, deciding that she might as well be the one to ask questions.

"I am on holiday to see friends in Basel. This is where my mother is from. I have many relatives here. My father is from Russia. I have been seven years living in Moscow. I lived in Basel before that time." Alexander leaned back and looked at Sierra with his gentle smile. "If you live in two different states, how did you then come to be friends?"

"We met in England last January on a…" Sierra thought a moment before answering. "We're Christians," she blurted out. "We were on a missions trip."

A warm smile spread across Alexander's strong face. A friendly chuckle emerged from his lips. "You will not believe," Alexander said, laughing. "I am also Christian. Four years now."

Sierra felt relieved and delighted at the same time. She and Christy both laughed in camaraderie with Alexander.

"We would call this a God-thing, Alexander," Christy said.

"Yes! Please. Call me Alex. Yes, this is good. You being Christian makes for easier conversation, no?"

"Yes," Sierra agreed. She was glad to see that Christy had

relaxed and that they didn't have to feel uneasy about Alex. Sierra liked the feeling that had come over the three of them. In the past she had discovered that when she was away from home and out of her familiar routine, she learned to trust God more. She had seen Him provide for and protect her many times in situations in which she was out of her element. Now God had provided another Christian for her and Christy to share their first meal with in Germany.

The server stood at their table, swaying slightly with the train's rhythm. He carefully placed before them a basket of hard, crusted rolls, a plate of thinly sliced ham and cheese, and a bowl of individually wrapped butters and jellies. They each received a small silver pot of coffee, and a pitcher of milk was placed before Sierra.

"This is what you ordered?" she asked.

"Yes." Alex looked concerned. "Is it not what you wanted? Did you not say milk for your coffee?"

"This is fine," Christy said quickly.

"It's fine. Really," Sierra said. She wondered if it would be tacky to pour the milk directly into her coffee cup and drink it all.

"I must tell you something," Alex said, pouring his coffee and looking long at Sierra. "There is a beautiful innocence about you. About both of you. It is as if I am gazing on the first tulips of spring."

Then, because she couldn't help it, Sierra burst out laughing. She wondered if her forehead had an invisible sign emblazoned on it that said "Sweet sixteen and never been kissed."

"Did I say something not correct?" Alex looked at Christy.

"It was sweet of you to say that. I guess we just didn't expect it," Christy responded.

Sierra checked herself. "Are you always this intense with people you've just met?"

"Yes," Alex said, looking serious.

Sierra swallowed her laughter. "I bet you are. You'll have to excuse me for laughing. I'm not used to guys like you."

"And I am not used to girls like you. This is a good compliment."

Sierra took a sip of her coffee. It was one part coffee and ten parts milk.

"You two must have boyfriends who wait in long lines for you. Do they do this—make long lines in front of your houses?"

It was all Sierra could do not to spew her coffee mixture when Alex said that. She quickly swallowed the murky, luke-warm beverage and said, "Christy has found her true love. I'm still interviewing all the guys in my long line."

Alex sat up a little straighter and tilted his chin. He flipped back the lock of dark hair that hung over his eye. "Then I should like to get in line. I am ready for interview. First question, please."

Sierra had never felt so charmed. She put her hand over her mouth to keep from laughing. "Okay. Here's your first question." She picked up one of the tiny containers next to the jelly. "What is this?"

"Oh, how do you call it? Ah...I do not know this in English."

Sierra shook her head and, with a "tsk, tsk," said, "I'm sorry. You'll have to go to the back of the line."

Alex laughed and then said, "You must try it. You will know it. Take some on the bread."

Both Sierra and Christy tried some.

"It's kind of like cream cheese," Christy said.

"Cream cheese," Alex repeated. "Yes, cream cheese. Now do I get to ask you a question?"

Sierra licked the last dab of the sweet cream cheese from her lip. "Sure. Ask me a question."

"How do you make your hair so?"

"So...what?" Sierra asked.

"I have never seen hair so...so beautiful."

Sierra shook her head again. This time she looked at Christy and said, "Some guys will say anything to get to the front of the line."

three

"MARTI?" Sierra slid open the door to their train compartment, and tall Alex ducked to enter with Sierra and Christy. "Marti, this is Alex."

"I am pleased to meet you," Alex said, extending a hand to Marti.

She ignored him. "Where did you meet this young man?" Marti asked the girls.

"In the dining car," Sierra said innocently. "We had breakfast together."

Marti looked shocked. Alex withdrew his hand.

"I do not mean to interrupt here. I will go. It was my pleasure to meet you, See-hair-a." He reached for her hand, but instead of shaking it, he held it warmly.

"And to meet you, Christy." Alex kept hold of Sierra's hand and nodded at Christy. "Perhaps we will meet again soon."

"It isn't likely," Marti said coolly.

Alex smiled. He slowly released Sierra's hand, gave a pleasant nod to all of them, and left.

"You didn't have to scare him off," Sierra said, lowering herself onto the seat across from Marti. Her right hand still felt the warmth of Alex's touch.

Marti's dark eyes blazed as she looked incredulously at Sierra. "Excuse me? I tell you and Christy not to talk to strangers, and you come back with some scruffy German boy and expect me to be delighted with your behavior?"

"He's not German. He's Russian," Sierra said under her breath.

"Russian!" Marti looked shocked. "What in the world are you doing speaking with a Russian?"

"Aunt Marti," Christy said calmly, "I know it seems as though we went against your wishes, but we didn't. We just happened to meet Alex in the dining car. He left his package on the seat."

"That was convenient," Marti said.

"No, it wasn't like that. He's a very nice person. He's a Christian. We felt totally comfortable around him. You would like him if you gave him a chance. Nothing was against your instructions, really," Christy responded.

"I told you not to speak to strangers. You deliberately went against my instructions. What kind of a trip will this be if you two don't follow my wishes?"

Sierra bit her lip to keep from saying anything.

Christy sat on the upholstered bench seat next to Sierra. "Look, Aunt Marti, we both appreciate your taking us on this trip, but the fact is, I'm nineteen years old, and I've traveled halfway across Europe by myself on a train. I think you know you can trust me. This whole trip is going to be really frustrating for all of us unless you treat Sierra and me like responsible adults."

"I'll treat you like adults when you begin to act like adults. Starting up conversations with Russians is not the way to prove you're responsible."

"He's only half Russian," Christy stated. "His mother is Swiss, and he grew up in Basel."

"And that's supposed to make everything all right?" Marti said. "I don't want you two consorting with strangers. Is that clear?"

Christy and Sierra looked at each other and then nodded.

"Yes," Christy said. "We'll go by your rules."

Marti leaned back, let out a long huff, and folded her arms across her chest. Sierra looked over and noticed Christy had closed her eyes. It seemed to be the only way to block out Marti's railings. Sierra followed Christy's lead and did the same.

Alexander...Why did Marti have to scare him off? I want to see him again. There's something special about him. I'm sure we'll see him when we get off the train. He's going to Basel, too. And we told him where we were staying. He'll come find me. I know he will. Sierra smiled to herself.

"When is that cart coming by?" Marti asked. "I'm awfully hungry. The service in these countries is nothing like it is at home. It's disgraceful, really."

"We can get you something," Christy offered.

"Don't think I don't know what you're trying to do, Christina. No, you may not sneak out to meet your foreign friend. Consider yourself grounded to this compartment. Both of you."

Sierra couldn't imagine how humiliated Christy probably felt. It was bad enough to be grounded in the first place, but even worse in front of Sierra—especially when Christy was only trying to be nice.

The train began to slow. Sierra gazed out the window as they pulled into a station, but she didn't catch the name of the town on a sign they rolled past. Several rows of track were laid on either side of the covered station, and dozens of travelers hurried across the landings. Large billboards advertised soft drink, chocolates, and cigarettes—all in German, of course. Sierra tried to break down the words to see if she could decode any of them. It made her wish she knew more languages. She had taken Spanish during her first two years in high school, but she didn't know if she would be able to converse in Spanish if the need arose. It amazed her that Alex spoke several languages and that his English was still very good. He was such a gentle-spirited guy.

Just then the door to their compartment opened, and Sierra looked up, hoping that Alex had been bold enough to return in spite of Marti. A gray-haired gentleman in a suit entered, carrying a black briefcase. He checked his train ticket for the seat number and then tucked it into his coat pocket, greeting them in German.

Marti put on a tight smile and looked him over.

His eyes moved around the room, politely acknowledging the three of them. He spoke to Marti again in German, motioning toward her seat by the window. She didn't answer him.

"I think you're in his seat," Sierra said.

"Just so," the man said. He had switched to English. "That is my seat number, but it does not matter to me. Please. I'll sit here."

Marti offered him an obligatory nod.

"You are, I suppose, three sisters traveling together?" he said as he settled into the seat.

"Oh, no," Marti said, suddenly coming alive with a ripple of laughter. "This is my niece and her friend. We're not sisters."

"You certainly look like three sisters to me," the man said. His voice was smooth, the look in his eye was keen, and his aftershave was strong enough to be considered an air freshener back in the States.

Oh, brother! Sierra rolled her eyes. *Does this guy think he is suave, or what? I can't believe Marti is actually flirting with him. At least Christy and I weren't flirting with Alex. We had a much deeper conversation. How can Marti judge us when she acts worse than we do around strangers?*

"We're on our way to Basel," Marti said. "Perhaps you can suggest a good restaurant. I'm afraid the cart hasn't found its way back here yet, and we're all very hungry."

"The service is not always what it should be on this part of the trip. I was going to get myself a cup of coffee," the man said. "May I bring back enough for all of us?"

"None for me," Christy said.

"Nothing for me," Sierra added.

"That would be very nice of you..." Marti paused, waiting for the man to give his name.

"Gernot," he volunteered. "And you are?"

"Marti," she said slowly, as if he wouldn't understand her unless she exaggerated her words.

Before Gernot could rise to get the coffees, the cart and attendant appeared at the door. Gernot insisted he buy the coffee and roll for Marti and even bought chocolate bars for all of them. For the next hour, Sierra pretended to be asleep. Actually, she did doze off and on, but it was hard not to stay awake listening to the spicy conversation between Gernot and Marti.

This is weird. Really weird, Sierra thought. *First, Christy and I get grounded for our innocent conversation over breakfast with Alex—and now we're locked in this compartment, listening to a middle-aged married woman carry on a flirting fest with a smooth talker who is wearing smelly aftershave.*

Feeling nervous about what might happen next, Sierra could only imagine what Christy was thinking and feeling. Sierra couldn't wait for the train to stop so she and Christy could talk all this over. They had to be almost to Basel by now.

Staring out the window, Sierra saw rolling green hills dotted with old timber-framed farmhouses. A forest of towering evergreens covered the rise to the south. She decided that must be the Black Forest, which meant they were close to Basel, since it was located just over the border from the Black Forest.

She wondered if Alex was looking out his window right now, too. Was he on the same side of the train? Was he seeing the same beautiful hills and thinking of her the way she was thinking of him?

Sierra mentally went over their conversation at breakfast after they had quit joking with each other. Alex had said that he'd studied on his own to improve his English and then taught himself French. He also spoke Russian, German and some Italian. He had already finished school but was hoping to be accepted at a university where he would study economics. Sierra sighed. Alex seemed so intelligent and fun at the same time.

The peaceful scenery rolled past. Sierra eyed green

grass, cows grazing on the hillsides, and tumbling brambles of wild berries. Children in shorts played in front of houses with red tile roofs. Everything seemed perfect in the scenic world outside.

Sierra couldn't help but think that if she could see Alex one more time, everything in her world would be perfect, too.

four

RIGHT BEFORE THEY ARRIVED in Basel, sweet-smelling Gernot offered to drive Marti and the girls to their hotel and treat them to lunch at his favorite bistro. Marti declined, explaining they already had lunch plans. Until that point, she had chatted happily with Gernot. But when he made the offer, Marti backed off in a hurry. Gernot still lingered at the Basel station, making sure they had all their luggage and knew which direction to go.

Marti thanked him and took off, walking with purpose across the long, crowded platform. Sierra did her best to follow Marti, but she kept turning to look for Alex. Any sign of him and Sierra was sure her heart would jump into her throat. She'd be happy with just one more smile and a wave from him.

Alexander didn't appear—not on the platform, not inside the train station, not in the line at customs, and not on the street where they caught a taxi to the hotel. Gernot seemed to have disappeared, too.

From the backseat of the taxi, Sierra took one last look

over her shoulder, scanning the stream of visitors coming and going from the Basel station. She saw no sign of Alex.

"He'll probably call the hotel," Christy whispered, leaning over and invading Sierra's thoughts.

"Am I that obvious?" Sierra asked.

"He really liked you, didn't he?" Christy said.

Sierra smiled timidly.

"He knows where we're staying and what our plans are for the rest of the week. He'll call. You'll see," Christy comforted Sierra.

The taxi slowed and stopped only a few miles from the train station.

"You want *how* much?" Marti said when they climbed out. Sierra and Christy gathered their luggage as Marti counted out the money.

Twenty minutes later in their hotel rooms, she was still muttering about the cab. "I've never paid so much for a cab!" She checked her watch and motioned for the girls to go to their room through the common door. "We have only forty-five minutes before we meet the school's director. You two hurry and get ready. I'm going to freshen up now."

Sierra stretched out on the wide bed with the fluffy, white comforter. "Freshen up? I'd rather take a nap."

"No," Christy said. "We have to stay awake, remember? Maybe you should try to wake yourself up with a quick shower."

"You go ahead. I'll just take a little catnap."

Christy jumped into the shower, and Sierra floated on her cloudlike bed. She remembered how good it felt to have Alex look at her with such admiration and how warm his hand felt as it covered hers.

"You're next," Christy said, tapping Sierra's foot and interrupting her dream.

"And you're cruel. I was about to get to the good part of my dream." Sierra rolled over, snatched a pillow, and, through bleary eyes, tossed it at Christy.

"You missed. Come on. The shower felt great, and clean clothes are going to feel even better."

Sierra dramatically peeled herself off the bed and staggered toward the bathroom. "I'm never going to make it."

"Sure you will. And if you know what's good for you, you'll be ready in five minutes."

"Right."

Sierra forced herself to snap out of her drowsy state. The last thing she needed was to invoke Marti's wrath. Sierra's shower in the blue-and-white-tiled stall was speedy, mostly because she didn't wash her hair. It was easier to pull back her mane than to wash and try to tame it. She smiled, remembering how Alex had said she had beautiful hair. He was a unique guy. Sierra turned to face the water, letting it pour over her face. When she finished her shower, she did feel better. Christy was right.

Pulling on a pair of clean shorts and a knit shirt, Sierra opened the bathroom door with a grand "Ta-da!"

Christy stood in the middle of their small room wearing a dress and trying to towel-dry her hair.

"Don't tell me I'm supposed to wear a dress," Sierra said.

"I'm sure it doesn't matter what you wear. I just know how my aunt expects me to dress. You're fine."

"This time, maybe," Sierra said, tossing her dirty clothes over the back of the chair next to the writing desk.

"But if we go anywhere that requires nice clothes, I don't have anything with me. Not even my gauze skirt. It ripped. Remember? That's why I borrowed your dress for Doug and Tracy's wedding."

"Don't worry about it. You look fine. I'm sure we'll manage to do some shopping before we leave Basel." Christy rummaged through her backpack and pulled out a small, over-the-shoulder leather purse. "Do you have your passport and everything? The school is back over the border in the Black Forest. We'll probably need our passports."

"I'll get mine," Sierra said.

Marti's long fingernails tapped on their common door. Sierra reached for her leather slip-on shoes and grabbed her backpack.

"Ready, girls?" Aunt Marti called out, then opened the door. A pouf of strong fragrance rushed in ahead of her. "Sierra, you're not dressed yet."

"I told her what she had on was okay," Christy said quickly. "She doesn't have anything but shorts and jeans. We need to go shopping while we're here."

Marti seemed to brighten. "That's a marvelous idea. Perhaps we can squeeze in a few shops on our way back this afternoon."

Sierra made a mental note. *When in doubt, tell Marti you want to go shopping.*

"Christy," Marti said, turning her attention to her dutiful niece, "you're not going with wet hair, are you?"

"It'll dry on the way," Christy said, heading for the door. "I have our room key, Sierra."

Marti and Sierra followed Christy to the elevator.

"This is a nice hotel," Christy commented as they

waited for the elevator to reach their third floor.

"It's not bad," Marti said. "Rather plain but clean. Efficient, like so many of these European places. But for the price I'm paying, I expected larger rooms at least."

"I think it's fine," Christy said. She flipped back her hair, and Marti looked put out.

"You girls and your long hair. I can't believe you're going out with it sopping wet. What is taking this elevator so long?" Marti tapped her foot impatiently.

Just then the bell above the door rang, and the doors opened. There stood Alex.

"Hello! I was coming to see you," he said.

Sierra smiled at Alex, then glanced at Marti. Sierra noticed Marti's face turning a shade of burgundy.

"That was very nice of you, but we must leave. We are in a hurry." Marti brushed past Alex and entered the elevator, where she pushed the button for the lobby. "Come, girls."

"Hi," Sierra said softly as she moved past Alex. He reached over, and his fingers touched hers for the briefest moment.

"Sorry, Alex. We're on our way out," Christy offered, trying to smooth things over.

"Yes, to the Schwarzwald Volkschule—I mean, the Black Forest People's School. My cousin has lent me his car for the afternoon. I thought I would drive you," Alex said. He stood outside the elevator while the three women remained inside.

Marti slapped her hand on the button to close the elevator door. "No, thank you," she said firmly, not looking at Alex as the doors closed.

Sierra turned from Marti and, in disbelief at what was

happening, looked at Alex. "I'm sorry," she said as the doors clanged shut and the lift took them rapidly down.

"You're sorry?" Marti looked at Sierra in shock. "Sorry for what? Sorry that you told a complete stranger where we were going? Yes, you *should* be sorry. I can't believe you girls were so foolish!"

"And you," Marti said, turning to Christy and pointing a long finger at her. "You know better than to do such a thing. Why didn't you stop your young friend here from divulging all our private plans?"

"I was the one who told him where we were going," Christy said firmly. "You're not being fair, Aunt Marti. Alex is a very nice guy. He's only trying to help. You even said the taxis are far too expensive. How else are we going to get there?"

"We shall take a cab, of course. One can never put a price tag on safety. Accepting rides from complete strangers while we're halfway around the world would be foolish. Now, if Alex is in the lobby when these doors open, I want you both to ignore him. If he persists, I shall notify the hotel management." Marti let out a huff as the doors opened.

Alex was nowhere to be seen. Sierra was glad for his sake. She feared what might have happened to him if Marti reported him. At the same time, Sierra felt sorry for herself. She was sure Alex wouldn't have the guts to show up again and risk offending Marti a third time. Sierra would probably never see him again. Unless...

No. Sierra shook the thought from her mind. It wouldn't be right to sneak out to meet Alex somewhere. It was obvious, however, that he wanted to see her again. He had flirted with her, letting his fingers brush against hers. It had felt wonderful.

Maybe I could sneak down to the hotel lobby tonight and somehow get a message to him to meet me there, Sierra schemed. *We could stay in the lobby—it wouldn't exactly be the same as sneaking out.*

Before she got too carried away, Sierra reminded herself that she was Marti's guest. Sierra's parents had given her "the talk" on the phone before she came, reminding her to be honest and respectful to Marti. Mr. and Mrs. Jensen had said, "We expect you to respond to Marti the same way you would to us when it comes to making decisions. This is not a time for you to test your independence, Sierra."

Yeah, but if my parents were here, they wouldn't mind. They would like Alex, Sierra rationalized.

Marti flagged a cab, and she, Christy and Sierra rode the twelve miles to the Schwarzwald Volkschule in silence. Sierra's heart and head were anything but silent, though. Why should she have to follow the rules if the person she was supposed to obey and respect wasn't being fair?

Sierra was sure that if she were traveling with her mom instead of Marti, this whole embarrassing mess never would have happened. Mrs. Jensen would have liked Alex immediately. Sierra just knew her mom would understand if she had to bend the rules a pinch to get around Marti, the tyrant. That is, if Sierra ever had the opportunity to bend those rules.

Her mind spun with possibilities. She and Christy did have a separate room. Maybe Alex would try calling. He wouldn't give up so easily. And Christy would have to be on Sierra's side. Quickly, Sierra concocted a plan. It was risky, but she had to take some chances.

She had to see Alex one more time.

five

"AND THIS IS THE COMPUTER ROOM," said Mr. Pratt, the school's director, as he completed the tour of the Schwarzwald Volkschule. He was a large, friendly man, and Sierra liked him the moment they met. She had a feeling Christy liked him, too, which was good. First impressions counted, especially when Christy needed to make a decision quickly. And the fact that Mr. Pratt was so likable probably made Christy feel better about the school.

"All assignments are to be turned in on disk. Those students who have laptops, of course, prefer to use those, but our equipment is available to all the students," Mr. Pratt continued.

"Very impressive," Marti said, admiring the rows of tables laden with computers. "This certainly is a fine institution. I must admit I didn't expect everything to be so modern."

"Well, Europe has been a bit slow to adopt the idea of individuals owning computers, but our school has been blessed with several generous donors who are very committed to keeping us state of the art and accomplishing our educational goals. We offer accredited college courses and require a hands-on practicum." Mr. Pratt checked his watch. "Please excuse me. I was expecting another guest this afternoon. He might be waiting in my office."

"We won't keep you," Marti said. "You've been gracious to allow us this much of your time. Although I'm sure Christy will be eager to see the dormitory situation. May we schedule another appointment to tour the dormitory?"

"We can do that right now, if it's convenient for you. Let me stop by my office a moment on the way out." Mr. Pratt turned off the lights and let them down the long, quiet hallway.

"How many students will be starting here in the fall?" Christy asked.

"We currently have close to 800 registered. That is the most we've ever had. Of course, for many of them, this center is only a place to keep their files."

"What do you mean?" Marti asked.

"We have several schools, which we call 'on location.' The students are registered here, but all the course work and professors are at various ends of the earth. For instance, we have fifty students enrolled in Israel and nearly one hundred who will study anthropology in Australia. Over a third of our student body studies on location."

"I didn't realize that," Christy said. "Can you tell me about the orphanage in Basel?"

"Yes, of course. You will be going there tomorrow, won't you? I believe they're expecting you at ten o'clock." Mr. Pratt opened the door to his brightly painted office and invited them inside.

"We'll need directions to give the cab driver," Marti said, stepping into the room.

Out of the corner of her eye, Sierra noticed someone sitting on the sofa against the wall. The person stood to greet them.

"Or I could drive you," the deep voice said.

"Alexander!" Mr. Pratt exclaimed. He rushed forward and began to speak to Alex in rapid German. The two exchanged warm greetings.

Sierra felt her heart flutter. She quickly turned to catch Marti's shocked expression.

"Please excuse me," Mr. Pratt said. "I haven't seen this young man for several years. He's been living in Moscow. Alex, I'd like you to meet—"

Before Mr. Pratt could finish the introduction, Alex interrupted him. "We've already met," he said, his eyes fixed on Sierra. "Perhaps you can give Christy's aunt some comfort. Let her know I am not such a strange person."

"Oh, I never..." Marti fumbled. "I mean, it was a strange situation, that's all. One can never be too safe these days, you know."

"I can assure you," Mr. Pratt said with an arm around Alex, "this young man is upright and dependable. You have no cause for concern regarding him. As a matter of fact, let's take a tour of the dormitory, and then you ladies can join us for coffee."

"Oh, that's quite all right," Marti said. "It isn't necessary."

"I insist," Mr. Pratt replied. "I'd like you to be my guests."

"Thank you," Christy said.

At least one of them was thinking clearly enough to respond graciously to Mr. Pratt's invitation. Sierra was too happy to even talk. She couldn't contain her smile.

Alex looked pleased, too. He casually fell into step beside Sierra as they marched down the halls, went out the school's front door, and walked across the street to the dormitory. Mr. Pratt explained that it was one of five large houses run by the school. Students ate together in the main dining room and, every Saturday morning, each student was expected to assist in chores around the house.

As they took the tour, Alex stayed by Sierra's side, taking his own tour of her life. The two of them hung back slightly from the others as Alex asked questions about Sierra's family, her school, her job at Mama Bear's Bakery, and her "hobbits."

"My hobbits?" Sierra asked with a giggle.

"What you like to do for fun," Alex explained. "For example, do you ski?"

"Yes."

"That is your hobbit, then."

"You mean my 'hobby.' Yes, skiing is kind of a hobby for me. Actually, I like most sports, thanks to my dad and my four brothers."

"And what are your favorites?" Alex held open the door for Sierra as they exited. She liked being treated like a princess.

"My favorite sports? I like hiking and backpacking."

"Oh, then you are going to like Switzerland very much. We must go for a hike together."

Sierra looked up at him. A wayward strand of his dark hair was just beginning to break free from the pack to form a curl. *He reminds me of Paul*, Sierra realized. Not in looks, but in manner. They both had strong personalities. And Alex looked at her the way Paul had when they first met. But Paul was older—definitely too old for Sierra. And he was far away in Scotland. Sierra was in Germany with Alex. Why was she thinking about Paul? And why would she want to compare Alex with anyone? He was unique and wonderful, and she loved that he was paying attention to her.

Mr. Pratt led them down the street four short blocks past a tidy little garden alive with columbine, sweet peas, and cherry tomatoes strung up against a low fence. He stopped at the front door of a tall, narrow, timber-framed house and said, "Please make yourselves welcome. You are my guests." He then opened the door and called out something in German.

A stout, stern-looking woman appeared before them, wearing an apron over her skirt and blouse. It seemed to Sierra that the woman was staring at them a little too obviously as Mr. Pratt spoke to her in German.

"Is that his wife?" Sierra whispered.

"No," Alex whispered back. "She died many years ago. This must be the housekeeper. He is asking her to prepare something of a meal for us. She is arguing that he didn't give her enough notice. He is going to see what there is to eat."

Sierra suppressed a giggle. It was fun having a personal interpreter. It was even more fun having him whisper in her ear.

Mr. Pratt directed them into the living room, saying he would join them in a moment. The four of them sat down. Alex, Sierra, and Christy perched on the sofa while Marti selected the winged-back chair. The living room was small but tidy. A picture of a canal and an elaborately carved bridge hung on the wall above the mantle in an intricate gold frame.

Sierra was gazing at the picture when Alex leaned over and said, "The Bridge of Sighs. In Venice, of course. Have you been there?"

"No."

"I have," Marti spoke up. "My husband, Robert, and I were there many years ago. It is a lovely city, isn't it, Alex? Overpriced accommodations, of course, but the food is good, don't you think?"

No one said anything. It seemed they were all too startled by this sudden change in Marti's treatment of Alex.

"My favorite, of course, is Paris," Marti plunged on. "No other European city compares. The food, the shopping, the museums..."

"Then you would like Moscow very much," Alex said. "It is a masterpiece of a city. When it comes to museums, nothing compares with the Hermitage in St. Petersburg. You must come for a visit."

It seemed to Sierra that Marti bristled slightly. There was no mistaking her body language. The thought of visiting any part of the former Soviet Union did not appeal to her one bit.

Fortunately, Mr. Pratt arrived with a plate of cookies in his hand. His cheeks were flushed. It appeared he was more in command at his school than he was in his own home. "Please forgive me for leaving you like this. Frau Weber will be right in with the coffee. You do all drink coffee, don't you?"

Sierra nodded with the rest of them. The truth was, she rarely drank coffee. Her idea of a good hot beverage was herbal tea, especially the fruit herbal teas. Apparently, everyone in Germany liked coffee. Her dad would definitely fit in here.

Dark, strong coffee served in small china cups arrived on a tray carried by the disgruntled Frau Weber. She let the tray down with a clang on the small coffee table and turned with a huff.

"So," Mr. Pratt said, regaining his composure, "please help yourselves, and Alex, do tell me how your family is doing."

Sierra enjoyed sitting back and listening to Alex talk. She held her cup of coffee carefully in her lap and took one tiny sip. Even with all the milk and sugar she had added, it was still too strong for her to stomach.

The warm August afternoon sun pouring through the open window soon made the living room feel small as Sierra sat wedged between Christy and Alex. She liked hearing about Alex's family, but she would have given anything for a glass of ice water and a seat by the window.

Alex spoke fondly of his mother and father to Mr. Pratt. Whenever he didn't know a word in English, he slipped in a German one, and Mr. Pratt would repeat the word in English for Marti, Christy, and Sierra's benefit.

Marti had recovered her charming self and even laughed at one of Alex's stories about his six-year-old sister. Sierra gave Christy a poke, and Christy poked her back. Marti's opinion of Alex had been transformed—and that could only mean good things for Sierra.

six

LATER THAT NIGHT, back at the hotel, Marti put Sierra's romantic hopes in check.

"Don't think for one minute," Marti said, "that I approve of you nurturing a romance with this Russian, Sierra. What would your parents think?"

Sierra knew what her parents would think. She was sure they would think she was old enough and mature enough to manage her own relationships. They always liked her friends. All of them. They would like Alex, too.

Before Sierra could defend herself to Marti, Christy stepped out of the bathroom. She was wearing her pajamas and had a toothbrush in her hand. "You saw for yourself what a great guy he is, Aunt Marti. He drove us back from the school, took us to dinner, and even paid for it himself. The guy is a gem! What's wrong with Sierra developing a new friendship? I'm all for it," she said.

"Go brush your teeth, Christina. This is between Sierra and me," Marti snapped back.

Christy stepped forward and stood next to where Sierra

was seated on the bed. Marti was standing in front of Sierra, which meant Christy formed a sort of human buffer between them.

"Actually, this is among all three of us," Christy said firmly. "Sierra is my friend. She's my guest on this trip. I'm enjoying Alex's company as much as she is. And when he picks us up and takes us to the orphanage tomorrow, this will be among the four of us."

Christy's toothbrush appeared to be shaking slightly in her hand. Sierra wondered if Christy stood up to her aunt like this very often, or if she was merely appearing brave and confident.

"If it's all right with you, Aunt Marti," Christy continued, "I'd like it if the three of us could come to a mutual agreement about Alexander now, so that there won't be any awkward situations tomorrow. He's a wonderful Christian guy. He enjoys being with us and doesn't seem to mind being our tour guide. I'd like it if you would approve of Sierra's and my friendship with Alex. Please trust us, and please be nice to him."

"I've been extremely nice," Marti said defensively.

"After you found out that Mr. Pratt approved of him," Sierra said, sliding her comment in carefully. The minute she said it, Sierra knew that she should have kept quiet and let Christy calm Marti.

Marti snapped back at Sierra, "You've missed the point entirely. You met him on the train, for goodness' sake. How did you know it would be safe to spend time with him?"

Sierra paused a moment before stating calmly, "Because he's a Christian."

Marti threw up her hands and turned her face to the ceiling. "Why can't I make you two innocent young dreamers understand what men are really like? It doesn't matter what they say. They can't be trusted. The sooner you grow up and realize that, the better off we'll all be." She shook her head and pursed her lips together. It seemed she had something more to say but was trying hard to hold it in. "You just don't know," she finally sputtered. "You two girls simply don't understand."

With that, she turned and went into her room, firmly closing the door. Sierra and Christy gave each other long, silent looks.

"What do you think she's trying to tell us?" Sierra asked. "Maybe she was burned by some guy when she was our age, and now she thinks it's her role in life to protect you and your friends from the same mistakes she made."

"Wow." Christy plopped down on the bed and stared at the closed door between the rooms. She was silent a moment, then said, "You could be right. I never thought of that."

"Your uncle seems so great," Sierra said. "I can't imagine that he would ever hurt her. Must have been some guy before Bob. Maybe some gorgeous football player broke her heart in high school."

"You have quite an imagination," Christy said.

"It could have happened. Has she ever told you anything?"

Tucking her legs under her, Christy said, "For a long time I thought Marti was hiding something from me, and then I found out that she'd had a baby right before I was born."

"You're kidding," Sierra said, getting comfortable on the fluffy, white coverlet. "What happened?"

"The baby was premature and had brain damage or something. She died the day before I was born."

"How awful," Sierra said softly.

"I know. That's why my aunt treats me the way she does. My mom told me years ago that everything Marti would have done for her own daughter she tries to do for me."

"Has Marti ever talked to you about any of this?" Sierra asked.

"Never. My mom says Marti doesn't talk about it to anyone. Mom told me something about Bob and Marti's not being able to have any more children, but I don't remember what she said. We've only talked about it once." Christy tilted her head and pulled her silky hair over her shoulder. "I never thought of what you said tonight. What if she did have her heart broken by a guy when she was young and then lost her only baby? Something like that would explain why she's so resistant to God."

"Exactly," Sierra said. "I think it would be pretty hard to trust a God who lets horrible things like that happen in your life."

Christy nodded thoughtfully. "But how much of what happens in our lives is because God lets horrible things happen, and how much of it is due to our reaping the consequences of our actions?"

"Is that what you think happened with your aunt?" Sierra asked, surprised at Christy's comment.

"Well, we've all blown it," Christy said. Her clear blue-green eyes carried a soft glow of understanding. "Even after we surrender our lives to the Lord, we still have that tendency to go our own way. And if Marti had a really wild past, a lot of her hurt and anger today probably comes from the consequences of her choices—not random acts of God."

Sierra propped her pillow against the headboard and leaned back. "I'd sure be curious to know," she said.

"Don't get your hopes up," Christy warned as she stood up, her toothbrush still in hand. "My aunt doesn't open up to anyone. Ever."

As Christy brushed her teeth, Sierra stared at the textured plaster on the ceiling. It was hard not to take Christy's warning as a personal challenge. There were ways of getting a person to open up. Badgering them sometimes worked. And if Sierra had the opportunity, she could try her relentless debating skills on Marti. No one should spend her life acting so guarded. Marti needed to unwind.

A self-righteous thought entered Sierra's mind: What if the reason she had come on this trip was to crack open Marti and make her break down some of her walls? What if Sierra was supposed to help Marti experience God's love? Sierra liked the thought that God might have chosen her for such an important task.

"You know what?" Christy said, returning from the bathroom and slipping into her bed. "I kind of like the school."

Sierra left all her Joan of Arc feelings to float on the plastered ceiling and came down to earth to join Christy. After all, the obvious reason they had come on this trip was so Christy could check out the school. The least Sierra could do was support her friend in this gigantic decision.

"Tell me your impressions of the place while I get ready

for bed," Sierra said. She rummaged in her bag for her nightshirt and toothbrush.

Christy ran through a list of all the logical pluses of the school. She gave all the reasons she should go there as Sierra washed her face and brushed her teeth.

"Obviously, you think it's a great school," Sierra commented. "So why do I hear you hesitating about it?" She crawled into bed and fluffed up her pillow. "Man, this is a comfortable bed!"

"I know. Like snuggling into a cloud," Christy agreed. "Anyway, I'm just not sure because…"

"Don't tell me," Sierra said. "It's Todd."

"Of course."

"How does he feel about your coming here? Last week he said it was totally up to you. Did he ever give you his true opinion?"

"That is his true opinion," Christy said, resting her head on her arm. "The night before we left, Todd told me that if we're meant to be together—which I took to mean if we're supposed to get married—then this year away at school won't change things between us. He says it will only make us appreciate each other more—the way we fell more in love when he went to Spain."

"I think you two appreciate each other plenty. Why don't you just go ahead and get married? You know you're right for each other. At least, that's what everyone else thinks. Don't you two feel the same way?"

Christy's face took on a contemplative, glowing look. To Sierra, it was the look of a woman in love. "You see, Todd has always been slow," Christy explained. "Or maybe I should say 'cautious.' His parents divorced, and he wants to be careful about his commitments and about making sure he means to keep all his promises. We've never really talked about marriage. I thought maybe we would after Doug and Tracy's wedding."

"I wish I had a picture of you and Todd when you walked out of the church arm in arm after the wedding ceremony," Sierra said. "You both had that Romeo-and-Juliet look down pretty well. I think Todd's hopelessly in love with you, but he isn't ready to admit it yet."

Christy smiled. "I know. And I love him. I know that. But I don't know if either of us is ready for marriage yet. Having me go away for a year might be the best thing for us. And like you said last week, we could start to write letters, which would be a whole new way to communicate for us."

"A very romantic way, too," Sierra said. "I've always dreamed of what it would be like to carry on a passionate correspondence with a guy I was crazy about."

"With Alexander, maybe?"

Christy's comment surprised Sierra. Actually, Sierra had been thinking of a correspondence with Paul. Ever since his brother, Jeremy, told Sierra a few days ago that he thought Sierra should write to Paul in Scotland, Sierra had let the idea build in her mind. Her reaction to Paul's brother had been, "If he wants to correspond, then let him write me first." She knew Paul would get the message exactly as she stated it. And somehow she also knew that Paul was just like her, and he wouldn't let go of a challenge.

"Yeah," Sierra finally said, "with Alexander."

"Wait a minute," Christy said. "You didn't sound too excited there. You weren't thinking of Alexander, were you?"

"No. Isn't that weird? After all the happened today, you would think Alex would be the only guy on my mind. I was thinking of Paul." Sierra had told Christy all about Paul, but she had never admitted to Christy or anyone else how stuck she was on him.

A slow grin spread across Christy's lips. "I didn't realize," Christy stated with an air of satisfaction.

"Realize what?"

"Paul is your Philippians 1:7 guy, isn't he?"

"My what?"

"Your Philippians 1:7 guy. Todd sent that verse to me once on a coconut from Hawaii. The verse says, 'I hold you in my heart.'"

Christy sat halfway up and leaned toward Sierra. Then, as if Christy were revealing a great secret, she whispered, "Sierra, you hold Paul in your heart, don't you?"

seven

WHEN SIERRA AWOKE the next morning, she felt as though she hadn't slept at all. Her dreams kept waking her through the night—and her dreams had been about Alex. When Sierra woke to the alarm, she only wanted to go back to sleep.

"Want me to shower first?" Christy mumbled.

"Be my guest. Take as much time as you want. Don't bother to wake me when you get out." Sierra turned on her side and pulled the comforter over her face to block out the brightness of the sun breaking through the window.

"Sierra," Christy said, plopping on Sierra's bed and gently shaking her shoulder, "wake up. We're in Switzerland! Alex is going to be waiting for us."

"I thought you were going to take a shower," Sierra said.

"I did. You fell back asleep. Come on. We need to get going. My aunt wants us to have breakfast downstairs with her in fifteen minutes."

"All right, all right. I'm coming." Sierra sat up and tried to open her eyes. "Do I look as wiped out as I feel?"

"You'll feel better after a shower, that's for sure," Christy said. "You'll see. It's a great shower. Lots of warm water. This is going to be a wonderful day!" Christy rose from the bed and began to sort through her stack of clean clothes as she hummed a little tune.

"I can't stand perky people in the morning," Sierra blurted out as she stumbled to the shower. "You'll remember that, Christina, if you know what's good for you."

"A shower will be good for *you*," Christy called out after her.

Sierra never would have believed it, but Christy was right. Sierra emerged from the shower feeling much more coherent than she had been ten minutes earlier. She wrapped herself in a towel, stepped into the bedroom and saw Christy sitting at the small corner desk, talking on the phone. She was wearing a short summer dress, and her hair was twisted on top of her head in a smooth roll, styled like many Swiss teenagers were doing. It was an elegant look, and it made Christy look five years older.

Christy looked up and smiled, still holding the phone to her ear. "So far I do. We're going to the orphanage this morning.... Okay, I will. You, too.... Okay.... Yeah, I promise I'll call you tomorrow at this time.... I miss you, too. 'Bye." She lowered the receiver and gazed at the silent black phone.

"Todd?" Sierra guessed.

Christy nodded. "He called me. I was going to ask Marti if I could call him in a few days, but he called me. He said he missed me and was praying for me. And he said to tell you hi, too. I told him about Alex."

"You did? What did he say?"

"He said he hopes you go for it."

"Go for what?" Sierra laughed, pulling on her shorts.

"You know, the relationship. The adventure. The chance to grow by giving a little part of yourself to someone special."

Sierra pulled her wrinkled T-shirt over her head and wrapped the bath towel around her wet hair. One uncooperative blond curl dangled down the right side of her face. "What are you telling me? Todd calls you all the way from California, and you spend his money discussing my love life—or rather, lack thereof?"

"Something like that," Christy said. "Remember how you told me what your dad said when he gave you your purity ring?"

Sierra glanced down at the simple gold band on her right hand. "What? That he was proud of me for setting such high standards or something?"

"No, remember after you left the restaurant? You told me your dad said to have fun while you were a teenager. Well, I agree with him. Take every relationship God brings your way, and enjoy what that person has to offer and what you can offer him. It's not all serious soul-searching when it comes to guys, you know."

Sierra put her hand on her hip. "You and Todd discussed all this while I was in the shower? Maybe we should have had a conference call so I could have received this advice right from the Big Kahuna's mouth."

"No," Christy said with a laugh, "we didn't discuss all this. I've just been thinking about it ever since you told me what your dad said, and I think he's right. You have to take a chance and open your heart to people, Sierra."

"You don't think I do?"

Before Christy could answer, Marti called through their closed door, "Are you two ready?"

"Almost," Christy called back.

Marti opened the door. She looked fully rested and ready to go in her straight denim skirt and freshly pressed white blouse. Her eyebrows crashed together when she saw Sierra with a towel wrapped like a turban around her head.

"You're not ready," she stated.

"We almost are," Christy said. "Can we meet you downstairs in a few minutes?"

"Do hurry," Marti said with a drawn-out sigh. "I'll be waiting for you in the dining room."

As the day proceeded, Marti's patience was tried half a dozen more times. It seemed she spent most of the day waiting for Sierra and Christy. First, they were late for breakfast, and then when Alex arrived, the girls had to run up to their room to pick up their backpacks.

When they met Alex and Marti at the car, Marti was planted in the front passenger seat. Alex opened the back door for Sierra.

As she climbed inside, Alex leaned toward her and said softly, "It is wonderful to see you again, See-hair-a."

Before she could respond, he gently brushed the back of his hand across her cheek. It was the most tender, affectionate gesture she had ever experienced, and it almost made her heart stop.

"It's good to see you, too," she said, her voice suddenly turning hoarse.

When they arrived at the orphanage, Alex offered Sierra his hand as she exited the backseat. He held it only a moment before opening Marti's door and offering her a hand as well.

She politely refused and walked ahead of them into the orphanage, stating over her shoulder, "We're ten minutes late, you know. They might not let us in."

The staff woman who greeted them assured Marti their late arrival was no problem, and they could take the tour now. Marti made it only to the first hallway on the first floor before she excused herself, saying she felt jet-lagged, but they should go ahead and take their time. She would wait outside for them on the long bench in front of the building.

Sierra and Christy exchanged glances. Sierra assumed it was difficult for Marti to be around so many children since she had lost her only child. Or maybe all the references to Christianity their hostess used as she explained the mission and philosophy of the orphanage had disturbed Marti.

Sierra felt drawn in and intrigued by the orphanage. She knew Christy was feeling the same way. Alex's presence added a deeper level of understanding as he quietly provided insights during their tour. Many children were from Africa, but most were from Bosnia. Some were Serbs, some were Croatians. Now everything Sierra had heard on the news about Bosnia had a face. These children were no longer faraway victims. The suffering was right here before her, and it was very real.

The sheer number of children in the orphanage disturbed Sierra. Their hostess said currently more than 300 orphans lived there, but only 3 percent of those would ever be adopted. There were so many children! Sierra's heart ached for them.

The building was once a factory and was large enough to hold even more kids. The guide said it had housed more than 425 orphans a few years earlier. The structure was restored with fresh whitewash on the walls and newer fixtures in the bathrooms. It was actually better looking and cleaner on the inside than it was on the outside. The efficient Swiss staff all wore tidy uniforms and appeared to run a tight ship.

Even though the children were clean, well fed, and looked as if they were being cared for, Sierra could tell something was missing. Their eyes all had the same sad look. They longed for a mother and father's love. Sierra knew their empty little faces would haunt her for the rest of her life.

After they had finished their hour and a half tour of the facilities, Christy, Sierra, and Alex joined Marti out front. She looked as if she were nearly at the end of her patience rope.

Alex offered to take them to lunch, and Marti accepted for them, briskly stating that this time she would pay.

"I know just the place we can go," Alex said, opening the car door for Marti. "This will be a real treat."

Then, opening Sierra's door, Alex gave Sierra's shoulder a gentle squeeze. She wondered if he was feeling the same way she was. They had looked into the face of terrible injustice. Any personal, earthly luxury seemed selfish. Lunch did not appeal to her.

Alex pulled out into the moving traffic. All around them, the summer day glowed. Sierra opened her window. It only went down halfway, but it was enough for the scents and sounds of Basel to come rushing into the car. She noticed a sign above a large old building that said in English: "The Salvation Army." It looked like a secondhand shop as well as a soup kitchen, similar to the Highland House in Portland, where she volunteered one day a week. Suddenly, the world seemed rather small. The poor and needy, orphans and sick people, were everywhere. It was overwhelming to think of how much help humanity needed.

"Is that the train station where we came in?" Christy asked, interrupting Sierra's thoughts.

"Yes. That one is the Badisher Bahnhof," Alex said, pointing to the station as they passed. Two cement lion statues guarded the entrance. Sierra hadn't noticed them before. Lions always made her think of Aslan from the Narnia tales, and Aslan made her think of Christ.

Does all this pain in the world break Your heart, too, Lord? It must.

Sierra thought about the conversation she'd had with Christy the night before. Christy had said that some of life's problems are "acts of God"—circumstances we many never understand—while other problems are the direct result or consequence of our sins. But Sierra knew that those 300 children hadn't done anything to deserve being orphaned.

As Alex drove across the Rhine River, Sierra gazed into the slow-moving waters and blinked back tears. This morning, those children had become her neighbors and were no longer distant images on TV. Pain in life was real.

eight

"MCDONALD'S!" Marti blurted out in disbelief. "You've brought us to a McDonald's?"

"Yes," Alex said proudly, looking for a parking place along the crowded street. "This is a very popular place for the university students. I thought Christy would like to see it."

"Well, we've seen it," Marti remarked. "Remember where this is, Christy. Now let's go find a nice, quiet café."

"You do not wish to eat here?" Alex sounded baffled. "You can always find a small restaurant, but McDonald's are not so many."

"They are everywhere in America," Marti said. "And if I don't eat at McDonald's in America, I'm certainly not going to eat at one in Switzerland."

"We will drive on, then," Alex said.

Sierra appreciated his flexibility, although she liked Alex's idea. She wanted to go inside the McDonald's to compare it with the ones at home.

They found a small outdoor café with several open

tables. Alex parked the car, and they sat under a green-and-white umbrella at a round table. The menu was limited. Marti ordered a salad and was sorely disappointed. At Alex's suggestion, Christy and Sierra ordered the Nurnburgers. What they got was actually a type of small hot dog or sausage. Alex also suggested they order Schwip Schwap to drink. It came to them in glasses, lukewarm, with no ice.

"I forgot about this part of European dining," Christy said as she tried her drink. "They don't put ice in the drinks."

"Do you like the Schwip Schwap?" Alex asked. "It was always my favorite when I was young."

To Sierra, it seemed terribly sweet. A sort of "suicide" combination of orange, lemon, and cola mixed together. It tasted flat without the ice. "It's different from what we drink at home," she said. She was still unsettled by her experience at the orphanage—her lunch was not appealing.

"I've been thinking about why the orphanage asks the students to make a one-year commitment to the program," Christy said. "Can you imagine how hard it is on those children to always have people they love leave them? That's the only thing that scares me about coming here."

"The children?" Marti asked.

"Being with them for so long and then having to leave," Christy explained.

"Gracious, Christy, you haven't even decided if you're going to attend the school, and already you're turning melancholy over leaving. You don't know how it will be until you come. You might be glad to leave after one year. The purpose is your education, not to save the world."

"Have you decided to come?" Alex asked.

His seat was the only one in the direct sunshine. He had put on a pair of slim sunglasses and was leaning back in his chair. Sierra thought he looked very different from the guys she hung out with at her Christian high school in Portland. Even though he was wearing a T-shirt and jeans, Alex looked like someone who had already lived a lifetime.

"I don't know for sure," Christy said. "Part of me is ready to sign up and start school here right now. Another part wants to go home and pretend this corner of the world is only something I imagined."

"It's real," Alex said. "All of it. But it's as real as your life in California. I am of the belief that it does not matter where one lives or what one does so long as everything revolves around God. Time is short."

Sierra shot a quick glance at Marti to see how Alex's words affected her. She hid her reaction well.

"You know," Christy said, leaning forward and not looking at Marti at all, "sometimes I think about that, too. I keep hearing more and more about the end times and how Christ is coming back, and it makes me wonder what I should be doing. I mean, if we are living in the end times, then shouldn't I be more concerned about witnessing to people rather than pursuing my education?"

Sierra had never thought of that.

"We should get going," Marti said.

Alex gave a slight nod; then, removing his sunglasses, he leaned in and looked intently at Christy. "Whatever God shows you to do, the reason should be always a...what was that word?" He reached into his back pocket and pulled out a small New Testament. Flipping through the pages, he found what he was looking for. "Here it is. This is Peter One in the fourth chapter."

"Do you mean First Peter?" Sierra asked.

"Yes, First Peter." Alex's strong face clouded over. "I know this in Russian and German. I do not know this word in English. It means 'very strong, coming out of the heart.'"

"Wait," Sierra said. "I have a Bible here in my backpack. What's the verse?" She pulled out her Bible and looked to see where Alex was pointing in his German New Testament. "Okay, here it is. First Peter 4:7–8: 'But the end of all things is at hand; therefore be serious and watchful in your prayers. And above all things have fervent love for one another.'"

"Yes!" Alex exclaimed. "That is the word: 'fervent.' This is a strong, steady love. This is what you must consider, Christy. Whatever you do, do it with a fervent love."

"There's some more here," Sierra said, reading on in the chapter, "'...for "love will cover a multitude of sins." Be hospitable to one another without grumbling. As each one has received a gift, minister it to one another, as good stewards of the manifold grace of God.'"

"We simply must get back to the hotel," Marti said abruptly.

The three of them turned to look at her.

"What?" Sierra asked.

"If you must know, I have a terrible headache. I tried to keep going so as not to spoil the day for everyone else, but now I must lie down."

"We will then go," Alex said, rising from the table and putting his Bible back in his pocket. He helped to pull out Marti's chair and offered her his arm.

"I'm not an invalid," she snapped. "I can get myself to the car."

As they drove back to the hotel, Sierra thought about the verses they had read. *"Love each other fervently." Do I know what that means? I love people, but is my love strong and steady?*

When they were about a block from the hotel, Alex calmly asked Marti, "Would it be all right with you if I show Christy and See-hair-a some of the other sights of Basel?"

"I don't think that's such a good idea," Marti said. "I think this is where we say good-bye. You've been quite gracious, and I do thank you."

Alex stopped in front of the hotel, and a uniformed attendant opened the car door for Marti and offered her a white-gloved hand to help her out. Alex opened the door for Christy and Sierra. He took hold of Sierra's elbow and gave it a little squeeze.

Sierra looked up into Alexander's dark eyes and knew that if he asked her right now to sneak out tonight, she would do it.

"I'm sure Aunt Marti will change her mind once she feels a little better," Christy said to Alex in a low voice. "Thanks for everything. Really. I appreciate it more than I can say. Not only the ride, but also your advice and encouragement."

"Girls," Marti called over her shoulder, "come now. Good-bye, Alex. And thank you."

Alex leaned over and touched his cheek against Sierra's. It happened so fast that she felt the blood rush to her face.

"I will call," he whispered.

Sierra nodded.

He got back into the car and drove away. Sierra looked

over her shoulder and watched him leave.

She didn't speak again until the door was securely closed between their room and Marti's. "Did you see that?" she asked Christy.

"Did he kiss you?"

"No. He touched my cheek with his cheek. Just barely. Is that a local custom or something?"

"I don't know, but it looked pretty romantic." Christy smiled and kicked off her shoes. "I hope he calls you."

"Do you think it would be okay if we sneaked out to see him?"

"Why do you ask that?"

Sierra walked across the room and looked out the window. "Because you and I know he's wonderful and being with him is wonderful, not to mention spiritually uplifting. But your aunt doesn't understand that because she's not a Christian."

"I don't think that makes it okay to go against her wishes," Christy said.

Sierra let out a sigh. "There has to be some way to justify it. I'd rather be sightseeing with Alex than confined to the hotel. Wouldn't you?"

"Yes," Christy said. She took the bobby pins from her hair and shook it so it fell freely over her shoulders. "But right now, I think we should take a nap."

"I hate to admit this, but I could fall asleep in a second," Sierra agreed, going over to her bed and running her hand over the comforter before flopping down. "But won't we have a hard time sleeping tonight?"

"I won't," Christy said, her eyes closed. She had stretched out and looked blissful.

"Wake me when Alex calls." Sierra rolled over onto her side and adjusted the pillow under her head.

"No way," Christy murmured. "If the phone rings, you answer it. He'll be calling for you, anyway."

"Okay," Sierra agreed. It was her last word before floating off to dreamland.

nine

THE EARLY EVENING SHADOWS were stretched across the wall of the hotel room when Sierra forced open her eyes. "Christy?" she mumbled. Sierra turned to see her friend snoozing in the same position she was in when she fell asleep.

Quietly rising, Sierra tiptoed over to the window. She liked the view from here. Across the road stood a large building that had the name *Rathaus* carved into its wall. She knew that meant it was the community or municipal building. There had been one in Germany, too, where the Schwarzwald Volkschule was located, and Alex had explained that every small town had one.

This one in Basel was painted a deep reddish color, the shade of bricks. Along one side was a mural of larger-than-life townspeople during the Middle Ages. Around the edges was a bright gold leafing. The area surrounding the Rathaus was cobblestone, and a row of shops in tall, building-block style structures lined the street. They had to be old, hundreds of years old. But the buildings were kept up nicely with flower boxes in all the second-story windows. The boxes spilled their apple-red geraniums over the sides. Sierra found the view soothing.

Behind the shops and the Rathaus, the evening sky busily rolled up its turquoise carpet. Sierra imagined that somewhere up there, God was preparing to unfurl night's inky black rug, the black rug that was sprinkled with tiny holes. At least that's what her Granna Mae had always told Sierra when she was little. Granna Mae has said God decided not to repair those ancient pinpoints in the night-time carpet because all those holes let the brilliance of heaven peep through.

I'm in Switzerland, she reminded herself. *This city must be beautiful at night. What if Alex and I went out tonight and strolled these ancient streets? Now that would be romantic.*

The phone rang. Sierra jumped. Actually, the noise it made was a warbling, electrical sound rather than a ring. She grabbed the receiver and said, "Hello, Alex?"

"Oh, I must have the wrong room," a familiar voice on the other end said. "I'm sorry."

"No, wait!" Sierra said before the male voice was cut off. "Dad?"

"Sierra?"

"Yes, it's me. Hi."

"Hi. How are you doing?" her dad asked.

"Fine. We're all doing great. Tired, but I was expecting that. How are you guys? Is everything okay?"

"Yes. Terrific. We were just missing you, and I wanted to see how everything was going."

Sierra gave her dad a quick rundown of the orphanage and the school.

"Good," he said. "And who is Alex?"

Sierra smiled, pausing before she spoke. Her dad never missed a beat. He knew all six of his kids so well. He had earned their respect, and the kids welcomed his involvement in their lives.

She told her dad about meeting Alex on the train, how he had turned out to be Mr. Pratt's close friend, and how he had been showing them the sights.

"Sounds like a great guy," Mr. Jensen said, "but I'm going to give you one fatherly command here. Are you ready?"

"Yes."

"Make sure Christy is always with you when you see him these next few days."

"Why?"

"A precaution, that's all."

"Dad, you would really like him. He's a super-strong Christian."

"I don't doubt it," her dad said. "And I hope you two have some really wonderful, memorable times together. Use the buddy system, though. Make sure Christy is always with you, okay?"

"Don't you trust me?"

"We trust you completely."

"Then what's the big deal?" Sierra asked incredulously.

"Oh, a couple thousand miles," he replied. "Your spending time with a guy in Switzerland isn't quite the same as having Randy over here for dinner."

"Randy's just a buddy."

"Okay, then Drake."

"I only went out with him once," Sierra said.

"Sierra."

She could tell by the firmness in her father's voice that it was time to stop the banter. Dad meant business.

"If, or should I say when, you see Alex again, you must be with Christy or Marti the whole time. Those are the orders from headquarters," he said.

"Got it." Sierra tried to sound lighthearted. The last thing she wanted to do was upset her dad or have him think she was going against his rules. He had been right too many times for her to second-guess his reasoning. "Say hi to Mom and everyone for me."

"Will do. You have a great time, now, okay?"

"I will. Thanks for calling. I love you guys."

"We love you, too. 'Bye, honey."

The click on the other end signaled the phone call was over, but the warmth of her dad's voice remained. Sierra had awesome parents, and she knew it.

"Was that Alex?" Christy asked, shaking off her jet lag as she sat up and stretched.

"No, it was my dad. Can you believe that? Here I'm thinking how wonderful it would be to sneak out to see Alex, and my dad calls and asks me to promise I'll only spend time with Alex if we're with you or Marti."

"Sounds like something my dad would say," Christy observed.

"And would you do what he said?"

"Probably." Christy stretched again and yawned. "I sneaked out once on a trip with my aunt and uncle to Palm Springs."

"You?" Sierra sounded shocked.

"Yes, some of my friends and me. It was so dumb. Now

when I think about it, I can't believe I let them talk me into it."

"Was it to see a guy?"

"No," Christy said, getting up and going over to the window to look out at the view. "We sneaked out to go to a store. It turned into a huge mess. We ended up at the police station, and everyone was mad at me for a long time. Definitely not worth the risk."

Sierra believed Christy when she said it was a bad idea. Sierra knew that her dad made the chaperone rule only because he loved her. Still, she couldn't deny that if Alex called and wanted to see her tonight, she would still be tempted to go.

But Alex didn't call. Marti woke up shortly after Christy did and briskly proclaimed her headache had gone away. Marti insisted the three of them go downstairs to the hotel restaurant for dinner even though it was after eight o'clock.

They were all hungrier than they thought, and the Wiener schnitzel and potatoes tasted wonderful. With their spirits renewed, they decided to take a stroll and window-shop in what their waiter had called the *alt stadt,* or old town, of Basel.

A cool breeze skittered off the Rhine River and kept them company as the three women walked and talked. They got along better than they had at any other time on their trip.

Sierra was hopeful that, if Marti stayed in this good mood, she might agree to let Sierra spend more time with Alex. Maybe they could go hiking as he had suggested. Or at least for a picnic or bike ride.

Ever since Sierra had arrived in Europe, Alex had been a part of everything she had done. It would be miserable to try to see the sights without him.

"Would you like to visit the school again tomorrow, Christy?" Marti asked as they looked in one of the shop windows. "Are there any unanswered questions you would like to discuss with Mr. Pratt?"

"No, I think I have a pretty good idea of what it's all about. I just need to decide if I'm going to attend or not before we leave."

"Yes, you do," Marti agreed.

"I'd like to do some more sightseeing," Christy said. Then she added smoothly, "A hike with Alex would be especially fun."

To Sierra's surprise, Marti didn't immediately rebuff Christy. They were nearly back at the hotel.

"Marti, I don't know if this helps you decide," Sierra said, "but when my dad called tonight, I told him about Alex. Dad said he hoped we would spend more time together, have fun, and make some memories."

"Your father said that?" Marti asked. "You're not making this up, are you?"

"No, that's what he said. He also said that whatever I did with Alex had to be with Christy or with you."

"That's what he told you?"

"Yes," Sierra said firmly. She wasn't used to having her word questioned.

"Then I must say I applaud you for telling me. Honesty is always the best policy."

"Yes, I guess it is," Sierra said, more to herself than to Marti.

Marti stopped walking and turned to face Sierra and Christy with one of the nicest expressions she had worn on the trip. It was obvious she was feeling better. "I must say I admire the two of you for the way you abide by your parents' directions. You are both quite different from how I was at your age."

"I hear you were pretty wild," Sierra said, seizing her opportunity to delve in. Christy pinched her. "I mean, I can just imagine you must have been rowdy if you were so different from us," Sierra said quickly, trying to cover her blunder. "Christy and I are actually pretty boring people when it comes down to it."

"Speak for yourself," Christy teased.

Marti resumed walking in step with Christy and Sierra. A moment later, she asked, "Christy, what has your mother said about me?"

"Nothing."

"No, you can tell me. What has Margaret been saying?"

"All she ever said was that you two were pretty opposite, and I know my mom was super obedient and had a boring social life."

"My social life was never boring, that's for sure."

"What was it like?" Sierra said, barging into the conversation. She thought this might be the right time for her to start tearing down the walls that Marti had built.

"That's quite a bold question," Marti said. She sounded surprised but not offended.

"Did you have lots of boyfriends?" Sierra asked. "I picture you with the captain of the football team or maybe the star basketball player. You would have made a cute couple—a tall guy and you, a sweet, petite girl."

Marti laughed. "He was actually a hockey player. And he wasn't all that tall. Just muscular and, oh, so aggressive! I believed he could stop the world from rotating if I only asked. Nelson was definitely a self-made guy. What Nelson wanted, Nelson got."

"That was his first name?" Sierra asked. "Nelson?"

Marti suddenly looked surprised, as if she hadn't realized what she had said. "You girls don't need to hear this. Forget I brought it up. That was all very long ago. What we should be doing is discussing our plans for tomorrow. Why don't we plan on breakfast at eight? We'll meet downstairs as we did this morning, only please try to be on time tomorrow. We can take it from there. I think some shopping is in order, don't you?"

Sierra wasn't ready to think about shopping. She had uncovered a corner of Marti's armor, and the name tattooed there was "Nelson."

ten

"NELSON," SIERRA REPEATED to Christy once they were back in their room. "Have you ever met anyone named Nelson?"

"No."

"I wonder what happened with him. She almost told us—did you notice that?" Sierra asked.

Christy nodded. "She was in a good mood, too. That was nice."

"Let's hope her good mood sticks around for a while."

The next morning Marti was still in a good mood when they met downstairs for breakfast. Sierra might have tried to make another crack in Marti's armor, except this time Sierra was the one in a foul mood.

She hadn't slept well. The nap had thrown her off, and so she wasn't able to fall asleep right away like Christy had. Instead, Sierra lay in the quiet room thinking and praying, half awake and half asleep for hours.

It didn't help that Alex hadn't called. *Why do guys do that?* Sierra fumed to herself. *They say they'll call, they act sweet and even*

*touch your cheek like they mean to keep their promise, and then you never hear
from them. Here I was thinking of what it would be like to sneak out, and then
he doesn't even call!*

The more she thought about her previous urge to sneak
out, the worse she felt. She wouldn't even dream of doing
something like that at home. Why had she allowed herself to
think it would be okay here? All she could come up with
was, at home, she respected her parents and their authority
over her. She didn't feel exactly the same about Marti.

"We can start with shops down the street where we went
for our walk last night," Marti suggested after her breakfast.
"I especially wanted to go back and buy that scarf I saw about
two blocks down. Was there anything in particular you girls
saw that you wanted?"

"Nope," Christy said. She had awakened in a sunny
mood. When Sierra emerged from the shower, Christy had
been seated at the desk, reading her Bible, writing in her
journal, and humming. Sierra threw a pillow at her, but
that didn't stop her happy little tune.

They entered the first shop, and Sierra watched Marti
turn into a different person. She greeted the friendly sales-
clerks and began to make flattering comments about their
merchandise. The clerks moved in closer and responded to
her in their professional English. Marti was in control.

"Why do you think Alex didn't call?" Sierra asked
Christy.

They hung back in the front corner of the store next to
a display of greeting cards.

"He probably had a good reason."

"Yeah, like, he's a guy and all guys are alike. They come
across all sweet and interested, and then someone more

interesting catches their attention and suddenly you're nothing to them."

Christy laughed softly.

"I wish you wouldn't mock me when I'm sulking." Sierra crossed her arms and gave Christy an exaggerated pout.

"It's funny," Christy said. "Not what you're feeling, but what you're saying sounds exactly like what I used to say about Todd a few years ago."

"Great. Now you're telling me that even Dream Boy Todd used to be an insensitive jerk. Is there no hope?"

"Oh, I could tell you stories! There's enough to fill a book." Christy leaned closer. "Todd has still been known to have occasional setbacks. Like with this trip. This is a big decision for me, and I think it involves Todd, too. But he keeps acting like it doesn't matter. Whatever I want to do will be fine with him. Makes me so mad when I think about it."

"I'm sure he's only trying to be nice and give you freedom to make your own decision."

"Are you defending him?" Christy said, now crossing her arms as well.

"Somebody should," Sierra remarked.

She and Christy eyed each other.

At that moment, Sierra realized that if she looked half as silly as Christy did, both standing there in their mutual pout positions, the two of them must be a hilarious sight. She started to laugh.

"What?" Christy said.

"Guys," Sierra said with a glimmer in her eyes. "Who needs 'em?"

"That's right," Christy agreed. "Who needs them? We're in Switzerland, for goodness' sake! We need to start having our own fun and forget about Todd and Alex."

"I'm with you," Sierra said. "We have the whole day ahead of us without a single guy on the schedule. What do you want to do?"

"I'm sure Marti wants to shop some more, but then she always wants to shop." Christy looked over at her aunt. "If you see anything, be sure to speak up. She'll buy it for you. I think her hobby is buying things for people."

"You mean her hobbit," Sierra said.

"Her what?"

"That's what Alex said instead of 'hobby.'"

"Alex?" Christy challenged. "I thought we were done with those undependable guys. It's just us women today."

"You're right," Sierra said, holding up her arm as if she were the Statue of Liberty. "Onward to freedom and liberty and shaking off our emotional chains."

As she spoke the last two words, her fist hit a revolving rack of note cards and tipped the rack off balance. It teetered dangerously.

"Look out!" Christy yelled to one of the customers who was heading for the door and about to be clobbered by the card rack.

Sierra's quick reflexes enabled her to catch the edge of the rack, and she jerked it back toward herself. The rack didn't hit the startled customer, but a dozen packets of note cards ejected in the sudden yank and pummeled the unsuspecting woman like snowballs. The rack, responding to Sierra's quick pull, toppled in the other direction. It landed on the greeting cards, crumpling dozens of them as it continued its crash course to the floor, where it pulled out the electric cord along the wall, causing the overhead lights and fans to turn off.

Everything suddenly went silent. Everyone in the store turned to stare at Sierra and Christy. A salesclerk marched over and plugged the lights and fan back in.

"Quick!" Sierra said under her breath. "How do you say 'Excuse me' in German?"

"Sorry," Christy blurted out. "Pardon us. *Merci. Por favor.*"

"That's not German!" Sierra hissed through her clenched smile.

"It was the best I could do," Christy said.

She helped Sierra right the toppled rack and began to scoop up the packages of note cards.

"Are you all right?" Sierra asked the still startled customer.

The woman answered in French and then in German. When Sierra understood neither, the shopper swatted her hand in the air and exited the shop.

"What happened?" Marti demanded, flying to their corner of the store.

"It was an accident," Christy said, calmly placing the note cards back in the rack. "Oh, these are cute. Did you see these with the wildflowers, Sierra?"

"Let's get some," Sierra suggested, placing the last of the note cards onto the rack.

"Couldn't you have decided they were cute without causing the entire display to fall apart?" Marti snapped. "They're ruined, so we'll have to buy all of them."

"They're not ruined," Sierra said. "They're packaged in

these sturdy plastic boxes. But the cards are a different story." She turned to look behind her. At least two dozen greeting cards were mangled.

Marti marched over and began to snap up the bent cards. She even took ones that were not bent but were in the vicinity of the damaged ones.

"You two wait outside and try not to destroy anything else, will you?" Marti whooshed past them and went to pay for the cards. Sierra and Christy silently left the small store and walked over to a streetlight to wait for Marti. A basket of bright yellow marigolds and tiny blue flowers hung over their heads.

"Don't do any more liberated-woman imitations, Sierra, or you'll bring that flower basket down on your head," Christy warned with a laugh.

"Is your aunt so annoyed that she'll never want to see me again?"

"She'll be okay. Don't worry about it. It was an accident. Besides, we got a year's supply of German greeting cards out of the deal. That might not have happened if the rack hadn't come after you."

They both started to laugh.

"I want the cards," Sierra said. "I think we should send them to all our friends and let them guess what the German greeting says."

"Let's do it!" Christy agreed. "They probably say, 'Sorry to hear about your kidney stones,' or "Congratulations on your retirement.'"

"Probably!" Sierra agreed. She shielded her eyes from the sun and looked across the street at a small wooden booth that was painted white and had green shutters. It looked like a playhouse complete with window boxes brimming with masses of orange, yellows, and blue flowers. "What is that little place? I didn't see it last night when we walked along here."

"It looks like an information booth. They probably have free maps. Should we get one?"

"Sure," Sierra said, leading the way across the cobblestone street.

An older man smoking a thin-stemmed pipe and wearing lederhosen and a green felt hat greeted them.

"*Guten tag,*" he said with a nod.

"Do you speak English?" Christy asked.

"Of course," he said.

"Is this an information booth?" she asked.

He silently raised his gray eyes to the large information sign above his head.

"We'd like a map." Sierra said, tucking her head in next to Christy's. "Do you have one that shows all the interesting places to go in Basel?"

"Yes." He handed them a brightly colored map with directions in four languages. "What would you like to see?" he asked.

"I'd like to go on a picnic in the Alps," Sierra said suddenly. "Like in *The Sound of Music.*"

"That was in Austria," Christy said.

"I know, but Austria and Switzerland share the same mountains, don't they? I think a picnic would be fun. We could take a bus, couldn't we? The taxis are so expensive."

"Yes, you can take a bus or you can take a train. Which mountain range would you like to see?"

Sierra shrugged. "Any of them. I like all mountains. Isn't the Matterhorn in Switzerland?"

"Yes, you could take a trip to Zermatt," the man said, opening a map of Switzerland all the way.

"I didn't mean an overnight trip. Just a day trip. For today. I thought we could go on a picnic today," Sierra said.

The man closed the map. "Then perhaps you would allow me to make another suggestion."

He opened a smaller map and, with a red pen, marked the bus line they should take. He pointed across the street to a yellow building where they would stand to catch the bus. When Christy and Sierra turned to see where he was pointing, they both saw Marti at the same time. She was pacing back and forth in front of the store with a frenzied look on her face.

"This is great. Thank you," Christy said, reaching for the map and hurrying across the street.

"*Danke,*" Sierra called over her shoulder. She knew Marti would be hopping mad that they hadn't told her where they were going. Their plan had been innocent—a quick detour before Marti got out of the store.

There she stood, her fist punching into her waist and her toe tapping. In her hand, she held a bag filled with mangled German greeting cards.

eleven

"I'M NOT UPSET," Marti said. With purposeful steps, she led Christy and Sierra down the street toward the scarf shop. "You explained the situation to me, and like I said, next time just tell me where you're going. You can imagine how I felt when I stepped out of the shop, having covered the expense of your catastrophe, only to discover you were nowhere to be found. How would *you* feel? I was terrified. I'm responsible for the two of you, and if anything ever happened, why, I'd never recover from it."

"We're really sorry," Christy said, keeping step with her aunt.

"I know. I accepted your apology the first time you offered it. Now let's stay together, and everything will be fine."

Sierra thought for a moment that it might have been better if Marti had exploded and yelled at them. It was terrible to go through her drawn-out scolding and repeated instructions. They entered the scarf shop, and Sierra and Christy played the roles of interested and attentive nieces, helping Marti select three scarves.

"I believe the next stop should be a clothing store for you, Sierra. You said you would like to buy a dress or perhaps a new skirt. I want to treat you. Did you see a shop that interested you along the way, or should we keep going?"

"It's okay, really," Sierra began. Christy pressed her finger into Sierra's back. It had become Christy's signal to tell Sierra not to argue with Marti. "Actually, I saw a shop about three doors back that had some gauze skirts in the window."

"Gauze skirts?" Marti questioned. "Those hippie clothes?"

Sierra paused before nodding. "We could look there."

"If you're sure that's what you want."

Marti led the way to the shop. When they entered, the fragrance of heavy incense greeted them. Little bells chimed over the door, and exotic music played in the background. Posters with satanic emblems hung on the walls, and fake green snakes crawled out of the ceiling. Sierra immediately turned around and went back outside.

"That was not my kind of shop," she said.

"Well, I should hope not," Marti said.

"I like natural-looking clothes like the ones in their window, but that's all I like. The clothes are nice, but the other stuff they're promoting in there isn't."

"Why don't we keep going down the street?" Christy suggested. "There are lots more shops."

The threesome slowed their pace a little as the sun warmed them and more people crowded the streets. To Sierra, it felt as if they were in the States and this was an elite outdoor shopping center built to resemble an old European marketplace. Only this was the real thing. People speaking different languages brushed past them while the scent of strong black coffee wafted from the tiny sidewalk bakeries. In all the windows, the small shops displayed their finest wares behind thick glass, hoping to entice shoppers into their stores.

Marti, Sierra, and Christy lingered at a shop that sold nothing but tea. The wall behind the long mahogany counter was lined from ceiling to floor with dozens of bins of loose tea leaves. The scent of the mixtures filled the room. Each time Sierra drew in a breath of the fruit teas, black teas, and rich Ceylon and oolong leaves, she felt as if she had just tasted something delicious.

"I have to buy some," she said to Marti and Christy. "Do you guys mind waiting a minute? I'd like to get in line and buy some tea."

"Here's some money," Marti said.

"Thanks, but I have enough. I'm only going to buy a small bag."

Sierra studied the names of various teas as she made her way forward in line. Every time a customer pointed to a bin, one of the two white-aproned clerks pulled it open and ladled out the leaves with a metal scoop. The tea was weighed in kilos, Sierra noticed. She decided half a kilo would be more than enough. Using gestures, nods, and the clerk's heavily accented English, Sierra was able to buy exactly what she wanted: jasmine spice. It smelled wonderful. She felt sophisticated and cultured. They exited the shop, leaving the exotic aromas behind as the door shut.

"That was fun," Sierra said. "Thanks for being patient."

"Not a problem," Marti said, pulling a lipstick tube from her purse and dabbing some color on her lips. "I could use a drink and maybe some lunch. How about you girls?"

"Do they have water anywhere in this country?" Sierra asked. "With all the snow in the Alps, you would think a drinking fountain would be on every corner."

"In here," Marti said, directing them into a bakery. "Bottled water is in the refrigerated case, Sierra. What would you like, Christy?"

"One of those," Christy said, pointing to a fat, flaky, blond-colored pastry in the case. A thin line of chocolate was drizzled over the delicacy.

The minute Sierra saw it, she said, "Definitely one of those for me, too."

Marti stepped forward and ordered for the girls. Sierra noticed that once again Marti's voice rose. She seemed to think the clerks could understand her only if she spoke loudly and exaggerated each word.

The trio took the white, glossy pastry bags outside. A father and son were leaving their seats on a window bench, providing an open seat for their group. Saying something in German, the man motioned for them to sit down. They nodded their thanks, and all three squeezed onto the brightly painted red bench.

"This is heaven," Sierra said, turning her face up to catch the warmth of the midday sun as she devoured her first bite of pastry. "What do they put in these? Mrs. Kraus needs this recipe so she can add these to the menu at Mama Bear's."

"It's probably marzipan," Marti commented. "Very popular in their pastries here."

"What kind did you get?" Sierra asked Marti.

"Nothing. A diet Coke is all I wanted."

"How can you be in Switzerland in a bakery like that and not get anything?" Sierra asked. This time Christy didn't try to stop her.

"Think of all the butter and sugar in those rolls!" Marti said.

"I don't have to think," Christy said. "I'm experiencing it."

"It will go right to your thighs," Marti warned.

"Here, have a bite of mine," Sierra urged.

"No thank you."

"Come on! One little bite. It tastes incredible! When are you ever going to be able to get a pastry like this again— and especially in Switzerland?" Sierra broke off the end of her roll using the bag as a glove and offered the sweet to Marti. "Please. Try it."

"I don't know why it's such an issue for you," Marti said.

Christy leaned over and said, "Come on, Aunt Marti! You're going to walk off all those calories this afternoon anyhow. Live a little."

Shaking her short dark hair to show she'd given in, Marti reached over and took the chunk of pastry from Sierra. The two girls waited for Marti's response.

Marti reluctantly drew the dainty morsel to her mouth and slowly took a bite. "Oh, that was good!" she said, savoring the pastry.

Sierra and Christy both giggled. "We told you! Go back in there and buy one for yourself."

"Do you think I should?" Marti's expression was like a little girl's. The transformation from dictator to uncertain child amazed Sierra.

"Definitely," Christy said. "If you don't go in there and buy one, Sierra and I are going to buy you one—and you know what happens when the two of us are let loose in these small shops."

"Say no more," Marti said, holding up a hand. "I'm on my way." She sprang from her seat. Grinning coyly over her shoulder, Marti entered the shop.

"You know," Sierra said, tearing off a piece of her pastry, "I like your aunt when she's on sugar."

Christy laughed. "She's a complex woman, isn't she?" Christy held up a piece of pastry and slowly placed it in her mouth.

"She's exhausted," Sierra said.

"I thought she said she slept well last night."

"No, I mean she's exhausted from hiding something deep inside for so long. It keeps trying to leak out, and she spends most of her time on guard, making sure she doesn't let up and allow her pain to surface."

"Whose psych book did you read?" Christy said, turning to study Sierra.

"Nobody's. It's only my humble opinion. You don't have to agree with it."

"That's the scary part. It makes sense. I might agree with you."

"All we have to do is wait for the right moment and ask the right question, and she'll let it all out," Sierra said.

"Don't count on it," Christy said.

The bell over the pastry shop door jingled, and Marti

stepped out with her own glossy white pastry bag in hand and a mischievous grin on her face.

She sat down and said in a lowered voice, "I also got us truffles. Did you see their chocolates? World class. Absolutely exquisite. Here's one for you, and one for you, and one for me. *Bon appetit!*"

Sierra gave Christy a look that said, "Told you. We're wearing down all her defenses."

Christy took a bite of her truffle and began to chew it.

"No, no, no!" Marti scolded. "You don't chew a truffle! You let it dissolve slowly on your tongue. Savor the experience."

Sierra took a tiny bite of the rich chocolate and let it dissolve in her closed mouth. It was good. Very good.

"You're right," she said to Marti. "Make the moment last as long as you can."

"Chocolate should be a tender experience," Marti said. She closed her eyes and drew in a deep breath. "I can't remember the last time I had chocolate like this."

"Did Nelson bring you chocolates?" Sierra asked.

Marti slowly opened her eyes and looked down at her pastry bag, then over at Sierra. People were milling around the street, entering and exiting shops. It seemed as though everything clicked into slow motion as Marti said, "Nelson brought me anything I wanted, including chocolates."

"Whatever happened to him?" Christy ventured.

Sierra admired Christy's bravery. But then, how hard was it for Christy to step over a wall Sierra had just brought down?

It appeared the answer was on the edge of Marti's chocolate-smudged lips, as if she were about to divulge some secret. Then her lips closed, and she seemed to swallow more than her last bite of truffle.

"Perhaps I'll tell you sometime," she said in a hollow voice. Marti reached into her pastry bag and broke off a portion of the flaky croissant. She chewed it slowly, mechanically. Sierra couldn't tell whether Marti was savoring the pastry or if she had lost her taste for everything and was only going through the motions. It seemed to represent the way Sierra believed Marti went through life—making all the right moves without enjoying any of it.

They sat silently in the strong heat of the August sun, eating their pastries, each swept up in her own thoughts.

twelve

SIERRA CHEWED HER PASTRY SLOWLY. She could feel the persistent sun on her face. Voices floated through the street. Overhead, she heard a bird call to its mate. The summer breeze blew across her bare legs, just lightly enough to make its presence known.

For many years, Sierra had compared the Holy Spirit to the wind, as it said in the Bible, noting that it was always there, no matter how faint the breeze. The wind went where it wanted to go, and its path was easy to detect because it moved objects and people. But no one had ever seen the wind.

Sitting on the bench in Basel, Sierra felt that something deep inside her was coming alive. Was it desire? Passion? A sugar rush?

No. This was something emotional and spiritual blended together. The stirring was strong and vibrant. It made Sierra realize she wanted to enjoy to the absolute fullest this life God had given her. She wanted to be more aware of the Holy Spirit's "breeze" blowing through her life.

She wanted its effects and presence to be evident in her. She knew she didn't want to turn out like Marti, living by schedules and goals, not tasting the sweetness that was before her.

Sierra realized that, lately, she had been setting up her life like Marti did. Sierra had rules, standards, goals for college. Her summer had been packed with working, volunteering at the homeless shelter, and being at church nearly every time the doors opened. For the first time, Sierra saw that she had organized a lot of the spontaneity and joy right out of life.

Then something else occurred to Sierra. She realized what her father had meant when he gave her the purity ring. He'd told her to enjoy herself. Sierra had all her goals in place, but where was the good clean fun in her life? This last-minute trip had awakened those impulses in her, and she liked it. This vitality felt good—freeing. And it felt right. Finally, Sierra was being true to who she was and who God had made her to be.

"What was that verse, Christy?"

Christy licked her fingers and wadded her empty pastry bag into a little ball. "Which verse? First Peter 4:8—that one Alex quoted yesterday?"

"Yes. What did it say about love?"

"I just read it in my Bible this morning and underlined it. It said, 'Above all, love each other deeply, because love covers over a multitude of sins.'"

"That's it," Sierra said. "Love each other deeply. How did Alex say it? Oh yeah, 'fervently.'" Sierra thought another moment and then said, "You do that, Christy. You love people fervently. I like that about you. I want to be like that."

Christy began to blush.

"You know what I don't understand?" Marti interjected. "How did you two become such good friends? When I was your age, Christy, I would never have enjoyed being friends with someone three years younger than myself. I certainly wouldn't have considered her to be a genuine friend."

"There's really only about two years difference between us," Christy said. "But it doesn't seem like even that much."

"It's because I'm so mature," Sierra said playfully in a deep voice.

Marti said, "I find that to be true."

"I was only kidding," Sierra said.

"I wasn't. You both are so much more aware of yourselves and of life than I was at your age. Mind you, I don't agree with the fervor of your Christianity, but I do think it's been an advantage for you both in some ways."

"It's not supposed to be an advantage," Christy said. "It's supposed to be my whole life."

"Oh, Christina! Can't you simply take the compliment without trying to correct me? I was being nice."

"I noticed that," Sierra commented.

Marti and Christy both looked at Sierra.

"I meant, I noticed you were being nice, Marti. I thought it was nice that you were complimenting us. Thank you."

"You're welcome. See, Christina? That's the proper way to respond to a compliment."

"I appreciate your comment, too." Christy said.

"Good," Marti said. She paused and then added, "I suppose we should get going. On to a dress shop?"

"How about a picnic?" Sierra asked.

"Isn't that what we just had?" Marti asked back.

"We picked up a map from the information booth," Christy said. "Sierra and I were thinking it would be fun to do some hiking and take a picnic snack up into the Alps."

"We're already taking a walk," Marti said, appearing unclear as to why a walk in the mountains would be more appealing than taking a stroll down this wonderful row of shops.

"Maybe tomorrow?" Christy asked hopefully.

"You'll have plenty of time to hike these mountains if you come to school here," Marti said, making her way into the crowds along the street.

Christy tossed her bag into a trash can. "Sierra won't."

"Sierra needs a dress," Marti said firmly. "We still haven't eaten at a really nice restaurant, and Sierra certainly won't be allowed in wearing those baggy shorts."

The rest of the afternoon was spent fulfilling Marti's goal of finding nice clothes for Sierra. They returned to the hotel by cab since they had walked so far and now had their arms loaded with bags.

"I'll ask the concierge to make reservations for us at seven," Marti announced as they entered the hotel lobby. "That gives you nearly two hours to rest, shower, and dress up. And do wear the black skirt, Sierra, not the gypsy one."

"Yes, Aunt Marti," Sierra teased in a nasal-sounding voice.

Marti turned sharply and gave Sierra an intensely disapproving look. Sierra knew she would never joke around like that again.

"Are you going to take a shower?" Sierra asked Christy

as they tossed all their bags onto the beds.

"I'm thinking about it. You know what? I think my arms got sunburned. Can you believe that?"

"The sun was pretty hot when we were sitting in front of the bakery," Sierra said. "My cheeks feel red."

"They are a little," Christy said, examining Sierra's face. "How do you do that?"

"Do what?"

"You look perfectly fresh, like you don't need a shower at all. Your hair is perfect and your face is perfect."

"My hair is never perfect. My hair has a mind of its own. It never cooperates with me," Sierra said, grabbing a handful of the long, unruly strands.

"Alex sure liked it," Christy teased. "Why don't you see if we got any phone messages?"

"You read my mind," Sierra said.

While Christy was in the shower, Sierra tried to figure out how to work the message retrieval service on the phone. An instruction sheet printed in German, English, French, and Italian was in the top drawer of the desk. It didn't help. Even the English instructions were hard to decipher. When Sierra finally pushed the right buttons, she was rewarded with the sound of Alex's deep voice on the other end.

"This is Alexander, and I am calling for See-hair-a. I will be at my cousin's house today helping him repair his automobile. If you do not already have arrangements for tomorrow, I would like to take you on a picnic. I will call again tonight, and we can make our plans. Ciao."

There was a click on the end of the receiver and a zing inside Sierra's heart. Alex hadn't forgotten about her. He wanted to take her on a picnic tomorrow. Or rather, to take

Sierra and Christy on a picnic. Marti had to let them go. Sierra hoped Marti would be in a good mood at dinner when Sierra asked permission.

It was hard to distinguish what kind of mood Marti was in that evening. Sierra and Christy had dressed according to her instruction, both wearing basic black evening attire. They took their time putting on makeup and talking about Alex and the picnic. Christy urged Sierra to leave it up to her. She would find the right approach with her aunt.

Marti wore a stunning black dress with a string of pearls and black high heels. As the three of them paraded through the hotel lobby, Marti carried herself like a movie star at the Academy Awards. A cab was waiting for them and drove them to the nicest restaurant Sierra had ever been to in her life. The place was small and intimate. The light was golden, and the music from the string trio reverberated off the delicately painted ceiling.

Sierra noticed that everyone was dressed up, and everyone was wearing black. She leaned over once they were seated and softly thanked Marti for the new skirt. Then she asked Marti to please order for her since she trusted Marti's judgment more than her own at a place like this. Marti was pleased.

Their dinner was cold cucumber soup, with baby carrots that were arranged like a bouquet on her plate, and a swirl of garlicked mashed potatoes. And then coffee and dessert. Sierra thought dessert would be the perfect time to bring up the picnic with Alex. Christy and Sierra nibbled on a rich chocolate torte while Marti sipped her espresso in a dainty cup, which according to Marti was called a "demitasse."

But Christy didn't say anything, so Sierra forced herself

to wait until Christy decided the time was right.

They took the cab back to the hotel. The *alt stadt* was lit up beautifully at night, and many people were strolling on the bridge across the Rhine River or walking along the storefronts. Marti paid the cab driver, led the girls back upstairs, and in the hallway said good night to them.

"Oh," Christy said suddenly. "We haven't decided yet what we're going to do tomorrow. Would you like to come to our room so we can talk about it?"

"I thought we would go back to the school tomorrow and meet Mr. Pratt. We only have tomorrow," Marti reminded them. "The next day we have to leave."

"Oh," Christy said again.

"Is that our phone ringing?" Sierra said, pressing her ear to the door. "Hurry up! Open the door."

"Who would be calling you?" Marti said.

Sierra burst inside and reached for the phone. "Hello?"

"Is this See-hair-a?" Just hearing Alex say her name with his distinctive accent brought a smile to her lips. "Yes, this is Sierra."

"This is Alex."

"Yes," Sierra said, trying to suppress a giggle, "I know."

"Did you receive my message?"

"Yes."

Christy was giving Sierra a "Well?" look.

"Who is it?" Marti asked.

"Would you like to go for a hike tomorrow?" Alex asked.

Sierra paused. "Yes, I would. But I'll need to talk to Marti about this."

"If it would be helpful, I will speak with her."

"Good idea." Sierra held out the phone to Marti. "For you," she said, biting her lower lip and giving Christy a sideways glance.

"Hello? Who is this?" Marti asked. "Oh yes, Alex.... What's that?... Tomorrow? I'm afraid we have plans already."

Sierra's heart sank.

"Why, yes, we are returning to the school.... No, in the morning." Then Marti was silent. To Sierra, it seemed like the longest pause in the world.

"Yes, all right then.... Thank you for calling. Good night."

Sierra watched Marti hang up the phone and felt like diving to grab the phone. Sierra's stomach sank when she hear the "click" of the receiver.

Christy and Sierra waited with wide eyes.

"Well?" they asked in unison.

thirteen

"DID YOU TWO ARRANGE THIS?" Marti asked with her hands on her hips.

"No," they said in one voice.

"You're telling me Alex decided on his own to call and invite you to go on a picnic?"

"Yes."

"He called earlier," Sierra explained. "While we were out shopping this afternoon. He left a message and said he would call back tonight. So, in a way, we did know about his invitation, but we didn't talk to him today."

"Why didn't you tell me he called earlier?" Marti asked.

"We're afraid of you," Sierra blurted out.

Marti let a rippling laugh escape. "Afraid of me? Why?"

"We really wanted to go," Christy explained. "We thought you might not agree unless we asked when you were in a good mood."

Marti lowered herself into the desk chair. "Is that what you think of me?"

"You haven't exactly been crazy about Alex," Sierra said.

She gave up all hope of seeing him again. Marti had responded so coolly on the phone that Sierra was certain Marti had ruined any possibility Sierra and Alex would get together.

"Your view of me is about to change." Marti slapped the top of the desk with her open palm. "Tomorrow morning at eight, we will meet downstairs for breakfast. At nine, Alex will take us to the school. After our meeting there, Alex will drop me off at an art festival in a small town not far from the school. He will then take the two of you out for a picnic lunch."

Sierra's heart soared. "That's great! Thank you!"

"See? I'm not such an old party pooper, after all. Now get some sleep. Tomorrow will be a busy day." With a swish, Marti left.

Sierra danced around the room. "I can't believe it! Your aunt has a streak of human kindness in her after all. This is going to be so great! A picnic in the hills! Is this going to be romantic, or what?"

"With me along, it'll probably be 'or what,'" Christy said. "I'm glad it worked out, though."

"Oh, yeah," Sierra said, reaching for her pillow to throw at Christy. "No thanks to you! When were you going to bring up the subject? On our plane ride home?"

"No," Christy said, ducking as the flying pillow came her way. "I was scared, just like you said. I've never admitted it before, but my aunt scares me sometimes. I like the way you get right at the heart of an issue and speak up truthfully. I have a hard time doing that."

"It gets me in lots of trouble," Sierra said.

"Not tonight, it didn't."

"Christy," Sierra said, flopping onto her stomach across the bed, "do you think it's right for me to be so excited about seeing Alex?"

"Of course. Why do you even ask?"

"Because I don't usually get all hyper about seeing a guy. It's weird. I mean, where could this relationship possibly lead? I probably won't ever see him again after tomorrow."

"Hold that thought. I'll be right back." Christy slipped off her shoes and grabbed her pajamas.

While Christy was in the bathroom, Sierra let her thoughts fly freely. When Christy returned in her pajamas, Sierra asked, "Did you ever go out with a guy only one time and that was it? I mean, was there ever an Alex in your life?"

"Sort of." Christy fluffed up her pillow and got comfy on the bed. "I was a counselor at camp one summer, and this guy, Jaeson, asked me to go out with him one night. Well, he didn't exactly tell me where we were going. He just asked me to go to a movie. I went, but once we had left our camp area, he took my hand and said he was going to teach me how to paddle a canoe."

Sierra let out a hoot. "Now that's an original line! Did you like this guy?"

"Yes, sort of, I think. Now, it seems unbelievable that I ever liked him, but I know I had strong feelings for him then. Looking back, though, I don't know if I ever really liked Jaeson or if I just liked the attention he gave me."

Sierra's emotions began to plummet. What if she were just after the attention? Earlier that summer, she'd gone through that with Drake, a guy from school. After their first and only date, she had decided she liked the *idea* of being asked out more than she liked actually having a relationship.

There were too many complications in trying to define the relationship, especially trying to define it to her friends.

But Christy didn't seem to have any problem with Sierra and Alex's relationship. It was strange—when Drake had entered the picture, all of Sierra's friendships became strained. But now, having Alex around hadn't changed Sierra and Christy's friendship at all.

Christy continued. "I'm not saying I'm sorry I went out on the lake with Jaeson. It was beautiful the way the moon rose and shone across the water. Jaeson had set up the canoe with candles and flowers. And he had peanut butter cookies he had saved from the first night of camp. It was all very sweet of him."

"Did you have permission to be away from the campers?" Sierra asked.

"No. And I've always felt bad about that part. It wasn't right that we sneaked out. No one found out, but it didn't matter. Leaving the main meeting was against the rules, and we could have gotten in trouble. It bothered me for a long time. I asked God for forgiveness, and then I even wrote a letter to the camp dean to confess. He wrote me a very nice letter back, but to this day I still feel bad about breaking the rules."

Sierra was glad she hadn't sneaked out to see Alex. She didn't have to, because everything was working out. She knew what Christy meant, though. Sierra would have felt bad for a long time, too.

"Can I ask the big question?"

"You want to know if Jaeson taught me how to paddle the canoe correctly? Yes as a matter of fact, he did."

"No," Sierra laughed, "you know that's not what I was going to ask."

Christy's lips turned up in a smile. "Did Jaeson kiss me?"

"Well, did he?"

"No." Christy looked off toward the ceiling with both arms behind her head. "I remember being so nervous. I thought he was going to kiss me, and then he reached over and brushed my cheek. But it was only because I had cookie crumbs stuck there. I must have looked like such a loser to him."

"I'm sure that's not what he thought."

Christy turned onto her side and propped her head up with her arm. "You know what I think? I think a lot of things aren't about what we think they're about. Like the canoe ride. It wasn't about Jaeson, our relationship, or our kissing or not kissing. What I remember most about that night—besides that big, fat, yellow moon and the way it came over the mountain—was that Jaeson asked me what my dream was. That's what that whole night was really about."

Christy sat up and gave her full attention to Sierra. "Jaeson asked me, 'What's your dream?' and I told him something I'd never told anyone else before."

Sierra too sat up and waited, feeling honored to share Christy's secret.

"Wow," Christy said in a moment of sudden revelation, "I haven't thought of this in ages. I told him my dream was to go to Europe. I said I wanted to visit a real castle and go for a gondola ride in Venice."

"That's what you told him?"

Christy nodded. "Isn't that wild? I had no idea then that I'd go to Europe twice in one year, or actually live in a castle like we did in England."

"Guess all that's left is the gondola ride," Sierra said. She could feel her sunburned cheeks tightening as she flashed Christy a big smile. "Kind of a God-thing that you remembered your dreams of Europe tonight, when you have to decide about the school."

Christy nodded solemnly. "I know. It is. Maybe God has been preparing me for this school for a long time, and it isn't such a whim after all."

They shared a comfortable silence before Sierra spoke up again. "Do you think your relationship with Jaeson was about your dreams and not about building a lasting friendship?"

"Something like that," Christy said slowly. "That night was about being brave enough to open my heart and tell my dream to Jaeson. To be honest, it doesn't really matter now whether or not I kissed him. As long as it was only a quick, innocent kiss. It would have mattered if we had, you know, done more. Then I would have been giving away part of my passion, and I want to save all my passion for just one man."

"Todd," Sierra answered for her.

"My husband, whoever he will be. I haven't given my passionate, intimate self to Todd—or to any guy. I've only kissed a few guys, but to me a short, tender kiss is way different from a passionate embrace and prolonged, heart-and-soul kissing. You know what I mean?"

"Not from personal experience, but yes, I think I understand. I never thought of it that way before. I thought the goal was not to kiss at all until you're standing at the wedding altar, like Doug and Tracy did."

"That's what was right for them," Christy said. "Doug is such a loving and affectionate guy. You know how he is, always hugging everyone. I think it would have been hard for him to only give a girlfriend a short, sweet kiss. And I think he knew that, too. He set a very high standard, and I totally admire him for sticking to it."

"So, what you're saying is that you and Todd have a different standard, but you think that's okay?" Sierra was trying to understand.

"Yes, I do. Todd and I have drawn the line at light kissing. We hug and hold hands, too. But that's it. And that's all it'll be for me until I marry, no matter whom I end up with. Todd told me one time that his goal was to give me his affection but not his passion. That made sense to me and that's where I draw the line, too. For us, affection can mean brief kisses. For someone else, that might be too big of a temptation or something."

Sierra was listening carefully to Christy's words. She knew it was wise advice. Their talk made Sierra think of her friend back home, Amy, who had told Sierra about a first date she'd had with a guy from work. Amy had said proudly that they had made out in his car for a long time.

When Sierra got home from this trip, she planned to have a lengthy conversation with Amy. She wanted to tell Amy some of the things Christy had just said. It would be better to talk with Amy than to judge her, which was the way Sierra had first reacted. Amy had gotten mad and defensive. Their whole friendship seemed to turn upside down in one conversation. Now Sierra was determined to find a way to make things right.

Sierra smiled at Christy. "I really appreciate your sharing with me, Christy. It's good to be able to talk to someone who has been there and has it figured out."

Christy laughed. "I wish I had the rest of my life figured out! I'm glad we can talk about all this stuff, too. You help me a lot with your insights—especially when it comes to my aunt. I'll be honest with you: I didn't know how well this trip would go."

"I had my doubts, too," Sierra said as she started to get ready for bed.

"It's going much better than I thought," Christy said, slipping underneath her covers.

"There's always tomorrow," Sierra said. She turned out the light. "It's a fresh new day with more note card racks to send crashing to the ground."

Christy started to laugh. "I couldn't believe that happened!"

Sierra laughed, too. "We should be safe in the wide open trails of the Black Forest. You can never be completely sure, though. I'll probably knock over a cow or something." Christy kept laughing.

They whispered and giggled like ten-year-olds at a sleepover until they were too drowsy to talk. Sierra never slept better.

fourteen

THE NEXT MORNING, specks of rain dotted the windshield as Alex drove the three women to the Black Forest People's School. A wreath of frothy mist hung over the green hills before them. Sierra tried hard not to worry that their picnic might be canceled.

Alex seemed to read her thoughts. "It is only the morning dew," he said, turning on the windshield wipers. "It will be clear before we go on our hike."

"If it doesn't clear up," Marti said, "you can come to the art festival with me. Alex tells me it's the largest in this region."

"It will clear," Alex said.

They arrived right on time at the school. While Christy and Marti met with Mr. Pratt, Sierra and Alex sat on a cushioned bench in the alcove of the school's entrance. Sierra decided at once that she liked this romantic setting. The polished wood floor reflected the massive light fixture that hung from the center of the rounded ceiling. The light looked like the top of a tree that had been cut off in winter, bronzed, and then adorned with rows of flickering candles on its frozen, outstretched limbs. The double doors to their left each had an oval in the center filled with a mosaic of clear, beveled glass. The morning light shone through the glass, creating lacy patterns at their feet.

Every word Alex and Sierra spoke echoed off the ceiling. They lowered their voices and spoke in hushed tones.

"We have much to talk of," Alex said, his deep voice still echoing through the room.

Sierra smiled. "Are you going to ask me about my dreams?"

Alex wrinkled his forehead. "Your dreams?" he questioned.

"Never mind," Sierra said. "What was it you wanted to talk about?"

Sierra noticed that Alex's dark hair was less cooperative than usual today. Instead of staying straight back with only one runaway clump, all his hair fell freely. It made him look like an Olympic skier who, upon completing his run, had pulled off his cap at the victory line. Sierra liked the look.

"What will you do when you return home?" Alex asked.

"I don't know," Sierra answered. Home was the last thing on her mind. "Work some extra hours, I guess, and get ready for school."

"This is your final year?"

Sierra nodded. "My senior year."

"And what will you then do?"

"Do you mean after I graduate from high school?"

"Yes. Then what?"

Sierra shrugged. "Go to college somewhere. I don't know where."

"I was told by an American that you must know these things early because some universities are difficult to enter."

"Some are. But I need to give it more thought."

Alex nodded his agreement. "More thought and more prayer. Am I right?"

He had been sitting only a few inches from Sierra, with his right arm resting on the back of the bench. He wasn't touching her, but she almost felt he was, since he was so close to, and focused on, her. Now he adjusted his position slightly, and for a moment his hand brushed against her shoulder.

Put your arm all the way around me and draw me close, Alex. I want you to.

Sierra's thoughts surprised her. But they felt natural. She remembered what Christy had said the previous night and wondered if she was feeling affection or passion. *Or is affection the beginning of passion?* Sierra asked herself. Then she had another mysterious thought: *What if I'm the kind of person who can't restrain myself and express only affection? What if my passions suddenly overpower me? Is that what happened to Amy on her date with Nathan?*

Sierra forced her thoughts back into the conversation.

"Oh, um, yes. Pray about my future," she said. "You're right. I need to do more praying and to start planning. This whole summer went by way too fast. What about you? When will you find out if you can get into the university?"

"Perhaps the letter will be waiting when I return home in two weeks." Alex's high cheekbones seemed to lift even more as a smile crossed his lips. "You should have known me last winter. I could not eat or sleep because of my worry over being accepted to the university. Now I have completely changed."

Sierra wasn't sure she understood what Alex was saying.

"Do you mean you aren't worried about getting into the university anymore?"

"Worry," Alex repeated thoughtfully. "I have changed my views on worry. Do you know the German word for 'worry' is the same as 'strangle'?"

"Is it really?"

Alex took both his hands and grabbed himself around the neck, demonstrating being strangled.

Sierra laughed softly. Her laughter echoed off the high ceiling.

"You have such song in your laughter. I'm beginning to know this song, and it brings me a good feeling." Alex reached over and took Sierra's hand.

She thought her heart would stop.

"There are songs all around us," he said, smoothing his fingers over the top of her hand. "Even in the touch of two friends. Shh. Listen. Do you hear the music our hands are making?"

Sierra definitely heard something. But it sounded more like bass drums pounding in her ears. She imagined it was her heart, but maybe it was music, music she was not used to yet. She smiled at Alex and said, "Tell me what you hear."

Alex closed his eyes and tilted back his head, resting it against the wood-paneled wall of their private alcove. He drew in a deep breath and squeezed Sierra's hand more tightly. "I hear the sound a river makes going over rocks on its way to the sea." Then softly he added, "There is a river of life in you, See-hair-a. See-hair-a of the mountains, not of the desert."

She felt relaxed as he spoke, comfortable holding his

hand and absorbing his poetic words. She looked down at their hands, clasped together and resting on her leg. Right above their hands was the ivy-leaf-shaped mustard stain on her jeans.

I don't think I'll ever wash these jeans again.

"What do you hear?" Alex asked without opening his eyes.

Sierra closed her eyes and leaned back her head. The hall was silent for a moment. "I don't know what I hear." Nothing she said would be able to match Alex's poetic words.

"Listen," Alex urged her. His voice was barely a whisper. His touch on her hand was light.

Sierra listened. She still didn't hear anything poetic. But she felt something. "I feel happy," Sierra said.

"Happy," Alex repeated. "One does not always feel this in life. Especially where I live. You are not choked with worry. This is good."

Down the hall they could hear voices. Marti, Christy, and Mr. Pratt were headed their way. Sierra didn't want their private time to end. She wondered if she should let go of Alex's hand or if he would let go of hers.

He stood, bringing her up with him, and then he let go of her hand. Not quickly, as though he didn't want to be seen by Mr. Pratt and the others. Alex lingered as he let go.

"Well?" Sierra asked Christy. "What did you decide about school?"

Christy looked at Mr. Pratt and then at Marti. When neither of them answered, she spoke up. "I called my parents and talked to them about everything."

"And?"

Christy nodded slowly. "I'm going to come here. I've made a year's commitment."

"Isn't that marvelous?" Marti asked. "Studying abroad is going to be fabulous for Christy. Don't you agree, Sierra?"

Sierra tried to read Christy's expression. She seemed happy and at peace with her choice.

"It's great," Sierra said. "I think you're going to have some incredible experiences."

Christy nodded. "I'm worried about a few things, but I think they'll work out."

"Don't worry," Alex said, repeating his strangling demonstration. "It will choke you."

Christy looked at Sierra for an explanation. "We'll tell you all about it on our picnic."

An hour later, Alex was leading Christy and Sierra along a dirt trail up the side of a hill. Marti had appeared to be content spending the afternoon taking in the art festival. She had left them cheerfully and asked them to be back in two hours.

"I was correct about the weather, was I not?" Alex said, pausing to survey the landscape.

The blue August sky willingly shared its open spaces with a host of plump and lazy clouds. All around them, a blanket of vibrant green grass covered the lumpy earth. To their right, a tangle of wild berry bushes kept the last of their summer treasure tucked inside their thorny caverns.

They had passed half a dozen cows on the climb up the mountain. Each cow wore a large bell around its neck, which played an enchanting strain of music as the cow grazed. Christy said she thought the cows were "cuter" than the cows at home, and Alex laughed. She told him she was qualified to make this distinction because her father was a dairy farmer, and she spent the first fifteen years of her life around cows.

Sierra drew in a deep breath. "The air is so rich here, and I love this view! I'm so glad we came. Hiking is my favorite hobby. It does something to my spirit to rise above the rest of the world," she said in satisfaction.

"I love it here, too," Christy said. "And it's so close to the school. I can't believe I'll be able to come up here any time I want. This is gorgeous!"

"Where would you like to have our picnic?" Alex asked.

"Right here," Sierra said. "This view is beautiful."

"Then we stop here."

Alex led them a few feet off the trail onto the grass. All three of them removed their day packs and pulled out their offerings for the picnic.

"I hope you are not too hungry," Alex said. "I did not bring a lot, and it is not specialty food."

"Don't worry about it," Sierra said. "We were more interested in the hike than the picnic. The food is a bonus."

"A bonus?" Alex repeated.

"It's extra," Sierra said, defining the unfamiliar word.

"Besides, Christy and I have a few goodies to share, too."

"Two candy bars," Christy said, cleaning out her day pack and placing the food in front of them.

"I have an orange left over from breakfast," Sierra said.

"Something here to drink," said Alex. "And some

cheese and bread." He pulled out a pocketknife and sliced off a hunk of cheese from the block in his hand, offering it to Sierra on the blade of his knife.

"It's practically a feast," Christy said when she accepted the next wedge of cheese Alex cut. "Now, are you going to tell me what the strangling was about at school? You kind of made me nervous."

"Alex did that when you said you were worried," Sierra explained. She broke off a corner from the loaf of bread resting on top of Alex's pack and explained how Alex had been worried about getting into the university. "We're not supposed to worry. Because worry strangles us."

"I sure don't want to go through life feeling strangled."

Christy reached for the bread with her free hand. She couldn't pull off a corner, so Alex held on to the loaf, and she broke off the bread with his help.

Sierra looked around at the perfect day. "Doesn't it seem as though we've stepped into a picture?" she asked. The breeze lifted the loose side strands of her hair and play-fully brushed them across her face. "Christy, you have to make this your thinking spot. It's so beautiful."

"I know," Christy said, drinking in the view with Sierra. "I'm getting kind of excited about coming to school here. Can you imagine how pretty this is all going to be in winter? I haven't seen much snow since we left Wisconsin. This might be my first white Christmas in five years."

Alex stretched out on his side and leaned on his arm. He reclined on the grass as if he didn't have a care in the world. "I've never known Christmas without snow," he said. "I much prefer the sunshine." He reached over and brushed the side of Sierra's bare arm with the top of his fingers. "The way the sun makes your skin warm like this, I like very much." He drew his hand back and broke off another chunk of bread.

Sierra closed her eyes and listened. What was that? She heard something. Maybe it was the distant chiming of the cows' bells or the birds singing in the trees. Whatever it was, when Alex touched her arm, she definitely heard music.

fifteen

"IT WAS MORE THAN A FUN PICNIC," Sierra explained to Marti as Alex drove them back to the hotel. "For me, it was a spiritual experience."

Marti laughed bluntly. "You know, my dear Sierra, I do believe you and my niece could manage to make a spiritual experience out of washing your hair. You mustn't become so absorbed with your heavenly thoughts, or you will be no earthly good to anyone."

Sierra glanced at Christy, who gave a silent signal to let Marti's comment go. From the moment they had picked her up at the art festival, she seemed a little wobbly in her movements. Apparently, the festival offered an abundance of wine-tasting opportunities, of which Marti took advantage. And Sierra heard the way Marti slurred the word "experience," Sierra was almost certain that Marti had tasted too much wine.

"What are you doing tonight?" Alex asked.

"We must pack," Marti said. "Sierra and Christy will not be available for dinner because we have plans."

"May I offer you a ride to the train in the morning?"

"Yes, you may," said Marti. "We must leave the hotel at seven o'clock. Will you pick us up?"

"Yes," Alex said. "I will be there at seven."

He pulled up in front of the hotel just as giant drops of rain began to splash against the windshield.

"That was convenient," Marti said. "Now I suppose you will think the rain coming back after your picnic is also spiritual."

None of them commented. Alex got out first and opened the door for Marti. Sierra and Christy climbed out and stood under the front canopy. The rain sounded like rapid-fire pellets on the overhang.

"It's really coming down." Sierra said.

"Thanks again for everything, Alex," Christy said. "We'll see you in the morning."

"Yes. At seven. I will be here."

He turned to Sierra and gave her a warm smile. For several seconds, they looked into each other's eyes, neither of them speaking. Then Alex wrapped his arms around Sierra and hugged her close. She wasn't expecting it and took a moment to respond before hugging him back.

Alex pulled away, brushing his chin against the side of her hair. "*Tschuss,*" he said.

Sierra assumed he was saying good-bye in German or French or maybe a combination of both languages.

"'Bye. I'll see you tomorrow."

He turned to dash back to his car. The rain was coming down so hard and loud that it seemed the canopy above them would burst open. A sudden flash of lightning lit up the sky, followed by a loud boom of thunder.

"Hurry," Marti called to the girls. "Hurry inside!" She looked panicked.

The second flash of lightning struck just as Sierra unlocked the door to their room. The lights in the hallway flickered. Three seconds later, the thunder came.

"This is not good," Marti said, following the girls into their room. "Don't turn on your television, and stay away from the windows."

"We used to have powerful thunderstorms like this in the mountains where I grew up," Sierra said. "I'm sure this storm is much more dramatic than the kind of storms you get at the beach where you live."

Marti didn't look comforted. She slipped off her shoes and made herself at home on Sierra's bed. "Wouldn't you know?" Marti said, shaking her head. "Now I wish Robert were here."

Sierra realized this was the first time during the entire trip that Marti had mentioned her husband. "Why didn't he come?" Sierra asked.

"Because of his face, of course," Marti answered bluntly. Recovering quickly from her brashness, she added, "What I mean to say is, his scars are still healing from the burns, and he shouldn't travel until after the plastic surgery is completed. He looks terrible. You know. You've seen him. Both of you. Do you think he should be traveling?"

Sierra could tell the alcohol was affecting Marti's judgment. Ordinarily, she would never be so frank about her husband. Could it be she was so obsessed with appearances that she was embarrassed by Bob's? It had only been five months since the gas barbecue accident had burned the side of his face, his neck, and his ear. Sierra didn't know much about burns, but she guessed Bob wouldn't be "presentable" by Marti's standard for a long time.

"Well? Do you think he should be traveling?" Marti again asked for an answer.

"I guess it depends on what the doctor recommends," Christy stated diplomatically.

"Doctors don't know anything," Marti muttered. "They said they could fix my baby, but they couldn't. They said they could fix me, but they couldn't. Why should I believe them when the say they can fix my husband?"

Sierra carefully glanced at Christy, who was seated on the edge of her bed. Christy seemed as startled as Sierra that Marti had so casually mentioned her baby. The great secret was out.

Another flash of lightning, trailed by roaring thunder, caused them to jump. Sierra sat down on the end of her bed and faced Marti. She decided if she was going to play detective about Marti's past, this was the moment.

"What happened to your baby?" Sierra said, trying to sound casual.

Marti blinked several times. "You know about Johanna?"

"I do," Christy said, moving over to Sierra's bed and closing the small circle. "Mom told me a few years ago. I'm really sorry she died. I wish you had told me about her, Aunt Marti."

"What good would that have done?"

"It would have helped me to know you better."

"Ha!" Marti laughed. "There's a lot you don't know about me. I was never like you, so open and sweet. I had secrets. Secrets hardly anyone knew."

"You don't have to tell us if you don't want to," Christy said. Her voice was full of compassion.

Marti drew in a deep breath through her nose. "No, I think you're old enough now. I promised myself I'd tell you one day. I suppose today is as good as any day. Your mother knows, but I asked her not to tell you because I thought you should hear it from me."

Sierra felt out of place. Here she had seen herself on a great mission to get Marti to open up to them. Now that she was about to talk, it seemed her confession should be between herself and Christy. Sierra didn't belong.

"Do you want me to go into your room while you and Christy talk?" Sierra asked Marti.

Another round of lightning and thunder punctuated the end of Sierra's sentence with a loud bang.

"You might as well hear this, too. You probably already figured out most of it," Marti said, turning her attention to Sierra. Marti's right eyelid seemed to droop slightly. Her usually sophisticated air was gone. "You don't miss a thing, do you, Sierra? No one your age should be as smart as you."

Sierra didn't know if she had been insulted or complimented. She leaned back and decided it would probably be best if she didn't say anything.

"Well? Go ahead and tell my niece. She hasn't figured it out yet," Marti said to Sierra.

"Figured out what?" Sierra said. "I really don't now what you mean."

"Johanna. Tell her about how Johanna was Nelson's child."

A wave of nausea hit Sierra. She didn't know why she

had thought it would be cool to unlock Marti's psyche.

Marti began her story. "We were in love. Very, very much in love when we started dating. I was fifteen. That's why I wanted you to come stay with me the summer you turned fifteen, Christy. I wanted to warn you about what can happen to nice girls who know nothing about men and life. I knew nothing when I was your age."

Marti shook her head and fixed her gaze on her niece. "But you were so different from me. I didn't know how to tell you. I didn't want to make you grow up fast like I did, so I didn't say anything."

An uneasy silence followed. It was as if they were waiting for the lightning and thunder to shatter the intensity of the moment.

"What happened?" Christy finally asked in a small, tight voice.

"I got pregnant when I was seventeen. I told Nelson, and I honestly expected him to marry me. But he left town. I never saw him again."

"That must have been awful for you," Christy said.

"I went to live with your parents, Christy. I told everyone it was because my older sister was pregnant, and she needed my help. No one knew I was pregnant, too. The baby came early and was, well...she was less than whole. I knew God was punishing me. But I didn't understand why He had to punish an innocent baby. Right after little Johanna died, your mother went into labor. I somehow felt responsible for that, too, because of the burden I'd placed on Margaret. You were born the next day, Christina, and you were perfect."

The lights in their room flickered again and then went out. It was early evening, but the storm raging outside made everything turn dark.

"I have a flashlight," Sierra said, reaching for her day pack on the floor.

"Is this one of your God-things, Christy?" Marti said with a bite to her waning voice. "This sudden darkness makes for an added touch, doesn't it? Dark—that's how I felt the day you were born. My sister was God's favored one, and I, the terrible sinner, was cursed. I moved to California and worked hard to put myself through secretarial school. My first job was for your uncle Bob. He fell in love with me and accepted me as I was. All I wanted was someone to love me and to have a daughter of our own."

Marti seemed to be running out of energy as she finished her story. "But your God doesn't forget, does He? I was diagnosed as infertile. The doctor said he could fix me, but he couldn't. You can't fight God, can you?"

"Sure you can," Sierra said. "You can fight Him and blame Him and be mad at Him all you want. He's still God. He's still in control of everything that happens. He still loves you."

Marti made a snorting sound. "Well, He has a very strange way of showing it."

In the dull lights of their room, Sierra couldn't quite make out Christy's expression. The beam from the flashlight was directed toward the bathroom, creating elongated shadows across the wall.

"He does love you," Christy added to Sierra's words.

Marti shook her head. "Love," she said. "You two have no idea what love is. You don't know what I'm talking about at all. If God is so loving and protective, then He's going to have to prove it to me." Marti leaned forward and, with some difficulty, tried to stand. She bent over to pick up her shoes and then stood up, her legs wobbling.

"Now you know, Christina. Your aunt is a horrible person, and God has given up on her. I suppose I should be glad you are such a good girl and He has smiled on you."

"God never gives up on anyone," Christy said, rising from the bed and taking quick steps in the darkness to stand beside her aunt. Christy put her arms around Marti and said fervently, "I love you, Aunt Marti. I'm sorry you have gone through such horrible things in your life. My love for you won't ever change. And I think you know deep down that God hasn't given up on you. He's just waiting for you to come to Him."

Marti received only a bit of the hug. She pulled away, and straightening up, she mumbled, "Well, He'll just have to keep waiting for me because I have a suitcase to pack and a train to catch in the morning."

With that, she took unsteady steps into her room and shut her door in exact unison with a vicious clap of thunder.

sixteen

"CHRISTY, ARE YOU AWAKE?" Sierra whispered in the darkness of their hotel room. They had gone to bed hours earlier. After Marti had left, they had ordered room service for dinner and packed their belongings while they discussed the intense conversation with Marti. The storm had continued outside, and now the noise of the pelting rain had awakened Sierra.

Christy didn't answer.

Rats! She's asleep. I wish I could fall back to sleep.

Sierra also wished Marti would have been more open to what Christy had said about how Marti needed to come to God. That's what had happened to Bob after the barbecue accident. For years, he had told Christy he didn't need God, but after the accident, he had done a complete turn-around. In the hospital, Bob had surrendered his life to Christ. His transformation had been instantaneous and obvious.

Sierra suspected Marti had not only turned a cold shoulder to God, but had also done the same to her husband now that he was a Christian.

Long into the stormy night, Sierra prayed. So much had happened in the past few days, and each of these events had been significant.

The rain pounded against their windows. The wind made a shrill, piercing noise that filled the dark room.

The clamorous storm reminded Sierra of the verse Alex had read in 1 Peter: "The end of all things is at hand; therefore be serious and watchful in your prayers. Above all things have fervent love for one another, for 'love will cover a multitude of sins.'" Sierra shuddered.

Now that she better understood Marti, Sierra wished she hadn't prejudged the woman so severely. Christy had done the right thing. She had loved her aunt unconditionally. Sierra closed her eyes and prayed for God to teach her that kind of love.

But by seven o'clock the next morning, her commitment to unconditional love was being tested. Marti was not feeling well. She yelled at Sierra and Christy for taking too long to get down to the lobby. Alex was there waiting for them, but when he greeted them, Marti acted as if she had never agreed to let Alex take them to the train station. She insisted he put down their luggage. They would take a cab. Alex could go home.

Marti's moodiness was driving Sierra crazy. She tried to face each of Marti's mood swings calmly, as Christy did. But when Marti started being downright mean to Alex, Sierra had to defend him.

"Yesterday you said you wanted Alex to take us to the train station," she said, giving Marti a hard look. "He went to all the trouble to come get us—don't you think we should go with him?"

Marti glared right back at Sierra. "Oh, I don't care!" she said at last. "Do whatever you want. I see that my opinion is of no value."

"I'll help you carry our stuff to the car," Sierra said to Alex. "Where are you parked?"

Alex led the way while Sierra followed with Christy. Marti trailed behind.

"Please don't let her get to you," Sierra said to Alex. "I'm sorry she treated you that way."

"This is not your responsibility," Alex said. "There is no need for you to apologize. I think the battle in her heart is very strong."

Sierra nodded. Alex seemed to understand what was going on perhaps even better than Christy or Sierra did.

They drove through the rain-drenched streets to the Badisher Bahnhof. A steady drizzle was coming from the gray clouds that hung over them, and the drab light muted the bright colors that had sparkled on these streets only the day before. A warm yellow light glowed inside the bakery, but all the other stores appeared dreary, like the day.

"Do you have your tickets already?" Alex asked.

"Of course we do," Marti snapped. "The minute we get to the station, I want this luggage loaded onto the train, and I want you girls to go immediately to your seats."

"Okay," Christy agreed.

Sierra was thinking of how she was going to say good-bye to Alex. He had made such an impact on her in the short time they had been together. She knew she had become a different person, partly because of him. Sierra needed to tell that to Alex. She wanted to say it privately, face-to-face, so that she could look into his dark eyes one more time.

She and Christy had been late arriving in the lobby that morning because Sierra had gone back to the room to write her address on a piece of hotel stationary. She wanted to find the right moment to give Alex that piece of paper. With that in mind, Sierra knew she couldn't promise Marti she would board the train the instant they got there. So Sierra kept quiet.

They pulled up in front of the station. Sierra was glad to see the two lions were still there, guarding the entrance and reminding her of Narnia and of Christ. She prayed silently, asking God to provide a chance for her to say good-bye to Alex the way she wanted to, the way she felt she must.

Entering the station with them, Alex carted their luggage to track number seven, where their train was beginning to board passengers. Marti rummaged through her purse and checked the papers in her hand. "My ticket!" she squawked in a panic. "I've lost my ticket! Here's Christy's and Sierra's, but mine is gone."

"Have you checked in your bags?" Alex asked.

"It's not in there!"

"Maybe we should check," Christy suggested, bending to unzip the top of Marti's suitcase.

"It's locked," Marti snapped. "Here, let me do that."

"I'll check in the car," Alex offered.

"And I'll go with him," Sierra blurted out. She was beginning to feel panicked, too. Not about the tickets, but about the possibility of never seeing Alex again. What if she could never tell him the words that were on her heart?

Before Marti could object, Sierra and Alex were dashing through the train station on their way to the car. Alex quickly unlocked it and began to look under the seats, while Sierra went through the backseat and checked the glove compartment.

"I don't see it," she said.

"I do not either. Maybe they have found it in the suitcase. We must go back before the train leaves."

Alex locked the car, and they began to run back to track number seven.

When they arrived at the front of the long train, both of them were breathing hard. They couldn't find Marti or Christy among the dozens of people standing along the platform. A young couple was saying good-bye, wrapped in each other's arms. That was how Sierra had wanted to say good-bye to Alex, but now everything was too frenzied.

"Where did they go?" Sierra asked, panting.

"Perhaps they found the ticket and boarded the train," Alex suggested.

"They wouldn't go without me!"

"Perhaps they think you will get on when you do not see them."

Sierra looked right and left. There wasn't a trace of Marti and Christy anywhere.

"What should I do, Alex?"

"I think perhaps you should get on the train. You will not otherwise make it to the airport to take your flight home."

Forgetting all her plans to give Alex a tender farewell and to slip her address into his hands, Sierra put her foot on the first step into the train and grabbed the handrail.

She paused. Something wasn't right. Her heart began to race the way it had on the airplane when she had the night-mare about crashing.

Sierra turned for one last look.

"Good-bye, See-hair-a," Alex called out, lifting his arms to her as if offering a benediction. "May God be with you always."

A loud bell chimed, and the train lurched forward. Sierra knew she needed to move inside, but she couldn't force herself to go further onto the train.

From somewhere down the platform, Sierra heard her name being called. The train made a hissing noise and began to pull slowly out of the station.

"Alex," Sierra cried, "I think I heard Christy. On the platform!"

Alex began to walk fast, keeping pace with Sierra as the train moved forward. He looked down the platform and then back at Sierra. "It is her! Christy comes! Jump, See-hair-a! I will catch you."

All the feelings of terror that had started in her racing heart now exploded into her stomach and throat, paralyzing her.

"You must jump!" Alex called. "I will catch you! Now!"

Sierra held her breath and jumped into Alex's waiting arms.

seventeen

SIERRA COLLIDED WITH ALEX'S CHEST. The impact made it impossible for him to stay standing. In one great tumbling motion, he fell to the ground, his arms tightly wrapped around Sierra as she came down with him.

"Ouch!" Sierra yelped.

"Ooof," was all Alex could manage.

"Are you all right?" Sierra asked, trying to get up off the ground.

Alex's eyes were wide. His mouth moved, but no sound came out.

"Oh, no!" Sierra said, reaching for his hand. "I hurt you, didn't I?"

Alex tried to force out a word, but instead he coughed a deep, long cough. Behind them the last few train cars were leaving the station, and the noise went with them.

"Sierra!" Christy cried, arriving beside them and kneeling down next to her friends. "Are you guys okay? I saw you jump. I thought you were going to die!"

"I think Alex almost did die," Sierra said.

She and Christy both helped him to sit up. His hair was pushed forward in his eyes. He shook his head and drew in a deep breath.

"It's all right," he said at last. "The air went from me."

"Oh, I am so sorry!" Sierra said. "I shouldn't have jumped so hard. I didn't mean to knock you over. I'm so sorry."

"It's all right," Alex said shakily and rose to his feet.

"Christy, where were you?" Sierra asked. "We didn't see you or Marti anywhere. I thought you must have boarded the train."

"We were down there." Christy pointed. "Marti's sitting on a bench and our luggage is on a cart. Maybe it was blocking your view of us. We were right where you left us, but I think you came in a different entrance, at the other end of the train."

"Did you find the ticket?" Sierra asked as they began to walk toward Marti. "Not that it matters. We just missed the train."

"No," Christy said, "we can't find the ticket anywhere. My aunt is about to blow a mainspring, as my dad always says. That's why I had her sit on the bench."

"I'm sorry to do this to you, Christy," Sierra moaned.

"Don't worry about it. It's definitely not your fault. I told Aunt Marti that God was in control, and we shouldn't worry. You know, it strangles people." Christy imitated Alex's strangling demonstration.

"What did Marti say?"

"She just about strangled me, so I didn't say anything else."

"Wise choice."

"Then it was so strange," Christy said. "I was sitting there on the bench with her, and all of a sudden I looked up, and way down at the end of the track I saw your day pack and all your blond hair, Sierra. I knew it was you."

"I'm glad you saw me," Sierra said.

"Me, too."

They arrived at the bench where Marti was seated with her arms tightly drawn across her middle. The scowl on her face was bitter.

The worst part was, Marti didn't say a word. Sierra expected to have to defend herself in a long yelling match. Marti, however, did not throw the first punch. She just sat there, staring at them, as if they were responsible for the problems.

"May I make a suggestion?" Alex said calmly, having finally caught his breath. "Perhaps we can check at the ticket desk to see if they have you on their computer. They can issue you a new ticket, and you can board the very next train."

This suggestion did not appeal to Marti. She wouldn't move. She wouldn't speak.

"We have to do something," Christy said. "Would you like it if I went to check on the tickets, and you could stay here?"

"No!" Marti stated emphatically. "I am not letting either of you out of my sight for another second. We will all go. Alex, get the luggage."

Of all the things Marti had said, her insulting command to Alex angered Sierra the most. Marti could say whatever she wanted to Sierra and it wouldn't really matter. Sierra knew none of the mix-up was her fault. After all, they were trying to help Marti find her ticket. Even if Sierra had been there, they couldn't have gotten on the train without Marti's ticket. There seemed to be no reason for her to treat Alex so horribly. And because Marti had occasionally been nice to Alex, her rudeness seemed even worse; there was no telling when she would be nasty to him and when she would be sweet.

"I can carry something," Sierra offered.

"I can, too," Christy said.

Marti led the procession with stiff angry steps. At the ticket counter, they had to wait in a line with six people ahead of them. Marti began to murmur about the lack of efficiency and the laziness of the workers. It was embarrassing to stand next to her. It took nearly ten minutes for them to reach the clerk.

The whole time Sierra was replaying her risky jump in her mind. She had dreamed of a movie-like romantic adieu with Alex. Instead she had leveled the poor guy and infuriated Marti. This day was not going according to plan.

"May I explain for you?" Alex asked Marti as they stepped up to the window. "If you think it would be helpful," he added hastily.

Too ruffled to show any more irritation, Marti clammed up again, so Alex took the opportunity to begin a swift explanation in German. The clerk answered in deep, rough German words. Alex was beginning to negotiate with him when an announcement came over the speaker system in German. This one sounded different from the destination announcements that were called out regularly.

Everyone in the station stopped to listen. Sierra noticed looks of surprise and annoyance appearing on faces.

"What are they saying?" Sierra whispered to Alex.

"All trains north have been canceled." He held up his finger to indicate he was still listening and she shouldn't speak.

"But we have to go north," Marti said. "That's all there is to it. How can they cancel all the trains north? What kind of country is this?"

Sierra watched Alex's face. Something stirred inside her. She bit her lower lip and watched Alex's body language.

His eyebrows rose slightly, then quickly plummeted. His lips formed a tiny "o," and he let out a slow stream of breath. People around the station began to murmur and then grew silent as they listened to the rest of the announcement. Alex squeezed his eyes shut and shook his head.

"It was your train," he said quickly. Then looking at Marti, Christy, and Sierra, he touched his fingers to Sierra's cheek. "The train you almost boarded went off the main track two kilometers from here. The rains weakened the ground. The mud went out under the track. They fear that many are dead."

"No," Sierra whispered.

Alex put one arm around her and one arm around Christy, giving them a comforting hug. The he went to Marti and put both arms around her, trying to hug her, but she wouldn't have it.

Pulling away from all of them, Marti looked wild-eyed at the news. "We could have all died," she said.

They stood silently, absorbing the thought. The clerk at the ticket counter spoke abruptly to Alex.

Alex raised a hand and said in English, "It does not matter now. *Danke*."

He led the three dazed women over to an open spot on a bench and gathered their luggage around them. "Please. I have a phone call to make. Will you wait here a moment?"

"We're not going anywhere," Marti said numbly.

As soon as Alex walked away, Sierra began to make suggestions. "We could take a bus. Or maybe see about renting a car. What do you think?"

"I think we almost died," Marti said.

"I know you're not going to like my saying this, Aunt Marti," Christy said, "but can't you see what just happened? God protected us. Your lost ticket wasn't a bad thing. It was a God-thing. It kept us from boarding that train. Remember last night you said that if God is so loving and protective, then He would have to prove it to you? I think He just did."

This time, Marti didn't yell at Christy for spiritualizing yet another situation. Instead, a tear coursed down Marti's cheek. Then another and another. She reached into her purse to find a tissue.

Sierra felt all shivery inside. It was as though she had been invited to see a miracle—the melting of Marti's heart.

"Where's the restroom?" Marti asked, suddenly rising. Her face was pale.

"I saw it back there." Christy pointed toward the bathroom. "Do you want me to go with you?"

"If you would," Marti said, already heading in the direction Christy indicated.

Sierra watched the luggage and waited for Alex to return. He came back with a broad smile. "My cousin said it is okay."

"What's okay?"

"That I take his car. I will drive you to the airport."

"That's great, Alex," Sierra exclaimed, happy to spend more time with him. "You know it's a couple of hours' drive, though, don't you? Of course you do. That's really nice of you. Marti and Christy went to the restroom. They should be back in a minute."

"I can load the car. Or do you think I should wait for them?" Alex asked.

"I don't know. Maybe we should wait so we don't upset Marti."

"This is good," Alex said. "I had hoped for a chance to tell you how good it was for me to be with you. I think for my life always I will remember you, See-hair-a."

Suddenly, their tender good-bye moment had come. Sierra was too startled to know how to respond. This wasn't at all the way she had planned it.

"I wanted to say the same things to you," Sierra said. She felt the pocket of her jeans to make sure her address was still there. Now that the opportunity had come, she felt shy about suggesting they write. Shyness was a new feeling for her.

Forcing herself to be vulnerable, Sierra reached over and touched Alex's arm. Earlier, she had planned to take his hand in hers, the way he had taken hers in the alcove, and then share her feelings with him. She had even hoped that he would have already taken her hand and told her his feelings. But he had spoken his heart without touching her, and now it felt clumsy trying to take his hand. Sierra gave Alex's arm a timid squeeze and let go.

"You have given me so much in these past few days, Alexander. I want you to know that your fervent love has opened up my passions."

He lifted an eyebrow slightly.

"Wait. That's not what I meant. You didn't hear that. What I meant was, you know, your verse. The one about loving each other fervently." Before Sierra could explain further, a male voice boomed over the speakers. Alex listened intently and then interpreted. "They are arranging for passengers with tickets to take a bus. Would you then like to take a bus instead of my cousin's car?"

"We don't exactly have three tickets to cash in," Sierra said. "I think Marti would be more comfortable in the car."

"You are right. Please excuse. I go to check on parking to make certain I have not exceeded the time."

Alex stepped away briskly, leaving Sierra by herself.

"That didn't go so well," she mumbled. *He probably thinks I'm wacky, telling him he opened up my passions. Boy, I sure haven't made things easy. First I knock him over, and then I scare him off. Father God, feel free to intervene at any time here.*

As soon as she thought it, Sierra felt terrible. God *had* intervened. He had gotten her off the train. Hundreds of other people hadn't gotten off, and now some of them were dead. Sierra's thoughts spun around. Finally, she was hit with the realization that she could have been dead right now.

Sierra was struck by the contrasting experiences she'd had these past few days. Life was absolutely wonderful, and life was absolutely horrible. Life was both.

Life was also a gift. God gave people life, and clearly He could also take it back any time He wanted.

He's God, Sierra reminded herself. *He can do whatever He wants.*

eighteen

WHEN CHRISTY AND MARTI returned from the restroom, Marti didn't look well at all. After a brief pause, Alex offered to drive them to the airport, and Marti accepted without flinching.

Sierra climbed into the car's backseat, feeling as though she were on borrowed time. She decided every moment of her life needed to count. God had kept her on this earth a little longer, and she wanted to make the most of the gift of life He had given her. She thought of the young couple she had seen saying good-bye at the train, and a lump formed in her throat. Was that young woman alive, or was she one of the train wreck's victims?

Turning her head, Sierra cried silently. The others in the car were quiet as well. Sierra's tears kept coming. The scenery along the way was a peaceful mix of green hills and fields of corn. She wondered how everything could look so calm and beautiful when something horrible had just happened. But she knew that often in life, there were no simple answers. Life was wonderful, and life was horrible. That was life.

These hard truths brought little comfort to Sierra as the car sped through one small town after another, each of them appearing like a village from a fairy tale. Most of the houses boasted small, tidy gardens packed with a variety of vegetables and bright flowers. The flashes of fresh color had a soothing effect on Sierra. But the sky continued to pout, threatening to rain its tears on them once more.

Marti rode with the front seat reclined and her hand on her forehead. Christy indicated silently that Marti had been sick to her stomach when they went to the bathroom in the train station. Sierra wondered if they would have to pull over along the way. She knew it was not fun to be sick when traveling, and she empathized with Marti. It didn't matter that Marti was probably sick from the combination of having too much wine the day before, along with being thrown into a nervous panic when they missed their train.

The narrow but well-paved road took them past a long, flat field where white sheep were grazing.

"Don't they look like big marshmallows on top of a birthday cake with green icing?" Sierra asked.

"What are marshmallows?" Alex asked.

They were all keeping their voices low out of consideration for Marti. Alex's voice seemed loud even when he talked softly, though.

Sierra explained marshmallows, and Alex described a favorite treat from Russia. He explained it as a long white cube that sounded to Sierra like a stick of butter the size of a bread loaf.

"You eat wedges of butter all by themselves?"

"I know butter. This is not butter. It is much more of a

delicacy." He described the treat and how it was made, trying to get Christy and Sierra to understand what it was like.

"That sounds like what we call lard," Christy said, wrinkling her nose. "We would never, and I do mean never, sit down to eat a slice of lard!"

"Pull over!" Marti shrieked.

Alex stopped the car alongside a grove of trees. Marti nearly tumbled from the car and got sick in the ditch that divided the road from the grove.

"Should I get out?" Christy asked.

"Did she want help when she was sick at the train station?" Sierra asked.

"No."

"Then she probably doesn't now either. Do you have a tissue or anything?"

Christy reached for Marti's purse in the front seat and pulled out a travel packet of tissue.

"Are you okay?" Christy asked her aunt, handing her the packet.

"I'll be fine," Marti said. "As long as you can do me a favor and change the topic of conversation."

"Sorry," Christy said.

"Drive on, Alex," Marti said, adjusting her seat and rolling down her window. "We can't miss that plane."

"I'll need to stop for petrol at the next opportunity," he said.

"Fine, fine. I'll pay, of course. Just drive faster."

They found a service station just before the entrance to the freeway, or autobahn, as Alex called it. Christy and Sierra went into the convenience store and bought Marti some water and mints. They also purchased drinks for themselves and Alex, some beef jerky, and a bag of cookies.

"It seems like a normal gas station in the States," Sierra said as they walked back to the car. "Except for the different brands of drinks and candy."

"And the prices," Christy said. "Do you realize the gas is more than twice what we pay?"

"I hope I remember that the next time I have to fill the car. I guess we don't appreciate a lot of things about life at home."

"That's for sure," Christy said as they settled back into the car. "I was thinking about how I'm going to get around here without a car. I guess I'll get used to the bus and train system. But it's going to be a whole new experience, trying to figure out everything."

"Thanks again for taking us to the airport," Sierra said, patting Alex on the back. He was pulling onto the autobahn and accelerating the car to keep up with the zooming traffic.

"How fast are we going?" Sierra asked.

"I don't know, but I remember hearing about these autobahns from a friend of mine, Alissa. She said people drove a hundred miles an hour, and I didn't believe her." Christy gave Sierra's leg a squeeze as Alex rapidly changed lanes. "I believe her now!"

They seemed to arrive at the airport in no time. The drive had definitely been faster than the train would have been.

Some of the color had come back into Marti's face after they arrived at the airport. Alex parked the car and helped carry in the luggage. He stood with them in line as they waited to check in for their flight.

"Are you feeling better?" Sierra asked.

"Yes, thank you." Marti reached into her purse. "Alex, thank you also. It appears you saved the day. Here's something for your trouble."

"It is not necessary," he said, holding up a hand to refuse Marti's money. "I wanted to do this for you."

"It was certainly kind of you. Thank you." Marti put back the money and glanced at her watch. "You should probably say your good-byes now. We're nearly to the front of the line."

Sierra had been wondering what would happen when this moment came. Would it be awkward to say good-bye to Alex in front of Christy and Marti? Should she try to explain to Alex what she meant earlier about her passions being awakened?

"Alexander," Christy said, stepping forward and shaking his hand warmly, "I'm so glad we met you that first day on the train. Thanks for everything."

"If I have another holiday here, perhaps I will see you at the school."

"I would love to see you again," Christy said.

Alex gave her a quick hug, kissing the air beside her cheeks—first the right side, then the left. Sierra had seen many Europeans greet each other in this way. She even had a friend from Italy, Antonio, who had kissed her on each cheek when he greeted her. He did that to all his female friends, so Sierra never considered it a kiss. Now, with the prospect of Alex saying good-bye to her in the same way, it suddenly seemed very much like a kiss.

He moved over to Aunt Marti and gave her the same warm gesture. She remained fixed in her rigid posture, but her expression was softer than it had been all day.

Now it was Sierra's turn. Her heart began to thump like a bongo drum, pulsing its rhythm to her throat. "Alex," she said in a low voice, leaning close so no one else could hear her, "I wanted to explain what I was trying to say before at the train station. You know, about your verse on loving others fervently. I don't think I know how to really love other people yet, but you do, and you showed me that kind of love by your living example. I'll never forget it. And I'll never forget you. I'm so glad I had the privilege of knowing you."

Sierra held her breath and replayed the words in her mind to see if she had been able to say what she meant. It was a little bumpy, but basically she had told Alex what she wanted to say. She smiled, satisfied.

Alex gave her a tender look, a look that gave her instant assurance he had heard her heart and understood what she meant. He leaned closer. His steady hand gently brushed a wisp of hair off her forehead.

Is he going to kiss me? Should I close my eyes? Maybe I had better leave them open. I could open one and close one. What am I thinking? I can't think straight! What should I do?

"*Meine Freunde,* I have in my heart," Alex said in his deep voice, "all these same thoughts for you. In heaven we will meet once again, and I will be glad for that day."

Sierra swallowed. "In heaven," she repeated. She knew he had called her "my friend" in German. Suddenly, she knew he wasn't going to kiss her. Not on the lips. And she knew Alex would never write to her either. Sierra's address remained in her pocket, but she knew Alex would remain in a tiny corner of her heart. And thankfully, Sierra had been able to tell him that.

"May the peace of Christ be upon you," Alex said.

"And upon you," Sierra repeated.

He leaned over, took her gently by both shoulders, and pressed his right cheek to hers. It felt cool against her blushing redness. She heard the sound of the kiss he sent into the air next to her ear. Then his head moved to her left cheek, and again, he kissed the air by her cheek.

Alex let go of Sierra's shoulders and, to her surprise, he put his right hand on his heart. Then Alex bowed to the three of them.

"May God be with all of you," he said with emotion.

Just then an airline employee motioned the three of them to the next open ticket stand to check in.

"Come, girls," Marti said.

Sierra and Christy followed Marti, and she handed the attendant their three tickets. Sierra turned to give Alex one last smile over her shoulder. Heaven could be a long time from now—or not. Either way, she wanted to remember that face until then.

nineteen

THE FLIGHT HOME WAS UNEVENTFUL. That in itself was a welcome relief. When the trio deplaned in Los Angeles, Sierra said good-bye to Christy and Marti before catching the next flight to Portland. They were all so tired that it turned into a rather emotional scene.

"Thank you so much for inviting me, Marti," Sierra said. "I know some of the things I said and did were pretty annoying, and I apologize. I learned a lot on this trip, and I really appreciated your generosity and kindness in letting me come along. Thank you. I..." Sierra paused. "I love you."

Marti didn't look as startled as Sierra thought she would. But Sierra herself was startled to have those words even come to her mind.

"You were refreshing to have on the trip, Sierra," Marti said. She looked at Sierra with a fondness Sierra hadn't seen before. "I appreciate your loyalty to Christy. At first I didn't understand the friendship you two have. But, I must say, you are a good friend for my niece. A little too strong on the religious side, but then Christy seems attracted to your kind. Oh, and don't think I didn't notice your efforts to convert me." Marti included Christy in her sweeping gaze.

"I must admit, after they announced that our train had been derailed, I was almost persuaded to bow to your God. I'm sure it was from the stress of the moment and my sudden sickness. I do feel back to myself now."

Although Marti was acting extremely self-reliant, Sierra thought she detected a new tenderness in her eyes.

Christy and Sierra glanced at each other.

Oh, Marti, you are so close. Just stop fighting and surrender your life! Sierra thought. She could tell Christy was thinking the same thing.

"I'm going to miss you," Christy said, hugging Sierra.

"I'm going to miss you, too. Send me your address in Germany, and I'll definitely write."

They pulled away from each other, and both had tears streaming down their cheeks.

"And I'll write back," Christy said. "I promise."

"If you want to know what to buy me for my birthday," Sierra said, wiping her tears with the back of her hand, "just send me one of those marzipan pastries from that little bakery."

"Okay," Christy laughed. "Should I send truffles for you, Aunt Marti?"

"No, dear, of course not. And don't you eat too many of them while you're there, either."

Both girls laughed. Their eyes met again, locking in silent, eternal friendship.

"I love you—fervently," Sierra said.

Christy smiled. "And I love you fervently. 'Bye, Sierra."

They hugged again, and then Sierra got in line to board her flight to Portland. An hour and a half later, her parents met her at the baggage claim. They hugged and kissed her and listened to her chatter about everything all at once.

They were standing by the luggage carousel, waiting for Sierra's bag to come rolling around, when a flashback hit her. Last January, when she had returned from England, Paul had stood beside her at this very carousel, in nearly the same spot. He had thought she had his suitcase, but the luggage tag proved it was hers.

Sierra remembered being judgmental of him on the flight home. Her approach had been to act grown-up and witty, and her final words had been "Have a nice life."

Sierra closed her eyes, embarrassed now at the memory. Who was she trying to be? Where was the fervent love in that comment? She remembered how mature she had felt. After all, she had just traveled to England and back by herself.

Now that didn't seem like such a grand accomplishment. It was nothing compared with surviving a trip to Europe with Aunt Martha.

A loud buzzer sounded, and the luggage conveyor belt began its cycle.

Sierra remembered Paul's last words to her that day: "Don't ever change, Sierra."

I have changed, Paul. Something major has changed in my heart. I know now that it's not enough to have all the right answers and obey all the rules. If I don't have love, I'm nothing.

She wished she could tell that to Paul. If she ever had the chance, she decided she would apologize for her brash past. Not that it was likely she'd have the opportunity. The best she could do was learn from her experience and resolve to show love.

After all, she thought, *love is supposed to cover a multitude of sins. Does that include a multitude of immature blunders?*

"This one is yours, isn't it?" her dad asked, reaching for Sierra's luggage.

"Yes," Sierra responded, returning to the present. "That one's mine."

When they got home, Sierra hugged her little brothers, kissed Granna Mae, and chatted with her family for nearly an hour.

"Did you bring us anything?" Gavin asked.

Sierra felt bad. She hadn't been looking for souvenirs when she had shopped with Marti. "I think I have some German greeting cards. They're a little bent but kind of funny. I didn't really shop for souvenirs. The only thing I bought was some tea. I'll bring some stuff next time."

"You're going again?" Dillon asked.

"I might. Does anybody want some jasmine spice tea?"

Sierra had no takers, so she made a steaming cup for herself. Then, saying good night, she went up to her room to crash, even though it was still light outside. "I think you'll like the surprise you're going to find up there," Mrs. Jensen said as Sierra climbed the stairs. But she didn't care what the surprise was. All she wanted to do was reacquaint herself with her fluffy pillow.

Sierra opened the door to a tidy room. Her mom must have gotten fed up with the clutter while Sierra was gone. The window was open, letting in a warm summer breeze. With all the mess cleared away, Sierra immediately noticed a piece of paper on top of her neatly made bed. The paper had been all crumpled but was now smoothed out. It was a letter to her with no envelope. The distinctive handwriting was in black ink, written in a mixture of printing and cursive.

"Paul," Sierra whispered into the air.

Sierra eagerly snatched up the letter and quickly realized it was one Paul had written last spring. Sierra had been so frustrated with him that she had wadded it up and tossed it into the trash. Obviously, the letter never made it to the city dump. It probably was lost behind her dresser or something until her mom found it while cleaning her room. Sierra didn't mind that her mother had probably read Paul's letter. In a way she was glad her mom had found it.

Smoothing the wrinkles on her lost-and-found letter, Sierra carried it over to her antique dresser and tucked it into the top drawer. She glanced into the antique oval mirror to see how scruffy she looked from the long trip home. But instead of her own reflection, Sierra saw an envelope wedged into the bottom right-hand corner of the mirror. It was addressed to her, and the return address was Scotland. And, most important, the writing was in familiar bold, black ink.

Her hand began to shake as she reached for it. As a child, Sierra's favorite adventure was having treasure hunts. On many birthdays and Christmases, her mother had written clever clues that had led Sierra all over the house and yard in search of her gift. It made her smile to think her mom probably had to clean her room just for the chance to place the "clue" letter, which would lead Sierra to the dresser drawer, where she would notice the mirror and the new letter. Sierra might never have found it otherwise.

With this newest correspondence in her hand, Sierra floated to the overstuffed chair by the window. It felt strange not to have to move the usual pile of clothes as she lowered herself into the chair. With her thumbnail, Sierra slit open the envelope and slowly took out the page of ivory parchment.

Dear Sierra,

This may come as a complete shock that I am writing you. I have to admit, it's a little surprising to me. Something has been very much on my mind since I left Portland in June. That something is you.

The night before I left for Scotland, I went to your house for dinner as a favor to my brother. Ever since he started to date your sister, Jeremy had wanted me to have a meal with Tawni's family and "be nice" to you. I fulfilled my promise to him and even took you out to coffee. To me, it was nothing more than a favor.

What I didn't count on was the way you got to me, Sierra. As I think about it even now, I feel something I have never felt before. You said something about God's having His mark on me, and that He's going to do something with my life. I believe He already has done something. He's brought me here, to the land of my kin. Spiritually, some would consider this to be a dark place where so many people are without hope. But in the short time I've been here, I've come alive.

I know God, Sierra. It's different from knowing about Him. I talk to Him, all the time. I go for long walks in the Highlands, and I sing out loud to Him. I can't believe I'm telling you this, except somehow I feel as if you, of all the people I know, will understand what's going on in my life.

How did you know God had "marked" me? Why did you pray

for me all those months, like you said? Where does your zeal come from, Sierra? For the first time in my life, I'm beginning to desire the same things.

I don't know if any of this makes sense to you. If you don't want to write back, believe me, I'll understand. But I'd like to ask you if you would start a correspondence with me. I'm not sure that you and I got off to the best start when we met in England. I think I was a different person then. Do you believe in second chances? I'd like a second chance at our relationship.

It's with great pleasure that I can tell you this...I've been praying for you, Sierra. And I will continue to, whether you write to me or not.

Sincerely yours,

Paul

Sierra read the letter again—slowly this time, moving her lips. It was sweeter the second time. And after the fourth time, she felt overwhelmed with tears. She blinked them back and read it a fifth time.

Paul is praying for me. I'll have to tell him about the train and about Alex, and I wonder if Jeremy told him about Doug and Tracy's wedding? Oh, and the Highland House. He's going to want to hear how things are going at the homeless shelter his uncle runs. There's so much to tell him.

Her mind raced with all the possible things she could write to him about. The words lined up inside her head and began to multiply until they smashed together in her jet-lagged mind.

I can't write anything until I sleep.

Going over to her bed, Sierra folded the treasured letter and placed it under her pillow. Kicking off her shoes, she curled up in her inviting bed. Exhaustion pulled its invisible blanket over her and passed a dark hand over her heavy eyelids. A contented smile curved across her lips.

She might not know exactly how to enter into this wonderful new relationship with Paul, but Sierra definitely knew she was ready to open her heart.

Book Eight

TIME WILL
TELL

one

SIERRA STOOD IN THE PARKING LOT and nervously nibbled on her thumbnail. She felt chilled in her shorts, T-shirt, and sandals. Leaning against her friend Amy's old Volvo, she waited for the back door of the restaurant to open.

Amy usually got off at eight. Sierra checked her watch: Eight-twenty. Where was Amy?

Gathering her courage, Sierra made her way to the front door of the Italian restaurant and opened it cautiously. She had planned that Amy would come to the parking lot and they could sit in her car to talk things through calmly. The last thing Sierra wanted was a confrontation in the lobby of Amy's uncle's restaurant.

Glancing around, Sierra noticed Amy wasn't at her usual spot behind the hostess podium. No customers were waiting to be seated. It was quiet. Exactly what Sierra had expected for a weeknight in September. That's why she had been certain Amy would get off at eight.

Sierra's buddy, Randy, was busing tables near the hostess station. Sierra sneaked up behind him, leaned over, and said, "Boo!"

Randy turned around, his crooked grin proving that her shock tactics had no effect on his composure. "What's up?" he asked.

"I was hoping to catch Amy. Do you know if she has left?"

"She and Nathan left together. I think he said they were going down to The Beet."

The Beet was a new teen club that had opened that summer in downtown Portland. It featured local bands and served only nonalcoholic beverages. Sierra had heard all about it the first week of school from Randy and the other guys in his band. They were on the alternate list for October, which meant their band had a slight chance to make their big debut.

"I didn't see them come through the parking lot," Sierra said.

"They left through the front door. They're probably going to walk over. All the free parking near The Beet is taken by this time of night."

"Oh," Sierra said quietly.

"How long have you been waiting?"

"About half an hour."

Randy gave her a sympathetic look. "You and Amy haven't talked yet?"

Sierra shook her head. "I've tried. All week at school she had someone else to talk to or someplace to go right after class. I've called her, I've left notes in her locker, and now..."

"And now you're waiting for her in the parking lot," Randy said, shaking his head.

His straight blond hair had grown out over the summer,

and he had to wear it pulled back in a short ponytail when he worked. He had already received a notice at the private Christian high school they attended advising him that his hair exceeded the acceptable length as stated on page 14 of the Royal Christian Academy Student Handbook.

"I know. You think I'm pathetic, the way I'm stalking her," Sierra said. "It's just that I'm not ready for our friendship to be over until we at least have a chance to talk about it."

"And Amy doesn't feel that way," Randy surmised.

Sierra shook her head and her turquoise-beaded earrings brushed her jawline.

"Don't give up," Randy said, giving her a quick squeeze on the shoulder. "Remind yourself of that verse you kept telling me when you got back from Switzerland." Randy seemed to have suddenly lost his memory. He looked at Sierra. "What was it you kept saying?"

"Love each other deeply, because love covers over a multitude of sins." Sierra recited the verse like a bored kid at vacation Bible school.

"That's the one. Keep telling yourself to love Amy like that. She'll come around."

Sierra sighed. "I don't know."

An older couple got up from their table, and Sierra moved to let them pass.

"I'd better let you get back to work," she said.

"Okay. I'll see you tomorrow at school," Randy said, heading for the table the couple had just vacated.

Sierra slipped out of the restaurant as quietly as she had slipped in. She climbed into her car and drove home with the windows rolled up and the heater on. It was too cold for this time of year, especially when it still looked like summer all around. Sierra wasn't ready for summer to be over. Without a doubt, this had been her best summer yet, full of travel, friends, adventure, and even a little brush with romance. In the same way she wasn't ready for summer to end, she knew she wasn't ready for her friendship with Amy to be over.

It had been a simple misunderstanding. Amy had taken an interest in Nathan when he came to work at her uncle's restaurant at the beginning of the summer. Nathan asked Amy out, and when she called to give Sierra an account of their first date, Sierra had jumped all over Amy for making out with Nathan in his car. Amy had hung up, and since then they had spoken no more than a few sentences to each other.

Sierra was gone for several weeks, and when she came back, it was a mad rush to get everything ready for school. It had been almost five weeks now since Sierra and Amy had talked, and from the looks of things, Amy and Nathan were still very much together.

Pulling into the narrow driveway of her family's old Victorian home, Sierra turned off the engine in the old VW Rabbit her parents had given her the week before. It was a mixed blessing to have her own car. Last year she had shared the Rabbit with her mom, which meant her dad paid for her insurance. Now that it was her car, the insurance bill was hers also. As long as she kept up her grades, her rate would stay the same, and her part-time job at Mama Bear's Bakery should cover her expenses. It didn't leave much money left over for exciting adventures such as the one she had spent her savings on this past summer.

Sierra sat in the warm car a few minutes. *Is it me? Am I making too big of a deal out of this face-to-face with Amy? Should I let it go? I want to prove to her I really am her friend, no matter what. How can I prove that to her if she won't respond?*

Locking the car door, Sierra shuffled through the damp grass to the front porch, where the amber light glowed above the door, welcoming her home. Amy had once accused Sierra of having the perfect family and the perfect home. At this moment, it felt perfect. Her parents were still in love after twenty-seven years of marriage. Granna Mae lived with them, or rather, they lived here with her—it was her house. And Sierra's four brothers and one sister were all living happy lives.

Sierra wiped her feet on the welcome mat before she went in. She thought back to when she had stood here a week and a half ago with tears streaming down her cheeks as her favorite brother, Wesley, had driven off to college in Corvallis in his fixed-up sports car. She loved her brother and had relied on him more than she realized this past summer.

Wes was the one she had told about Alex, the tall Russian she had met on her trip to Switzerland. Sierra also had confided in Wes about the letter she had received from Paul three weeks ago. Paul, her mysterious friend with the blue-gray eyes, was going to school in Scotland. She hadn't shown Wes the letter, but she did describe to him how Paul said he went hiking through the Highlands of Scotland, singing aloud to God. Wes hadn't laughed. Instead, he had folded his arms, nodded, and said, "Now there's a brave heart for you. Keep praying for that one, Sierra."

She had taken his advice and not only continued to pray

for Paul but had also written him—twice. He hadn't written back.

As Sierra opened the front door, her mom poked her head around the corner from the kitchen. Sharon Jensen had a worried look on her face and the phone to her ear. She waved at Sierra with a flutter of her fingers.

Sierra headed for the study, her favorite room in the house. It was also her dad's office and Granna Mae's old library. Sierra liked to retreat there to do her homework and smell the mixed scent of leather and old books. She had left her backpack in the den that afternoon while doing homework. When she pushed open the door, she saw that her father was at the desk, also on the phone. He didn't look up when she came in.

Quietly gathering her textbooks and stuffing them into her pack, Sierra heard her dad say, "Okay, honey, we'll talk again in a few days. You do know that Mom and I support you in this decision, don't you?…Okay…. Good. Call us and let us know what you decide…. Bye-bye."

There were only three women Howard Jensen called "honey," and two of them were in this house at this moment. The other "honey" was Sierra's sister, Tawni, who had been living in Southern California for the past few months so she could be closer to her boyfriend, Jeremy. As her dad said good-bye and hung up the phone, Sierra began to feel a little nervous about Tawni.

"Is everything okay?" she asked when her dad turned to her.

"Tawni has a big decision ahead of her." Mr. Jensen's usually happy eyes were clouded over.

Just then Sierra's mom stepped into the den. She didn't

notice Sierra sitting in the corner chair. "Oh, Howard, I don't know about this. What do you think?"

Mr. Jensen glanced at Sierra, and his wife followed his gaze.

Mrs. Jensen pursed her lips, working up a smile for Sierra. "I didn't see you there, Sierra. How did your time go with Amy?"

"We didn't talk," Sierra said. "She'd already left. I'll try again tomorrow, I guess."

"That sounds like a good idea."

Sierra could tell her mom wasn't thinking about Amy.

"Is Tawni all right?" Sierra asked tentatively.

"Yes," Mrs. Jensen stated, looking at her husband.

Neither of them offered any more information.

Rats! Sierra thought. *Something is going on, but they're not going to tell me. Is it something to do with Jeremy?*

Sierra glanced at the clock. She looked back at her parents and caught them sending each other the silent message *Don't say anything*.

"I'll get out of here," Sierra said. She felt like adding, "So you can have your big, private conversation about Tawni without me hanging around." But she held her tongue and slipped past them, closing the door behind her. She knew she should appreciate that her parents kept Tawni's situation confidential. If it had been she, Sierra would want to count on them to keep her news quiet.

Trudging up the stairs to her bedroom, Sierra muttered to herself, "This is so frustrating. All I can do is wait. Wait for another chance to talk to Amy. Wait for Paul to write. Wait to see if Mom and Dad will include me in Tawni's problem. Wait, wait, wait. I hate waiting."

Sierra opened her bedroom door and tossed her back-pack into the corner by the closet. Her relaxed attitude about cleaning up expressed itself all over the room, making it hard for her to find a place to flop down and have a decent pout party. Sierra had to admit her room was a startling sight. Clothes, books, bags, socks, plates, CDs, hats, papers, and a crazy variety of "stuff" covered her large upstairs bedroom with no semblance of order. She could usually find what she wanted, and she believed more important and interesting things were to be done than sort and organize belongings.

If everything else in her life was on hold, Sierra decided she might as well add her room to the list. She would wait until tomorrow to clean it.

two

TOMORROW TURNED into the next day and the next until finally, on Friday night, Sierra was back in her room, trying to think of a way to make sense of the mess. The rest of her life was still in disarray. Her parents had answered her questions about Tawni by saying they would leave it up to Tawni to tell Sierra and her brothers. She knew then the decision couldn't be to get married or move back home or anything that radical because her parents wouldn't have hesitated to share that information with all of them.

Still no word had winged its way to her from Paul. Then there was elusive Amy, who kept disappearing down the hallway at school whenever Sierra tried to approach her.

Resigning herself to trying to do something about her room, Sierra set about the task. The exercise of picking up, sorting, and putting away helped restore order in more ways than one. As she stuffed clothes into her dresser drawers, she devised a plan for meeting with Amy. The next morning Sierra didn't have to be to work at Mama Bear's until ten. She would take a picnic breakfast to Amy's and wake her up.

They could sit on Amy's bed, eat breakfast, and have the heart-to-heart talk they needed. Amy couldn't walk away from Sierra in her own room.

Sierra smashed down the junk in her trash can and added another handful. She stacked her books on the floor beside her bed and smoothed back the comforter on top of Tawni's old bed. Scooping up a huge armful of dirty clothes, Sierra made her way to the basement, where she started to feed all her dark-colored clothes into the gaping mouth of the washing machine. That was only the first load. She had hauled down enough for at least two more loads, which meant she would be up and down these stairs all night.

The basement's smell brought mixed memories. When Sierra was a child, this had been a great hiding place when her family came to visit Granna Mae. Once Sierra had wedged her skinny frame behind the stack of Christmas decoration boxes and pulled an old trash can filled with rakes and shovels beside her to close off the opening. For the first five minutes or so, she felt wonderfully sneaky. She smiled, hugging her knees to her chest and waiting for someone to come look for her.

Then the thrill wore off. The icy cement floor had turned her bottom numb, and the once-exotic swampy fragrance now stuffed up her nose and made her eyes itch. She had no room to stretch her cramping legs.

Unable to stay in hiding any longer, Sierra had pushed the trash can back herself, stood up, and shaken her legs to make the tingles go away. Then slowly taking the stairs, she made her way to the front yard, where she found her sister and all four brothers huddled around a cardboard box from which a neighbor's six kittens mewed for attention.

Clicking on the washing machine and drawing her thoughts back to the present, Sierra remembered how at the time she didn't care about the kittens. She wanted to know why no one had come looking for her. Why hadn't they cared enough?

A smile came to her face as she remembered the way Tawni had begged their dad to let her keep one of the kittens. He had refused. Mr. Jensen was a dog man, not a cat man. Not even the helpless ball of caramel fur Tawni held up to his face, with tears in her eyes, changed his mind that summer afternoon. However, that Christmas, Tawni received an all-white kitten. She named it Snowflake, and it lived in a cozy bed beside the dryer.

Taking the basement stairs two at a time, Sierra left the musty smells and childhood memories behind. She decided to fix her breakfast picnic now while waiting for her laundry. Finding some bagels, she packed them in one of her mom's wicker baskets hanging on a peg in the kitchen. From the refrigerator, she took a tiny jar of blackberry jam from the door rack, two oranges from an open bowl on the shelf, and a couple of eggs marked with happy faces. The black pen faces were Mrs. Jensen's code for Sierra's younger brothers, Gavin and Dillon, to let them know which of the eggs were hard-boiled. Two years ago Gavin took what he said he thought was a hard-boiled egg and cracked it over Dillon's head. After all the boys' wailing and hollering, their mom had devised the happy-face code.

Covering the now-full basket with a dish towel, Sierra felt pleased with her picnic and her plan. Just then her two younger brothers came in with their dad. They each had a miniature wooden car to show Sierra.

"I'm going to paint mine tomorrow," Gavin said. "Hot red so it'll go fastest."

"Those turned out nice," Sierra said, examining Dillon's car up close.

Both her brothers had entered a toy boxcar derby contest at the city park.

Mrs. Jensen stepped into the kitchen with a tray of dirty dinner dishes. "Granna Mae is already asleep. I think you boys need to head to bed now, too."

After the usual round of groans and complaints, the boys made their way up the stairs.

Mr. Jensen stepped into the entryway and called after them in a strong whisper, "Not so loud. Don't wake Granna Mae."

"What have you been doing all night?" Mrs. Jensen asked Sierra.

"Picking up my room a little."

Her mom's eyes seemed to brighten. "Really? Good for you."

"I have some laundry going, and I put together a breakfast picnic for tomorrow. I plan to go over to Amy's and wake her up."

"You two still haven't talked?"

"No. And it's hanging over me like an overdue term paper."

"I hope you settle it soon," her mom said, checking the dishes in the dishwasher, trying to determine if they were dirty or clean. "Unresolved relationships can really wear a person out."

Mr. Jensen stepped back into the kitchen in time to pick up the last bit of their conversation. "You talking about Tawni?"

Mrs. Jensen and Sierra both turned to look at him. Mrs. Jensen's look said, *What are you doing?* while Sierra's begged, *Tell me more!*

"I guess not," Mr. Jensen said, reaching for a glass in the cupboard and pouring himself a drink of water. He sipped the water slowly, watching both of them over the top of the glass. Without offering any information, he placed the empty glass on the counter and, with a wry grin to his wife, said, "Carry on, then. As you were." With a mock salute, he headed out the back door to his workshop.

"Is there anything I should know about Tawni?" Sierra asked her mom after he left. "I mean, I already know she's trying to make a big decision, and now I can guess it has to do with a broken relationship. It isn't Jeremy, is it? She isn't going to break up with him, is she?"

Mrs. Jensen had concluded that the dishes were dirty and was trying to wedge in the last few glasses. She didn't say anything but worked silently, pouring the soap into the dispenser. As she clicked the knob to "On," her words seemed to come.

"I'm not sure what to say, honey. I think Tawni would prefer we not tell you until she's made her final decision. It'll only be a few days, and I think she would feel better about our doing it that way."

"But we're a family," Sierra said. "Why should families keep things from each other?"

Her mom sighed and leaned back against the counter, folding her arms across her middle. A frustrated look came over her face. "You're right. That's been our policy all along. We keep things open and honest in the Jensen clan. But I think it's better that we wait for Tawni to decide what she wants to do, and then we can all talk about it."

Sierra couldn't begin to imagine what would be so secretive. Returning to the basement to put her clothes in the dryer and start a new load, Sierra could only hope her sister's secret was something good. Maybe like her Christmas kitten. Maybe Tawni's news was something like that.

And then again...

three

THE NEXT MORNING Sierra dressed for work and left at seven-thirty with her picnic basket. She drove to Amy's house with a prayer for peaceful reconciliation on her lips. Sierra rang the doorbell three times before Amy's groggy, grumpy father opened the door in his robe.

"Oh, I'm sorry I woke you up. I wanted to surprise Amy. I brought a breakfast picnic for us."

Mr. Degrassi gave Sierra a baffled look.

"I'm Sierra. Sierra Jensen. I know I haven't been over for a while…"

"Amy stayed at her mother's last night," Mr. Degrassi said. Without any further explanation, he closed the door.

Sierra nearly dropped the basket. *At her mother's! What does he mean? Amy's mom moved out?*

Stumbling back to her car, Sierra realized how out of touch with Amy she had become. Earlier in the summer, Amy had confided in Sierra that her parents had been fighting and Amy had overheard them talking about divorce. Sierra had tried to convince Amy that it wasn't serious. All parents have misunderstandings. Everything would work out fine, she had told Amy. Obviously, Sierra had been wrong.

Stunned, she drove home. When she turned onto 52nd Street, she noticed Randy was mowing the lawn at one of his regular yard jobs. He had started his own lawn maintenance business in the spring and then took the part-time busboy position at the restaurant during the summer. With two jobs and all the hours he put into the band, which practiced three nights a week in Randy's garage, he had been busy all summer.

Sierra pulled up to the curb and parked the car. Taking the basket with her, she walked toward Randy, waving and calling his name.

"Yo!" Sierra called out again, only a few feet away.

Randy looked up and shut off the lawn mower. "Hey, what's up?" he asked.

"Did you know Amy's parents aren't together anymore?"

"Yes."

"Why didn't you tell me?"

"I thought everybody knew."

"I didn't know. I went over there this morning and found out from her dad. He didn't look too happy."

Randy looked at the basket. "What's that?"

"A picnic."

"Food?" Randy asked.

"I had this great idea to surprise Amy with a breakfast picnic, only she stayed at her mom's last night. I can't believe this. How has Amy taken it all?"

"I don't know. At work she pretty much keeps to herself

and then leaves with Nathan when she gets off. I think her mom moved into an apartment over on Halsey. I heard Amy telling someone at work a few weeks ago."

"When did all this happen?"

"While you were gone."

Sierra shook her head and sighed. "I feel awful for her."

Randy nodded and motioned toward the basket. "So, what's in the basket?"

"Why? You hungry?"

Randy's half-grin told her it was a pointless question. "Hot cinnamon rolls from Mama Bear's, I hope," Randy suggested.

"No, low-fat bagels. Sorry. I packed it for Amy and me."

"Bagels are good," Randy said, taking the basket from Sierra and leading her over to a part of the lawn he had already mowed. He sat down and pulled back the dish towel. "Do you have anything to drink?"

"No."

"I have some drinks in my truck." Randy sprang up and returned with two cans of cream soda. It didn't seem the likely beverage to accompany hard-boiled eggs and bagels, but Sierra didn't complain. She was just glad she had Randy to talk to. It seemed he was her only close friend.

"What do you want first?" Sierra asked. "The bagel or the egg?"

"Is this a variation on that age-old question: Which came first, the bagel or the egg?" Randy grinned at his own joke. "Give me both. I'll make a sandwich." He pulled out his pocketknife and wiped it on the leg of his jeans. Then he created a breakfast bagel.

Sierra looked around the quiet neighborhood as it

began to wake up. "Do you think it's okay that we're sprawled out on these people's lawn?"

"Sure. They won't mind."

Sierra opened her bagel and spread it with the jam. Overhead she could hear doves cooing in the trees. A row of perky-faced pansies from the flower bed watched Randy and Sierra enjoy their morning feast. The pleasant, peaceful setting didn't match Sierra's emotions. She willed herself to downshift and enjoy this time with Randy, who was quite possibly her one and only true friend this school year. She knew one question that was guaranteed to get him talking.

"So, how are things going with the band?"

"Vicki came to hear us practice last night," Randy said, snapping open the lid of his soda can. "She thinks we're sounding pretty good."

Sierra hadn't heard the band practice for weeks. She had sat in on a jam session once, but it drove her crazy to listen to the same piece of music over and over.

"That's good. Have you guys come up with a name yet that you can all agree on?"

"Almost."

"Do you mean the name of the band is 'Almost' or you've almost come up with a name?"

Randy chuckled. "I should throw that one into the mix. 'Almost.' That would be a pretty radical name. What I mean is that we almost had a name, but Ben was pretty sure it was already taken. It was 'White Horse.' Vicki said she'd search online for us to see if the domain is still available."

"That's nice of her." Sierra thoughtfully chewed her bagel and swallowed her feelings about Vicki.

Last semester Vicki had asked Randy out to a formal

benefit dinner, and Sierra had labeled her a flirt. Maybe it wasn't a fair assessment of Vicki, but the two of them had gotten off on the wrong foot when Sierra had moved to Portland. Sierra had overheard Vicki and another girl talking about her in the locker room Sierra's first week of school. The other girl said she thought Sierra was stuck-up. Sierra had marched around to their side of the lockers, blasted out that she wasn't stuck-up, and then marched out.

Looking back, that seemed a ridiculous way to handle the situation. She had only proved they were right by over-reacting. The unfortunate result was that Sierra had then labeled Vicki as someone to avoid. It hadn't helped a bit when Vicki asked Randy out. At that point, Sierra was just beginning to feel as though Randy was her close friend, and then Vicki seemed to be wiggling in between them.

At the end of the school year, Vicki had been assigned to the same special project team as Randy and Sierra when they helped out at the Highland House, a homeless shelter where Sierra still occasionally volunteered. Vicki hadn't exactly put her heart into the project. She hadn't even managed to show up most of the time.

Suddenly, Sierra felt an interest in listening to the band practice again. She knew it was crazy. She only wanted to hear the band because Vicki was hanging out with Sierra's friends and she didn't trust her.

Maybe if Vicki weren't so gorgeous, Sierra would have felt differently. Vicki's silky, light brown hair hung down her back. She wore it parted down the middle and was forever flipping it over her shoulders. Her thin, arched eyebrows framed her green eyes and gave her face a centered look. When a person looked at Vicki, the first things he saw were her eyes.

Sierra felt inferior when she compared herself with Vicki. A person's first impression of Sierra, she imagined, would be her unruly hair. She knew she had nice eyes. They were a blue-gray color, and she had been told they seemed to change with the weather. Her figure had always been closer to a tomboy's than a beauty queen's, though Sierra had noticed this fall that some of her school clothes had gotten tighter on her: Either she had shrunk everything in the wash or her body was actually launching into her final, late-bloomer stage of development. She hoped it was the latter.

Realizing she had been quiet for a long time, she wrapped up her private thoughts and asked Randy how the lawn-care business was. He didn't seem to have noticed how quiet she had been, since he had been busy eating.

"I've cut back some for the fall, but I think I'm going to have to quit my job at the restaurant. They scheduled me for sixteen hours this week, but with school and the lawns, I don't have enough time for the band."

"Have you given your notice yet?"

"No, I was thinking and praying about it this morning. What do you think?"

"I think you can't do everything. Something has to go."

"I make more money on the lawns, and I can get them done if I work all day Saturday. That gives me weeknights for the band."

"Sounds as if you could leave the restaurant and it wouldn't hurt your finances too much," Sierra said.

"I asked my parents last night, and they said it was up to

me. They said they would support my decision, whatever I end up doing."

"Don't you hate that?" Sierra said. "I sometimes wish my parents would just tell me what to do instead of leaving it up to me."

"I know. Funny, isn't it? A few years ago I was complaining to my parents that they wouldn't give me enough freedom to make my own decisions. Now they are, and I'm complaining again."

Randy popped the last bite of his bagel into his mouth. A crumb of egg yolk clung to the corner of his lower lip. Sierra motioned for him to brush it away.

He wiped his mouth and said decidedly, "I'm going to give my notice this afternoon at the restaurant."

"How many more lawns do you have to do today?"

"Eight."

"Are they all as big as this one?"

Randy looked around. "Some. Some are smaller. I don't know. It takes about an hour at each house. Except some of the ones around here. They only take half an hour or so. I do ten houses. Makes for a long Saturday, but like I said, the money is great."

"I'd better let you get back at it," Sierra said. "Thanks for sharing my little picnic with me."

"Anytime," Randy said with a smile. "It's too bad Amy wasn't at her dad's, but her loss was my gain." He patted his stomach contentedly.

Sierra gathered up the basket and drove to work. The bakery already had a line of customers inside when Sierra arrived. She washed her hands, put on her apron, and took over for Jody at the cash register. The soothing scent of freshly baked cinnamon rolls circled the bakery, enticing more customers to come inside every time the door opened and some of the aroma escaped.

Sierra knew she had a great job. She loved the people she worked with, especially Mrs. Kraus, who ran the bakery. She had understood when Sierra went to Southern California during the summer. Then when Sierra called to say she was going to be gone for another week because she had the chance to fly to Europe with her friend Christy, Mrs. Kraus had assured her not to worry about a thing. That short but meaningful jaunt to Switzerland and Germany had changed Sierra deep down, helping her to understand more about relationships and not to force them into boxes that didn't fit them. She didn't always apply that principle well, but she was trying. And Amy was one of the people with whom she wanted to try.

As Sierra cleaned out the coffee filter from the espresso machine, she noticed two customers running in the door, soaked from the sudden downpour of autumn rain. The shimmering wonder of summer had officially ended.

four

SIERRA DIDN'T DISLIKE THE RAIN, but she didn't love it either. It was just something she lived with in Portland. Sometimes, when the gentle taps danced on her bedroom window, it had a soothing effect on her. Other times it meant a forced retreat from a softball game or a canceled walk with their Saint Bernard, Brutus.

When she finished work and drove home, Sierra went upstairs to her partially cleaned room, where she grabbed her favorite pair of jeans and one of Wesley's OSU sweatshirts, which she hadn't realized she had confiscated, and headed for the bathtub. It had been a long time since she had had a good soak.

As she rubbed the cinnamon roll and coffee fragrances from her skin, Sierra tried to think about nothing. She had checked the mail, but no letters had arrived from Paul. Big surprise. She didn't want to speculate anymore on Tawni's problem, and she was pretty discouraged about trying to talk to Amy.

Relationships are supposed to be two-way streets, aren't they? I'm not supposed to be the only one pursuing, am I?

She wasn't exactly sure if she was thinking about her relationship with Paul or with Amy. It didn't matter. They both seemed to be in the same mode: silence—like Tawni's unspoken decision.

Whoever said silence is golden obviously never had the kinds of friends and relatives I have.

Then, because it was much too quiet in the bathtub, Sierra cut short the soak and slipped into her bum-around-the-house clothes. She headed downstairs, looking forward to the noise and activity of her family.

She found her mom, Granna Mae, and Dillon in the kitchen. Mom was setting paper plates on the counter, and Dillon was checking his race car to see if the paint had dried.

"You might leave a fingerprint," Sierra warned. "It's better to let it stay on the paper towel until tomorrow."

Dillon looked as though he was having a hard time deciding if he should heed his sister's advice or go with his impulse. His impulse won. He looked around sheepishly to see if anyone had noticed. Sierra was still watching him.

"It's almost dry," Dillon said and then left the room, casually trying to rub the smudge of red off his fingertip.

"Caught red-handed," Sierra called out after him with a laugh.

"What was that?" Granna Mae asked, turning around from the sink where she was rinsing out a china cup.

"I was talking to Dillon, Granna Mae," Sierra said. "What's for dinner, Mom?"

"Dad went to get some Chinese food."

"Perfect," Sierra said, her mood beginning to pick up.

"Oh," Granna Mae said. Her face scrunched in disapproval. "I don't believe I'd like Chinese food. I'd prefer some soup." She headed for the pantry and asked over her shoulder, "Would anyone else like some?"

"No thanks," Sierra answered for them both.

"Here, let me do that for you, Granna Mae," Sierra's mom said.

"I can do this fine by myself, Sharon."

"But I'd like to help you, Mother."

Granna Mae turned and gave Sharon a bewildered look. "I'm not your mother, am I?"

"Your son, Howard, is my husband," Mrs. Jensen said calmly. "You're my mother-in-law."

"Yes, I know that." Now Granna Mae sounded irritated. She had a can of chicken and rice soup in her hand, which she plopped down on the counter. "And this is my house. All you people are here in my house, and you're trying to keep me from making myself some soup."

Mrs. Jensen backed off. Sierra knew that when Granna Mae got confused, it was better to say very little. However, Granna Mae didn't seem confused. Everything she said was true. This *was* her house. When it became apparent that she couldn't live here by herself, Sierra's large family had left Pineville in northern California and had moved in. It meant big adjustments for all of them. But never in the last year while they had lived here had Sierra heard Granna Mae declare this was her house, as if she needed to stake her claim.

"We're not trying to keep you from anything," Mrs. Jensen said calmly. "I thought maybe I could help."

"Help me to open a can of soup? I don't think I need

help. In all my days, I've never needed help opening a can of soup."

Granna Mae continued to mutter as she fished out a can opener from the drawer. Poor Granna Mae couldn't get the can opener to catch on the lip of the can, a simple process for steady hands but an exasperating chore for someone with shaky ones. At last she got the opener to cooperate, and she turned the handle with great effort. Sierra wanted to step in and do it for her, but she knew it was better to let her grandmother do this herself.

With the can opened and the lid barely hanging on by a catch in the metal, Granna Mae bent over and hunted for a soup kettle. She pulled one out from the cupboard and dumped the soup in. Then she slowly turned the knob to light the gas flame. Sierra marveled at how difficult everything seemed to be for her grandmother.

As the soup heated up, Granna Mae returned to the pantry for a box of crackers. She took a bowl from the cupboard and a spoon from the drawer. She seemed to be in her own little world. Sierra didn't talk to her or try to help. Instead, she wiped the counter around the sink, the way she cleaned up at work, and chatted with her mom. But both of them were watching Granna Mae out of the corners of their eyes.

When the soup was bubbling, Granna Mae found a pot holder and carefully ladled the soup into her bowl. She carried the bowl to the dining room table, leaving Sierra and her mom alone in the kitchen. For the first time, Sierra began to understand the kind of pressure her mother had been under all these months as she lovingly cared for her mother-in-law, following her around the house and making sure she wasn't endangering herself or others. It was worse than when Dillon was a toddler. At least Dillon could be kept in a closed-off area. Granna Mae could open doors, turn on stove tops, and even possibly wander off someday.

"Is there anything I can do to help out?" Sierra asked.

"You mean with dinner?"

"No." Sierra lowered her voice. "With Granna Mae."

Her mom shrugged. "She's been doing pretty well lately."

"I know, but don't you have to keep an eye on her all the time?"

Her mom nodded.

"Why don't I do something like take her out for an afternoon so you don't have to think about her?"

"It's okay, Sierra. This is your senior year. You have a job. Your life is full already."

"There's room for my grandma in it," Sierra stated a little too loudly before lowering her voice again. "I'd like to do something."

Mr. Jensen and Gavin arrived just then with the tall white bags filled with boxes of Chinese food.

"Let's get this food on while it's still hot," Mr. Jensen said. "Gavin and I almost tore into it on the way home."

Mrs. Jensen reached for some serving spoons and said to Sierra, "It's fine with me if you arrange something. Make sure it's okay with Granna Mae first. She does better if she has time to think through any changes in her schedule."

Sierra went into the dining room, where Granna Mae was rising from her chair. Sierra again resisted the urge to help her.

"Are you sure you don't want some Chinese food?" Sierra asked. "It smells really good."

"No, no. I'm fine. The soup is too hot, though. I thought I'd take it up to my room and let it cool."

"I'll take it for you," Sierra said, quickly reaching for the bowl before Granna Mae's shaky hands had a chance to lift it.

"Thank you, Lovey. I'd appreciate that."

Sierra suddenly breathed easier. It seemed that whenever Granna Mae was thinking clearly, she called Sierra "Lovey." It was to Sierra what the childhood call of "Olly, Olly, Oxen-free" used to mean when she played hide-and-seek. It meant the coast was clear. Come out of hiding. Everything is okay now.

Sierra followed her grandmother up the stairs, each step a greater effort to conquer for the woman than the last. Again, Sierra was overwhelmed with the thought of how hard everyday life was for her dear grandmother.

"Can I get you anything else?" Sierra asked after Granna Mae had settled herself in her recliner.

"No, no. This is lovely. Thank you." She smiled sweetly as if she were dismissing Sierra.

Heading downstairs, Sierra thought of how, when her family had first moved in, she had thought it unkind of her parents not to include Granna Mae in all the family's meals together. Now Sierra was beginning to understand. With the noise and activity that come with a big family, it was much more calming for Granna Mae to eat by herself in her large, comfy bedroom.

By the time Sierra returned to the kitchen, everyone had dished up and gathered around the dining room table.

It was then that Sierra remembered she was going to ask Granna Mae about the two of them scheduling something to do. She would ask her later. Right now an alluring box of sweet-and-sour pork was calling to her.

Sierra scooped out the last of the pork, thankful that Dillon hadn't taken it all since that was his favorite. Sierra unwrapped a set of the wooden chopsticks and was about to pop the first tender morsel of pork into her mouth when the phone rang. With plate in hand, she picked up the receiver. It was her sister.

"Hey, Tawni," Sierra said, imitating Randy's usual greeting. "What's up?"

"A lot, actually," she said.

"I suppose you want to talk to Mom and Dad," Sierra said, balancing the portable phone on her shoulder and drawing the chopsticks full of sweet and sour pork to her mouth.

"Actually, I'm glad I caught you. I'd like to ask your opinion about something."

The meat tumbled from Sierra's chopsticks onto her plate. She put down her food and leaned against the counter, hardly daring to believe her own ears. Such words had never crossed her sister's lips.

"Sure," Sierra said, trying not to sound shocked or overly excited about being invited into the big decision. "What's going on?"

five

"WHAT HAVE MOM AND DAD TOLD YOU?" Tawni asked.

"Nothing."

Tawni sighed into the phone. "Aren't they the best, Sierra?"

Now Sierra was completely lost. "The best what?"

"The best parents. I thought they might have said something to you, but I should have known they would keep my confidences. I appreciate them so much. Just wait until you move out. You'll see how great you have it at home."

Sierra thought she was going to be let in on some great secret, but all Tawni seemed to want to talk about was their parents. Sierra already knew she had great parents. That was not a secret. She drew the chopsticks back to her mouth, devoured her first bite of dinner, and answered Tawni with an "Ah-hmmm."

"I'm trying to make a big decision," Tawni went on. "I talked to Mom and Dad about it the other night, and of course I've talked to Jeremy about it endlessly, and my other friends. I'd like to hear your opinion before I take the next step."

"Ah-hmmm," Sierra answered again.

"Are you eating?" Tawni asked.

Sierra swallowed. "Boy, am I! Sweet-and-sour pork. I got the last of it."

"Oh," Tawni moaned. "Don't tell me it's from that Chinese place downtown. I miss their egg rolls."

"Egg rolls," Sierra repeated, the suggestion sending her on a search through the rest of the bags and boxes. "No egg rolls, unless everyone else already got them. There's some rice left and some cashew chicken." Sierra stuck one of her chopsticks into the box and pulled out a chunk of chicken. "Oh, the chicken's good."

"Stop it!" Tawni practically screamed into the phone. "You're torturing me!"

"Then I guess we're even," Sierra said without thinking. "I've been tortured trying to figure out your big news."

Tawni paused and then blurted out, "I've found my birth mother. She lives in Reno. I'd like to meet her, but I don't know how to approach her."

Sierra plopped onto a stool at the counter. "How did you find her?"

"One of Jeremy's friends at school needed a project for his summer course in humanities. A bunch of us were sitting around one night, and I suddenly said, 'You can find out who my birth mother is and save me the price of a professional search.' He thought it was a great idea, and so I became his project."

Sierra waited for Tawni to go on. It seemed she wanted the story to be drawn from her bit by bit. Sierra willingly coaxed out the next bit.

"What's her name?"

"Lina. Isn't that a pretty name? Lina Rasmussen."

"And she lives in Reno?" Sierra found her imagination suddenly flooded with images of a middle-aged showgirl who would be a gigantic disappointment to Tawni when she met her.

"She works at the university there," Tawni said, shattering Sierra's colorful image.

"What else do you know about her?"

"A few things," Tawni said slowly. "She was fifteen when she had me."

"Fifteen? Oh, man! Can you imagine? No wonder she gave you up for adoption."

Sierra regretted her flippant statement as soon as she made it. Tawni's adoption had always been a sensitive issue with her.

"I'm sorry," Sierra said quickly. "I didn't mean for that to sound that way."

"No, that's okay. Jeremy said about the same thing. He said that considering the alternative, he was really glad Lina gave me up for adoption."

"You mean, considering the alternative would have been an abortion?" As soon as Sierra said it, her hand flew to her mouth. "I did it again. I'm sorry, Tawni. Nothing I'm saying is coming out right. I'm just so shocked."

"Don't worry about it. You're completely right. Lina could have easily gotten an abortion, and I wouldn't be here today." There was a catch in Tawni's voice. "I guess that's why I wanted to find her. I want personally to thank her for choosing to give me life. I want her to know that her choice was the best one."

Tears flooded Sierra's eyes. "I think that will mean a lot to her."

"I know it doesn't always go well when an adopted child tries to make contact with her birth parents," Tawni said quickly. "One girl at work told me about a cousin of hers who found her birth father. She contacted him by phone, and he hung up on her. She wrote him a letter, and he never responded. I guess some people bury the memory so deeply they can't handle being reminded that they had a child."

"Are you going to call Lina or write her or what?"

"I'm not sure. That's why I wanted your opinion. I thought the next step would be clear after I talked with Mom and Dad, but they said it was up to me. Then Mom called back today and said she and Dad were split in their opinion. Dad thinks I should call her. Mom thinks I should write."

"And what do you think?"

"I don't know. Jeremy thinks I should just show up on her doorstep so she won't have the chance to hang up on me or not respond to my letter."

"That seems a little pushy," Sierra said. "I mean, how would you feel if you went through whatever she went through at fifteen, and then almost twenty years later, this person shows up on your doorstep?"

"Exactly. That's why I kind of like Mom's idea of a letter. That way I can say some of the things I really want to, like thanks for giving birth to me. That way if she's not comfortable responding, at least I've achieved my goal of telling her what I wanted."

"Do you think any of this bothers Mom or Dad?" Sierra asked.

"I don't know. At first they seemed pretty surprised but real supportive. You know how they are. Then today, I don't know. Some little things Mom said made me wonder if she's feeling strange about this, like she wants me to get it over with quickly."

"After all, she raised you," Sierra said.

"I know. That's why I'd never refer to Lina as being my 'real' mother. I'd only refer to her as my 'birth' mother. Mom is and always will be my real mother. I told her that."

Sierra adjusted her position on the stool. "Well, I know you've wanted to do this for a long time. I remember your telling me you were going to hire a lawyer. It looks as if maybe God is working things out."

"That's what it seems like to me," Tawni said. "Jeremy is probably more excited about this than I am. He says I need to solidify my identity."

"What does that mean?"

"That I need to become more secure in who I am and who God made me to be. I don't know what I think." Tawni sighed and went on. "Some people I know who are adopted say they rarely think about where they came from genetically. It's not been that way for me. It's bothered me for a long time. I want to see if I have her eyes. Maybe she would tell me I laugh just like my birth father. All the time I was growing up in this big family, people—complete strangers—would say things like, 'You don't look much like either of your parents.' Or I'd hear, 'All those Jensen kids sure resemble each other. All except the older daughter.' I guess it bothered me more than I ever realized."

"Yeah, but did you hear the rest of their comments?" Sierra asked. "They would say, 'That Tawni is much better looking than that younger daughter.' That's what I've had to live with. The shadow of the beautiful Tawni was a long one I couldn't get out from under."

Tawni sounded surprised. "Sierra! You of all people should know that we're not supposed to compare ourselves with others."

"Isn't that what you're doing?"

Tawni paused. "I guess maybe I am. This is what Jeremy has been telling me for a long time. That's what he meant by me solidifying my identity. Mentally, I know my self-image is supposed to be based in Christ, and I should be seeking to find out who God made me to be. But I guess I don't understand that yet in my heart."

Sierra nodded. She understood. It was wonderful having her sister open up to her like this. Neither of them spoke for a moment. Sierra took another bite of her dinner.

"Are you and Jeremy getting pretty serious about each other?" Sierra asked.

"Sometimes I think so. Other times I'm not so sure. He's never brought up the subject of marriage, if that's what you're asking. He's committed to finishing school, and he's committed to our friendship. We haven't opened up any other doors of possibilities. By the way, how are things going with Paul? You said a few weeks ago that he wrote you. Has he written again?"

"No. I wrote him twice and then decided to wait to hear from him before I contacted him again. It's hard to tell with guys, isn't it? You think they give you a green light, and then it turns yellow. You don't know if you should chance it and run through or hold back and assume that it will suddenly turn red on you."

Tawni gave a lighthearted laugh that came from a well of deep understanding. "You have it figured out, Sierra. That's exactly how it is with guys."

Sierra stared out the kitchen window. "I mean, I opened up my heart and told him things that I don't tell just anybody." She hadn't expected the tears that suddenly welled up in the corners of her eyes.

"And now you feel vulnerable," Tawni said. "You handed him your heart, and you're afraid he's going to tromp all over it."

Sierra sniffed. Her answer was a hoarse "Yes."

"It'll be okay," Tawni said quickly. "Even if he never writes you back, it's okay. Don't close up, Sierra. Don't lose that free-spirited exuberance of yours for any reason. Be yourself. Even if being yourself means you say or do things you regret. All relationships are a process. You'll learn as you go. We all do."

Sierra reached for a napkin from the basket at the end of the counter and wiped her eyes. "I wish I understood relationships better and that I had them figured out ahead of time." Sierra was thinking of Amy as well as of Paul. "If I knew what the other person was thinking or what that person was going through ahead of time, I'd know how to think and act and respond."

"Sorry," Tawni said. "It doesn't work like that. Sometimes all we can do is take the little bit of info we have and go with it. It makes you trust God absolutely."

"I guess that applies to Paul and me as much as it applies to your writing or calling your birth mom, doesn't it?"

There was silence on the other end of the line.

"You're right," Tawni said.

"All your friends and family are giving you the feeling it's a big green light to go ahead and call her, but then you find out it might suddenly turn red and you'll be breaking all the rules if you try to run it."

"Yes," Tawni answered quietly. "That's exactly what it is. I guess I have to take my own advice and go with the little bit of info I have. I have to trust God absolutely in this."

"So, how do you know if you did the right thing?" Sierra asked.

"I guess only time will tell."

six

SIERRA SPRINTED into her literature class just as the bell rang. Mrs. Chambers gave her a friendly, scolding look. As Sierra sat down and took her notebook from her backpack, her heart was pounding. She was late because she had been talking to Amy in the hallway.

When Sierra had spotted Amy at her locker right before class, she had taken Tawni's advice and gone with what appeared to be a green light.

Sierra walked up to her friend and simply said, "Hi. Can we talk after school?"

Startled, Amy said, "Okay."

Sierra suggested they meet at her locker after school and that was that. She was trying to trust God absolutely, as Tawni had said.

"I'm handing out an assignment that is due on Friday," Mrs. Chambers said, passing papers down each row. "This is a list of American authors and the titles of some of their works. I want you to read and evaluate one of the works listed. If you would like extra credit, you may do two evaluations. The questions for you to answer are on the second piece of paper."

Sierra skimmed the list and recognized the names of only about half of the authors.

"Do not save this until ten o'clock on Thursday night," Mrs. Chambers said, perching on the edge of her desk. "You will need to go to the library and check out these books to read the sections listed. I have a few of the books in my library at the back of the room. You may check them out, but only until Friday."

Mrs. Chambers gave them a few minutes at the end of class in case they wanted to check out one of her books. Sierra took advantage of the opportunity and reached for a book of poems by Emily Dickinson. Vicki stood beside her and took a book by Henry Wadsworth Longfellow.

"Sierra," Vicki said, "I was wondering if you wanted to do something together sometime."

Sierra gave her a puzzled look. "What do you mean?"

Vicki's smooth cheeks began to flush. "I don't know. Go shopping or something."

Sierra tried to hide her surprise. "Sure. We could do that."

"How about today after school?"

"I already have plans for today."

"Tomorrow maybe?"

"I work tomorrow," Sierra said.

"Oh. Well, another time," Vicki said. "Let me know when you have some time."

"Okay," Sierra said. She looped her backpack over her shoulder and gave Vicki a suspicious look. *I didn't think she liked me. Is she trying to get to somebody through me? Who could it be? Randy?*

Sierra put away her suspicions about Vicki and spent the rest of the afternoon concentrating on what she was going to say to Amy after school. She had it all planned out and felt only a little nervous as she stood by her locker, waiting for Amy to show up.

Randy came by and said, "I gave my notice at the restaurant. Did I tell you already?"

"No. Did you give them two weeks' notice or what?"

"I offered two weeks, but he said I could be off at the end of this week if I worked the lunch shift on Saturday."

"What about your yard business?"

Randy shrugged. "I'll get somebody to help me."

Sierra noticed that his hair was back in a ponytail and tucked under his collar as if he were trying to hide it.

"What happened with the warning you got about your hair?" Sierra asked.

"Nothing."

"What are you going to do? Get it cut?"

"I don't know. Everyone was saying at lunch today that it's a dumb rule. They think I should petition to get the rule changed to say that if your hair is clean and neat, it doesn't matter what length it is."

"So you get to be the one to challenge the fifty-year history of Royal Academy?"

Randy shrugged again. "I'm not exactly the rebel sort."

"Does everyone think you are because you're growing out your hair?"

"I grew it out for the band," Randy said. "I think it gives us more of a connection with the kind of people who go to The Beet. What do you think?"

"I don't know. I haven't been to The Beet. And I haven't noticed the other guys' hair in the band. Are you sure you want to go to the wall on this one?"

Randy readjusted his backpack. "I don't know."

"Are you going to talk to your parents about it?" Sierra asked.

"I probably should."

Randy looked past Sierra and gave a chin-up greeting to someone behind her. "Hey, Amy. How's it going?"

"Hi, Randy," Amy said. Her dark eyes centered on Sierra.

"Hi," Sierra said.

"Well," Randy said, apparently reading the situation, "I'd better get going."

"That's okay," Amy said. "Don't leave on account of me. I just wanted to tell you, Sierra, that I forgot I have someplace I need to go this afternoon."

Sierra felt her heart sink. "How about later tonight?"

"I work tonight," Amy said. "And then I have a ton of homework."

"When would be a good time?" Sierra asked. "I really want to talk to you."

Amy smoothed back her dark, wavy hair. "I don't know." She smiled at Randy, not making eye contact with Sierra. "I need to get going. I'll see you guys." She hurriedly turned.

Sierra watched Amy practically run down the hall and out the double doors that led to the parking lot. A heavy cloud of apprehension and frustration came over Sierra. Randy must have seen it.

"Hey," he said, leaning over to make eye contact with

her, "you tried. Don't beat yourself up like this. Give it a little more time."

"A little more time, huh?" Sierra said. "Why is it that everything in life seems to require a little more time? I'm tired of waiting! Why can't relationships move along smoothly without all this...this...What is this?"

"Life." Randy looked serious. "This is life. It's nothing like the brochure, is it?"

"I don't like it," Sierra said, giving him a pout. "Why won't she just talk to me?"

Randy shrugged.

"It's so frustrating."

"I imagine it must be," Randy said.

Sierra sighed and readjusted the backpack slung over her shoulder.

"Come on," Randy said, tugging on Sierra's sleeve. "I'll buy you a taco and a milk. That'll cheer you right up."

Sierra pulled away. "Will you stop with the taco and milk?"

"You're the only person I know who orders milk with a taco."

"So?"

Randy led the way out of the school building. "I'm buying," he said.

"Who's driving?" Sierra asked when they hit the parking lot.

"Me. My truck is over there."

They were on their way to Lotsa Tacos, which was only two blocks away, when Randy asked, "Did Mrs. Chambers give your class the same assignment we got?"

"Probably. We're supposed to read and evaluate one of

the works of an American writer. Did you get one of the books from the back of the room?"

"No," Randy said. "Did you?"

"Yes."

"Do you think she would mind if we did our evaluations on the same author?" Randy asked.

"I don't know why not. I was planning to do mine tonight. I'll give you the book tomorrow. Make sure you turn the book back in on Friday because it's checked out in my name," Sierra said.

They decided to go inside Lotsa Tacos rather than drive through. Sierra brought her backpack with her and pulled out the Emily Dickinson book while Randy ordered their food. She skimmed the preface and flipped through the book, happy to see that all the poems were fairly short.

Randy returned with six tacos, a large soft drink, and a carton of milk.

"Didn't you have lunch?" Sierra asked.

"Yes. Why?"

"Never mind."

Randy sat down and motioned to the book. "Is that the book for lit class?"

"Yes." Sierra held it up for him to see. "Emily Dickinson. It's a collection of her poems."

"Poems?" Randy echoed. "I thought we were supposed to read short stories or something."

"Poems are better than short stories. They're images in a tiny box wrapped up real pretty."

"Terrific," Randy said, punching his straw on the table so the paper wrapper tore off. "I always wanted to do a report on pretty little images all in a row."

"Hey," Sierra said, quick to defend Emily's poems, "don't be like that. What about your music? When you write lyrics to a song, aren't you sort of writing a poem?"

"Hmmph," Randy said.

"Hmmph?"

"Yeah, hmmph. I don't know if I want to agree with you or not."

"Here, let me read you one. You might get some inspiration."

"Inspiration, huh?"

"Yes, listen to this. 'Out of the more than 1,700 poems Emily Dickinson wrote, less than a dozen were published during her lifetime. The first volume of her poetry was published four years after her death.'"

"When did she die?"

Sierra scanned the introduction. "I don't know. It says she was born in 1830." She felt a tinge of adventure, reading words that had been written more than a hundred years ago by a woman who had died never knowing she would be famous one day.

"Here, listen." Sierra leaned across the table and read,

In lands I never saw, they say,
Immortal Alps look down,
Whose bonnets touch the firmament,
Whose sandals touch the town.
Meek at those everlasting feet
A myriad daisies play.
Which, sir, are you, and which am I,
Upon an August day?

"What is that supposed to mean?" Randy said, munching his taco.

Sierra felt her heart pick up its pace with a contented little jig. She knew what it meant to see those immortal Alps whose bonnets touch the firmament and sandals touch the town. She had picnicked last August in a field of daisies on those very slopes. Alex was the "sir" from her personal poetic picnic. And just like Emily, she had only soft questions about the roles she and Alex were to play.

Gazing out the window at the clear autumn sky, Sierra felt transported above the roar of the engines at the stoplight outside. She had opened her heart to Alex just a little last August, and it had proved to be an enriching, growing, and encouraging experience.

Suddenly, she felt okay about those two transparent letters she had written to Paul. Even if he never answered, she had grown from writing them. Maybe Paul was encouraged. That was what she wanted. Maybe in some relationships all the questions were never fully answered.

And maybe they didn't need to be.

seven

"HELLO? SIERRA?" Randy said, waving a hand in front of her face, blocking her gaze of the endless sky and bringing her thoughts back to the noisy fast-food restaurant. "Where did you go?"

She smiled but kept her answer to herself. "Should I read you another one of Emily's poems?"

"That depends. Will it send you on another trip?"

"I don't know," Sierra said. "Shall we live dangerously and find out?"

She turned to another page in the book and read,

> The way I read a letter's this:
> 'Tis first I lock the door,
> And push it with my fingers next,
> For transport it be sure.
>
> And then I go the furthest off
> To counteract a knock;
> Then draw my little letter forth
> And softly pick its lock.

There was more, but Randy interrupted her. This time he was the one looking out the window and apparently being transported to another world.

"Check it out!" Randy said. "That's the new turbo diesel 780. The black one there. They just came out. That's the first one I've seen."

Sierra glanced over her shoulder at the stream of cars. She had no idea which vehicle he was referring to, and she didn't much care. She was more interested in reading about this woman who knew what it was like to wait for a letter and then go hide away to "pick its lock" to fully savor it all alone. The image brought another smile to Sierra's lips.

"Are you going to eat that?" Randy nodded at her untouched taco.

"No, you can have it," she said, returning to her book and reading the rest of the poem to herself.

After Randy inhaled the taco, Sierra read another poem to herself.

"You know what?" she said to Randy. "I've changed my mind. You can't use this book. I think I'm going to have it for more than just tonight."

"You actually understand what she's trying to say?"

"No, not all of it. But parts of it apply to things that are interesting to me."

Randy wadded up the paper wrappers and carried the tray to the trash can without making a comment. Sierra followed him, carrying her still nearly full carton of milk.

"I'll get another book tomorrow," Randy said. "You can keep Emma all to yourself."

"Emily," she corrected him.

"Whatever," Randy said.

They climbed back into the truck and drove to the school parking lot.

Driving home, Sierra thought about the poems. She wondered if she could finish reading the whole book tonight and start on her report. It would be good to get a head start this semester. She was so captured by the three poems she had read that she wanted to slowly drink in the book before beginning her report.

Sierra parked in front of the house, and out of a habit she had developed recently, she opened the mailbox to fish out the stack of mail. Pulling open the screen door, she walked into the kitchen and plopped everything down on the counter.

"Hello!" Sierra called out. "I'm home."

"I'm down here," her mother called from the basement.

Sierra flipped through the mail, making a stack of bills and advertisements for her parents. There was a letter for Granna Mae and two other envelopes.

She suddenly stopped and held her breath. The two envelopes both bore her name and address, written in bold, black letters. The stamps in the top right corner showed a side portrait of the Queen of England. Each stamp had been canceled with a thick circle of ink and showed the date of September 12. The name in the top left-hand corner was the name she had repeated for months in her whispered prayers: Paul Mackenzie.

He didn't forget about me. These were mailed over a week ago. Paul has been thinking about me, too!

Sierra's heart was fluttering like a butterfly caught in a

net. She couldn't stop smiling. No one was around to see her carefully lift the two letters and steal away to her favorite chair in the study.

Just like in the poem, Sierra closed the study's door and locked it. She pulled her chair over to where the late afternoon sun spilled through the French doors. There, in a spotlight of autumn glory, she sat down and held both letters, one in each hand.

Which one do I open first? Maybe Paul put the date on them on the inside.

Sliding her thumbnail under the flap, Sierra opened one of the letters and drew out the single, folded page of white onionskin paper. It crinkled when she lifted the two folds, revealing the familiar bold letters that came from Paul's hand. The date at the top was September 7.

Sierra didn't know if she could bear to open the next letter and leave this one unread. But it would make more sense to read them in order. She opened the second one more hurriedly. That three-page letter bore the date of September 10.

Pursing her lips together, Sierra went back to the first letter and read each word slowly.

Dear Sierra,

I haven't heard back from you, and I realize you may never write. As I said in my last letter, I would understand if you don't want to start up a correspondence.

Sierra looked up and spoke to the swirling stream of dust specks riding on the afternoon shaft of light. "He didn't get my letters!"

She read on.

There is one more thing I wanted to say to you, and then I'll let you be. Months ago on the airplane you said something that has stuck with me. I wanted you to know. You asked how I felt now that my grandfather was gone. Do you know, you're the only one who ever asked me that? So many people tried to tell me how I should feel. They still do that here. They say, "Oh, you'll get on fine," or "You should feel proud to have been kin to such a man."

Sierra, only you asked how I felt. I wanted to thank you for that. It's given me some freedom to feel all the things I need to.

May the peace of Christ be upon you.

Paul

Sierra folded up the letter. She eagerly began to read the next letter.

Ah, dear Daffodil Queen,

Pulling the paper close, Sierra looked to the ceiling and bit her lower lip to stifle a giggle.

"Ah, dear Daffodil Queen," she repeated aloud. Paul had once seen her walking down the street in the rain with an armful of daffodils and had teased her about it. This time his title sounded sweet to her ears.

I have read and reread your two wonderful letters at least half a dozen times, and they still make me smile. You have such a way with words. I could actually see some of the stories as you told them to me: your father taking you to the restaurant where your friends all worked and presenting you with the purity ring; Doug being chained to the Balboa Island ferry; and your surprise trip to Switzerland.

I laughed aloud when I read about how you and your friend knocked over the card rack inside that proper little shop in Basel. I know exactly what that's like. There's a tea shop my grandmother goes to every Wednesday and Saturday to meet her friends. She took me along my first week here, intending, I'm sure, to show me off to the dear women of the town so they could see if I was a suitable match for their granddaughters. We sat at a very small table by the window. As soon as the tea and biscuits were served, I accidentally kicked the leg of the decrepit table and brought the whole spread, china teapot and all, crashing to the floor.

Sierra tilted her head back and laughed. She could just see the little tea shop, since she had been in one in Ireland. She knew how serious the little ladies were about having a proper, quiet teatime.

Poor Paul. How embarrassing!

I began classes at the university several weeks ago, and now my life consists of books, books, and more books. Perhaps that's another reason I enjoyed your refreshing letters so much.

How was your first week of school? You said that you were having a misunderstanding with your friend Amy. I've wondered how that all turned out.

Last year I had a lot of friends at school, and I always had someone I could do something with. Here, I have very few friends. I don't know if it's me or them. Last year I didn't have many friends who were what you would call a good influence on me. I haven't found anyone here who holds to the values I now embrace. So I spend a lot of time by myself rather than at the pubs with the others. It's actually been good for me. My grades are all high so far. I spend the weekends at my grandmother's, working around the place.

Have I told you about my grandmother's home? It's a cottage, really. The original foundation was laid something like 200 years ago. It's been renovated a dozen times. The most recent improvements were made about four years ago. My grandmother has a microwave and a new central, wood-burning stove for heat, but she'll never have a dishwasher or trash compactor. There are two acres of hilly, rocky land that have been in the family for generations. They used to keep sheep on the land, but now all Grandma keeps is a collie named Laddie and a small garden, which did poorly this summer because of the unusual heat.

I'm writing this on the train to Grandma's. My stop is the next one, so I'll bring this to a close. I'm already looking forward to your next letter. Perhaps there will be one waiting for me at the cottage. Please tell me everything that has been happening in Portland. Have the autumn rains begun yet? Or are you enjoying those brilliant blue skies and warm sunshine as the leaves begin their transformation? We've had very little rain here, but everyone is ready for the wet to return.

I send this with my prayers for you, Sierra. May the peace of Christ be upon you.

Paul

Sierra let the pages drift to her lap as the rhythm of her pulse slowed. The sunlight waltzed through the French doors warming her arms the way Paul's letter had just warmed her heart. She didn't want to move from this chair. She didn't want to lose this feeling. Ever.

eight

FOR THE TENTH TIME in the last few days, Sierra "picked the lock" on her wonderful letters from Paul as she sat in the quietness of her room to read them again. After she read them, she prayed for Paul as she had done many times. She prayed that God would make his path straight and that his heart would be responsive to all the things God was teaching him. It gave her comfort to know that even though they were so far away from each other in miles, they could be close in spirit. Paul was praying for her. He had said so.

Sierra had written Paul back right away Monday night after she had read his letters. It took her three hours to carefully craft her reply. She had given him her e-mail address and suggested they correspond by e-mail since it would be much quicker. Stopping at the post office Tuesday after school, she sent the long letter off by air mail. It would be hard to wait for his answer. If they could correspond through e-mail, they could chat on-line and answer each other the same day.

Now it was Wednesday evening, and Sierra had just

returned from the youth group Bible study at church. She went up to her room, where she shut the door and read her letters in private. There was something decisive and serious about Paul's handwriting. Each character was etched bold and black on the onionskin paper. Sierra noticed the way he crossed his *t*'s with an upward stroke. This gave the whole page a feeling of optimism. The letters seemed to reflect Paul's personality as Sierra was beginning to know him: thoughtful yet hopeful.

"Sierra?" Her mom called out from behind Sierra's closed door. "Are you busy?"

"No. Come in."

Mrs. Jensen entered and sat on the edge of Tawni's bed. The top half of the bed was covered with a mound of unfolded clean clothes that Sierra had brought up from the laundry on Monday.

"I just talked to Tawni," her mother said.

Sierra nodded, waiting for her to go on. Before her mom came in, Sierra had folded Paul's letter and slipped it under her pillow, where she had kept his letters since the day she had received them.

"Tawni has decided to write a letter to her birth mother and wait for a reply. She wanted me to tell you what she finally decided."

Sierra nodded again. She was trying to read her mom's expression to see how she felt about all this. She appeared calm.

"How do you feel about all this?" Sierra asked. She felt a little strange, talking to her mom as an equal, asking about her feelings.

"I'll be honest: It disturbed me at first. There's so much

that could happen or be said that could never be erased. Tawni has always been sensitive in certain areas. I was worried this would cut her deeply and leave quite a scar."

"It is kind of like venturing into the unknown," Sierra said.

"The more I've talked about it with your father and with Tawni, the more I think she's doing the right thing. This is a good step for her to take. I think the letter is a good idea."

"I do, too," Sierra agreed, leaning her elbow on her pillow and thinking of the hidden treasure under it. "Letters can really communicate a lot, can't they? I mean, you can go back and read a letter over and over and take your time to respond."

"You're right," her mom said. "I hope Tawni is prepared to never hear back, if that's what happens." She reached over and patted Sierra's leg. "The hardest thing for me is to realize you two are both old enough to make these kinds of life-affecting decisions."

"I think Tawni and I are both realizing that relationships can be complicated and there aren't always easy answers."

"That reminds me," Mrs. Jensen said. "Whatever happened with Amy?"

Sierra shook her head. "I don't think we're ever going to talk." She related what had happened at school on Monday and how Amy had made it clear she didn't want to discuss anything with Sierra. "It makes me feel awful," Sierra said. "Have you ever lost a friend like this?"

Her mom thought a minute. "Yes." She hesitated. "It's happened to me several times over the years. People change. Friendships change. I chose to take a different direction with a friendship when we moved here to Portland. I guess I was the Amy in that relationship. I simply didn't have the time or energy to keep in touch with this friend at the level she wanted. My life here is so different and in some ways more demanding than it was before. I'm afraid I hurt her feelings."

Sierra wondered if that was what was going on with Amy. Now that Amy was wrapped up in her relationship with Nathan, she didn't have the time or energy to keep a friendship going with Sierra.

After Sierra went to bed that night, she thought about Amy and the loss of their friendship. It wasn't even so much that Amy had a boyfriend. It was the way their friendship had ended. Sierra realized now, quite clearly, that she had a different set of values and goals for her own dating life. She had formulated what she called a creed, which outlined her standards in writing. She had assumed that Amy had the same set of values and that she would only go out with a strong Christian and would be deliberate about staying morally and physically pure. That didn't appear to be Amy's goal.

Before Sierra fell asleep, she wondered if she should write a letter to Amy. Her letters from Paul had meant so much to her. Tawni had decided to write a letter to her birth mother. Perhaps a letter would accomplish what Sierra wanted in making peace with Amy, even if they didn't remain good friends. Sierra knew it would have to be carefully written. As she lay in the silence of her dark bedroom, Sierra lined the words up in her mind, arranging and rearranging them like vowels and consonants in a game of Scrabble.

When she woke on Thursday morning, Sierra realized

she had dreamed about her letter. In her dream she had handed the carefully written sheets to Amy in the school cafeteria, only to watch Amy drop them into the trash can, unread. As unsettling as the dream had been, Sierra still felt her idea was a good one. If only she could figure out what to say and the right way to say it.

There was no time to act on her idea that day because she worked after school and then helped serve dinner to the homeless who lined up at the Highland House. She didn't get home until after eight, and the first thing she did was go into the study and turn on her dad's computer. She checked the e-mail, just in case Paul had received her letter already and had written her back by e-mail. No messages waited for her.

Sierra opened a writing program and started to draft her letter to Amy: "Dear Amy, I want to tell you how sad I am that our friendship has gone on hold."

No, that didn't sound right. Deleting the line, she tried again.

Sierra kept reworking the letter, trying to express what she wanted to say without its sounding too strong. It was a lot harder than she had thought it would be. Her parents came into the study to say good night before they went to bed.

"A girl named Vicki called while you were at work," her mom said. "I left the note with her phone number upstairs on your bed."

"Thanks."

Her dad glanced at the computer screen. "Finishing up your homework?"

"I'm about to. I was just working on something else."

"Well, be sure to turn everything off when you go to bed." He patted her shoulder and gave her a quick kiss on the top of her head.

"I will," Sierra said.

She felt self-conscious about her words on the computer screen. They appeared so final there. Is that how they would seem to Amy? What if she tried her best to choose all the words so they sounded right to her, but somehow they didn't sound the same way to Amy?

Saving her efforts in a file marked "Amy," Sierra put away the letter and unzipped her backpack. The first book she pulled out was Emily Dickinson's poems.

"Oh, no!" Sierra groaned. She had forgotten about the writing assignment due the next day. With a glance at the clock, Sierra shook her head.

I can't believe I'm doing exactly what Mrs. Chambers said not to. I waited until ten o'clock on Thursday night.

Since schoolwork came easily for Sierra, over the years she had managed to get good grades with minimum effort. But now that she was beginning her senior year, it was important to her that she get straight As. This last-minute effort with the poetry evaluation was not the way to start off in English.

When Sierra turned her paper in the next day, she asked if she could do an additional report for extra credit.

Mrs. Chambers gave her a wistful look. "No, sorry. Next assignment maybe."

Sierra made a mental note: *No mercy from this teacher. Don't put off any assignments in this class.*

After class Sierra was returning the book to the library

at the back of the room when Vicki came up beside her. Vicki waited until Sierra looked at her.

"Hi," Vicki said.

"Hi," Sierra echoed.

"I called yesterday when you were at work. I was wondering if you wanted to do something tonight."

Sierra looked Vicki in the eye. She wanted to say "Why?" but she managed to refrain and offered a smile instead.

"I thought maybe we could get something to eat or go to the movies. I didn't know if you were already doing something tonight."

"No."

Vicki smiled. "So what do you want to do?"

"Well..." Sierra shrugged. Then she heard herself say, "Why don't you come over to my house?"

nine

"WHO'S COMING OVER?" Mrs. Jensen asked that evening.

Sierra was sitting on the floor in the family room going through the file drawer of all the DVDs.

"Vicki Navarone," Sierra said without looking up. "She goes to Royal Academy. Do you remember my saying anything about her before? She helped out at Highland House with Randy and me last spring."

"I remember your talking about Vicki, but I don't remember your saying you were friends."

Sierra looked up. "I didn't think we were." She turned her attention back to the DVDs. "I thought Tawni had all these in alphabetical order."

"She did when she lived here. I'm afraid no one has kept up the system."

The doorbell rang, and Sierra hopped up to answer it.

"That's Vicki. Are you sure it's okay if we watch a movie in here? The boys won't be crashing in on us, will they?"

"Gavin is over at Jason's, and I'll make sure Dillon stays upstairs. Have a good time."

Sierra felt apprehensive as she opened the front door. She never would have guessed that Vicki would have any of her Friday nights free, let alone want to spend one of them with Sierra.

"Hi. Come on in," Sierra said. "I was just going through our stack of DVDs to see if anything looked interesting."

"Sounds great! I love your house. That swing is so cute." Vicki had on a pair of shorts and a gray sweatshirt that said "Georgetown." Her silky, long hair was twisted up in a clip, and she didn't appear to have on any makeup.

"It's my grandma's house," Sierra said as Vicki entered and appreciatively glanced at the lighting fixture and wood trim in the entryway. "She lives with us, or rather, we live with her. Sometimes she gets kind of confused, so don't be surprised if she comes in and starts doing or saying things that don't make sense."

Vicki nodded.

They went into the family room, and Sierra returned to the movie options, where she read off some of the titles.

"That sounds good," Vicki said as Sierra read. "I like that one. Oh, that's a great movie! I cried the first time I saw it."

Suddenly Sierra stopped. This was all too unexplainable to her. Even though she knew she should think before she spoke, she didn't.

"Vicki, I have to ask you something. Why in the world are you here? I mean, why do you want to sit around my house and watch DVDs? I know you could be out with a whole lot of other people who have more exciting social lives than I do."

Vicki blushed.

"What exactly do you want?"

"I want to be your friend," Vicki said.

"Why?"

"Because I—"

"I mean," Sierra said quickly, trying to cover up her brashness, "we didn't exactly hit it off last year."

"I know," Vicki agreed.

"So what's changed?"

"Me," Vicki said without blinking. "I've been wanting to tell you…"

Sierra sat, attentively waiting.

"This summer I went to a church camp and I made a commitment to Christ. I've gone to church all my life, but I never realized I needed to surrender my life to God to have a relationship with Him. I became a Christian."

"You did? I mean, that's so great!" Sierra said. She felt like jumping up and hugging Vicki, but it still felt a little awkward between them.

Vicki smiled. "I can tell that God's been working in my life. He's been changing me, Sierra. On the inside. I don't want to hang out with the same people I used to spend time with. I don't want to get caught up in the whole party thing again. I want to stay strong in my walk with the Lord. That's why I wanted to get in with your group."

"My group?" Sierra held back the laugh she felt welling up inside. "I don't exactly have a group."

"I know that you, Randy, Tre, and some of the others from Randy's band are true Christians, and that's how I want to be, too."

Sierra lowered her head and shook it slowly. "Vicki," she said. The laughter in her throat had turned into an uncomfortable lump. "I feel really bad."

"Why?"

"I haven't exactly given you any reason to believe I am, as you say, a 'true Christian.' I mean, I am a Christian, and I feel the same way you do—I want to grow in my relationship with the Lord. But I've never treated you the way I should have, as a Christian. I'm sorry, Vicki."

"Don't be sorry," Vicki said quickly, reaching over to give Sierra's arm a squeeze. "I never treated you very nice, either. I knew you were different, though. You acted as though you were trusting in something or Someone bigger than yourself. You were what I wanted to be."

Sierra shook her head. "I have a long way to go."

"So do I."

There was a soft moment of quiet between them.

"I was hoping we could walk the long path together," Vicki said.

Sierra smiled. Vicki smiled back. It seemed their new friendship was somehow eternally sealed.

"Do you still want to watch one of these?" Sierra said, motioning to the stack of DVDs on the floor beside her.

"It's up to you," Vicki said.

"I'd rather talk," Sierra said, getting off the floor and settling on the couch across from Vicki. She tucked her bare feet underneath her and said, "Tell me about your summer. I want to hear about the camp and everything."

"I want to hear about your summer, too," Vicki said. "I heard you went to Europe."

"Just Switzerland," Sierra said, since "Europe" sounded so grand. "Well, and Germany. It was only for a week."

"Still!" Vicki said, opening her eyes wide. "I've always wanted to go to Europe. Anywhere in Europe. Did you buy a lot of souvenirs?"

Sierra laughed. "No. Can you believe it? About all I bought was some tea."

"Tea? I love tea."

"Do you want some now? Let's go in the kitchen."

The two friends talked and laughed over their cups of tea as if they had done this a hundred times together. The phone rang, and when no one else answered it, Sierra picked it up on the fourth ring.

"Hey, Sierra!" There was a lot of clanging of pots and pans in the background.

"Randy?"

"Yeah. Hey, Sierra, what are you doing tomorrow morning?"

"Working."

"What time do you go in?"

"Ten o'clock. Why?"

"I need some help. I have to be here at ten-thirty, and I couldn't find anyone else to do my lawns for me tomorrow. Can I hire you to help me mow lawns from seven o'clock to nine-thirty?"

"Hire me? You don't need to pay me. I'll help you. Where do you want me to meet you?"

"That depends." Randy hesitated.

Sierra looked at Vicki over her shoulder and raised her eyebrows as if to say, "Wait until you hear this one."

"That depends on what, Randy?" Sierra asked.

"Do you think you could use your father's lawn mower? If you can, I'll send you to the houses off of Hawthorne, and I'll do the others. There are only three lawns, and they're all close to your house."

"I think I know at least two of the houses," Sierra said.

She had met Randy at his lawn jobs more than once. "Give me the addresses and tell me what to do. I'll be there."

"I owe you," Randy said gratefully.

"Oh, do I get to hold you to that?"

"Sure," he said. "How about if I drop off the addresses and the instructions on my way home from work tonight?"

"What time would that be?"

"I get off at ten o'clock. I'll leave the paper in the mailbox. Make sure you get started by at least seven-thirty, or you won't have time to finish."

"Got it," Sierra said.

"Oh, and hey, Sierra."

"Yeah?"

"Thanks again."

"Don't thank me yet, Randy. You don't know if I can do what your customers expect."

"Don't worry. These three yards aren't too complicated. Make sure you wear boots. I don't have workmen's comp for my employees."

"You do offer vacation benefits, don't you?"

"Not for the kinds of vacations you go on."

In the background, Sierra heard someone call Randy's name.

"I have to go," Randy said. "I'll leave the paper in your mailbox."

"Okay. See you later."

Sierra hung up, and Vicki met her gaze. Her thin eyebrows arched up, silently questioning.

As Sierra stepped over to the counter where Vicki sat, an idea came to her. "Vicki, what are you doing tomorrow morning?"

ten

BY SEVEN-FIFTEEN the next morning, Vicki and Sierra were marching side by side up the street to the first of Randy's lawn accounts. Sierra pushed the mower like a baby carriage, hoping none of their neighbors were up early enough to see their strange parade. Sierra wore jeans, a long-sleeved denim shirt, her dad's old cowboy boots, and a pair of stained, suede garden gloves. Her hair was wrangled under a baseball cap. A thick, curly ponytail hung out the back opening.

Vicki sported a sleeker landscaper's look. She wore jeans, a short-sleeved knit shirt, and an expensive-looking pair of sunglasses. Her hair was pulled back loosely in a clip. She carried a pair of long-handled shrub clippers, a rake, and a dozen black garbage bags.

"I've never mowed a lawn before," Vicki said with a giggle. "I can't believe I agreed to do this with you."

"I'm beginning to wonder why I told Randy *I'd* do it," Sierra said. "I'm glad you came with me. It'll go a lot quicker."

What Sierra didn't tell Vicki was that she had never actually mowed a lawn before, either. Her brothers and father had always kept up the yard at home. While she had helped out plenty with the yard and garden over the years, she had never done the mowing.

"This is the first one," Sierra said, pulling the piece of paper from her pocket. She double-checked the address and read Randy's instructions aloud. "Mow front and back lawn. Small dog in backyard."

"Does that mean we're supposed to mow the small dog in the backyard?" Vicki said.

Sierra laughed. "Let's hope not."

"Should we start in the front or back?" Vicki asked.

"Front, I think. I'll start this thing, and we can take turns."

Sierra bent over the gas-powered lawn mower and gave the start cord a yank. To her amazement, it revved up immediately.

"Okay," Sierra said calmly as if she had done this dozens of times. "Here I go."

She pushed the mower straight up through the grass to the front steps. Turning around to go back the other way, she decided it would be more orderly to start on the other side of the yard. That way she could follow the line of the flower bed. To change her pattern, Sierra cut across the lawn in a huge diagonal and carefully followed the edge of the flower bed toward the house.

Vicki, who had been standing on the sidewalk watching, burst out laughing. "Look!" she shouted over the sound of the mower. "You made it look like Zorro was here." She motioned to the Z in the grass.

Sierra paused to see what she had done. In the spirit of the moment, she called out, "Watch this!" Then she made another long, diagonal line, crossing the first. "It's a bow tie," she called out over the roar of the lawn mower.

Vicki laughed and pointed at Sierra's masterpiece.

The front door of the house opened, and an older woman, wearing a long green robe and moccasins, stepped onto the front porch. "What are you doing?" she shrieked.

Sierra bent to turn off the lawn mower. The only problem was, she had no idea how to make it stop. The mower rumbled on as she tried to answer the distressed woman.

"We're filling in for Randy," Sierra yelled.

"What?" the woman yelled back, her hands on her hips. It appeared she hadn't noticed the giant bow tie yet.

"I'll tell her," Vicki yelled to Sierra. She ran up to the porch and spoke with the woman.

Sierra fiddled with the mower, trying to stop the engine. Nothing worked. She could see the woman gesturing wildly with her hands as she talked to Vicki. Vicki hurried over to Sierra while the woman remained on the porch.

"She says we woke her up and that Randy doesn't do her lawn until after nine o'clock. She wants us to come back at nine."

"At nine! What about the bow tie?"

"I don't think she noticed it. Maybe if we leave really quickly, she'll go back inside. Can't you turn off that noisy thing?"

Sierra shook her head. "I don't know how."

Vicki stared at her with disbelieving eyes. "We'd better get out of here quick. Isn't the next house only a few doors down?"

"Yes, but what am I going to do with the mower? How do I get it there?"

Vicki shrugged. She glanced over her shoulder at the woman and offered a friendly wave, indicating they were on their way.

"Turn that thing off!" the woman yelled.

"Come on! Grab the clippers and stuff and let's go."

Sierra tipped the mower on the back two wheels and carted it off the woman's lawn. As fast as they could trot, the two mechanically challenged young women pushed the "live" mower down the sidewalk to the next house.

"Here," Sierra said, motioning for Vicki to grab the mower handle with her free hand. "Hold her steady."

Sierra slipped her hand into her back pocket and pulled out the instruction paper. She double-checked the address and jerked her thumb in the direction of the house they were to work on next.

"This one," she said loud enough for Vicki to hear over the rumble of the mower. "No dogs."

Vicki nodded and put down the gardening gear.

Sierra took the wild mower by the horns and forced it onto the tough grass. This time she carefully made her way up and down the perfectly square yard in tidy rows. Vicki went to work on the tall, spindly grass that sprouted at the sidewalk line. They both worked quickly, as if they were going to get caught and yelled at again. The front door never opened, nor did the front curtains part. If the tenants were home, they seemed unfazed.

Twenty-five minutes later, Sierra wiped the perspiration from her forehead and tried again to turn off the mower. It still wouldn't stop.

"It must be stuck," she yelled to Vicki. "We'd better go to the next house before it runs out of gas."

They trotted down the street looking like kids in a three-legged race. Both of them had one hand on the mower handle and carried garden tools in the other.

"Next block over," Sierra said, directing Vicki with a tilt of her chin. They turned left at the corner.

A man in jogging apparel came up the block toward them. A smile spread across his face. "Throttle stuck?" he hollered at them as he stopped jogging.

"I guess," Sierra called back.

"Mind if I have a look?" He bent down and began to fiddle with the contraption.

Sierra noticed more people were outside now. It made her feel as if they were becoming a neighborhood spectacle.

Why did I ever agree to do this for Randy? At least Vicki is being a really good sport. This would be much more embarrassing if I were by myself.

Suddenly, the motor stopped. Peace returned to the neighborhood.

"Thank you so much," Sierra said. "Do you think it will turn off okay if I start it again?"

"Let's try."

Their knight in shining running apparel gave the cord a yank, and the engine started its annoying rumble all over again. He then flipped back the lever on the handle, and it immediately stopped.

"Thank you so much," Vicki said, taking off her sunglasses to beam her appreciation at the man.

He took her praise and fixed his gaze on her face. Sierra

didn't blame him. She had done the same thing when she had met Vicki. She guessed now it was something about the way Vicki's green eyes were framed by her thin, arched brows. It gave her a look of intrigue, like a smooth-skinned actress in an old spy movie. Sierra hadn't always admired the mysterious look. But since their long heart-to-heart talk last night, Vicki and her captivating looks didn't intimidate Sierra anymore.

"Hope it works for you," the man said with a nod.

He took off jogging again, and Sierra pushed the mower to the next house.

Vicki walked in step with Sierra and said, "Do you suppose he was our guardian angel?"

"Our what?"

"An angel of mercy sent to help us," Vicki said.

"In running shoes?"

Vicki laughed. "It's says something in the Bible about how we can entertain angels without knowing it. I read it a few nights ago in Hebrews."

"What are you saying?" Sierra asked. "You think that guy found us 'entertaining'?"

Vicki laughed again. "Maybe."

"Where does it say that?" Sierra asked.

"It's in the book of Hebrews. Somewhere in the last chapter."

"I'll have to look that one up," Sierra said.

"Where have you been reading?" Vicki asked. "In the Bible, I mean. What part are you reading now?"

"I kind of skip around," Sierra said. "I was reading in the Old Testament, but when school started I began to read in Romans. I'm only about halfway through." It sounded more like a confession than an answer.

"You make it sound so bad," Vicki said. "I think it's great that you're halfway through. I mean, how many students at our school do you think even read the Bible on their own? And it's a Christian school. Don't ever apologize for reading the Bible, Sierra. No matter how fast or slow you're going through it."

"You're right," she said, pushing the mower onto the third lawn on their list. "I always want to read my Bible because I want to, not because I have to. It's my way of listening to God. I don't want it to be a duty. Do you know what I mean?"

Vicki nodded. She put the garden tools down on the sidewalk and tilted her head, giving Sierra a sunny grin. "You know what I've been doing?"

Sierra waited for Vicki to reveal her secret.

"I've been reading my Bible like it's a letter to me. I got the idea from my counselor at camp. I go in my room, shut the door, and read every word with my heart open. My counselor said to imagine that God, the One who knows me and loves me more than anyone else ever will, wrote those words just for me, because He did. That's what the Bible really is, isn't it? God's love letter to us?"

As Sierra watched, the morning sun peeked over the full elm tree behind her and sprinkled its amber blessing on Vicki's expectant face.

"'Tis first I lock the door...then draw my little letter forth and softly pick its lock,'" Sierra recited in the golden, piercing moment.

"What?" Vicki asked.

Sierra smiled and shook away the Emily Dickinson quote. "I know what you're saying about reading letters and how that can be a wonderfully private time. God's love letter. I like that."

Vicki smiled back, her face aglow.

eleven

SIERRA AND VICKI managed to finish the second lawn in plenty of time to return to the "bow tie" yard. When they got there, the woman was waiting on her front porch, dressed and wearing a scowl on her wrinkled face.

"What are you two trying to do?" she called as they headed up the walkway. "What did you do to my grass?"

"We're helping Randy out today," Sierra said, probably louder than she needed to. The way the woman was yelling, she appeared to have a hearing problem. Either that or she was really angry.

"I know that, but what have you done to my grass?"

The woman pointed at her yard. From the woman's perch on the porch, Sierra imagined the bow tie must have been quite evident.

"We're sorry," Sierra said, standing on the bottom step that led up to the porch. She didn't dare take another step forward. "We're going to fix it now. Then we'll mow the backyard. Is that okay with you?"

"Of course it's okay with me. That's what I pay for.

Make sure you clip those rose bushes on the side yard." She seemed to eye Vicki with even more skepticism than Sierra. "They need a good trimming."

Vicki nodded, and the woman came down the stairs to direct Vicki to the rose bushes. Sierra started up the lawn mower and went as fast and as precisely as she could across the width of the lawn. Vicki and the woman hadn't returned, so Sierra guessed that Vicki was receiving a detailed lesson on rose-bush trimming.

When Sierra finished the front lawn, she headed for the backyard. Vicki was patiently enduring the woman's criticism, which she offered with each delicate clip Vicki took of the massive climbing rose bush.

"Done already?" the woman asked Sierra.

Sierra tried to appear cheerful. "Yes. I'm ready to mow your backyard. I think you'll be pleased with how the front turned out. Should I go through this gate?"

The woman studied Sierra a moment. "You certainly can't go through the middle of my house with that thing."

"No," Sierra said, swallowing her laughter, "I certainly can't."

"Then go. Shoo." With a brisk flex of her wrist, the woman dismissed Sierra and went back to inspecting Vicki's work.

The backyard was very small. The dog, a black and white mutt, appeared frightened of the mower and cowered in his doghouse. Sierra mowed the lawn in less than ten minutes, which was a good thing since she definitely needed a shower before work and it was after nine o'clock. However, the woman had other plans.

"Right here, next to the garden hose," the lady said to Sierra. "Those are weeds. If you don't pull them now, they'll be as big as my fist by next Saturday." She made a feeble fist with bony knuckles to prove her point.

Sierra picked at the tiny weeds.

"No, no, no! You have to pull them by the root, or they'll grow back. Go ahead. Dig down there. Get out the root."

Sierra did as she was told, bending and digging for almost half an hour all around the house. Wherever the woman spotted something growing that didn't meet her fancy, she yelled at Sierra, "There, right there. Don't you see it? Pick that out of there."

Vicki was still working on the rose bush. Every now and then the woman would call over her shoulder, "You are cutting those at an angle, aren't you?"

"Yes, ma'am," Vicki would answer patiently.

Finally, at nine-forty-five, Sierra stood up and said, "That's all for today. We really have to go now. I'm sure Randy can get whatever we missed next week."

The woman looked surprised. "Randy never does this for me," she said. "He only cuts the grass."

Sierra and Vicki exchanged pained expressions.

"That poor boy has two jobs, you know. He doesn't have time to weed my yard."

"Well, we would do more if we could, but I have another job, too, and I need to be there by ten o'clock." Sierra stretched her stiff neck from side to side and leaned back to remove the kinks from her spine.

"Well then, go. Shoo!"

They gathered their things and headed down the street.

"Oh, and thank you, girls," the woman called out.

Sierra looked over her shoulder and saw the lady smiling at them. It was the first time Sierra had seen her smile all morning. She looked rather normal. Almost pleasant.

They hurried from the house, pushing the mower at top speed over the lines in the sidewalk. Clang, clank, clank, clang.

When they were a block away, Vicki said, "I know that verse in Hebrews said we're supposed to show kindness to all strangers, and we might be entertaining angels without knowing it. Even though I'm sure we entertained that woman thoroughly, I have serious doubts about her being an angel in disguise."

They both laughed.

"Could you believe it when she said Randy never has time to weed because the poor boy has two jobs?" Sierra said, huffing as she walked. "I should have started out by telling her I had two jobs, too."

"What time do you have to be at work?" Vicki asked.

"In two minutes."

"You're kidding. We should have left earlier," Vicki said.

"I know. But it was so hard to get away. She kept finding weeds that weren't even there!"

They ran up the driveway at Sierra's house, and she pushed the mower into the garage.

"I have to fly," Sierra said to Vicki. "Thanks so much for helping me. I couldn't have done it without you."

"It was fun," Vicki said. "I hope you have a good day at work. See you later."

Sierra was about to dash into the house. Then she

stopped. Vicki was opening her car door.

"Hey," Sierra called out. "Vicki, I'll call you later."

Vicki waved and nodded. It all felt so natural, as if they had been close friends for years and did this every Saturday morning. The ease with which they had slipped into each other's lives amazed Sierra.

She didn't end up calling Vicki until Sunday afternoon. The answering machine picked up the call, so she left a message asking Vicki to phone her back.

The only call that came into the Jensen home for Sierra that evening was from Tawni.

"How are you doing?" Tawni asked her.

"Pretty good. I helped Randy mow lawns yesterday. That was an experience."

"I hope he paid you," Tawni said.

"No, it was a favor."

"You could never get me to mow anyone's lawn as a favor," Tawni said.

"This is how I see it," Sierra said, settling into her favorite chair in the study by the French doors. "One of these days I'll want Randy to do me a favor, and I'll use the opportunity to remind him of how I saved the day for him."

"What do you hear from Paul?" Tawni asked.

"I told you about the two letters I received on the same day, right?"

"You mentioned it the last time I called. That's why I asked. Did you write him back?"

"Of course. Right away. I sent him our e-mail address, and I've checked every day. But he hasn't written back."

"Give it some time," Tawni said. "Did I tell you I wrote to Lina?"

"Mom said you were going to. What happened? Did you hear from her?"

"No, not yet. I know it's not the same thing as waiting to hear from Paul, but I do understand what you're feeling. Waiting is just awful. I keep thinking I should have said this or that differently. Once those words are on paper and out the door, there's no changing them."

"I know," Sierra agreed. "But with Lina, I'd think waiting to hear back from her would be much more nerve-wracking than my waiting to hear from Paul. What are you going to do if she doesn't respond?"

"I don't know yet."

"What if she writes or calls and asks you to meet her? Would you go?"

"Absolutely." Tawni paused and then said, "I've opened a new savings account just to be prepared to buy an airplane ticket in case she invites me to see her."

"You must be a nervous wreck."

"Sometimes I am. Most of the time I'm okay. A strange feeling comes over me every now and then. It's as if I really don't want to know what she's like. I don't want to see her. It's enough to know her name and make up my own image of her. Then, other times, I think I'd give anything to hear her voice or look into her eyes just once."

Sierra felt herself choking up. She had never fully understood her sister's feelings on any subject. Now, in a tiny way, she thought she understood what Tawni was saying. This whole issue was much larger for Tawni than Sierra had ever realized.

"I hope she calls you," Sierra said. "As a matter of fact, I'll start praying that she does."

"Thanks." Tawni's voice was warm and welcoming. "I appreciate that."

"Did you want to talk to Mom and Dad?"

"No, just tell them I called and that I got the job for the catalog shoot." Tawni's voice was flat.

"That's great! Don't they pay really well?"

"Yes."

"You don't sound very excited. What catalog is it?"

"It's a line of western wear. I don't remember the name. I get to spend four days wearing cowboy boots and forcing myself to smile beneath the brim of a cowboy hat. This will be a real stretch for me."

Sierra laughed. Even while they were growing up in a small mountain town near Lake Tahoe, Tawni never wore anything that looked country western, even when everyone else did. Now she was getting paid to dress up like a cowgirl.

"Don't worry," Sierra teased. "They'll probably play country-western music during the shoot to put you in the mood."

Tawni groaned. "If anyone ever tells you the modeling life is glamorous, don't believe them for one second. The torture we models must endure."

"Well, y'all would know, wouldn't ya, pardner?" Sierra teased.

"Right," Tawni said. "You should be the one in the photo shoot. You and your beat-up cowboy boots."

"Hey, don't make fun of those poor ol' doggies. They served me well yesterday while I was mowing lawns."

"I'm so happy for you," Tawni said sarcastically.

It didn't carry the bite her sarcastic tone used to have when they shared a room and continually bickered at each other. This time it sounded funny, like one friend teasing another. It was nice.

The only problem was, at moments like this Sierra remembered her unsettled friendship with Amy and a sickening feeling returned to her stomach. She and Amy had once been able to tease each other and talk about the things they really cared about. Vicki seemed as if she were about to become that kind of friend, but how do people switch from one friend to another without any remorse?

After Sierra hung up the phone, she sat for a long time in the snug chair. She prayed for Tawni—that if it was what God wanted, Lina would call or write and that the two of them would be able to settle that relationship. Then she prayed for Amy. She guessed it was time just to let their broken relationship fade away.

twelve

"WHAT'S THE PLAN FOR FRIDAY?" Randy asked.

He was stretched out on the school's grass during lunch. It had rained the day before, but today was clear and glorious. The autumn air felt crisp and cool. Bright orange sunshine came rushing at them, not directly overhead as it had in the summer, but at an angle. If Sierra had had a pair of sunglasses with her, she would have been wearing them.

"I don't know," Sierra said. "It's only Tuesday. Besides, I didn't know anything was planned. Is there a school football game or something?"

Sierra and Randy were joined by six other students who chose to eat outside rather than inside or to drive to a nearby fast-food place.

"The football game is an option," Randy said. "I was talking to Vicki, and she said she hung out at your house last Friday. Now that I don't work at the restaurant anymore, I thought we should all get together and do something."

"Sounds good to me," Sierra said. "Where is Vicki, anyhow?"

"I think she went to get something to eat with Drake and Megan."

Sierra took a bite from the apple she had brought with her that morning. An apple, a bag of onion-flavored potato chips, and a carton of cold milk—that was Sierra's idea of a perfect lunch. She considered asking if Drake, whom she had dated once, was now dating Megan. But Sierra knew better than to try to keep track of Drake's dating roster. All that mattered to her was that she wasn't on his list. Not at the top, not at the bottom. Not on the list at all.

Thinking of Drake's social life made her think of Amy. Sierra hadn't seen her yet this week. Amy had wanted to go out with Drake last spring and had tried to set up a casual date with him. She had included Sierra in the plans. They never did fix dinner for Drake and Randy the way Amy had tried to arrange. It hadn't been a big deal to Sierra, but it seemed to have been for Amy.

Sierra slowly chewed her bite of apple as the conversations swirled around her. She still felt bad. She had failed as a friend to Amy by not understanding what was important to her and working with her to help get some of those important things.

"By the way," Randy said, snitching a chip from Sierra's bag, "thanks for covering for me on Saturday. You and Vicki saved my skin."

"I'll remember that next time I need a favor. Believe me, it's hard work. My back was aching by the end of the day. It didn't help that I also mopped the floor at Mama Bear's."

"The weeding is what does it to you," Randy said, tipping

Sierra's bag of chips upside down and shaking out the last few crumbs. "Mrs. Probst used to try to get me to weed for her. I did it once. Once was too much."

Sierra gave him a smirk. "It would have helped if you had warned me. She's the one with the dog in the backyard, right?"

Randy nodded.

"She got Vicki to trim her huge climbing rose bush, and she personally escorted me around the entire yard, pointing out everything she thought was a weed. Let me tell you, I pulled more green-tinged items from her flower bed than you even knew were there."

"You did?"

"Yes, and I was late for work because of it. All I can say is, it's a good thing Mrs. Kraus is so understanding."

"I guess this means if we do something Friday night, I have to pay for you."

"For Vicki and me," Sierra said. "Vicki worked her little fingers to the bone, too."

"Okay, McDonald's for both of you Friday night." Randy reached for his can of root beer and emptied it.

"McDonald's nothing! I'm thinking Anthony's Steak House. Don't ribs sound good to you?"

"Ribs, huh?" Randy didn't sound too thrilled about the idea of paying for three people at a place like Anthony's.

A tall senior named Tyler strode across the grass and joined their small group. He was the kind of guy Sierra considered to be conservative, studious, and a little on the shy side. This afternoon his countenance was far from subdued.

"Hey, Randy, I heard about the ultimatum on your hair. Way to go, man!"

Sierra looked at Randy for an explanation. His hair was still the way he had been wearing it since school started: long and pulled back in a ponytail.

"What happened?" Sierra asked.

Randy shrugged. "Nothing. I wrote a letter to the administration, that's all. They sent me a second notice, saying I had to get my hair cut, and I wrote them back explaining why I was growing it."

"He's not telling you the whole thing," Tyler said. Now everyone was listening. "Randy gave them an ultimatum."

"It wasn't an ultimatum. It was a letter."

Tyler jumped in. "The notice they gave him was the second warning about cutting his hair to codebook standards. If he doesn't do what they say by Friday, he could be expelled."

"Are you serious?" one of the other guys asked.

"My dad's on the board," Tyler said. "He was saying that they haven't had to deal with this kind of rebellion for years. There are always discipline problems, but not many acts of rebellion like this."

Randy shook his head, looking nothing like the rebel Tyler was making him out to be.

Tyler went on. "And since they decided not to change the school policy book, they're going to start coming down hard on any students who don't comply."

"Over the length of a person's hair?" Sierra asked. "What does that matter?"

"My dad says the issue is not the hair. It's the policy,

because Royal students are supposed to set an example to the community," Tyler said.

Sierra looked at Randy. He was sitting back, taking it all in, seemingly unaffected.

"What did you say in your letter?" Sierra asked.

"I just gave them my reasons for having my hair like this, and then I told them it was up to them to decide. I said I'd go by their decision, whatever it was." Randy offered Sierra a crooked smile. "I gave them until Thursday to respond."

Tyler made a fist and raised it as if this were his battle. "You're the man, Randy! Way to go! Hit them with an ultimatum right back."

"I don't get it," Sierra said. "Why the ultimatums?"

She looked at Tyler, who had sat down next to her and was grinning from ear to ear. Sierra noticed that Tyler's hair was short and stubby on top, which wasn't especially attractive with his long face and broad forehead.

"It's the sheer brilliance of his response," Tyler said. "He's turning their big guns back on them. The revolution is coming!"

One of the girls in the group laughed and threw a wadded-up lunch bag at Tyler.

Sierra craned her neck and squinted against the afternoon sun to look more closely at Tyler. Why was he suddenly on this crusade? Did he have a battle of his own to fight with his father or with the board of directors?

"It's not that big of a deal," Randy said, leaning over and lowering his voice. "They sent me a notice at the beginning of school and quoted some rule in the handbook. So I read the whole handbook. There's a lot of stuff in there that doesn't seem to apply anymore. I pointed that out in a letter to them."

"Like what?"

"Like it says all students are supposed to stand during the morning flag salute, Bible reading, and prayer."

"What's wrong with that rule?" Sierra asked.

"Nothing. But when was the last time you had a first-period teacher who remembered to do the flag salute? Or read the Bible even once in class during the whole semester? And how many of your teachers pray before class?"

Sierra thought back. "Not many. I see what you mean."

"The handbook uses that verse in I Corinthians that says long hair is a disgrace to a man." Randy shrugged and went on. "I pointed out that in the community where I live, work, and hang out, my hair isn't considered long. It's only considered long here at school. Then I told them why I was growing my hair out. It's for the band. I quoted those verses in I Corinthians 9 in which Paul says since he's free from the law, he has willingly become all things to all men so that by all possible means, he might save some."

Sierra was astonished at Randy's calm demeanor as he stated his case.

"That's telling them," Tyler said enthusiastically. "Fight fire with fire. They don't have the right to go around dictating what we should do and wear."

Sierra could see who the real rebel was.

"Then," Randy concluded, "I told them about our mission statement for the band, which is to reach out to our peers on their own turf and communicate the good news of Christ to them. I said to do that effectively I believe I should wear my hair the way it is."

"That was it?" Sierra asked. "That was the whole letter?"

"And then the last paragraph."

"That was the ultimatum part?"

"I said I would willingly submit myself to their authority since they were the ruling body God has placed over me at this school. I said whatever they decided I'd abide by, but I needed to know by Thursday so I could comply with their previously stated deadline."

"And what if they tell you to cut your hair?" Sierra asked.

"Then I'll cut my hair."

"You don't care?"

"Not as much as everyone else seems to."

"If they make you cut it," Tyler said, "I think we should all cut our hair. We'll all get buzzes."

"Yeah, right," one of the other guys said sarcastically.

"I'm not cutting my hair," a girl named Bethany said. "It's taken me four years to get it this long."

"Exactly," Tyler said. "And that's why Randy shouldn't have to cut his, either."

Bethany pointed at Tyler. "You're the one who wants to fight this battle. Why don't you grow out your hair and see what your dad says?"

Tyler froze. Everyone waited for him to respond. "Like that would ever happen," he muttered under his breath.

"I think Randy handled it really well," Sierra said. "Besides, aren't we supposed to be more concerned about what's on the inside of a person than about appearances?"

Before anyone could answer, the bell rang, signaling lunch was over. They rose as a group and returned to class, murmuring about the Thursday deadline. Sierra thought they looked like an unlikely band of rebels, especially with Randy as their reluctant leader.

"What do you think is going to happen?" Sierra asked Randy as they walked into class side by side.

Randy shrugged. His undaunted, easygoing grin appeared.

"Time will tell," he said.

thirteen

BY THE END OF SCHOOL on Wednesday, Randy still hadn't heard the verdict regarding his hair from what Tyler was now calling the "PTB," or the "Powers That Be." Everyone at school seemed to know about it, and Sierra had noticed a group of students quizzing Randy at his locker before lunch. Randy didn't make it into the cafeteria, and Sierra wondered if he'd had a chance to eat at all.

After school she joined a dozen or so students who had gathered around Randy in the parking lot at the back of his truck.

"I think you should write them another letter," one of the girls said. "Tell them we all feel the same way. They shouldn't put such strong restrictions on us."

"Don't they trust us?" another girl said.

"We need a petition," one of the guys said.

A few more students gathered, and suddenly everyone seemed to be voicing opinions at once. Sierra was amazed at how calmly Randy was taking all this. He kept mentioning quietly that the PTB had until Thursday and this was only

Wednesday. There was no need for radical action.

"Wait until tomorrow," he said. His steady voice carried over the ripples of murmurings from the students who seemed eager for a fight. "You guys seem to forget that I told them in my letter I would go by their decision, whatever it is. They're the authority over us here."

"Yeah, but what if their decisions are wrong? How can it be right to submit yourself to a bunch of leaders who are out of touch with reality?" The comment came from a short guy wearing glasses and looking startled that everyone had suddenly turned to look at him. "I mean, it only makes sense to go by their decision if it's a good one."

"That's right," another guy said. "We're the ones who are in touch with our culture. They are all way out of touch."

"They don't know what's really important," a girl chimed in. "We should be able to make our own rules as students and not have to go by their outdated laws."

"I think they should just let us all do what's right for each of us as individuals and only worry about our grades. That's why we go to school, isn't it?"

"My aunt said when she came here, they made all the girls wear dresses."

"Now that's discrimination! They can't do that anymore, can they?"

"I think they have to give students their rights now. And I say if we want the right to wear whatever we want or have our hair the way we want it, who are they to tell us what the rules are?"

"Yeah!" A common voice of agreement arose among the twenty or so students who had now gathered.

"You guys," Sierra said, finally finding her voice, "this is so totally out of the book of Judges, I can't believe it!" She had enough steam for herself and Randy, since he had chosen to respond passively. "Don't you remember last year in Bible class? The last verse of the last chapter in Judges says, 'Everyone did what was right in his own eyes.' That's why their nation fell apart."

"That was way back in Bible times," Tyler said, stepping forward and looking eager to debate. "What does that have to do with this situation? It doesn't apply at all."

"Oh, yes it does!" Sierra stated firmly, feeling her heart pound. "Everything God tried to teach them He still tries to teach us today. Can't you guys see that Randy is handling this the right way? He's willing to yield to the authority over him, but first he respectfully made his side known. We should all be supporting him, not trying to put him up as a cause for reform around here or something."

"Bravo," said a deep voice behind Sierra. She heard someone clapping and turned to see Drake, the star athlete, standing there with eight or nine people around him. "I'm on Sierra's side," he said, smiling at her.

"My side?" Sierra looked around at the crowd that had now grown to at least thirty students, almost all seniors. "There isn't a 'my side.' I'm just speaking up for Randy because everyone is trying to turn this into something it isn't."

"And as Randy said—" Bethany spoke up loud enough for everyone to hear. "There's nothing to debate until after the board makes their decision. And Randy plans to go by their decision, whatever that is. Why is everyone trying to turn this into a fight?"

"Let's meet here tomorrow after school," Tyler said. "Then we'll know if it's time we all started to take sides. It's way past time for some changes around here, and as I see it, this is only the beginning."

The murmuring started up again as the crowd slowly dispersed. Sierra could feel her heart still pounding. On impulse, she slugged Randy in the arm.

"What was that for?" he demanded, looking shocked that she would hit him.

"Why didn't you speak up for yourself?" Sierra challenged.

"Because I'm a pacifist. Unlike some other people I know," he said, rubbing the spot where she had clobbered him. "Ouch!"

"Sorry," Sierra said, forcing herself to calm down. "It just gets me that everyone is ready for a revolution, and they don't even know what they're fighting for. They're trying to make you their symbol or something. Doesn't that bother you at least a little bit?"

Randy shook his head. "It's like my mom always says, 'This, too, shall pass.'"

Sierra gave him a skeptical look.

"Relax, Sierra. They'll get over it. There's nothing to fight for. If the PTB say, 'Go to the barber,' I go to the barber. That will be the end of it."

"Somehow I have my doubts," Sierra said.

Vicki came up beside Sierra. "Hey, guys, what's up? Someone in the hall said there was a meeting out here or something and to meet back here tomorrow."

"It's nothing," Randy said.

"It could end up being something," Sierra countered.

"We'll see," Randy said. "I have to go home and put some ice on my arm before it swells up."

"Somebody hit you?" Vicki said, looking first at Randy and then at Sierra.

"Yeah," Randy said dryly. "My campaign manager slugged me."

"I'm not your campaign manager."

"Okay, my own private crusader, then."

"I wouldn't have to crusade for you if you would fight your own cause."

"I don't have a cause, remember?"

Vicki stomped her foot on the asphalt. "Will somebody please tell me what is going on?"

"She hit me," Randy said, pointing at Sierra and sounding like a little boy. "And I'm going home to my mommy." His hurt, puppy dog look was awfully cute.

"Come on," Sierra said to Vicki while shaking her head at Randy. "I'll fill you in. Do you want to meet me at Eaton's Drugstore? I promised my mom I'd take Granna Mae there after school to get her out of the house for a while."

"I have to go home," Vicki said. "I want to go to church youth group tonight, but my parents say I can only go out during the week if I have all my homework done, and I have a ton of it tonight."

"Then I'll see you at youth group, and I'll tell you everything," Sierra said.

"Okay, see you."

Sierra headed for her car at the other end of the lot. Randy revved up the motor of his truck when he passed her and gave her a broken wing wave as if she had maimed his arm for life. Sierra waved back. She felt foolish. Slugging Randy was something she would do to one of her older brothers. She hadn't even realized she had hit him until after she had done it. As much as she considered Randy her buddy, she had never hit him like that before.

"You know, Sierra Mae," she coached herself as she started the car and drove out of the school parking lot, "sometimes I think you're all grown up and sweet and mature, and then you get this ball of fire in you that explodes. When will you outgrow the feistiness?"

She was afraid she already knew the answer, and the answer was "Never." The Jensen family had a history of women who could hold their own in any situation and who never stopped feeling that ball of fire until the day they died.

Granna Mae used to be that way before her mind went fuzzy. Sierra remembered being in the car with her grandmother a few summers ago. They came to a stop sign in a residential area and saw two boys on the sidewalk contentedly eating Popsicles. An older boy on a skateboard came by, scooped up one boy's Popsicle, and took off down the street.

Granna Mae squealed the car's tires as she turned the corner in pursuit of the kid on the skateboard. The boy looked over his shoulder at her and tried to go faster, but he hit a rut in the sidewalk and took a tumble. Granna Mae pulled the car to the curb, got out in a huff, grabbed the boy by his shirt, and gave him a vigorous scolding. The Popsicle had bitten the dust on the tumble, but Granna Mae extracted $1.12 in change from the culprit. She then drove back and delivered the money to the forlorn boy on the sidewalk.

As if that weren't enough, when the boys said they had bought the Popsicles from the ice cream truck, Granna Mae drove up and down seven streets before they heard the cranked-up music blaring from the truck. She then bought two ice cream sandwiches—one for herself and one for Sierra—and a new Popsicle, which she hand-delivered to the waiting victim.

There was no doubt the Jensen women fought for truth and justice. Years ago Sierra's mom had teased Granna Mae, saying all she needed was a bright red cape and she could get a full-time job protecting the world. Granna Mae had taken the teasing well. Sierra watched and learned because she had not always been so good-natured when her mom had teased her and said that she was just like Granna Mae. Sierra doubted that her mom had ever felt a ball of fire in her stomach, at least not of the same intensity as the fireballs that rolled around in the bellies of the Jensen women. For that reason and many others, Sierra felt tightly linked to her grandmother—even more than she did to her own mother.

Because of Granna Mae's spunky history, her feeble condition was frustrating to the whole family. They only knew her as strong, not weak.

Sierra could see how taking care of Granna Mae was wearing on her mom. That's why Sierra had volunteered to help out in any way she could. So far the best and only plan she had come up with was to take Granna Mae out to some of her favorite places at least once a week. This afternoon the plan was to go to Eaton's Drugstore not far from their house. Eaton's had been in the neighborhood as long as Granna Mae had lived there. For more than fifty years, she had spent many hours at their lunch bar. It had been Granna Mae's tradition to take each of her own nine children to Eaton's after their first day of school and buy them chocolate malts. She continued the tradition with her grandchildren when they moved to Portland, but this year she didn't seem aware that school had started.

Sierra arrived home well past three-thirty, the time she usually got home. Her mother had Granna Mae all ready to go, and the two of them were waiting on the porch swing.

"Sorry I'm a little late. Are you ready to go to Eaton's for a malt, Granna Mae?"

She nodded. Her soft face was graced by a compliant expression. Sierra couldn't be sure if Granna Mae understood what was going on.

Mrs. Jensen gave Sierra an appreciative look and said, "Dinner won't be ready until six-thirty."

Sierra didn't know if that meant "Please take her and give me a break by staying away until six-thirty," or if her mother was merely giving Sierra a time reference on dinner.

"Okay," Sierra called back. "We'll be back by then." She wanted to make it sound as if they were going to have so much fun they would have to tear themselves away from Eaton's to make it home by six-thirty.

As Granna Mae lowered her thinning frame into the passenger seat of Sierra's car, Sierra wondered how much her dear grandmother was understanding today. Did she even know where they were going? Did it matter to her? Was this one of her bright days, and was she picking up every innuendo, including the one about not coming back until dinnertime?

The only way Sierra could know was if Granna Mae called her "Lovey." Only right now, as they drove down the street to Eaton's, Granna Mae wasn't saying anything.

fourteen

GRANNA MAE AND SIERRA entered the small drugstore and headed for the original Formica counter lunch bar. The red vinyl stools were exactly as Sierra remembered them as a child. Even the menu board above the long mirror didn't appear to have changed, except for the prices.

Sierra tilted her head and gave her companion a pleasant smile. "What do you think, Granna Mae? A chocolate malted, maybe?"

It startled Sierra to hear the tone of her own voice. She sounded like her grandmother. The tilt of the head and the inflection were exactly the way Granna Mae used to approach Sierra years ago.

What do you think, Sierra Mae? A chocolate malted, maybe?

Even that she said "malted" instead of "malt" was evidence of imitation of her grandmother. Something felt oh so strange. They had reversed roles. Now Sierra was the one driving the car to Eaton's and paying for the ice cream. Granna Mae had become the child.

"That would be lovely," Granna Mae said in response to Sierra's question.

For a moment, Sierra thought she said "Lovey," and she was about to feel relieved. But "lovely" was an altogether different word from Sierra's nickname of "Lovey."

"A chocolate malt, please," Sierra told the older woman behind the counter. "With two glasses."

"And a cup of coffee, please," Granna Mae ordered for herself.

Sierra smiled. "And one cup of coffee, please." It was hard to hold on to the image of her grandmother being a child if she was drinking a cup of coffee. Sierra was glad Granna Mae had ordered the coffee and that she had ordered it for herself. These were all good signs.

Sierra realized this was what her mother must go through every day as she kept an eye on Granna Mae. It was a constant guessing game. Is Granna Mae thinking clearly? What does she want? Can she ask for it herself? Will she be hurt or offended if I try to do something for her that she normally does for herself? Each of the clues Granna Mae sprinkled along the trail of the day had to be collected and analyzed. This could be an exhausting routine.

The door opened, and a little bell rang out its cheery chimes as a customer entered. Sierra glanced up. Her heart sprang into her throat. The customer was Amy.

Amy didn't see Sierra but headed straight for the pharmacy at the back of the store.

Until that moment, Sierra had been thinking it might be okay to let the friendship with Amy fade away. Now she suddenly felt differently. She remembered the time she had hidden in the basement as a child, waiting for someone to come find her. It struck her that perhaps Amy had pulled a trash can full of garden tools close to herself, in a manner of speaking. She was getting cold and cramped but wasn't willing to come out on her own.

I have to say something. But what? Maybe if I start talking, it'll come to me.

Sierra practically launched her tensed body from the stool as if there had been a spring on her seat.

"Granna Mae," she said slowly, "I'm going to the back of the store for a minute. If she serves you the chocolate malt before I get back, go ahead without me." Sierra realized she was speaking the way she would instruct a toddler, but she wanted to make it clear. "I'll be right back, okay?"

"Okay," Granna Mae said. "Don't rush yourself on account of me."

"Okay," Sierra agreed. She strode to the back of the store, moistening her dry lips and telling herself she shouldn't feel so shaken. This is what she had been wanting for weeks. Sure, it wasn't the best location for their talk, but it looked like the best she was going to get. She wanted to cry out, "Olly, Olly, Oxen-free" to signal Amy she could come out of hiding now.

"Amy, hi." The words tumbled out backward of how she had intended. "I was over at the counter with my Granna Mae when I saw you come in. How are you doing?"

Amy studied Sierra carefully. The expression on her face didn't change. She didn't even appear surprised to see Sierra. Her face held a flat, empty look.

"I'm fine. How are you?" Amy asked.

"Good. I haven't seen you at school all week."

Amy paused, looking at Sierra.

"I hope you haven't been sick or anything," Sierra said.

"No."

"Oh," Sierra said. "Good."

It was silent between them. No other customers were at the pharmacy window, and the pharmacist was in the back, apparently filling Amy's prescription. This was as good as it would probably get as far as a private spot for their long-overdue conversation.

"So," Sierra tried again, "how have you been?"

"Fine."

"Good."

Amy appeared reluctant to budge even an inch toward Sierra. Sierra knew she could always use dynamite words to break open Amy. At least that technique had worked in the past. Not today, though. This had to be done right. It was a delicate procedure, trying to gain back a lost friend.

"Have you been at school, and I just haven't seen you?" Sierra ventured.

Amy looked down and then back up, barely making eye contact with Sierra. "I don't go to Royal anymore."

"Oh. I didn't know. Why?"

Another pause.

"Is it because of your parents?" Sierra ventured carefully.

Amy nodded. She didn't look remorseful, nor did she look as though she was willing to share any more information.

"That's too bad."

"It's okay."

"Are things any better between your parents?"

"I guess so. In some ways. It's actually better now that they're not living together. They treat each other a lot nicer, and they both are trying to spend time with me. So it's okay."

Sierra was glad Amy was opening up a little. Taking advantage of the opportunity, Sierra said, "I'm sorry I wasn't home this summer while you were going through everything with your family. I tried to call from California, but I couldn't get a hold of you. I left messages."

"You did?" Amy said.

"Yes, several times. Then I went to Switzerland, you know. But it was all so sudden I didn't have time to call anybody."

Amy nodded.

"When I came back, it was crazy getting ready for school, working, and everything. I tried waiting for you after work one night, but you had already gone. Then I showed up at your house that one morning with a picnic breakfast."

"When was that?" Amy asked.

"A couple of weeks ago. Didn't your dad tell you? I think I woke him up, so he wasn't exactly happy to answer the door."

"He didn't say anything," Amy said.

"Oh. I thought he would have. I brought breakfast over. I thought maybe we could talk."

"Look, Sierra," Amy said, putting one foot forward as if trying to keep her balance. "I'm glad you're telling me this. I didn't know you had called me and come by. No one told me."

"I've been hoping we could talk. I don't like the way things are between us."

Amy stood a little stiffer. "I know you think we need to have this huge talk and get everything out in the open, but I don't feel that way. There are a lot of things better left unsaid. You have your life and your new group of friends and I have mine. Can we leave it at that?"

"I don't want to leave it at that," Sierra said stubbornly.

"Well, sorry, but you don't have much choice." Amy's dark eyes began to take on a spark of the old spirit. "I don't choose to be your friend anymore, Sierra. That's that."

"It doesn't have to be 'that,'" Sierra said, feeling lame as she said it. She urgently wanted to express what she still felt in her heart toward Amy.

Amy shook her head and looked away. "You have certain high expectations and goals that you force all your friends to live up to, and let's face it: I don't match up, do I?"

Sierra didn't know how to answer. She tried to choose her words carefully. Amy seemed like a rocket about to launch, and Sierra didn't want to be seared in the billowing white heat that would come with the takeoff.

Before she could decide what to say, the pharmacist stepped up to the window and called out, "Degrassi?"

"Yes," Amy said, turning on her heel. "I don't have anything else to say to you, Sierra. Good-bye." Amy spoke the words firmly without looking back.

Sierra didn't know what to do. If she had been by herself and didn't have Granna Mae with her, the fighter in Sierra would have followed Amy out of the drugstore and into the parking lot, which would have been a much safer platform for potential rocket blasts. Sierra wasn't afraid of pursuing Amy, and she wasn't afraid of what Amy might say to her. At least it would be out in the open. But she couldn't leave Granna Mae alone any longer.

As Amy stood at the counter paying for her prescription, Sierra turned and went back to the lunch counter. So much for "Olly, Olly, Oxen-free."

Amy doesn't seem to be playing the game I thought she was. I figured she would be happy I kept after her until I "found" her. How could I have been so wrong?

Just as Sierra came to the end of the aisle that opened up to the soda fountain area, her heart stopped. There sat a chocolate malt in a silver container with two empty glasses. A cup of coffee rested on its saucer, still full. The two bar stools were vacant.

Granna Mae was gone.

fifteen

"GRANNA MAE," Sierra called out, frantically glancing down each of the aisles. "Did you see which way my grandmother went?" she asked the woman at the counter.

"No, I didn't see her get up."

Sierra fled out the door into the parking lot. "Granna Mae!" she called out, not caring how silly she looked.

Amy exited the drugstore. When she noticed Sierra, she turned away and kept walking to her car.

"Amy, you have to help me. I've lost my grandmother!"

Amy paused and gave Sierra a skeptical look.

"She was with me at the soda fountain, but when I went back, she was gone. No one in there saw her leave. You have to help me find her. You know how she gets."

Amy hesitated and then let out a frustrated sigh. "Where do you think she went?"

"I have no idea."

"She's lived here almost all her life. She knows this neighborhood," Amy said. "Is there any place she likes to go? A park or something?"

"I don't think so. And if she's not thinking clearly, she could have wandered off anywhere and not known where she was. I think we should split up and drive around the blocks. That's what my mom and I have done before. Could you look on the next four or five blocks on that side?" Sierra said, pointing to the northwest side of the street. "I'll canvass this side."

"All right," Amy agreed.

"Meet back here after you've combed the blocks. And be sure to look in odd places like front porches and side yards."

"I'm not going to snoop in people's backyards," Amy said.

"Well, okay, but just call out for her. She knows you. She would get in the car with you if you asked her. Meet back here."

Sierra slid into her car and cranked the engine. Her heart was racing as she drove up and down the streets surrounding Eaton's Drugstore, calling out for her grandmother. "Yoo-hoo, Granna Mae!"

There was no sign of her anywhere.

This is awful, awful, awful! What am I going to do? I never should have left her alone. Not even for a minute. What am I going to do?

She canvassed the sixth block and still saw no sign of Granna Mae. Even on a good day, Granna Mae couldn't have made it much farther than this if she left the drugstore on foot. Still, Sierra drove down two more blocks, just in case.

Her search proved futile.

Maybe Amy found her. Oh, I hope Amy found her.

Sierra was in such a hurry to get back to the drugstore that she didn't look before making a turn at the corner and was nearly hit by a car that was going way too fast. She slammed on her brakes as the driver zoomed past her, giving her a dirty look as if she were the only one in the wrong.

Calm down. Getting yourself killed will not help the situation.

Forcing herself to be extra careful the rest of the way back to the drugstore, Sierra hoped and prayed with all her might she would turn into the parking lot and there would be Amy with Granna Mae in her car.

Amy's old beat-up Volvo was in the parking lot, but only Amy sat in the car. Sierra squeezed into a parking spot and hopped out of the car, running over to where Amy sat with her engine still running.

"I didn't see her," Amy reported. "I hope everything is okay. What are you going to do now?"

Sierra pounded her hand against the side of Amy's car door. She let out a fearful, frustrated sigh. "I guess I have to go home and tell my parents."

Amy pursed her lips together. "Well, I have to go, Sierra. I hope everything is okay."

"Thanks, Amy. Thanks for trying. I really appreciate it."

The two of them paused and made eye contact. No fireballs or flaming rockets traversed the space between them.

"That's okay. 'Bye."

"'Bye," Sierra said reluctantly. She got back into her car.

On the way home, she decided to scan the neighborhood again, just in case either she or Amy had overlooked something.

What if Granna Mae went back to the drugstore?

Sierra turned around and headed for the drugstore.

She hurried inside only to find the counter cleared. It was after five, and the fountain was closed. After walking up and down each of the four aisles, she asked the pharmacist if he had seen her grandmother. He hadn't. The woman who had been working at the front register had gone home, as had the woman who had been at the fountain. A high school student was now the cashier. She said she had been there for only ten minutes, and she didn't remember seeing an older woman who fit Granna Mae's description.

"Thanks anyway," Sierra said. She forced herself to realize she needed to go home, tell her parents, and call the police. There was no way to describe the way she felt at that moment. All her life her parents had lectured her about being careless and misplacing important things, like her passport, for instance. How could she look at them and tell them she had misplaced Granna Mae?

Everything inside Sierra began to go numb, from her head down. The drive home seemed like the longest drive in the world. She barely felt the bump of the slightly raised curb as she pulled into the driveway. When she turned the keys in the ignition to shut off the car, she had no feeling in her fingers. If she would have slammed her foot in the door while closing it, she wondered if she would know it.

The sentences ran through her mind like a wild game of crack the whip. Every sentence held her limp body at the very end of it and snapped her back and forth with a jolting force. She had felt nearly this bad once when she was seven and had broken one of her mom's vases while trying to get it out of the cupboard for a handful of wildflowers. She had swept up the pieces without getting cut on the glass and kept it all in a grocery bag in the garage. Then she waited until after dinner to tell her mom. That was the most miserable dinner of her life.

Tonight there was no waiting until after dinner.

Sierra took the front steps two at a time, suddenly aware that this wasn't about her failure or about her getting punished for losing Granna Mae. This was about her grandmother's safety, and the sooner she told her parents and called the police, the better it would be for Granna Mae.

"Mom!" Sierra cried out as she burst through the front door. "Dad!"

"In here, Sierra," her mom called out calmly from the living room.

"Mom, I—"

Sierra ran into the living room and stopped short. There sat Granna Mae on the living room sofa, as large as life and unharmed. Her mother sat on one side of Granna Mae, and her dad on the other. All three of them looked at Sierra with raised eyebrows, waiting for an explanation.

"Are you okay?" Sierra said, rushing to her grandmother and taking her hands. "What happened?"

"That's what we would like to know," her dad said. "Mr. Svenhart brought her home."

"Mr. Svenhart? Why?" Sierra looked first at her father, then at Granna Mae, then at her mother for an explanation.

"He said she was sitting there all alone, and he was concerned." Mr. Jensen gave Sierra a stern look. "Where did you go? Granna Mae says you got up to go to the bathroom, and when you were gone such a long time, she went to the bathroom to check on you, but you weren't there. She waited at the counter, but you never came back."

Sierra slapped her forehead. "The bathroom," she muttered. "Of course. The only place I didn't look."

Mrs. Jensen leaned forward. "Sierra, this is serious. Where did you go?"

"I didn't go to the bathroom. I went to the back of the store, by the pharmacy. Only for a few minutes. I saw Amy, and I went back to talk to her. It seemed like it might be the only chance I'd have to get things right with her. We talked for just a few minutes, and then I went back to the counter, but Granna Mae was gone. Amy and I went in separate cars and drove all around the neighborhood searching for her."

Mr. Jensen looked upset. "Meanwhile, Granna Mae is sitting there, all by herself, at the counter for nearly an hour."

"I am so sorry," Sierra said, looking into Granna Mae's confused face and giving her hands a gentle squeeze. "I didn't mean to leave you like that. I thought you had left."

"Why would I leave? I thought you were having some difficulty in the bathroom. And then you were gone."

"I know. I'm sorry. I won't do that again."

"That's right," her mother said. "You won't do that again."

Her voice contained a frustrated edge. Sierra felt terrible. Here her mom had expected a few hours' break from Granna Mae, but instead Sierra had delivered a boatload of anxiety to all of them.

"I really am sorry," Sierra said.

She hated it when these kinds of things happened. It all seemed so innocent: a trip to the soda fountain, a chance to talk with Amy. And then it all turned around and bit her.

"Don't fret," Granna Mae said, letting go of Sierra's hand and stroking back a tendril of blond hair from Sierra's grief-stricken face. "It's all over now, and we're all safe and sound."

"Would you like me to bring some dinner up to your room, Granna Mae?" Sierra asked. "Some soup, maybe?" She realized she was tilting her head and using the same voice she had used in the drugstore, the voice that mimicked the way Granna Mae had addressed Sierra when she was a child.

"That would be lovely." Granna Mae got up and excused herself to go up the stairs.

Sierra bit her lower lip. Again Granna Mae had used the word "lovely" when Sierra was so eager to hear the word "Lovey."

"This is much more serious than I think you realize," her mother said the minute Granna Mae was out of the room. "What were you thinking, Sierra?"

"It's like I told you. I saw Amy, and I thought I could talk to her for a few minutes."

"You can't leave Granna Mae like that. Not even for a moment. You know that."

"I know. I was wrong. I'm sorry."

"Go easy on her," Sierra's dad said, patting his wife's arm. "Everything turned out okay."

"This time," her mom said. "What about next time?"

"We'll all make sure there isn't a next time," Mr. Jensen said, his voice calm and soothing.

Mrs. Jensen let out a deep, stored-up sigh. "If only it were that easy, Howard. You don't know what it's like." She got up and headed for the kitchen.

"What do you mean I don't know what it's like?" he asked, following her. "I live here, too. She's my mother. I know what it's like."

Sierra considered trailing along. Her impulse was to do things for her parents whenever she upset them, sort of a system of balances in which she did two helpful things to make up for her one colossal goof. However, it seemed better to stay back, at least for a few minutes, to let the two of them talk this through. She would wait five minutes or so and then make Granna Mae's soup. Soup was supposed to help whatever ails a person, right? What kind of soup could possibly make any of them feel better tonight?

sixteen

JUST MINUTES after her mom and dad had exited the living room, the phone rang.

"Sierra, it's for you," Mrs. Jensen called out.

Joining her parents in the kitchen, Sierra took the portable phone from her mom and went over to the small, walk-in pantry in search of a can of soup.

"Hello?"

"Sierra, it's Amy."

Sierra stopped looking for soup and stood up straight. "Hi, Amy."

"I wanted to see if your grandmother is all right."

"Yes, she was here when I got home. A neighbor brought her back. You're never going to believe this, but she was in the bathroom while we were out looking for her."

There was a pause, and then Amy laughed. It sounded so good to hear her laugh again. "And you thought she was wandering the streets in a daze."

"I know. I didn't even think to look in the bathroom."

"Is she okay?"

"I think so." Sierra cupped her hands over the mouthpiece. "My parents are pretty upset, though." She could hear them still quietly "discussing" Granna Mae's condition at the kitchen counter.

Amy hesitated. "I just wanted to make sure your grandmother was all right."

"I appreciate your calling. Thanks."

"And I wanted to say that I appreciated your telling me that you tried to call and come over to see me. I didn't know that, and I guess I jumped to some conclusions."

Sierra closed the pantry door and pulled the chain on the overhead light. It was a tight squeeze, but Sierra didn't want to do anything to disrupt this moment she had waited for so long. "I've jumped to conclusions about you, too, and I know that wasn't fair."

"I meant what I said, though," Amy added quickly. "I don't want to sit down with you and have a huge discussion about my life."

"Okay."

"I'm not like you, Sierra. In some ways, we're similar and I think that's what first drew me to you last year. But I don't have all the same beliefs you do. I don't know if I ever did. I just tried to fit in, you know? And now I don't want to live with those kinds of expectations on me anymore."

"Amy—"

"Don't start in on me, Sierra. I'll hang up if you do."

"All I want to say is, okay," Sierra said quickly.

Amy didn't hang up.

Sierra kept talking. "Let's start from here. That's all I wanted to say. I care about you, Amy, and I want to stay in touch. Whatever is comfortable for you is fine with me. I just don't want to feel that we're supposed to ignore each other because we've changed in the last few months. I've changed, too."

There was no response, but Sierra could hear Amy was still there.

"I can live with that."

"You know, Amy, I just thought of how you jumped in and helped me look for Granna Mae. Only a friend would do that. I guess you and I don't have to try to *be* friends. We just *are* friends."

"I'm not used to having friendships that keep going," Amy said. "I'm used to hanging out with someone and then going on and making new friends. So I'm not guaranteeing anything on my end to keep our friendship going. But I won't ignore you anymore, either."

Sierra felt as if a weight had been lifted off her.

"Maybe it's like you told me a long time ago," Sierra said, leaning against the pantry wall. "How did you say it? We're orbiting in different spheres, but every now and then our paths will cross. When they do, I want you to know that I'll be there for you the same way you were there for me today with Granna Mae."

"Thanks, Sierra." Amy's voice sounded tender. "I appreciate it. And I'll be there for you, as long as you don't have any expectations."

"I hope everything goes well for you at your new school."

"Thanks."

"Are you still working at your uncle's restaurant?"

"Yes."

"Maybe I'll run into you there sometime."

"Maybe."

"Well, call me anytime you're really bored. I'll probably be around."

"Okay. Thanks. I'll see you later."

"'Bye, Amy." Sierra hung up, and leaning her head against the pantry wall, she let out a relieved sigh. It wasn't exactly the heart-to-heart conversation she had hoped to have with Amy, and it wasn't the outcome she had expected. But she was glad they had finally talked. Now she at least felt in some ways that the tension was settled.

What gnawed at Sierra were Amy's words about her beliefs. What did Amy mean when she said she didn't share Sierra's beliefs and maybe never really had? Did she mean Sierra's standards for dating? Or her beliefs in God? What was really going on inside Amy? Sierra knew she wasn't invited into Amy's heart, but at least she had limited "visitation rights." For now, she would be happy with that.

Opening the pantry door and stepping into the kitchen, Sierra found her parents were gone. Were they still discussing Granna Mae? Or was that conversation over and settled, the way Amy and Sierra had settled their conflict? Sierra guessed that everything had evened itself out for the time being. The next time something happened to Granna Mae, though, it was pretty certain the discussion would be opened again. That meant that more than ever Sierra needed to be on guard so she wasn't the one initiating any potential conflict over Granna Mae.

Sierra opened a can of minestrone soup, poured it into

a pan, and began to prepare a dinner tray for Granna Mae.

"What a day," Sierra said to herself. She glanced at the clock and decided she'd better not plan to go to youth group tonight. Her mom would probably start dinner any moment, and Sierra knew it would be good if she helped out. That would leave no time for homework if she went to church, and she had a lot of it tonight. She remembered that Vicki was expecting her to be at church and decided she would call Vicki as soon as she delivered the dinner tray to Granna Mae.

The rest of the evening passed uneventfully, which was a good thing for Sierra. She helped with dinner and with the dishes. Everything seemed calm and back to normal with her parents and Granna Mae.

After eight o'clock Sierra lugged her backpack into the study with the intent of starting her homework. She turned on the computer and checked the e-mail. There were four for her dad, one for her mom from Sierra's brother Wesley, and two junk ads. Nothing from Paul.

Sierra wondered if her friend Christy Miller, who was going to school in Switzerland, had an e-mail address. Sierra had seen the computers in the library at Christy's school. Certainly Christy could receive e-mail, if Sierra only knew where to send them. She had Christy's address and decided to write her a quick letter to get her e-mail address. It would mean sending another letter overseas and having to wait at least a week for the response.

Waiting was awful. It seemed terrible to have to wait days and weeks to hear from Paul. So much had happened already since she had written to him. Life was going by at the speed of, well…life. Her snail-mail to Paul and his letters back weren't able to keep up the pace.

Sierra stopped typing her letter to Christy and stared out the window at the black night. *I wonder what Paul is doing right now. Is he at school? Studying? Going for a hike in the Highlands he seems to love so much? I wonder if he's thinking about me. And what would he be thinking?*

"Oh, Father God, I'm so glad You are everywhere at the same time. Would You please wrap Your invisible arms of love around Paul wherever he is, whatever he's doing. Let him know how much You love him and how much You care about everything that happens to him. Please direct him in his studies to do the best he can and to learn the things that will have value in the future. Prepare him for the work that You have designed for him. And keep him safe, Lord. Give him good friends, I pray, and excellent times with his grandmother. Strengthen him on the inside. Thank You, God, for hearing my prayers and for answering them in Your way and in Your time. I love You, God."

Sierra smiled to herself. She had prayed many months for Paul. In the beginning those prayers carried a different sort of emotion than what she felt now. Praying for Paul, fighting for him with her whispers to God, had been more an act of obedience. She did it because she felt the urgency to do so. Now that she and Paul were corresponding, it was different. His letters made her feel as if she had access to a little corner of his heart. That closeness made it a whole lot more fun to pray for him. A wonderfully calm, contented feeling came over her when she prayed for Paul. It was amazing how a couple of letters could open up a relationship in such a warm way.

It reminded Sierra of how Vicki called the Bible God's love letter to her. *How would I relate to God if I didn't have His love letter to read? What would I think of Him? How would I talk to Him?*

Sierra stared out the window, pondering that thought. She had never considered that before. *Everything God wanted to say to me, He wrote down. And I can read it any time I want.*

The memory of the refugee children at the orphanage she and Christy had visited in Switzerland suddenly overwhelmed Sierra. *Have those children ever heard of the Bible? Has anyone ever told them how much Jesus loves them? How hard it must be for them to believe that after all they've been through.*

Quickly finishing her typed note to Christy, Sierra poured out her heart.

> It occurred to me that what you're doing in Switzerland, working with those children in that orphanage, well, it's God's work. I didn't see it when we were there. But tonight it seems so clear to me. If someone doesn't tell them about God, how will they come to believe in Him? And if they don't hear the Bible in their own language, how will they get to know Him? We have so much here in America, and I guess sometimes I forget that the rest of the world doesn't have the freedom or opportunity to sit down and just read the Bible whenever they want.

Sierra had to stop typing. The tears in her eyes made the computer screen go blurry before her. *Why didn't I ever realize this before? There are people all over the world who don't even have a copy of the Bible in their own language.*

It felt strange, being overwhelmed and so suddenly emotional like this. She had heard this kind of information from missionaries for years. She had even been on a missions trip and had visited the orphanage in Switzerland with Christy. Yet it had never hit her as it had in this moment: The Bible was God's love letter to the world, and there were people out there who had never received it, never read it.

Sierra pushed away from the desk and wiped her tears with the back of her hand. She hurried from the study and ran up the stairs to her room. It was a disastrous mess, as always. She knew where all her letters from Paul were. She kept them in a dresser drawer. A few days ago Sierra had tied them with a black velvet ribbon and tucked them under her pillow. Sierra checked, and the letters were all there, nice and flat.

Quickly scanning her room, rummaging through her dirty clothes, and kicking her shoes out of the way, Sierra searched for her Bible. She had read it two nights ago and had plopped it on the floor along with her science textbook. The floor, especially the floor in her room, was no place for such a treasure. She remembered how she had once crumpled up an early letter from Paul and tossed it aside in the same manner.

There the Bible was, peeking out from beneath a bath towel. Sierra snatched it up and held it close.

"I'll never do that again," she whispered.

Stepping over to the nightstand by her bed and clearing away the empty glass and the plate of cookie crumbs, Sierra placed her Bible next to the light.

All love letters are treasures and deserve a place of honor.

Feeling changed inside but not exactly sure why, Sierra went downstairs. She was determined to finish her homework as soon as she could so she wouldn't be too tired to read her Bible.

seventeen

THURSDAY AFTER SCHOOL, a large group of students gathered in the parking lot around Randy's truck. Everyone was talking at once about what was going to happen with Randy, his hair, and the administration's decision. It was all speculation because Randy hadn't arrived yet.

"He's still in there with them," Tyler announced, jogging out to join the group. "They might be there for a long time."

Sierra glanced at her watch. "I have to go to work," she told Vicki. "Since I was late on Saturday, I can't be late again."

"Do you want me to come by to tell you what happened?" Vicki asked.

"Would you?" Sierra said, giving her friend an appreciative smile. "That would be great. I'll see you then."

Sierra wedged her way through the crowd and hurried to her car. When she had talked to Randy after lunch, he had quietly told her he had been thinking about something the leader had said at the youth group meeting the night before. Randy didn't tell her what it was, only that the lesson was out of Romans 14. Sierra hadn't reached chapter 14 yet in her reading.

As she drove across town to Mama Bear's Bakery, she thought how blown out of proportion this whole incident seemed. What solution would please everyone?

She arrived at work a few minutes early, which was good because the place was unusually busy, and she was needed up front right away. Sierra went to work making special orders of coffees and lattes for the dozen or so women who flocked around the counter. They appeared to be some sort of group and very happy to be together. One of them had a chubby baby in her arms. All of them seemed to be speaking at once.

A tall woman with cinnamon-blond hair and a gentle, curious gaze asked Sierra, "What is the difference with all your coffees? We don't have this where I am from."

"Oh. Where are you from?"

"I live in the Netherlands. There coffee is just coffee, not an experience, as it seems to be here."

She smiled, and Sierra smiled back as she went down the list and explained each of the items on the coffee menu.

The woman listened with care and then said, "I see. Well, I'd like a cup of coffee. Just coffee, black. Thank you."

Sierra poured the coffee from a fresh pot and handed the mug to the woman.

"How much is it, then?"

"Nothing. It's my treat," Sierra said. "Welcome to Oregon. I hope you have a good visit."

The woman's face lit up. "Thank you! How kind of you! Thank you."

She turned to join her friends at the tables they had pulled close, and Sierra took a dollar from her own pocket and put it in the cash register.

"Why did you do that?" Jody, her coworker, asked. "Now they'll all come up and want free coffee."

"You think so?" Sierra said. "I don't think so. If I can't offer a stranger a cup of cold water in Jesus' name, I can at least offer a cup of hot coffee, black."

Jody shook her head. "I don't know what you're talking about."

Sierra shrugged. "I felt like entertaining an angel."

Jody turned and walked toward the back of the shop, still shaking her head. "When I come back, I want you to start speaking English again."

Sierra wiped off the countertop with a warm, clean towel and smiled to herself as she listened to the group of women talking and laughing. It appeared to be some sort of reunion. The door of the bakery opened, and a petite, well-dressed woman stepped in. Immediately, squeals of joy rose from the group as several of the women hopped up to hurry over and greet her.

As Sierra watched these women, she thought about how valuable friendships are, friendships of every kind. She was so glad she had had a chance to talk with Amy. It was great that Sierra and Vicki were now spending time together. And Randy was the best buddy a girl could ask for. She loved having a friendship with Christy and her other older friends, who never treated her as though she were below them, even though she was younger. Then there were all the friends in Pineville she had grown up with. She hadn't kept in contact with them like she thought she would; yet she knew if she went back to her old hometown today, all her friends would be happy to see her, and they would pick up their friendships right where they had left off.

Now Paul...she thought of how to classify Paul. Was he a friend? A good friend? More than a friend? The strange thing was, she didn't feel that she needed to know. Not right now. Right now it was just what it was. Nothing more, nothing less. She had a wonderful, warm, encouraging correspondence going with a great guy, and that was all she needed to know.

Jody returned from the back with a tray of hot cinnamon rolls. Sierra drew in the tantalizing fragrance as she passed.

"I might just have to have one of those today," Sierra said. She went through spells when she didn't think she could eat another cinnamon roll since she was around them so much. But today it sounded like a good idea.

"Some of my friends might stop by later," Sierra said. "Would you mind if I took a break when they come?"

"Not at all. As long as you don't start passing out free cinnamon rolls to everyone."

"I won't. I paid for the coffee, you know."

"Yes, I saw." Jody pulled out the used coffee filter from the machine and motioned to the pot of steaming java. "Why don't you go offer them some free refills?"

Sierra carried the pot over to the gathering of women and smiled. "More coffee for anyone?"

"Yes, thank you," said the woman from Holland.

A second woman held out her cup and asked, "Do you have any more cream? We used ours up."

Sierra was on her way to get a small pitcher of cream

when the door opened and Randy and Vicki came in. Sierra turned, but when she saw them, her first thoughts were so caught up in Randy's hair issue that she called out a combination of "hair" and "Randy" and said, "Hey, Harry!"

One of the women at the table heard her and repeated loudly enough for her group to hear, "Harry! You guys, it's Harry!"

The women burst into laughter. All eyes were on Randy.

"I'm sorry," one of the younger women said. "It's a little joke for our group. Harry is our invisible hero."

Randy offered them a crooked grin and took the outburst in stride.

"You guys want something to eat?" Sierra said. "I'll be right with you."

She took the creamer to the table, and a woman with dark eyes said, "We're sorry if we embarrassed your friend. We get a little crazy when we're together."

"That's okay. He's not easily rattled."

Sierra returned to the counter where Jody had already served up a cinnamon roll for Randy and a pot of apple spice tea for Vicki. They went to a table at the front of the shop where Sierra joined them with her cinnamon roll and milk.

"I have a fifteen-minute break," Sierra said, tearing off a piece of roll and catching the drips of white frosting with her fingers. "So talk fast and tell me everything."

Randy gave his customary shrug. "I still don't know what I'm going to do."

"Didn't the PTB meet with you?" Sierra asked.

"They met with me, but they didn't give me an answer.

They said my letter made them take a careful look at how some things were being done at the school. Then they said that since I handled it in such a responsible way, they would leave the decision up to me."

Sierra looked at Vicki, who nodded as if she were as amazed as Sierra. She knew how much Randy disliked it when his parents left important decisions up to him. He must be going through torture right now.

"You should have seen the mob in the parking lot," Vicki said. "They all acted as if it had been some great victory. They're sure Randy will not cut his hair."

"And you don't know if that's what you want to do?" Sierra ventured a guess, trying to read Randy's expression.

"I have to look at my reason. I told them it was so I would fit into my community and be accepted with the band and everything. But you know what? If you think about it, no one in the band cares. No one in my little community of musicians cares if my hair is short or long or if my head is shaved. It's only the administration at the school that cares. I don't think I have a very strong argument, really."

"Randy, they gave you freedom to do what you want," Vicki said. "I don't understand why you wouldn't just let it grow and be happy they saw your point."

"That's it, though. I don't know if I have a point."

"Now is a fine time to decide that." Sierra glanced at the clock and felt annoyed that her break was already half over. "Can't you walk away from the whole thing and be done with it?"

"I don't know."

Vicki shook her head. "Some people think they should impeach the student body president and elect Randy. As they see it, he caused the board to break down and do things the way the students want them done by letting us make the choices."

"I don't want to make anybody stumble and fall over this. That's the verse from Romans I was telling you about, Sierra. Shane talked about it last night."

"I remember that verse," Vicki chimed in.

"What was it?" Sierra was frustrated she didn't have the inside scoop on this verse they were talking about, but even more frustrated that she only had three minutes left to her break.

"It says something like 'Make every effort to do whatever leads to peace.'" Randy sighed. "Whatever I do, it should lead to peace and not more division at the school."

"I have to get back to work," Sierra said, pushing her barely eaten cinnamon roll in front of Randy. "You want the rest?" She stood and put her arm around Randy's shoulders. "I know you'll make the right decision."

Randy looked up at her and rippled his eyebrows with skepticism. "And how do you know that?"

"Because," Sierra said, her smile pouring over Randy like a blessing, "I'm going to be praying for you."

eighteen

SIERRA PRAYED LONG and hard for Randy on Thursday night. She also studied for hours. When she was going over the material for her English test the next day, she came to a portion in the material about Emily Dickinson. She read it eagerly, hoping to know more about this woman who wrote the poem about the "immortal Alps" and "picking locks" on special letters. What she read startled her.

"'As a child, Emily Dickinson attended the First Congregational Church of Amherst with her family. Of all her family, Emily alone resisted the revival that swept through the town in the mid-1800s. She stopped going to church sometime in her late twenties. Emily had few friends and kept to herself, spending nearly all of her fifty-six years at the Dickinson homestead.'"

Sierra looked up from her reading and felt sad. She knew from reading some of Emily's poems that she had a gentle reverence for God. She even had written about how God keeps His promises to sparrows and feeds them. She referred to Christ as "our Lord" and wrote of the love of Calvary.

So why had she stopped going to church? What had happened to her? What kind of friends did she have? Did they judge her or love her?

Sierra made a firm commitment that she would stick with Amy, no matter what. She wouldn't give up their friendship as if it were of no value to her. Her thoughts also turned to her friendship with Paul. Was Paul the kind of guy she would remain friends with no matter what? She hoped so. It was certainly that way with Randy. Why wouldn't it be that way with Paul?

Her homework wasn't finished until after ten. Sierra crawled into bed and eagerly opened to Romans 13. She wanted to get to chapter 14 where Randy said he had found the verse on trying to make every effort for peace.

Chapter 13 didn't end up being a quick read. The whole chapter was about having the right attitude toward those in authority over us. It all seemed to apply to the events of the past week, especially since Randy handled things so well by telling the board he would go by their final decision, whatever it was.

By the time Sierra had read through chapter 14, she understood why Randy was having a hard time deciding what to do. The chapter made it clear it wasn't always a matter of what was right for us as individuals. The test of love, the kind of love God calls us to show to others, includes being considerate of the weaknesses of others and what would be an obstacle for them in their walk with the Lord.

Sierra was so into the passage that she went on to chapter 15. When she reached verses 5 and 6, she pulled out her pen and underlined them, reading aloud as she drew the straight line with the edge of her book marker.

"'May the God who gives endurance and encouragement give you a spirit of unity among yourselves as you
follow Christ Jesus, so that with one heart and mouth you
may glorify the God and Father of our Lord Jesus Christ.'"

Even though it was nearly eleven o'clock, Sierra hopped
out of bed and trotted to the phone in the hallway. She
brought the phone back to her room, and sticking her cold
feet under the covers, she dialed Randy's number. He
answered on the second ring.

"Hi. Were you asleep?"

"I wish," he said.

"I found a verse. Listen, you have to hear this." Sierra
carefully balanced the Bible on her upraised knees and followed the verse with her finger as she read.

"Did you get that part about the unity among yourselves?" Sierra asked. "That's what we need at our school.
Not a revolution. We need to come together and be of one
heart and one mouth. That's how we'll be an example in
our community. We need a spirit of unity."

"Read the verse again."

Sierra read, and she could hear the pages flipping on
Randy's side of the phone line.

"Sierra," Randy said slowly, "you're right. You're 1,000
percent right. Will you help me out tomorrow?"

"Sure. What do you want me to do?"

"Stand up in chapel and read that verse."

"What?"

"I agreed to say something in chapel tomorrow morning, since this has become such a big deal. But I'm not
going to be there."

"What do you mean you're not going to be there?"

"I'll explain tomorrow. Just promise me that when you get to school you'll tell Mr. Ackermann I asked you to speak on my behalf, and I'll get there as soon as I can."

Randy, whose favorite word was "Whatever," had turned from complacent to wired in minutes. Sierra couldn't believe how excited he sounded.

"Would you mind giving me a little more information to work with here?"

"It'll make sense tomorrow. Trust me. Sierra, you're amazing. You'll never know how glad I am you called. Thanks a million. I owe you big time."

"Does this mean you're agreeing to pay for Anthony's Steak House tomorrow night for Vicki and me?"

Randy laughed. "Okay, okay. I'll pay. I'll see you at school." He hung up without saying good-bye.

Sierra held the receiver away from her and looked at it as if the beige piece of plastic had jilted her. "What was that supposed to mean?" she asked the silent phone. It did not answer.

The next morning before she left for school, Sierra tried to call Randy again, but his mom said he had already left.

"Oh, and Sierra," his mom added before Sierra could hang up, "thanks so much for your help. Randy said you gave him a verse last night that cleared everything up. You don't know how hard we've been praying."

"Can you tell me what's going on with him this morning?"

"I think he would prefer to tell you himself."

Sierra hurried to school. A dozen students were already inside the building, gathered around Randy's locker, apparently waiting to congratulate him for having broken through the rules of the PTB. One of the girls held a fistful of helium balloons. Sierra remembered the girl because she had worn a small silver ring in her pierced right eyebrow on the first day of school. The second day of school she wore two earrings there. The talk was that she had been sent home. Sierra didn't remember seeing the girl with earrings in her eyebrow since then. Today both earrings were back, and she was waiting expectantly for Randy, her new hero.

Even though Sierra felt like going over to Randy's locker and telling all of them he wasn't coming, or at least wouldn't be there until later, Sierra resisted the urge. They would only ask questions to which she had no answers.

First period went slowly. Chapel came right after first period, and Sierra hurried to get a seat near the front. She had talked to Mr. Ackermann, and everything was set. Vicki caught up with Sierra and sat beside her. The principal began chapel by asking all the students to stand for the flag salute. This had not been the habit, and everyone was surprised. He asked them to remain standing for the Scripture reading and for prayer. The freshman English teacher read from Psalm 8, and the football coach prayed. It was refreshing to see their teachers participate in chapel like that and lead the students spiritually. Sierra wished Randy were here to see how the suggestions in his letter had made a powerful change already.

After some general announcements, the principal introduced one of the men on the school board. An elderly gentleman wearing a tweed jacket stepped up to the microphone.

"It's the PTB," Vicki whispered to Sierra.

"He doesn't look so threatening, does he?" Sierra whispered back.

"As most of you know, one of Royal's students has written a letter to our board this week. That letter has prompted much discussion. I must say, the discussion has been good. The board has decided to make one exception and to allow Randy Jenkins, for the benefit of his ministry, to keep his hair long. None of the rules in the student manual have changed, and no other student will be allowed this same privilege."

An immediate rumbling rose from the student body. Sierra felt that yucky feeling she had experienced in the parking lot when everyone was coming up with plans of what seemed right to him or her. It was as if a little ball of fire had ignited in the room, and she felt uncomfortable thinking about what might happen next.

The administrator continued. "I'm told that one of our students has something to say." He checked his notes. "Sierra Jensen, will you come up, please?"

Vicki reached over and gave Sierra's arm a squeeze. Sierra held her Bible with sweaty palms. As she stepped onto the stage, one of the students called out, "You tell 'em, Sierra. Equal rights for all of us."

The administrator stepped over to the microphone and loudly called the room to order. He motioned for Sierra to step forward.

Opening her Bible to Romans 15 and swallowing hard, Sierra addressed her peers. "Randy asked me to read this verse this morning. It's Romans 15:5–6. 'May the God who gives endurance and encouragement give you a spirit of unity among yourselves as you follow Christ Jesus, so that with one heart and mouth you may glorify the God and Father of our Lord Jesus Christ.'"

Sierra looked up at the sea of waiting faces. She had the microphone and felt she should give some explanation as to why last night at eleven o'clock it sounded like such a great idea to read this verse to the school. "You guys, we have to be united. The only thing that will show our community that we're true believers is if we have one heart and speak with one mouth rather than taking sides about things that only matter on the surface."

She had just finished the last two words when she saw Tyler rise in his seat. Before he could do or say anything, the back doors swung open, and someone came rushing in wearing a baseball cap. Sierra assumed it wasn't anyone from her school, since hats weren't allowed—another one of the frequently challenged rules in the student handbook.

The guy ran down the center aisle of the auditorium and walked up onto the stage. Not until he was next to her did she realize it was Randy. He wore a black baseball cap and from the back hung his blond ponytail.

When the student body realized it was Randy, they began to applaud, as if he had scored a glorious victory for all the wannabe individualists. Not only had he conquered the hair rule, but now he also was blatantly breaking the hat rule.

Sierra cast him a skeptical glance. The principal stepped onto the stage briskly and headed for the microphone.

Randy turned to Sierra and, with his crooked grin, said, "Watch this."

"Mr. Ackermann," Randy began. "Fellow students."

The principal marched over next to Randy at the

podium. Sierra stepped back and then, deciding she was conspicuous, made her way down the three stairs and sat next to Vicki.

"What's he doing?" Vicki whispered. "What's with the hat?"

"I don't know," Sierra said. She suspected she was about to see her buddy do something crazy that would bring his new fan club to their feet with applause. If that happened, Randy could quite possibly be expelled from school.

"Don't do it, Randy," Sierra whispered under her breath. "Don't do anything you'll regret later."

"Did Sierra read that verse to you?" Randy asked, leaning too far into the microphone, causing it to feedback with a horrible squeal.

He leaned back. The principal stood right beside him, his hands folded in front of him, looking like a secret service agent.

Randy had everyone's attention, and so he began to speak. "I want you guys to know that the most important thing to me during this year at school is that we learn how to work together as a team. Like that verse says, we need to be one heart with a spirit of unity. I said in my letter to the board that I was growing my hair out so I could fit into the music community of Portland where my band plays, because that's my mission field. But the truth is, those people accept me exactly as I am, no matter how I look."

Sierra pursed her lips together and kept listening. Randy sure had everyone's undivided attention.

"This is my senior year," Randy went on. "Only one more year of my life will be spent here at Royal. Or actually, only nine more months. I want to thank Mr. Ackermann and the school board for granting me the freedom to choose what to do with my hair. And this is what I've decided."

With that, Randy ripped off the baseball cap and stood tall before a hushed crowd.

nineteen

SIERRA'S MOUTH FELL OPEN in surprise. Randy had cut his hair—short. It wasn't a severe, military-style short, but it was short. His ponytail had been cut off and was attached to the back of the baseball cap.

Randy waved the cap in the air and said, "I can wear this for concerts. For the next nine months of my life, I choose to go by the rules here at Royal and wear my hair like this." He leaned forward and used his left hand to rough up his inch-high hair. "What I want to say to you guys is unity. That's how people will know we're believers. Not by how we look, but by the way we act."

There was a pause, as if everyone were trying to evaluate Randy's actions and statements and decide whether to agree or not.

Sierra rose to her feet and began to applaud. She didn't care if anyone else joined her. Friends support friends, and right now she wanted everyone to know that she totally supported her buddy.

Vicki joined her. Then the rest of their row. Not everyone

stood. Sierra noticed that Tyler didn't. Several guys were huddled together, murmuring and looking as if they were making fun of Randy for being so dramatic.

Mr. Ackermann stepped to the microphone, his expression showing his relief. "Thank you, Randy. You are a fine example of Christian maturity in a teenager."

Sierra heard that phrase used again after school, only this time it was said by two girls who stood across from Randy's locker.

"There's our school's fine example of Christian maturity," one of them said sarcastically.

"We were counting on you, Randy," the other girl said. "You let us down."

Sierra felt like tossing a smirk toward the girls and walking off. Randy went right over to them and started to talk with them, taking their verbal jabs in the face. It felt uncomfortable to Sierra to go over there now, since she would look like a snoop. So she went on to her locker and tried to figure out what books she needed for the weekend. Randy was still talking to them when she closed her locker door.

At lunch Randy, Vicki, and Sierra had decided they would meet at Sierra's at five-thirty, go out to dinner, and then go to the football game. Sierra didn't need to hang around to talk to Randy about anything else. Obviously, he wanted to keep the conversation going with those girls.

Sierra glanced over her shoulder at Randy one more time and then headed down the hall to the parking lot. Something gnawed at her. It was that verse. The part about the spirit of unity. She wasn't even trying to show unity with those girls.

Drawing in a breath of courage on the wings of a prayer, Sierra turned around, went back to Randy and the girls, and approached them with a smile.

"You're right," Sierra heard one of the girls say to Randy. "I know what you're saying, but people aren't like that. You can't tell people to be a team and think they're going to automatically do that."

"Hi," Sierra said, breaking in. "I'm Sierra."

"We know. We saw you up there today."

"I don't know your names," Sierra said, trying to sound genuine. Both the girls were new to the school this year, but Sierra hadn't paid much attention to them.

"I'm Tara, and this is Jen," the quieter one said.

"Are you guys going to the football game tonight?" Sierra asked.

They looked at each other.

"We hadn't thought about it," Jen said.

"We might go," Tara said hesitantly.

"We're going," Randy said. "I'll look for you and save some seats if you want to sit with us."

Tara smiled. "Thanks."

Jen offered a reluctant smile. "It's tough to be mad at a guy who's trying so hard to be nice." She reached over and rubbed his fuzzy scalp. "We'll see you later, Peach Head."

The girls turned to go and Sierra called out after them, "'Bye. See you at the game." Then turning back to Randy she raised an eyebrow and said, "Peach Head?"

Randy shrugged. "I've heard worse today."

"Do you think anyone got the point? Didn't most people agree with you?"

"Yeah, most people agreed."

"So you think it's possible for our school to have some kind of unity?"

"I don't know," Randy said. "I hope so."

They walked together toward the parking lot, and Randy asked, "Is Vicki going to be at your house or meet us at the restaurant or what?"

"She's coming to my house. Remember? We'll see you there around five-thirty."

"Five-thirty," Randy repeated. "See you."

Sierra drove home thinking about how easy it had been to talk to Tara and Jen once Randy had broken the ice. And she never would have guessed that she and Vicki would have become such good friends. It made Sierra realize that if she started to take the initiative to make friends, this could be her best school year yet. And how fitting it would be, as Randy had said, to make their senior year one of unity in which the students worked together as a team. Maybe not everyone would want to make the effort, but Sierra knew she could. And she should. There was no reason she couldn't go out of her way to try to promote unity at school.

When she pulled into the driveway at home, her father was sitting on the swing on the front porch with Granna Mae beside him. It was a cool, pleasant October afternoon. A thin gray layer of clouds covered the sky, and a thick patchwork comforter covered Granna Mae's lap. Gavin and Dillon sat on an old rug on the porch playing a board game. Brutus, their big dog who thought he was part of the family, was tethered to the front pillar by a long rope. When he saw Sierra, he bounded toward her, barking and slobbering excitedly.

"Calm down, Brutus," Sierra said, slipping her hands behind his ears and roughing up his fur. "It's only me."

She held him by the collar and escorted him up the steps to the gathering on the porch. "What's going on?" she asked.

"Not much," Mr. Jensen said.

"Where's Mom?"

"She took the afternoon off," Gavin said. "We get pizza for dinner."

"She's doing some shopping," Mr. Jensen said, adding to Gavin's interpretation of the agreement Sierra had heard her parents make. One afternoon a week her dad would come home at noon so her mom could do whatever she wanted or needed to and not have to worry about Granna Mae. It meant her dad had to bring work home or work Saturday morning, but he had said that wouldn't be a problem.

"I'm supposed to remind you to check the oil in my car this weekend," Sierra said.

"That's right. Thanks for reminding me."

"And I'm going out to dinner with Vicki and Randy, and then we're going to the football game. I don't think I'll be home until after ten-thirty. Is that okay?"

"Call if you're going to be any later," her dad said. "Your curfew is eleven."

"I know," Sierra said. She reached over and squeezed Granna Mae's hand. It felt warm. "How was your day, Granna Mae?"

She smiled at Sierra as if she didn't know who Sierra was or what she had just said. It tugged at Sierra's heart, but she forced herself to smile back at her grandmother. "I love you," she said and kissed the top of Granna Mae's soft, wrinkled hand.

"I love you, too," Granna Mae responded.

"I'm going to go change for tonight. I sure hope it doesn't rain." Sierra said.

"It's not supposed to," Mr. Jensen said. "The weather report was cloudy, but no rain until Sunday."

Sierra stepped over Gavin's outstretched legs and opened the front door. As soon as she went inside, the phone rang. She took off her backpack and picked up the remote phone in the kitchen. It was Tawni. The two of them chatted away like friends for ten minutes. Sierra told her about Randy's bold move, and Tawni told Sierra about her western-wear photo shoot.

"If I ever hear another country-western song, I think I'll scream. They played that music all day."

Sierra laughed. "I told you they would."

She had been sitting at the kitchen counter but decided to take the phone into the study and turn on the computer to see if an e-mail from Paul might be waiting for her.

"All I can say is, the money is very good, and I'm thankful for the work."

"Did you hear back from Lina yet?" Sierra asked.

Tawni went quiet for a moment and then said, "No. And I think it's okay. Not that I've given up hope, but I think the important thing was that I got to say what I wanted to, which was thank you. If I were truly selfless, I wouldn't require a reply. But I'm not. Maybe someday she'll respond."

"I'm sure it must have been a shock to her," Sierra said, turning on the computer. "Give it some time. Maybe she needs a few weeks or something to think all this through."

"I know," Tawni said. "I've thought of that. Believe me,

I've thought of every possible angle. I don't have a problem waiting."

"Did you want to talk to Dad? Mom's not here."

"No, just tell them hi. I was doing my weekly check-in with the family."

"Do you miss us?" Sierra asked, grinning, knowing how her blunt questions always drove her sister crazy.

Tawni laughed. It was a cover-up kind of laugh. Then she said, "All right. Yes, I miss you guys. There. Now you know. Are you shocked?"

"No," Sierra said. "We miss you, too. I miss you."

A clumsy void of words followed their mutual confessions.

Tawni was the first to speak. "Well, I better hang up before I spend all my photo shoot money on this call."

"Say hi to Jeremy for me."

"I will. He's coming over tonight, and we're going out to dinner. I'm treating him to steak, now that I'm a rich woman."

"Sounds fun," Sierra said. "Talk to you later. 'Bye."

Tawni hung up, and Sierra scanned the computer screen, which showed all the retrieved e-mails. There were only two. Both for her dad from work. Nothing from Paul.

Sierra closed down the system and was about to leave the room when she decided to spend a few minutes in her favorite chair. It seemed a welcoming spot in which to feel sorry for herself. She noticed a picture on the seat of the chair. Looking closer, she realized it was a postcard. The picture was of a grand castle on a hill at sunrise. The sky behind the gray stone building was aqua blue with streaks of pink and mauve.

Sierra wondered who would send her dad such a post-card. Turning it over, she saw her name written in bold, black letters.

> *Sierra,*
>
> *Here's a pix of our famous Edinburgh Castle. I hope you can come to Scotland and see it one day. I'll write more this weekend but wanted to send this off to say thanks for the letter. It made me smile. Also, I don't think I'd like us to start e-mailing each other. There's something strong and enduring about old-fashioned letter writing. I like waiting for your letters.*
>
> *Time is our friend, Sierra. Let's enjoy the leisurely pace.*
>
> *Paul*

Sierra smiled as she turned the postcard over and studied the romantic shot of the castle. Then she read the card again. It was a good one. Not mushy. Not aloof. Just right. He had been thinking of her. He said he would write more later. And he said time was their friend. She liked that. Paul was right. E-mail did bring with it an urgency and immediacy. Why rush?

She closed her eyes and held the postcard to her nose and lips as if she could draw in the fragrance of Paul's Scotland through the picture. She knew it was silly.

Sierra opened her eyes and looked around. How did the card end up in the chair? She could guess. Her dad, who knew her heart, must have been the one to pick up the mail this afternoon. He must have known that she would come here, to her favorite chair, and would find the post-card like a hidden treasure. The thought made her smile.

She rose and headed upstairs to put on warmer clothes

and to tuck her postcard under her pillow. That was the only way to properly dream upon a castle. And that's where Edinburgh Castle belonged. In the "there" and "later."

Vicki would be here in a few minutes, and tonight Sierra would enjoy a fun evening with her friends of the "here" and "now." And the best part was, good ol' "Peach Head" Randy was buying.

Book Nine

NOW PICTURE
THIS

one

"SOMEBODY ANSWER THE DOORBELL," Sierra's mom called from the kitchen.

Sierra paused at the top of the stairs with an envelope in her hand. She had just arrived home from school and had found the eagerly awaited letter from Paul. Wanting to hide in her bedroom and soak up every word, she had taken the stairs two at a time. But she found her room invaded by Uncle Matthew; his wife, Abby; and their three young boys. The Jensen household was expecting a record-setting thirty-one family members for Thanksgiving dinner tomorrow.

"Howard, can you answer the door?" Mrs. Jensen called to her husband, since no one had responded to her first plea.

Sierra wedged her slim frame into the corner alcove at the top of the stairs, out of view from the entryway, and carefully opened the envelope postmarked "Edinburgh." She unfolded the onionskin paper. Paul had written with bold, black letters at the top of the letter:

When it rains it seems the world
Takes on a somber hue

My soul is hushed
I lift my pen
And write a song for You.

Sierra drew in a quick breath and read Paul's poem one more time. Closing her eyes, lost in a dream, she tilted her head back and hit the wall a little too hard. The glass globe on the wall's antique light fixture tilted off its perch and tumbled to the floor before Sierra realized what had happened. It hit the rug with a dull thump and split in two. Sierra carefully picked up the pieces and tried to fit them back into the light fixture's base. But the pieces wouldn't stay in place.

Downstairs the voices of Aunt Emma, Uncle Jack, and their twin daughters, Amanda and Kayla, filled the entryway. Howard Jensen's booming "Hello! Come in, come in!" welcomed them.

Above the rush of excited voices, Sierra's mom called from the kitchen, "Sierra, I need a hand in here."

"Coming." Sierra quickly folded the letter into the envelope and tucked it in the front pouch pocket of her sweatshirt. *I'll be back*, she silently vowed to the letter, giving it a pat. *Just as soon as I can.*

Then, taking the broken globe with her, Sierra hurried downstairs to greet her relatives. She handed her dad the two pieces of glass. "Upstairs, first light on the right. Sorry. I bumped the wall."

"Put it over there on the entry table." Worry lines creased Howard Jensen's forehead. "I'll see to it after I get the door back on the china cabinet."

Sierra followed the caravan of company into the

kitchen. Sierra's mother, in the thick of her pumpkin pie preparations, greeted them, promising hugs as soon as she placed the pies in the oven.

"Sierra, open the oven door for me, will you?" her mom asked. She was trying to sound nice even though Sierra knew she was frazzled.

"You were supposed to wait and let us help you with that, Sharon." Emma stepped over and brushed a kiss across Sierra's mom's cheek. "Thanks for doing all this and putting up with the craziness. It means a lot to have so many family members together again."

"We're glad everyone could make it," Sharon Jensen said graciously. "It'll be fun."

Sierra suppressed a grin at the word "fun." She knew this kind of pressure was not her mom's idea of a great time.

"Where's Granna Mae?" Emma asked about Sierra's grandmother.

"Upstairs, I think." Sierra's mom carefully balanced a pumpkin pie in each hand as Sierra held open the wobbly oven door. She knew if she let go of the door that it would tilt to the side. Her dad had worked on it last week, but it was crooked again and needed to be held steady.

Sierra was about to close the mouth of the ancient dragon oven when her mom said, "Wait. Two more pies."

"Sierra," her dad called over his shoulder, "I'm going to set up Jack and Emma here in the study. Could you run upstairs and let Granna Mae know they're here?"

The last thing Sierra wanted was to start running errands for everyone. She had a letter waiting for her. A wonderful, romantic letter warming her pocket.

"Wait a second," her mom said. "Before you run

306 🦗 Robin Jones Gunn

upstairs, Sierra, could you check on the boys for me? I think they're still in the backyard, but I haven't heard or seen them for the past half-hour. And don't let Brutus in the house."

Sierra sighed and reluctantly headed for the back door. A swirl of huge, amber-colored leaves had collected in front of the doorway. They were sent flying down the stairs and back into the yard when she opened the screen door.

"Dillon! Gavin!" Sierra called. "Where are you guys?"

The only response was the bellowing "Woof!" of Brutus, their lovable "lug of a fur ball," as Sierra's older brother Wesley called the dog. Sierra was glad Wes was coming home from college for Thanksgiving. This was his senior year, and even though Corvallis was only two hours away, Wes had hardly been home all fall. Of Sierra's four brothers, she was closest to Wesley. Something inside her suspected he had a girlfriend. He had told their dad that he might bring a guest home with him, but Mr. Jensen hadn't thought to ask if the guest was male or female.

Wes had volunteered to pick up Tawni, Sierra's only sister, at the airport on his way home. The two of them and the possible mysterious guest were expected to arrive after nine that night.

"Sorry, Brutus," Sierra said, stuffing her chilled hands into the pouch pocket of her sweatshirt. The letter warmed her fingers when she touched it. "You can't come in for the next few days, buddy. Get used to that doghouse."

The chain on his collar kept Brutus from venturing beyond the lawn's edge. He barked loudly, as if complaining about his confinement.

"I know. It's rough on all of us, Brutus. You should

see where I have to sleep. Tawni and I get the floor in Granna Mae's room, along with Nicole, Aunt Frieda, and Molly. It's a tight squeeze. And Dad says Aunt Frieda snores."

Brutus responded with what Sierra supposed was a sympathetic bark. A shiver ran through her. She could feel the chilling raindrops hit her long blond hair. Oregon's moisture made her hair curlier than it was naturally, which frustrated her. Only the weight of her hair kept her from being a total fuzz head.

Most of her friends had long, sleek hair, but they were continually telling Sierra they loved her wild, free-flowing curls, which matched her personality. Sierra would trade hair with any of them.

She pulled the hood of her oversized sweatshirt over her head. "You'd better stay out of the wet, Brutus. Where are Gavin and Dillon; do you know?"

Then she noticed that the light was on in her dad's workshop. The small structure was originally a playhouse complete with shutters and gingerbread trim along the roof. But Howard Jensen had turned it into a haven for his power tools and workbench.

A person approaching the dollhouse would expect to find little girls in big hats playing tea party at a small, lace-covered table, but instead the doors opened to a pint-sized hardware store with pegboard walls and fluorescent overhead lighting.

Sierra pushed Brutus away with her leg before he could jump up on her as she sprinted through the rain.

She approached the workshop and called out, "Dillon, Gavin, are you guys in here?"

Opening the door, she found her two elementary-school-age brothers busily moving equipment around in the tight quarters. A stack of blankets was on the workbench.

"What are you guys doing? Didn't you hear me calling you?"

"We're going to sleep out here."

"Says who?" Sierra asked, her hand automatically snapping to her hip as she took on her motherly voice.

"We don't want to sleep in Mom and Dad's room with those other boys."

"You mean Jared, Bob, and Marshall? They're your cousins. What's wrong with them? You guys are all about the same age. You'll have a good time."

Dillon and Gavin looked at each other skeptically.

Sierra realized the five young boy cousins hadn't been around each other since they were babies. They didn't have a relationship even though they were related. Sierra knew what that was like. She had felt the same way toward Nicole and Molly five years ago, when they had been together for Christmas. The three preteen cousins had a rocky beginning with a misunderstanding over who would sleep in which bed, but they had ended up friends before the holiday was over. And that time they all had beds to sleep in, not an allotted corner of floor space like this year. Sierra understood how her brothers could feel outnumbered by three boys they didn't know and yet were expected to treat nicely.

"Why don't you guys wait until after you've spent some time with them? You might like them. Besides, it's going to get cold out here."

"We don't care. We brought all the blankets."

"Yeah, and I'm sure Mom's not going to be crazy about

that. She'll need blankets for all the people sleeping in the house. Come on. Let's go in. Mom and Dad are counting on us to be hospitable."

"What's that mean?" Gavin asked.

"It means you be nice. Come on. And bring the blankets with you."

Sierra opened the door and motioned for the boys to dash through the rain back into the house. They took their time, lugging the blankets and looking like refugees leaving their homeland.

"Come on," Sierra said, jogging ahead of them to get out of the persistent rain. "You're getting the blankets wet."

Brutus emerged from his doghouse and bounded out to meet them.

"Back!" Sierra yelled. "Don't even think about jumping on us. You stay in your house."

"Yeah," Gavin echoed. "Be a-spittable, Brutus. At least you get your own bed tonight."

Sierra opened the back door, kicking away the now soggy yellow leaves and calling to her brothers to hurry up. When they entered the warm, fragrant kitchen, and Mrs. Jensen saw the stack of blankets, her eyes grew huge.

"What are you doing? Did those get wet? Sierra, why didn't you stop them?"

"I...they..."

Mrs. Jensen ran a hand over the top blanket and snapped at Sierra, "Take these down to the basement and put them in the dryer on low. Make sure it's low, or these wool ones will be ruined. Don't put more than two in at a time. You boys get cleaned up. I don't want you going outside anymore. It's too wet."

310 <Robin Jones Gunn

Sierra briskly grabbed the blankets from her brothers and tromped down to the cold, musty basement, muttering all the way, "'"Get the boys, Sierra-ella.' 'Check on your grandmother, Sierra-ella.' 'Stoke the fire, wash the floors, scrub the hearth, pluck the chicken, mend the...'"

Before she could continue her exaggerated chore list, Sierra noticed her dad coming up the basement stairs with a plunger in his hand. Their old house often had plumbing problems.

"The upstairs bathroom is already clogged." He looked as stressed as his wife, and his jaw was set as if to say, "Get outta my way."

Sierra flattened herself and the bundle of blankets against the wall as her dad marched past her. Apparently she wasn't the only one who was suffering from a Cinderella complex this holiday.

As he passed by, Sierra's dad's concretely set jaw opened only wide enough for him to mutter, "This is going to be a long weekend."

two

ALL SIERRA WANTED TO DO was to find a quiet place to hide so she could read Paul's letter. But as soon as the first round of blankets was in the dryer, she still needed to check on Granna Mae. She loved her dear, though often confused, grandma. The letter would have to wait a few more minutes while Sierra flew up the stairs to check on Granna Mae.

If the rest of us are this stressed, she wondered, *how is Granna Mae handling all the activity?*

This large Victorian house was actually Granna Mae's; she had lived here her entire married life, and her nine children had grown up here. Sierra's father was the oldest, and Emma was the youngest. The second oldest son, Paul, had died in Vietnam. The rest were still alive, and three of them—Frieda, Matthew, and Emma—were coming with their families for the Thanksgiving weekend.

Almost a year ago, Sierra's family had moved in with Granna Mae because she could no longer live on her own. Her condition varied; some days she was bright as a berry,

312 ~ Robin Jones Gunn

but other days she needed to be watched constantly so she wouldn't wander off in a daze.

Sierra knocked softly on Granna Mae's bedroom door. When Sierra didn't hear a reply, she called out, "Granna Mae, may I come in?"

She pushed the door open and peeked inside. Granna Mae was asleep in her cozy recliner by the window with the radio softly playing classical music. Sierra tiptoed past the bed mats lining the floor, and reaching for a quilt from the end of Granna Mae's bed, she slipped it over the sleeping woman.

Outside, the rain pelted the windows. Sierra pulled down the shades and closed the heavy curtains to quiet the room and buffer the chill from the original 1915 windows. She stepped away, intending to leave the room, but then she stopped. Her pile of clothes and other belongings she would need for the weekend were stacked against the wall by the dresser, next to her bed mat. Her mom had insisted that Sierra and her little brothers clean their rooms exceptionally well and then take the things they needed over the weekend to the room where they would be sleeping so they wouldn't disturb the guests who had claimed their rooms.

In the middle of Sierra's stack on the floor was her favorite birthday gift. She tiptoed over to draw it out of the clothes. The instant her fingers touched the cool metal frame, Sierra smiled. She pulled out the picture and held it close in the dimness of the quiet bedroom. Soft violin and cello music floated from the radio as she took in the picture's image: Paul.

The framed photo showed Paul standing in hiking gear deep in the Scottish Highlands, with the wind whipping his dark hair across his forehead and giving his cheeks a ruddy glow. Apparently he had been talking when he turned to face the camera because he looked as if he had just burst out laughing. Sierra focused on his eyes. One eyebrow was up slightly, and his blue-gray eyes almost shimmered, as if they caught the reflection off some pristine lake below him.

From where he stood on top of a rocky crag, the view behind him went on forever. And what a hopelessly romantic view it was: bright blue skies and velvet green hills dotted by windswept clumps of rose-tinted heather.

To Sierra, this wasn't just a picture. It wasn't merely a photograph. What she held in her hands was a window. A window framed in shiny brass. A window that allowed her to look out of her little corner of the world to see the view from Paul's life.

Since June, when Paul had gone to Scotland to stay with his recently widowed grandmother and to attend school in Edinburgh, Sierra had wondered what his world was like. She had prayed for this unique guy ever since their chance meeting at Heathrow Airport in London last January.

When Sierra's sister, Tawni, moved to Southern California and began to date Paul's brother, Jeremy, Paul's and Sierra's lives intersected again. Then, when she was given an assignment from her Christian high school to help out at the Highland House, she discovered that Paul's uncle Mac ran the homeless shelter. Paul even worked there at the same time Sierra did.

Yet, despite all the bizarre coincidences and connections, Paul showed no special interest in Sierra. He had embarrassed her one night at Carla's Café, a charming coffeehouse in downtown Portland, when he had asked if she had a crush on him.

Sierra's answer apparently surprised Paul. She had stated that she wondered if maybe God brought people into others' lives at different times for specific reasons. She told Paul she thought they had met so she could pray for him, since, practically against her will, she had been prompted innumerable times to do just that.

Much seemed to have changed inside Paul during the first few months he was in Scotland. By the end of the summer, he had contacted Sierra and asked her to correspond with him. He suggested they write via "snail-mail," instead of e-mail, which she preferred, since he wanted their words to take their time traveling back and forth and not to be shot instantly from one end of the world to the other.

For weeks now they had been corresponding. Sierra wrote to Paul nearly every day, even if it was just a postcard or a few lines on a piece of notebook paper in class. And Paul wrote to her often. His words brought descriptions of the classes he attended, the people he spent time with, the funny things his grandmother said, and the way the autumn sun looked against the windowpane of his grandmother's cottage right before it slid behind the hills. Paul also wrote about what was on his heart—his feelings, his prayers, his quiet thoughts. He shared openly with Sierra, and she did the same.

All along she had had only words to aid her in looking into Paul Mackenzie's life. Now she had a window in her hand. Through this brass-framed window she saw more than the hills, the heather, and the brown leather jacket Paul had worn when they first met. She could now see the face, the eyes, and the smile of the guy who had turned her emotions inside out. No one had ever done that to her before—not like this.

Sierra felt a smile pull up the corners of her mouth as she ran her fingers across the clear glass of her picture, her window. She remembered how her fingers had trembled when her mom handed her the package from Paul on the day before her birthday. Sierra had ripped open the padded mailing envelope right there in the kitchen while her mom and her little brother Gavin watched. The gift came wrapped simply, in tan-flecked tissue tied with thin jute cord. Sierra remembered carefully pulling off the jute, thinking she could use it to macramé something—a bracelet, maybe. The tiny attached card said, "Happy Birthday, Daffodil Queen," which was Paul's nickname for her.

When she pulled out the picture, Gavin said, "That's all you got? Just a picture?"

Sierra wanted to cry when she looked at Paul's handsome face. If her mother and Gavin hadn't been there, she most certainly would have kissed the glass.

Now, in the stillness of Granna Mae's room, while the echo of another round of voices filled the entryway and circled up the stairs, Sierra pressed her lips to her index finger and touched Paul's windburned cheek with her finger. She knew she still had his unread words waiting for her in her pocket.

Balancing his picture on her crossed legs, Sierra reached for the letter and adjusted her position so she could get as much light as possible from the one low-lit lamp on Granna Mae's nightstand.

She unfolded the paper and read, her lips moving silently:

When it rains it seems the world
Takes on a somber hue
My soul is hushed
I lift my pen
And write a song for You.

Sierra, my friend, it's a rainy night here. Can you tell? I'm at my grandmother's. I read your last letter on the train on the way home from school for the weekend, and I must confess I read every word twice. All three pages.

I think what you said about your sister is true. It was good for her to write that letter to her birth mother, even though she hasn't heard back from her—even if she never does.

Jeremy e-mailed me last week that he thinks Tawni is going to go back to school. Has she told you yet? He's been encouraging her to start with some night classes at the community college. I thought about you and all your big decisions about college next year. I remember what it was like having to send off all those applications before November 1 during my senior year. I'm glad you found out about the scholarship application and sent it in time. I imagine you'll have no trouble landing any scholarship you apply for. I hadn't realized you were a 4.0 girl. I should have guessed. You always do seem to have an answer for everything.

A sudden knock on the door made Sierra jump. Before she could stuff Paul's picture back in her stack of clothes or tuck away the letter, the door opened and her oldest brother, Cody, stepped in with his wife, Katrina, and their irrepressible toddler, Tyler.

"There's Auntie Sara," Cody said, using Tyler's nickname for Sierra as he released Tyler's hand so he could run over to Sierra where she sat cross-legged on the floor.

Sierra shot a cautious glance over at Granna Mae sleeping in the recliner. Cody followed her eyes and quickly apologized.

"Sorry," he said softly. "I didn't realize Granna Mae was napping."

Before Sierra could move, Tyler pounced on her. The heel of his little hiking boot crashed into the glass in Paul's picture.

"Tyler!" Sierra yelled.

He pulled back, startled by her response. The bend in his leg caught the corner of Paul's letter and tore the onionskin paper in two.

"Tyler!" she yelled again.

"Sierra," Katrina said with a definite scold in her voice.

Sierra grabbed the pieces of the letter and stuffed them into her pocket. With the other hand, she quickly reached for Tyler's curious fingers as they were going for the shards of broken glass. "Don't touch. It will cut you."

"What's going on?" Granna Mae asked, blinking and pulling the blanket off her lap.

"It's okay," Cody said, going over to his grandmother and giving her a hug.

Katrina scooped Tyler off of Sierra's lap just as the startled and confused boy burst into tears. Without a word, Katrina headed for the bedroom door. Sierra knew her sister-in-law was mad.

"I'm sorry," Sierra said to her retreating back.

Tyler squirmed in his mom's arms, trying to get down.

"Auntie Sara!" he cried. "I want Auntie Sara!"

Carrying her wailing son, Katrina left the room and closed the door behind her. Sierra heard Tyler's cries fading down the hallway. Cody, meanwhile, was trying to settle Granna Mae back down in her chair. In a soothing voice, he told her what was going on.

Sierra could still feel her heart pounding. How could so much have gone wrong so fast? Blinking to keep back the tears, she looked at the broken glass frame still balanced on her leg. At least the glass hadn't sliced into the photo or through her jeans, or so she hoped.

Rising and walking to the trash can by the door, Sierra let the broken pieces slip into the trash. She lifted the picture and examined it more closely. A tiny shard of glass still stuck in the photo. She tapped the back of the frame over the trash, dislodging the sharp fragment. Checking the photo again, she bit her lower lip when she realized the shard had left a mark. It was a tiny cut over Paul's heart.

three

"HE DIDN'T MEAN TO DO IT," Katrina said firmly to Sierra.

The two of them stood in the back corner of the kitchen while the rest of the group went through Mrs. Jensen's "chow line" and scooped their own bowls of soup from three large pots she had simmering on the stove. Everyone had arrived except Wesley and Tawni. The noise level in the tiny kitchen was unbearable. This many people had been at Sierra's birthday party the weekend before, but the noise hadn't irritated her the way this laughter and chattering did.

"I know," Sierra said. "He startled me, that's all. I didn't want him to get cut on the glass."

"I appreciate that," Katrina replied. "I'll be glad to replace whatever was broken. Was it a picture frame?"

Sierra nodded. "Don't worry. It's okay. The frame is fine. I can buy glass for it."

She smiled. Katrina smiled back.

"Where's Tyler now?" Sierra asked.

"He fell asleep on Gavin's bed. He didn't sleep in the

car on the way here as I hoped he would, so he crashed as soon as he stopped crying."

"I'd better check on him," Sierra said. "He might be frightened when he wakes up, if he doesn't know where he is."

Katrina nodded. "Thanks, Sierra. Do you want me to bring some soup up for you?"

"No, but you might want to see if anyone is taking some up for Granna Mae. I'm afraid we've rattled her, and Dad thought it would be better if she ate in her room rather than coming down for dinner."

"I'll check on her," Katrina said.

Sierra smiled as she slid past the swarm of relatives and retreated to the quieter upstairs. She stopped by the hall closet to grab a flashlight off the upper shelf. When she was little, she thought this was a magical closet that led directly to Narnia. Tonight she would have welcomed a journey into that fictional world. A cup of tea with Mrs. Beaver would have been a treat.

Tyler was sound asleep on Gavin's bed, so Sierra positioned herself snugly in the beanbag chair in the corner. She kept the flashlight low and pulled the torn letter from her pocket, determined to read the entire missive before the evening was over. Scanning the sentences until she caught up to where she had left off, she read:

…You always do seem to have an answer for everything. I mean that in a good way. You know what you want and what your life is all about. I wish I'd had that much clarity when I was your age. I guess God just allowed me to take a little more of a winding trail to get to that point. But here I am. And I can honestly say I've never felt this much peace or this close to God. It's a good thing. Or what is it you

said your friends say? It's a "God-thing"? Yes, it's definitely a God-thing.

My grandmother has insisted we ration the heating fuel this fall. I told you her cottage is old—make that ancient. When it's cold and wet here, it's really cold and wet. I have turned into a man of many layers. Even sitting around the house, I wear at least three layers with a wool sweater on top. I tried wearing my down jacket to dinner tonight, but Grandma said I was being rude and hit me with a wooden cooking spoon. (It didn't hurt a bit—couldn't feel a thing through all the layers!)

So as I write this in my "thrifty Scotch" bedroom, I'm wearing my down jacket and am wrapped in a wool blanket. Don't tell Granny, but I pinched one of her wee candles, and I have it lit here on the writing desk to thaw out my fingers between paragraphs....

Ah, there; warm again. Now, what was I saying? It's a dark and stormy night here. The raindrops fling themselves at my window like desperadoes shouting, "Let us in! It has to be warmer in there than it is out here!" Ha! Little do the raindrops know it's the same temperature in here as it is out there. And in here one must deal with "the Grandmother." Out there all they have to deal with is the wind. Hmm...I'm thinking I might join them.

May the peace of Christ be upon you, dear Sierra.
Paul

Sierra drew in a deep breath and turned off the flashlight. She always felt the same when she finished reading one of Paul's letters: wonderfully warmed and terribly disappointed. She felt disappointed that his words had stopped and the little bit of him she had in her hands had come to an end. And she felt warm on the inside. She wondered if Paul felt the same way when he read her letters.

Quietly lifting the shade on the window behind her, Sierra peeked out at the rainy world. The raindrops were just as Paul had described them: desperadoes beating against the glass. It made her wonder if Paul had any idea he was such a wonderful poet. She decided to tell him that in her next letter, a letter she would begin to write now.

With soft steps, she made her way over to Dillon's desk and reached for a pen and a blank piece of paper in the drawer. Returning to the beanbag chair with a book for a lap table, she balanced the flashlight on the windowsill so it shone away from the peacefully sleeping Tyler. Sierra began her letter.

Dear Poet,

You are, you know. I loved your "When It Rains" poem. Your timing is perfect because it's raining here, too. And I'm also thinking of you. Downstairs about a gazillion relatives have congregated so we can all be together for Thanksgiving tomorrow. But I've found a quiet spot beside a window where the desperado raindrops are now begging me to let them in. The funniest thing is that none of them sound like a western desperado. They all have Scottish accents! Did you send them here to harass me? And if so, why didn't you come along with them? I would have let you in, and I can guarantee it's warmer inside here than it is outside on this dark and stormy night.

She continued to write as Tyler slept. She filled four pages before the bedroom door opened. The light from the hallway flooded the room, and someone flipped on the bedroom light. Sierra squinted, trying to see who it was. Tyler woke up and immediately started to cry.

"Oh, I'm sorry," Caleb, her fourteen-year-old cousin,

said. "My mom told me to bring my stuff up 'cuz I'm sleeping here. Why's he crying?" Caleb dropped his gear on the floor and cracked his knuckles nervously.

"It's okay," Sierra said, going to Tyler's side to comfort him. The minute she touched him she said, "Oh, baby, you're burning up."

She put her hand on his hot forehead. Tyler only cried louder.

"Caleb, tell Katrina to come up right away."

Caleb fled the room.

"You want a drink of water, Tyler?"

"I want my mommy!"

"She's coming, Little Bear. Here, let's take off this sweatshirt."

Tyler squirmed and resisted, but Sierra kept at it, knowing he would feel better.

"There. Now let me take off your socks. We have to cool you down."

Just then Katrina flew in the open door. She took over immediately, calmly asking Sierra to bring a cold washcloth and to find the liquid Tylenol in Katrina's cosmetic bag in the bathroom. By the time Sierra returned, Tyler had stopped crying and was sucking on his first two fingers as Katrina rocked him in her lap. After Sierra did all she could to help, she gathered up her papers and told Katrina she would slip out now.

"Homework?" Katrina asked, eyeing the many pages.

"Oh, no," Sierra said, feeling herself blush. "Just a letter."

"Oh?" Katrina responded, with a knowing smile. "You'll have to tell me about him sometime."

Sierra nodded and left. She hadn't told many people about Paul and their growing relationship. She had e-mailed Christy several times and had asked advice once or twice. And she had told her best friend, Vicki, a little bit. Tawni, of course, knew because of her close relationship with Paul's brother, Jeremy. But that was about it. It wasn't the same as having a boyfriend who showed up on her doorstep every other day. All Sierra had were letters that showed up every now and then, and she was usually the one who collected the mail. So no one knew how frequently Paul was writing her.

Standing in the hallway, Sierra felt lost. She didn't know exactly where to go. She probably shouldn't barge into her own room to put away the letter in case someone was trying to sleep. And she knew Granna Mae and possibly other people were in Granna Mae's room, so Sierra didn't feel comfortable barging in there. She opted for keeping the letter in her backpack, which hung on the coat rack downstairs.

Gently folding the two onionskin sheets together and sliding it into her sweatshirt pocket, Sierra headed downstairs. The noise level rose with each step down. Just as she reached the entryway, the front door opened, and Wesley and Tawni stepped in.

"Hello!" Wesley greeted her, his booming voice sounding just like their father's.

Sierra received his warm hug and looked over his shoulder to see if his new girlfriend stood behind him. Only Tawni was there, shaking the rain off her jacket and smoothing back her long hair. The last time Sierra had seen her sister, Tawni's hair was a deep mahogany. Tonight it was white-blond, a much lighter blond than her natural color, and she wore long, layered bangs. She looked like a different person.

"Man," Tawni said, slipping off her coat before stepping all the way in. "When it rains here, it sure pours. What a night!"

"Oh, you don't know the half of it," Sierra murmured in her sister's ear as she reached out to hug her.

To Sierra's surprise, Tawni kissed her lightly on the cheek. This was new, too. Tawni had never been one to initiate affection. But she held Sierra close an extra moment and whispered, "I have something to tell you. Promise you won't tell anyone?"

Pulling away, Sierra looked into the face of her oh-so-changed sister and gave her an expectant expression. Tawni raised an eyebrow and tilted her head, waiting for Sierra to promise.

"I promise." Sierra whispered the words so not even Wesley could hear them above the chatter in the living room and kitchen.

"Tawni, Wes!" Uncle Jack burst upon them and called over his shoulder to the rest of the group the glad announcement that the last of the clan had arrived.

The swarm of relatives buzzed toward them. Just before the lovely queen bee, Tawni, was swept up in their frenzy, she turned to Sierra and mouthed the word "Later."

four

NO ONE SLEPT WELL in the Jensen home that Thanksgiving eve night. Tyler's fever didn't break, and he woke up crying every few hours. Caleb couldn't sleep in the same room with Tyler, so he took his sleeping bag downstairs. Uncle Jack tripped over him when the older man went looking for a glass of milk sometime around three o'clock. Marshall had to go to the bathroom, causing the upstairs toilet to overflow again. He cried out frantically for his mom, and Sierra's dad appeared to help. But it didn't matter. The whole household was awake from all the commotion except, thankfully, Granna Mae, who had talked in her sleep between midnight and two o'clock, waking the five on her bedroom floor. Sierra had lain awake long hours, worrying that Granna Mae might get up in the middle of the night and stumble over one of them.

The night's fiascoes, mixed with the ceaseless rain and wailing winds, made for a houseful of grouchy people at breakfast. Everyone had a different story to tell about his or her experience in the night.

Sharon Jensen had risen early, or perhaps never went to bed by the look of the dark circles under her eyes. She put the huge turkey in the oven before dawn and managed to set enough coffee and bagels out on the counter to soothe the savage beasts that lumbered down the stairs. One thing the Jensens all liked was strong black coffee. Mrs. Jensen kept the coffeemaker perking so the rich aroma filled the house.

Having had her fill of stories around the kitchen counter, Sierra slid past two of her aunts, who were insisting Sierra's mom give them something to do to help with the dinner. Sierra pulled a china cup and saucer from the cupboard and prepared a breakfast tray for Granna Mae.

Just as she placed the buttered toast and small tumbler of juice on the tray, her mother touched Sierra's arm and said, "Thank you, honey. May I assign Granna Mae to you for the next day or two? Make sure she gets her meals, okay? I thought I had that covered, but it's gotten away from me."

"Sure, I'll take care of her. Is there anything else you want me to do?"

"Just the dishes whenever you can. I'm sure I'll have the dishwasher running around the clock."

Sierra hated to do the dishes. She didn't know why; she just did. If she thought of doing them on her own and went about the task, it was no big deal. Then she felt she was helping out without being told. But if she was asked to do them, a spirit of rebellion rose inside her and whatever happiness she felt vanished.

This morning she clenched her jaw and forced herself to smile and nod to her frenzied mother. Sierra knew deep down that it was the least she could do to help out, especially since she had done so little yesterday.

Sierra had to watch her every step on the way to Granna Mae's room. She successfully navigated the minefield of people's belongings and found Granna Mae dressed and making her bed. The white-haired soul appeared clear thinking and well rested.

"Oh, Lovey, you are too good to me." Granna Mae smoothed back the quilt and sat down at the little corner table Howard Jensen had built to make his mother's bedroom meals more convenient. It sat next to the window, covered with a floral tablecloth and set with the hen and rooster salt and pepper shakers that had resided faithfully on the kitchen counter for as long as anyone could remember.

Sierra placed the tray on the table and asked if she could bring anything else.

"No, no. This is wonderful. I imagine you're eager to spend time with all your cousins. You don't have to stay." Granna Mae picked up her favorite china cup and drew it to her lips with shaky hands.

Sierra realized she hadn't spent time with any of her relatives, since she had preferred to "be" with Paul the night before. The way she felt this morning, the only relative she wanted to talk to was Wesley, to find out why he hadn't brought home a guest. She also wanted to pry Tawni's big secret out of her. During the restless night, Sierra had made up lists of what the news could be. She narrowed it down to four possibilities: Tawni's going back to school, as Paul had written; hearing from her birth mother; becoming engaged to Jeremy; or landing a great modeling job. Tawni modeled full-time, but not every assignment was to her liking, such as a western-wear catalog shoot that had subjected her to country music for an entire day. And not every assignment paid well.

Sierra had considered coaxing the news from Tawni during one of the many awake sessions during the night, but then others in the room might have heard them. Besides, Tawni wasn't much of a night person.

But before Sierra knew it, the morning had fled, with Sierra running first downstairs to help out in the kitchen and then upstairs on some urgent errand and then back down the stairs, over and over again.

By two o'clock, the Jensen flock were gathered in the dining room and spilling over into the adjacent living room, where more tables were set up. The nicely browned turkey graced the center of the dining room table. The rain had stopped about an hour earlier, and weary autumn sunbeams tunneled their way through the clouds, weaving themselves through the lace curtains along the south side of the dining room. Only the bravest sunbeams made the long journey, and when they arrived on Granna Mae's best ivory linen tablecloth, they danced for joy among the cranberries and the mashed potatoes.

The Jensen family stood and held hands. Tyler was back to his sweet self and wanted to be next to Sierra to hold her hand. Katrina had blamed the fever and rough night on a molar that had broken through on the bottom right side of Tyler's mouth sometime in the night. Sierra wondered how mothers ever figured out these things.

Granna Mae stood at the head of the table, smiling contentedly and appearing delighted to have so many of her family members together. The merry sunbeams seemed to find her soft hair a pleasant place to end their journey, and there they stayed. Sierra smiled at the sight of her grandmother standing straight and still, oblivious to her beautiful "halo."

The rooms grew silent, and Granna Mae pronounced a blessing on the family. "May the Lord continue to show His grace and mercy to our family. May we live each day for Him with hearts full of love. And may we never cease to be thankful."

"Amen," one of the men echoed.

"Howard," Granna Mae said, turning to Sierra's dad, "would you do us the honor of giving thanks to our heavenly Father?"

"Sure. Let's pray."

As they bowed their heads, Mr. Jensen began to pray eloquently, as well as at length. The family had much for which to be thankful.

Sierra's chair was next to her mother's, close to the kitchen. As her father continued to pray, Sierra's nose picked up the scent of something burning. Dozens of fragrances had run through the house that day, but this was a new scent and not a pleasant one. Sierra let go of Tyler's hand and slipped into the kitchen. She checked the stove and saw that all the burners were turned off. Then she turned to the oven and noticed thin ribbons of smoke wafting through the door.

Grabbing a pot holder, she pulled open the door. Long flames rose from the pan of sweet potatoes and lunged toward her, hungry for the oxygen around her. Sierra let out a scream and put up her arm to block her face from the fire. Her mother appeared instantly and kicked the oven's door shut. It wasn't enough to contain the fire. The flames crawled up the cupboard, where Sierra's mom kept miscellaneous supplies that didn't fit in the pantry. Immediately, the stench of melting plastic filled the air. Sierra realized the arm of her sweater was smoking and pulled it off. She checked the arm of her turtleneck shirt. The flames hadn't gone through the sweater.

"Everyone out!" Sharon Jensen yelled. "We have a fire."

Pandemonium broke loose. Sierra felt her mother pushing her away from the oven and toward the back door.

Howard Jensen appeared in the kitchen and yelled, "Where's the fire extinguisher?"

"In the basement," his wife responded.

Sierra considered going after the extinguisher, but someone was pushing her out the back door. Everyone was talking and yelling at once. As soon as they burst through the door, Brutus leaped from his doghouse and barked and barked.

Wesley was behind Sierra. He seemed to be taking a head count. Some of the family had exited the front door, and two of the younger boys had run around to the back of the house and were excitedly asking, "Is the fire truck going to come?"

"Sierra," Wesley said, "run next door to call the fire department."

"We'll go with you," the two boys said.

Sierra didn't wait for them. She took off running. This all felt vaguely familiar. She had been the one to make the emergency call last spring in California when Christy's uncle Bob had been burned by a fire from an exploding gas barbecue. That experience helped Sierra keep her thoughts clear this time.

Mr. DeVries opened his front door before Sierra even reached his steps. "What's all the noise about?"

"Fire," was her simple explanation as she ran into his kitchen and dialed 911. Taking a deep breath, she calmly relayed the information. The fire trucks arrived in less than five minutes, and the family was ordered to cross the street. Everyone had a different theory on what had happened. Sierra repeated again exactly how she had discovered the fire. She scanned the group and breathed easier when she spotted Granna Mae. Her grandmother looked shaken, but Emma had her arm around the older woman's shoulders.

"It was the marshmallows on top of the sweet potatoes," Aunt Frieda explained to a group of neighbors who came bustling up to the Jensens. "Sharon put the tray back in the oven and set it on broil. She planned to brown those marshmallows for only a minute. Then we forgot and sat down to eat, and my brother had to pray the world's longest Thanksgiving prayer."

"You make it sound as though it was my dad's fault," Dillon said, stepping boldly between Aunt Frieda and the neighbor. "It wasn't his fault. It's an old house, and stuff in it breaks all the time. There was probably something wrong with the oven."

"I don't see any flames," Caleb said. "Can't we go back over there to see if they smashed down the door with their axes?"

"We'll wait until the firefighters tell us we can go back,"

Uncle Jack said. "Or until Howard comes out and waves us back."

Sierra froze. Where was her dad? Had he gone into the basement for the extinguisher? He hadn't gotten caught in the fire, had he? She scanned the growing clump of spectators. Neither her father nor her mother was in the crowd.

five

"WESLEY, WHERE ARE MOM AND DAD?" Sierra tugged on her brother's arm. The rain had begun again, and she shivered in her thin turtleneck. She had left her sweater on the kitchen floor.

"I thought they were here," he said, looking around.

"I haven't seen them," Sierra said. "What if they went down in the basement, and the firefighters don't know they're trapped?"

"Everyone else stay here," Wesley ordered, taking Sierra by the arm and running across the street in the rain.

Just as they reached the other side, a firefighter came out the front door and waved to the family members, indicating they could return.

"Where are my parents?" Sierra asked. "Are they okay?"

"They sure are. Thanks to them your house is okay—or at least most of your house. Your dad used a fire extinguisher to put out the fire. All we did was check for hot spots. Everything is okay. Looks like you folks will still have your Thanksgiving dinner, minus the yams and with a smoked turkey."

Some of the others who arrived in time to hear his comment chuckled, but Sierra thought the guy couldn't have made a worse joke.

Nearly an hour later, the family was ready to gather around the table again. Everyone had wanted to inspect the damage personally. The oven would need to be replaced and the cabinets over the oven rebuilt, but the fire hadn't spread elsewhere, which everyone considered amazing.

The smell was the awful part. Everything was permeated with the stench of smoke. All the windows and doors were open, and the heater ran full blast. Sierra laughed to herself when she looked around the table and noticed a number of relatives wearing their coats. Paul would have felt right at home. She couldn't wait to add a lengthy P.S. to her letter to him.

Howard Jensen prayed again. This time his prayer was a short but humbling one. Everyone agreed with the "Amen" as they realized even more vividly all they had to be thankful for.

The food was passed around with no attempt to warm it. Sharon Jensen had tried to put the food in the microwave in stages, but everyone convinced her it would be fine just the way it was. Howard Jensen carved, and everyone dished up. In shifty-eyed silence, they began to eat, each waiting for the others to say something.

Finally, Sharon Jensen put down her fork and said in a voice choked with tears, "This is awful! It all tastes like smoke." Then she burst out laughing.

The pressure seemed to release for all of them as they laughed, cried, and joked about the food along with Mrs. Jensen. In the end, no one ate much except the olives, which for some reason didn't taste smoky. The entire dinner was sent to the trash cans outside instead of being neatly wrapped and stacked in the refrigerator, supplies for late-night turkey sandwiches.

The only salvageable part of the dinner was the pies. Mrs. Jensen had stored them in a large ice chest in the basement when she ran out of counter space in the kitchen. As she cut the pies, the doorbell rang, and one of the neighbors appeared with a pumpkin pie in her hand.

"We had an extra pie, and I thought maybe it would help, with the fire and everything."

"Thanks," Sharon Jensen said graciously. "We were just about to serve dessert."

Before the pie was served, another neighbor came by. This one delivered a plateful of sliced turkey and two pumpkin pies. Mrs. Jensen thanked her and added the pumpkin pies to the seven already lining the counter.

"Years from now we'll all look back and remember this as the year we ate pumpkin pie and nothing else," she said as Sierra watched her cut the generous slices.

After the feast of pumpkin pies, two whole pies were left. The table was being cleared when the doorbell rang and another neighbor stood there, offering a bowl of leftover stuffing and two pumpkin pies.

"None of us had room for pie," the neighbor stated. "I thought maybe your family could put them to good use."

Sierra heard her dad thank the woman and then deliver the goods to the kitchen counter.

"It seems for every pie we eat, another one shows up," Wes said.

"And to think I knocked myself out making all those

pies yesterday," Mrs. Jensen said, and she burst into another round of laughter and tears.

Even though Sierra had planned to sneak upstairs to write Paul, she decided she should stay to help her mom before she fell apart completely. For almost two hours, she washed everything that was handed to her. The kitchen's entire contents reeked of smoke and needed to be cleaned. All the aunts seemed to enjoy hunting out the smoke-tainted items. They celebrated their discoveries by delivering them to Sierra saying, "Ew! Smell this plate" or "Phew! This candleholder really stinks!" Sierra kept washing, emptying the sink, filling it with more soapy water, and washing some more.

For a while Aunt Emma dried dishes. Then Sierra's mom took over. Wesley came in at the end of the first hour, as if they were part of a tag team. He said there was a request for more coffee from the living room. That got Mrs. Jensen away from the sink long enough for him to pick up a towel and work on the row of glasses Sierra was washing. Aunt Frieda insisted that all the shelves be wiped off before anything could be returned, so the glasses had to wait until she was ready for them. She also took on the task of taking down the curtains to be washed.

Sierra's cousin Molly had been assigned by her mother, Frieda, to wipe down the walls, the top of the refrigerator, and the cupboards. The only problem was that Molly kept dunking her sponge into Sierra's dishwater. Instantly, the water would turn sooty gray. It was driving Sierra crazy. She knew everything needed to be washed off, but why couldn't Molly use the paper towels and spray cleaner as Mrs. Jensen had suggested and Sierra kept reinforcing? Wesley solved the problem by providing Molly with a mixing bowl full of sudsy water and a new sponge.

"I heard you were thinking of bringing a guest home for Thanksgiving," Sierra said to Wesley. "I bet you're glad now you didn't bring her."

"Her?" Wesley said. He shook his head. "I invited a guy from Japan. He had never heard of our American custom of Thanksgiving. But he decided to go with someone who lives in Corvallis rather than be gone all weekend with me. I'm sure he'll be sorry he missed all the excitement here."

"Rats," Sierra said. "I thought for sure you were bringing home a girlfriend."

"Nope, not me."

"No interesting women at school this year?" Sierra asked.

"Plenty of interesting women. Just not the right one."

"What would make her the right one?" Molly asked.

"I have a list," Wes said quietly.

"A real list?" Molly asked. "A written-out list?"

Wes turned to her and nodded. "Don't you?"

"Well, in my head, yeah, but nothing on paper."

"Put it on paper," Wes challenged. "It will help to clarify what you're looking for."

"Like, what do you put down?" Molly was short with round glasses and an upturned nose. She was usually so quiet that Sierra was surprised to hear her quizzing Wes.

"Character and personality qualities, life goals, you know. It's not a physical shopping list: five foot two, eyes of blue, or anything like that."

"Give me an example of one of the things on your list," Molly prodded.

Wesley hesitated. "Well, she has to be a believer and have a growing relationship with the Lord."

"What else?"

Wesley looked at Sierra, and with a teasing smile he said, "I'd like someone who is emotionally healthy. Preferably an emotional virgin."

"A what?" Molly wrinkled up her nose.

"You know, a woman who has been saving her heart for the right guy. Someone who hasn't been falling in and out of love since she was twelve and now, at twenty-three, is a big tangle of broken pieces from her past relationships."

"You're a dreamer," Molly said with a shake of her head. She was a year younger than Sierra but had always acted more mature and serious than her cousin. "No girls like that are left. Especially by the time they're twenty-three."

"Oh, I don't know," Wes said, giving Sierra another grin. "Some seventeen-year-olds have managed to guard their hearts. A guy can always hope a few wise women don't come with a truckload of emotional baggage when they're ready to start a serious relationship."

"What about you?" Aunt Emma said, jumping into the discussion. "Can you honestly say you're emotionally damage-free? I seem to remember a certain young beauty who showed up at Christmas one year when you were in high school."

"I never said *I* was an emotional virgin." Wes turned and leaned against the counter, his hands resting on the tile as if he were bracing himself for the verbal onslaught that was sure to come from this roomful of women.

"Isn't that just like a man?" Aunt Frieda spouted. "They

want the woman to be perfect, but they don't think they have to be."

"I didn't say that," Wesley stated. "It's just my ideal. I do understand reality."

"How could you if you're twenty-three and still carrying around a list of requirements?" Aunt Frieda was the only one in the family who had been through a divorce. She had let everyone know that she had felt unprepared for a realistic marriage because she believed all she had to do was marry someone who said he was a Christian.

For the next ten minutes, Frieda challenged Wesley to adjust his thinking to a more realistic view. She emphasized the Scriptures that said Christians are supposed to love one another and help the weaker ones along. "Not a single verse says we should marry only people who are completely pure because, if you haven't noticed, no one fits that description. We all fail. True love means sticking by the other person in his or her failures and loving that person no matter what."

Wesley didn't argue with that but added, "What about 2 Peter where it says we're to live holy lives?"

"We all fail," Frieda insisted. " 'Holy' means complete, doesn't it? We're made complete when we surrender our lives to Christ. He's the one who makes us 'holy.' It has nothing to do with emotional baggage."

"I think it does," Wes said. "We have choices every day of what we choose to keep in the storehouse of our hearts. All I'm saying is I'd like to meet a woman who has relatively few boxes of explosives in her storehouse."

Molly laughed, which helped break some of the tension that had been building. Sierra had finished the last dish and wanted to get out of there. She felt warm from the dishwater. She also felt a little nervous that Wesley might use her again as an example of someone with a storehouse full of empty boxes. That wasn't true. She had collected a few emotional mementos along the way. She had told Wes about some of them, like Drake and Alex. Wes had never suggested to her that he saw anything emotionally inappropriate in those relationships.

But Wes didn't know much about the box marked "Paul," which now filled the storehouse of Sierra's heart. She thought of Wes as understanding how special that relationship was to her. But in reality, how could he? He hadn't been home for weeks. He probably didn't even know she and Paul were corresponding.

Slipping out of the kitchen and pulling her green backpack off the coat rack in the entryway, Sierra retreated to Granna Mae's room. To her surprise, the bedroom was empty. She pulled out Paul's photo, which was tucked in the bottom of her mound of now untidy clothes. He was still smiling at her, even though he had that tiny slice above his heart.

She stared at the picture for a long time and wished Paul were here right now. They would go for a long walk together, hand in hand. It wouldn't matter that the rain fell on them or that the wet, molding leaves would fly against their legs. They would be together—close together. To Sierra that's all that mattered.

If she couldn't hold Paul's hand, she at least had his picture and his words. And she could give him back her words. In the solitude, Sierra pulled out a piece of notebook paper and wrote at the top:

P.S. This will probably be the longest P.S. you've ever seen. It might even be the longest one in the world. It's been less than twenty-four hours since I wrote you, but you're not going to believe what happened here today.

Sierra twirled the end of the pen across her smiling lips and thought how, in a small, secret way, she was spending time alone with Paul. Even with a house full of company.

SIX

"IS EVERYONE IN?" Sharon Jensen looked over her shoulder from the driver's seat of the family van. All of the passenger seats held Jensen women, seat-belted and ready for an outing that was, in Sierra's opinion, more important to her mom than to anyone else. It was Friday afternoon, the final day of the reunion, and her mom was determined to take all the women to tea in downtown Portland.

Sierra had resisted going. It had been another restless night for everyone, and Sierra wanted to sleep in. She had to work Saturday, and Sunday was filled with church and activities, so this was her only real day of vacation. Even though she had spent little time with her relatives because she kept finding quiet corners to write to Paul, Sierra enjoyed the isolation. She knew she was related to these people, but right now, at this point in her life, she wasn't interested in them.

Granna Mae was in the front passenger seat, and Tawni and Sierra were wedged in the back with Aunt Frieda, who had a wide berth. Frieda was leaning forward, chattering with Aunt Emma in the next seat up. Sierra's teen cousins, Molly and Nicole, were playing a finger yarn game with the seven-year-old twins, Amanda and Kayla.

"Tell me your big news," Sierra said, leaning close to Tawni so no one else could hear. "I didn't get a chance to ask you yesterday."

Tawni had pulled her hair back in a stylish twist. The strands framing Tawni's face tickled Sierra's nose when she leaned close to her sister's ear.

"I've decided to go back to college in January," Tawni announced.

"That's what Paul said you were thinking about."

Tawni looked surprised. "When did Paul talk to you? And how did he know?"

"Jeremy told him, of course. And I haven't talked to Paul. He told me in a letter. We've been writing each other. A lot," she added for emphasis.

Tawni picked up the clue and looked pleasantly surprised. "Jeremy hadn't told me. Are you and Paul e-mail buddies?"

"No."

"No? You write pen-and-paper letters?"

Sierra nodded. The van went over a bump as Mrs. Jensen drove onto the Hawthorne Bridge. The vehicle carried the yakking band of women through the pouring rain toward the heart of the city.

"I'm impressed," Tawni said. "I didn't realize you two were, well, what are you? Dating by mail?"

Sierra smiled. She liked that. "I guess you could call it that."

"How often do you write?"

With a shrug, Sierra said, "I don't know. Every day. Every other day. Sometimes twice a day."

Tawni's blue eyes grew wide. "This is serious, little sister. Why didn't you tell me? Why didn't Jeremy tell me? Do you think Paul has told him?"

"I don't know," Sierra said. She suddenly felt a pinch in her stomach. What if Paul hadn't said anything because he didn't think it was that big a deal? What if their correspondence was only a big deal to her? But how could that be? The guy was composing poetry for her and sitting alone on Friday nights, talking to her on paper. Sierra tried to bolster her confidence. Of course this relationship was as important to Paul as it was to her. He had made that clear plenty of times—hadn't he?

"Maybe you shouldn't say anything to Jeremy," Sierra said cautiously. "I mean, if Paul wants to tell him, brother to brother, I wouldn't want to steal his thunder."

"You mean like Paul stole mine by telling you I'm going to Reno?" Tawni said.

"What do you mean, going to Reno? I thought you said you were going back to school."

"I am. At the University of Nevada, Reno." Tawni looked like a woman whose mind and will were set in stone.

"Why Reno? What about Jeremy? Why don't you go to school in San Diego, where you live? I mean, what about all your modeling opportunities? Who do you know in Reno, of all places?"

"No one yet," Tawni said with a sly edge to her voice.

"I don't get it," Sierra said. "Is Jeremy transferring there?"

"No. He has only one semester left. He graduates next

June, just like Wes. Jeremy figures he can live through his final semester without me. He even thinks his grades might improve."

"Do Mom and Dad know about this?"

"Not yet. I'm keeping it a secret until I receive the acceptance papers. There have been some small problems with my transcripts."

"I still don't get why you would go to a university where you don't know anyone and you're out of state so you'll have to pay more."

Tawni just smiled. "Maybe and maybe not."

Before Sierra could extract any more information from her sister, Mrs. Jensen pulled the van into a parking space and turned off the engine. "I have several umbrellas here," she said, offering the Portland essential gear to everyone.

Sierra looked out, and the first shop window she saw had the words "Carla's Café" printed in gold letters under the scalloped, striped awning. She smiled and nudged Tawni. "Did you know we were going to Carla's? This is the place you brought Paul and me that night before he left for Scotland."

"We're not going there," Tawni said. "Mom found another place around the corner. It's an old hotel that serves high tea in a separate parlor. Didn't you hear her talking about it this morning? The parlor still has a lot of the original furniture from when the hotel opened for business in the late 1800s."

"I guess I didn't hear her," Sierra said, scooting across the seat. She stepped onto the sidewalk with the happy, chattering women and cast a melancholy gaze at the front window of the café. Someday she hoped Paul and she could return to sit by the front window. Their conversation would be different now. Paul wouldn't have to ask if she had a crush on him. He would know, as she knew, that what they had was much more than a childish crush.

"Sierra," Tawni called, "are you coming with us?"

The others had already scurried down the street and disappeared around the corner. Sierra stood alone in front of Carla's with the rain dampening her hair. She didn't mind. She had gotten much wetter than this one day last February when she was walking home with a big bouquet of daffodils as a gift for Granna Mae. She was soaked then, and Paul had seen her while driving by with his friends. That's when he had started calling her the Daffodil Queen.

"I'm coming," Sierra said, still lost in her dreamworld and not caring at all about sitting around with a bunch of relatives for a tea party. She would much rather go inside Carla's and sit in the chair she had sat in last time and imagine Paul sitting across from her. She could dream up all the things they would talk about and the way he would reach across the table to take her hand. He would squeeze it gently and smile in a way that would say, "I'm so happy we're finally together, Sierra."

She sighed as she rounded the corner, with Tawni three steps ahead, holding her umbrella close to the top of her head to protect her perfect hairdo. Mrs. Jensen had asked that Sierra dress up, and she had managed to put together an outfit consisting of a long skirt, a pair of warm socks, and her dad's old cowboy boots. Her long, wheat-colored sweater hung over the brown and cream straight skirt. She was keenly aware that her outfit wasn't dressy and stylish like Tawni's. But Sierra felt like Sierra: comfortable, unpretentious, original.

Now, if she could only convince Aunt Frieda to stop giving her disapproving looks, she would be fine. Fine enough to almost enjoy this tea party—for her mother's sake, if nothing else.

The parlor of the old hotel was charming. The women were seated in groups of four at several small, round tables that were arranged on the same side of the room as a baby grand piano. When they entered and took their seats, the pianist played Beethoven's "For Elise," which had always been one of Sierra's favorites. She sat next to Granna Mae, and the twins took the other two chairs.

A waiter appeared wearing a white shirt and black vest, with a towel over his arm. He explained the delicacies that were being served that afternoon and went through the list of available teas. Sierra ordered an Oregon specialty tea, marionberry. It came in a china pot with a silver strainer, since it was leaf tea and not in a bag. The twins loved all the attention given to dainty details: the decorated sugar cubes, the tiny silver creamers, and the cucumber sandwiches cut in star and heart shapes. The hotel even served pumpkin pie in cube-sized squares with dots of thick whipped cream on top.

"I don't want my pumpkin squares," Amanda said. "I'm kind of tired of pumpkin pie."

"Me, too," Kayla said.

"That's okay," Sierra assured them. "You don't have to eat the pumpkin pie if you don't want to. I'm kind of pumpkin-pied-out myself." She knew she wasn't the only one who had eaten a slice of cold pie that morning. Wesley had joined her, and so had their dad.

Granna Mae participated warmly, acknowledging when she was spoken to, but not always having an answer. Sierra could tell this was one of those times when Granna Mae's mind was beginning to slip through the fragile fingers of reality and slide into a world of confusion.

"This cranberry nut bread is very good," Sierra said to her. "Do you like it?"

Granna Mae smiled politely as if she had no idea who Sierra was or why she was talking to Granna Mae. She ate, which Sierra considered a good thing because when she had brought breakfast up to her grandmother that morning, she had only nibbled on the toast. Sierra now poured some English Breakfast blend through the strainer into Granna Mae's cup.

"More sugar for you?" Sierra asked, looking for some kind of response, any kind of response.

"Can I do it?" Amanda asked. She turned to Granna Mae and said, "One lump or two?"

It was obvious the twins would long remember this experience, and Sierra almost felt glad she had come along to play "little girl" again.

"One, please," Granna Mae responded to Amanda, stirring the tea in her cup with a fairly steady hand.

The girls grew restless before the older women did, and Sierra offered to take them to the hotel gift shop. They left Granna Mae with Mrs. Jensen and Tawni and off they went, Sierra in her rather un-tea-partyish outfit, and her twin cousins in their pretty party dresses, with starched bows in their hair. The girls each took one of Sierra's hands and nearly skipped with joy at the special attention they were getting.

"When I grow up, I'm going to dress just like you," Amanda said. "You're cool, Sierra."

"I want to be just like you, too," Kayla agreed. "I want to go to Europe like you do all the time, too."

"I don't go all the time," Sierra said.

"My mom said you did. She said you went twice this year because you're a free spirit."

"Kayla," Amanda scolded, "you make it sound like a bad thing."

"No, I don't. Mom said she was a free spirit, too, before she married."

"Aunt Emma said that?" Sierra asked as they entered the gift shop.

"Yes," both girls answered in unison.

Sierra smiled. "You have a very cool mother, you know."

Kayla shrugged. "I guess. But not as cool as you."

Sierra and her little fan club began to poke around in the charming gift shop. One antique table was covered with a collection of teapots and other tea goodies from England. A red plaid tin of Scottish shortbread caught Sierra's eye, and she was glad she had stuck a twenty-dollar bill in her boot. It served as her purse when she didn't feel like carrying her backpack. She thought about buying some shortbread cookies to eat while she sipped a cup of tea and wrote her next letter to Paul.

She had finished the long letter with the even longer P.S., which she had added to several times, and had slapped two airmail stamps on it because it was so thick. Even now it sat in the mailbox waiting for the postal worker to pick it up.

"Look at these sewing kits," Kayla said, lifting a needle-point kit up to Sierra. It came from a basket at Sierra's feet where dozens of small stitching kits were marked half off.

"That's nice," Sierra said, only glancing at the Scottish

crest that said "MacIver" across the top of the package. "Do you like to embroider?"

"I do," Kayla said. "Amanda doesn't. But this is ugly. They should have flowers or something."

Sierra glanced at the package again and saw what Kayla meant. The MacIver clan crest was a circle with a boar's head in the middle. She made a face at Kayla and said, "Yikes! Who would want to embroider that?"

Returning her attention to the lovely china cups, cookie tins, and small silver teaspoons, Sierra noticed a tin of Scottish Breakfast tea. She knew that would be the perfect tea to go with her shortbread. Collecting her private tea-party fixings, Sierra shuffled toward the register. But then the MacIver crest floated through her thoughts, and she suddenly turned around.

"Kayla, did they have any other Scottish clan crests in that basket of needlepoint kits?"

Kayla nodded, and Sierra dove into the basket, a woman on a mission. If she could find Paul Mackenzie's family crest, she would have her problem solved of what to buy him for Christmas. She could embroider the crest and frame it for him. Paul would love it. As long as it wasn't something disgusting like a boar's head.

seven

SIERRA FILED THROUGH THE BASKET of needlepoint kits, searching for "Mackenzie." She found one at the back of the basket. Drawing it close, she studied the crest. It was a mountain with three pillars of flames rising from it. For a fleeting moment she thought it looked like the flaming sweet potatoes and marshmallows she had battled in the oven yesterday. The Latin words surrounding the mountain were *"Lucero non uro."*

"I wonder what that means," Sierra muttered as she triumphantly rose with the prize in her hand. She had enough money for the needlepoint, cookies, and tea, but her change back was only seven cents. "Good thing we don't have any sales tax in Oregon," she said to Kayla and Amanda. "Otherwise I would have had to borrow some money from you."

"Why did you buy that? Are you going to sew it?" Amanda asked.

"Yes. It's going to be a gift for someone who is very special to me. And this is that person's last name." She pulled the kit from the bag. "Mackenzie." Sierra loved the way the name rolled off her tongue.

"What's that supposed to be?" Amanda asked, pointing to the crest.

"A mountain on fire, I guess," Sierra said. She gave Kayla and Amanda a big smile. "It's a whole lot better than a pig's head, don't you think?"

They laughed. Sierra enjoyed her little cousins.

"Do you think the moms are ready to go yet?" she asked.

"Not our mom. She's always the last one to leave anywhere. There's always just one more person she wants to talk to," Kayla said.

"That's how it is with us free spirits," Sierra replied. "We always have one more person we want to talk to."

The only person Sierra wanted to talk to at the moment was Paul. She wished she could prepare a proper tea party for him with her shortbread and Scottish Breakfast tea. The thought stayed with her and formulated into a plan.

As the group of Jensen women scurried to the van through the rain-drenched streets, Sierra's plan came together. For Christmas she could send Paul a tea party in a box. All he would have to do is open each of the little wrapped boxes in order, according to the number on them. First the tea, but not Scottish or British tea. She would buy some Oregon marionberry tea or maybe some Coffee People coffee beans, which were big in Oregon. She would write out instructions for him to start the coffee or tea while he opened the other gifts. Then he would unwrap the goodies. They should be from the Northwest. Maybe some smoked salmon or honey biscuits with blackberry jam.

The more Sierra mulled her plan over, the more excited she grew. This could be fun. She would include a long letter in the box, of course, and the finished clan crest—and what else? Maybe a picture of her. Yes! That would be perfect. A little window for Paul to look into her world and watch her face as he read her words.

"Are you even listening to me?" Tawni said, poking Sierra's arm as they sat squeezed together in the back of the van.

"What did you say?"

"I asked what you bought in the gift shop."

"Oh. I bought some tea and cookies." For some reason she hesitated to tell Tawni about the Mackenzie needle-point. Would she think it was a silly idea? Jeremy was obviously a Mackenzie, too. Would Tawni wish she had gotten one for Jeremy? There was only this one Mackenzie kit in the store.

"Is that all?"

"Well, I also bought something you might think is dumb, so if you do, don't say anything, okay?"

"Why would I say anything?"

"Just don't, okay?"

"Okay."

Sierra pulled the kit from the bag and showed it to her sister with no explanation.

"You're going to sew that?"

"Sure. It can't be too hard. Don't you think it will make a great Christmas present for Paul?"

"You're going to finish that by Christmas?"

"Yes," Sierra said defensively. "It's not very big."

"Yes, but look at all those tiny stitches. Don't they call that petit point? I'd never have the patience to attempt something like that."

At least I don't have to worry that Tawni will want to steal my gift idea, Sierra thought.

"Well, have fun," Tawni said flatly. "If you don't finish it before Christmas, you could always send him a framed picture of yourself."

"I was thinking of doing that, too," Sierra said. She wondered if her mom had told Tawni that Paul had sent her a picture for her birthday.

"That's what I'm giving Jeremy. I have some good shots from one of the photographers, and I thought I'd have several framed while I'm here. I'll give Jeremy the best one and send one to Mom and Dad."

Sierra considered Tawni's giving away professional model shots different from her own idea of taking a picture in the backyard. She wanted to send a little window to Paul, not plaster a billboard across his room.

She noticed the writing on the back of the stitchery kit and held it close to read the fine print. "Listen to this," she said, reading aloud to Tawni. "'The Mackenzie clan claims to be descended from Colin, progenitor of the Earl of Ross. He died in 1278 and was succeeded by his son Kenneth.'"

"In 1278?" Tawni questioned.

"That's what it says."

"How amazing that anyone could trace his history back that far. Or at least people whom he knows he is descended from." Tawni let out a noticeable sigh.

Sierra decided to let it go. Every now and then Tawni would become depressed over being adopted and not knowing where she came from genetically. A few months ago, Tawni had tracked down her birth mother and had written her a letter. Tawni hadn't heard anything back. Even though Tawni had said she felt the important point was that she had written the letter, Sierra could tell at this moment that Tawni felt discouraged. Sierra decided to plunge ahead and read the rest of the Mackenzie history.

"The clan crest is a mountain inflamed with the motto 'Lucero non uro,' which is translated, 'I shine, not burn.' Mackenzie also uses the crest badge of a stag's head and the motto 'Cuidich 'n righ,' which is translated, 'Help the king.' The Gaelic name is 'MacCoinnich.'"

"Sierra," Tawni snapped, "I get the point. Mackenzie is a Scottish name. All right. Why are you obsessing over this?"

"I'm not. I just thought you would be interested in the history of Jeremy's family."

"That's only on his father's side," Tawni said. "He's part whatever his mother is, you know. And so is Paul. There's such a dilution of nationalities over the years that nobody can really say they're completely French or Scottish or whatever."

Tawni's words were so sharp that Sierra decided to slip the needlepoint kit back into the bag and change the subject. All she could figure was that if Tawni couldn't identify her birth heritage, then no one else should be able to.

But Tawni's lack of support didn't diminish Sierra's enthusiasm in starting on the project as soon as they reached home. She went up to Granna Mae's room, where her grandmother was lying down. Sierra curled up in the chair by the window, and as the raindrops pattered against the pane, she quietly hummed and began her project. She had never done anything like this before. But she could read directions, and she could thread a needle. Everything was included in the kit. How hard could this be?

The next day, Saturday, at work, Sierra pulled out her needlepoint during her afternoon break. She was determined to get a lot done because the night before she had been persuaded by her parents to participate in the hour-long good-bye to their holiday guests, and after that the massive cleanup began. She didn't crawl into bed until after eleven, but at least it was in her own bed, and her room was the cleanest it had been in months, thanks to Tawni's diligent assistance.

Sierra worked at Mama Bear's Bakery, known for its cinnamon rolls. When the weather was cold and rainy, as it had been lately, Mama Bear's was packed with customers seeking comfort in a steaming cup of espresso and a warm, gooey cinnamon roll. Since the place was filled with customers this Saturday, Sierra's break was shorter than usual. The owner, Mrs. Kraus, frantically asked Sierra to bring more coffee beans out of the storage room. The needlepoint project was stuffed into her backpack.

Sierra didn't pull it out again until that night. Removing herself from the rest of the family, she hid in her room, trying to line up the tiny stitches. On the way home from work, she had bought a new frame to get the right size glass to replace the broken glass in Paul's picture. She also had bought some wrapping paper and a roll of film. If the rain cleared tomorrow after church, Sierra planned to find someone to take pictures of her.

But the rain continued. Mr. Jensen took everyone out

for lunch after the service. Sierra was starving, having eaten only a slice of pumpkin pie for breakfast as they ran out the door for church. Gavin and Wesley had done the same thing. The family was down to only one pumpkin pie.

Sierra ate her lunch quickly and then sat there, wishing she could get back to her needlepoint. She decided she needed to always carry it with her. That way she could work on it at times like this, while everyone else sat around the table talking. Actually, she found it pleasant to be back to just the immediate family of her mom and dad, Wes, Tawni, Sierra, Gavin, Dillon, and Granna Mae. A crowd still, but a comfortable, familiar crowd.

Mrs. Jensen was saying something about the family's going skiing during Christmas vacation or maybe during a long weekend in January.

"If we went in January, we could go to Tahoe," Sierra suggested. "That way we would have a free place to stay with Tawni in Reno."

"In Reno?" her mom said. "Why would Tawni be in Reno?"

All eyes went to Tawni, who was giving Sierra a furious, icy stare. Sierra suddenly remembered that Tawni had said she was waiting to tell her parents about her plans.

Sierra pursed her lips together and reached her hand across the table to touch her sister's arm. "I'm sorry. I forgot."

Tawni still looked mad.

"You heard from Lina?" Mrs. Jensen said slowly to Tawni.

Then it all became clear to Sierra. Tawni's birth mother, Lina Rasmussen, lived in Reno. She was a professor at the university. That was all Tawni knew about her.

"No," Tawni said quietly, drawing in a deep breath through her flared nostrils.

Mr. Jensen leaned in, next to his wife. His skin began to wrinkle between his eyebrows. "Do you want to talk about this, honey?"

Tawni looked away for a moment and then turned back, taking them all in with her composed gaze. She almost seemed to have switched to a different face, one that was ready for the camera.

"There's not much to talk about," Tawni said. "I've applied to go to school in January at the University of Nevada, Reno. I haven't been accepted yet, so I wasn't going to say anything until it was official."

"This is a surprise," her dad said. "I'd feel more comfortable with these kinds of big decisions if you would talk to your mother and me first."

"There wasn't anything to talk about."

"Don't do that," Wesley said, jumping in with his big-brother voice. "Don't pull away, Tawni. We all know you're going through this thing about your birth mom, and we've supported your searching for her and contacting her. But if you haven't heard from her and you're thinking of just showing up on her doorstep, or worse, enrolling in one of her classes, I think that's a pretty big deal, and you should talk with us about it."

Tawni looked shocked. "Is that what you think? You think I'm going to UNR to stalk Lina or something? I'm going because they have the kinds of courses I'm interested in. I can't believe you guys are all against me on this."

The tension was thick around the table, and Sierra felt it was her fault.

Then the waitress appeared with a smile and said, "Did anyone leave room for pumpkin pie?"

"No!" they all answered in sharp unison.

eight

SIERRA FELT MISERABLE. She knew Tawni had been invited to have Thanksgiving with Jeremy's family in San Diego, but she had chosen to come to Portland because all the family was gathering and her parents had paid for her flight home. Sierra wondered now if her sister wished she had gone to Jeremy's instead, or at least had coaxed Jeremy to come home with her and support her in this Reno decision.

After lunch, Tawni had to catch her flight back to San Diego. The whole family was in the van when they dropped Tawni off at Portland International Airport. Tawni politely and sweetly said good-bye to each of them with the expected hug. But a chill was in the air instead of the warmth with which Tawni had greeted them a few days before.

"I'm sorry," Sierra whispered again as they hugged. "Please forgive me." Sierra had tried to remember if Tawni had specifically told Sierra not to say anything or if it had only been implied. It didn't matter. Tawni was mad. It would take a while for her to melt.

"I forgive you." Tawni said the words, but they stung as

much as if she had said, "You're such a brat." Their relationship hadn't been this awful for years.

When Sierra reached home, Vicki called and said a bunch of Sierra's friends were going out that night. Sierra would have loved to get out of the house, away from family, and be with her friends for a few hours. But she had made a commitment to help out that night at the Highland House with its new teen hotline. She knew she couldn't cancel, so she told Vicki she couldn't go. Immediately, she began to feel sorry for herself. Randy, Vicki, and the rest of her friends were going to have one last blast of fun before returning to school, while Sierra was going to be responsible and do her duty. It was a bitter pill to swallow.

Her only consolation was that maybe the phones wouldn't ring much, and she could spend the time working on her needlepoint. To add to her unhappiness, she was concerned that the day was nearly gone, and she hadn't gotten any pictures taken. She needed to start on that project right away. Maybe tomorrow.

Only a few people were at the Highland House when she arrived. Parking in back, she hurried to the office. The director, Uncle Mac, was there with a college-age girl, and they both were on the phones when Sierra walked in. Uncle Mac waved and motioned for her to go to the third phone, which was located in a small cubicle against the wall. The Highland House had started this outreach a few months earlier, and their facilities and resources were limited. That's why Sierra wanted to help. With her work and school schedule, she didn't have much time to volunteer, and this hotline program seemed to be the best way to contribute to the Highland House's work.

Taking off her jacket and settling into the cubicle, Sierra put her Bible, her notes from the training course, and her needlepoint on the table in front of her. She had just threaded the needle when the phone rang. Glancing out of the cubicle, she saw Uncle Mac motion for her to pick it up, since he was still on a call, as was the other girl. Sierra reached for the phone on the second ring.

"Highland House Teen Hotline," she answered. "This is Sierra."

Her heart began to race. Even after all the training she had received on how to respond to the calls that came into this homeless shelter, she felt uneasy about how this, her first call, would go.

"I read one of your brochures," said the female voice on the other end of the line. "The one on purity."

"Yes?" Sierra was familiar with the brochure. It explained the health reasons for abstinence and included some verses from the Bible about purity.

"Well, I have a question."

From the girl's voice, Sierra guessed she was around Sierra's age or younger. That was the strength of the teen hotline program, according to Uncle Mac. Teens were more willing to talk to another teen than to an adult when it came to certain problems.

"I was wondering," the girl said slowly. "I mean, I agree with what this brochure says about being pure and saving yourself for marriage and everything, but what if..." Her voice faltered. Sierra thought the girl was crying.

"Yes?" Sierra prodded gently.

"What if you're not pure? What if…" The voice broke into a sob.

"It's okay," Sierra said. She flipped through her training notes until she found the paper marked "Purity."

"What if," the girl asked, "you want to be like that—pure, I mean—but it's already too late?"

"I understand," Sierra said. "It's okay."

"I can only stay on the phone for a few more minutes," the girl said. "Is there anything you can tell me?"

Sierra drew in a breath of courage. "There is a way to start over. God made a way for all of us to start fresh with Him and with others. In I John 1:9, the Bible says that 'if we confess our sins, He is faithful and righteous to forgive us our sins and to cleanse us from all unrighteousness.'"

Sierra looked up from her notes and tried to make her answer to this caller sound more natural. "What that means is that all we have to do is admit to God that we messed up. Once we tell Him we need Him and ask Him to forgive us, He makes us clean. We have a fresh start."

The caller didn't say anything. Sierra looked up at the wall and glanced at the sign over the bulletin board. "At the Highland House," she said to the caller in as gentle a voice as possible, "our motto is, 'A safe place for a fresh start,' and that's exactly what Jesus is willing to offer you. A fresh start on the inside."

Then speaking almost as rapidly as she felt her heart was beating, Sierra finished with, "What I'd like to encourage you to do is first make a commitment to the Lord and fully surrender yourself to Him. Then make a commitment to yourself and to your future husband. Promise that the next time you have sex will be after you're married. Don't settle for less than God's best for you."

There was silence on the other end. For a moment Sierra worried that the caller had hung up and that all her advice had evaporated into thin air.

"Do you really believe all that?" the caller asked.

"Yes, of course," Sierra answered quickly.

"I mean, did you just read that, or do you really agree with what you said?"

"I believe it," Sierra said firmly. "I agree with it because everything God says is true. If He promises to make us clean when we come to Him asking for forgiveness, then that's what He does. It's based on His promises and His Word. Not on what we feel."

"Well, I have to go," the caller said. "Thanks. I need some time to think about what you said."

"Call any time."

A click sounded on the other end, and Sierra's heart sank. She would have felt so much better if the caller had said, "Oh, thank you so much! That's exactly what I needed to hear. I'm going to pray right now, and I know everything will be better." Instead, the click of the line going dead echoed in Sierra's ear.

Two hours later, when her shift ended, she talked to Uncle Mac about how she felt. The next six calls had gone about the same.

"The first call I took was the hardest, though," Sierra said. "It made me feel as though I didn't know what I was doing. I mean, I have the answers here and here," Sierra said, pointing to her head and to the notebook in front of her. "And I believe them here." She patted her heart. "But it has to be hard to see things clearly when you're caught in the middle of a situation."

Uncle Mac nodded. "It is hard. We're complex human beings. It's not just our minds or our bodies that direct us. We have complicated emotions and that blessed and cursed free will God gave us. We choose every day, all day long, what we want to do."

"I know, but what if someone didn't choose for herself? What about the first caller I had? All she said was that she wasn't pure like the Highland House brochure described. What if that hadn't been her choice? I mean, what if she had been, you know, raped? I was going through the information on asking forgiveness, but what if it wasn't her choice that she wasn't a virgin anymore?"

Uncle Mac nodded knowingly. "First she needs to know she didn't do anything wrong. Did you give her the 800 number in the back of the manual for the sexual abuse counseling service?"

Sierra bit her lower lip and shook her head. "I forgot."

"You'll remember next time. It takes a while to become familiar with all the material and remember what to say in each situation. There's no sense worrying about it now. Trust that God used your willing heart as you talked to her and pray that He'll lead her to the next step."

With a sigh, Sierra said, "This is a lot harder than I thought it was going to be. Each situation is different, isn't it?"

"Yes, and each person is different. That's how God sees us: unique and wonderfully made. He works in each heart and life in a different way. The only sure direction, the only true answer to any problem, is to come to God and turn everything over to Him."

Uncle Mac gave Sierra a few more pointers and thanked her for volunteering her time. As she gathered up her things to leave, the Mackenzie-crest needlework slid off the table. Uncle Mac picked it up.

"'*Lucero non uro*,'" he said in surprise "That's my family crest. Do you know what our motto means?"

"I think it's 'I shine, not burn.'"

"Exactly," Uncle Mac said, looking impressed. He paused and then said with a smile, "Do you mind if I ask who this is for?"

"It's for Paul." Sierra felt a little awkward. Did Uncle Mac have any idea Sierra was dating his nephew through the mail?

"Really." It was a statement, not a question. He looked as if he were processing the information, trying to decide what he thought of this connection between the two of them. A gentle grin came across his face. "For any special occasion?"

"For Christmas," Sierra said, carefully putting the needlework in her backpack. "If I get it done, that is. It's taking a lot longer than I thought."

"Ah, but therein lies the value," Uncle Mac said, walking her to her car. "All things that hold lasting value in our lives take a long time to work on. Even relationships. Especially relationships."

As Uncle Mac opened her door, Sierra knew he was trying to convey some message to her. She wanted to tell him this relationship wasn't one-sided. Paul wrote to her all the time, and he was as committed to their relationship as she was. But that kind of validation probably needed to come from Paul, not from Sierra. She decided not to say anything in her own defense. Instead, she would mention it to Paul and let him enlighten his own uncle.

Just before Uncle Mac shut Sierra's car door, he smiled at her and said, "Thanks for your help tonight. You did fine. If I could give you any words of wisdom, I'd encourage you to think of 1 Corinthians 13."

"The love chapter?" Sierra asked. She had expected him to say, "Go home and read your counseling manual again so you'll be better prepared."

"Yes, the love chapter. What's the first characteristic listed?"

Sierra thought quickly. "'Love is patient'?"

"Exactly. 'Love is patient.' There, that's my word of wisdom for you." He closed her door and waved.

Sierra drove the short distance home trying to decipher Uncle Mac's message. Was he saying she needed to be patient with herself as she learned how to do this counseling? That she needed to be patient with the people who called in? Or was he trying to protect his nephew by telling her that if she truly loved Paul she would be patient?

"'Love is patient,'" Sierra repeated aloud as she parked the car in front of her house. "I can be patient."

nine

"HOW WAS YOUR WEEKEND?" Randy asked Sierra on Monday morning. He leaned against her locker, greeting her with his usual cheerfulness and crooked grin.

"Well, let's see," Sierra said. "Our house caught on fire on Thanksgiving Day, my sister is mad at me, and last night on the Highland House hotline, I think I did permanent damage to every single person I talked to. I guess it was a good weekend. How was yours?"

"Your house caught on fire?" Randy said, extracting the crisis that most intrigued him.

"While my dad was praying, the marshmallows on top of the sweet potatoes caught on fire and ruined the oven and the cabinets above it. The house still smells awful. We're supposed to get the new oven tomorrow."

"Did the fire engine come?"

"Yes, the fire engine came."

"Cool."

Sierra shook her head at her take-everything-in-stride buddy. "It was not my favorite Thanksgiving. How was yours?"

"Boring compared with yours."

"Hey, I heard from Vicki that your band is going to play at The Beet next Friday. That's great, Randy!"

He nodded, not appearing overly impressed with his own success. The Beet was a nightclub for teens in downtown Portland that offered music and nonalcoholic beverages on the weekends. Randy and his band had been together for only few months, but they had worked long, hard hours to get their sound just right. A gig at The Beet represented a breakthrough.

"Now here's the big question," Sierra said, slamming her locker shut as the bell rang. "What are you guys going to call yourselves?"

"We've narrowed it down," Randy said. "It's either The Smarties or The Slaymeyets."

"Where did that one come from?"

"The book of Job where he says, 'Though he slay me, yet will I hope in him.' Get it? Slay-me-yet."

"It sounds like Slimey-ettes."

"I know. That's the problem."

"So you have to come up with a name by Friday."

"Basically, yeah."

Sierra and Randy entered their first-period class. He put his arm around her and gave her shoulder a friendly squeeze. "All suggestions from friends will be cheerfully considered."

Sierra laughed. "Okay. I'll get serious about thinking up a name for you guys now that you're practically employed and everything. They are going to pay you for Friday night, aren't they?"

Randy shrugged. "We didn't ask."

As Sierra slid into her seat, a few possible names came to mind. For fun she jotted them down, just to see if they sparked other thoughts.

By lunchtime Sierra's list contained seventeen names. She read them off to her friends, who had gathered at Lotsa Tacos for a quick, off-campus lunch.

"How about The Moths?" Tre asked out of the blue as Sierra went down her list. Tre was from Cambodia, and Sierra often wondered what he thought when his friends became loud and rowdy, since his nature was to be reserved.

"That doesn't give a pretty image," Vicki said. She sipped her diet soda and scrunched up her petite nose. Vicki was gorgeous, in Sierra's opinion. As a matter of fact, Vicki was everything Sierra thought she was not. Vicki's green eyes and silky brown hair complemented her delicate features and smooth skin. Whenever Sierra looked at Vicki, Sierra wished she didn't have freckles and that a swish of a mascara wand would do to her eyes what it did to Vicki's. Paul had said when he first met Sierra that he liked her not wearing makeup.

The whisper of a memory of Paul made Sierra swallow. She wondered if anyone noticed the way a smile crept up her face and refused to leave. She wished Paul were here now, with her buddies. He would like them. He would have great comments to make. He might even have the perfect name for the group on the tip of his tongue.

"The Moths," Randy repeated, trying to decide if he liked it. "Maybe. You know, moths are drawn to light, and we're drawn to God's light."

"Yeah, but moths flock to the lightbulb and then get

fried," Vicki pointed out. "Not a real spiritual image there. How about the Lightbulbs? You know, like when a cartoon character gets a good idea and a lightbulb appears over his head? You could have a cute logo."

"That's what we need," said Warner with a huff. "A cute logo." He was the band's very tall bass player and Sierra's least favorite member of the group. Warner was always putting his arm around Sierra, and she couldn't get him to understand that she didn't like it. She appreciated it when Randy put his arm around her because they were buddies. But when Warner did it, he seemed to place so much weight on her that she felt smothered. Plus he would never let go on his own. He kept his arm around her as if he hoped people would think they were together.

"You know, we could abbreviate it," Randy suggested. "What do you think of The LB's?"

"It makes me think of boarding school in Peru," Margo said. She was a missionary kid who had started at Royal Academy a few months ago, when her family had come home on furlough. She had been hanging around with their gang for several weeks. "When we did reports for Bible class, they used to say, 'Make sure to make a note if you use the LB.'"

"What's that?" Tre asked.

"The Living Bible. It's a modern paraphrase of the Bible, and we had tons of them in the library at school," Margo said.

"I like The LB's," Vicki said.

"Could have double meaning," Sierra suggested. "You know that old saying about how we're the only Bible some people may ever read, so we're like walking, living, breathing Bibles."

"And lights," Randy added. "We're supposed to be lights in the darkness. That's our band's purpose. I like the name. What do you guys think?"

Tre nodded. Warner gave a stoop-shouldered shrug.

"I think it's great!" Vicki said.

Margo glanced at her watch. "I think we'd better get back, or we'll be late again and end up sitting around in detention on Friday."

"You didn't say what you thought of the name The LB's," Warner said to Sierra as they left Lotsa Tacos. He plopped his thick arm across her shoulder, and she felt the same weight inside that she felt across her back.

Grabbing his wrist and removing his arm, Sierra said, "I like the name. I don't like it when you lean on me like that."

Warner looked surprised. Sierra didn't think he should be, since she had told him the same thing before. This time she wanted to make sure he got the message.

"Look, Warner, I mean it when I say I don't want you to put your arm around me anymore. Okay?"

"I'm just being friendly," he said defensively.

The others climbed inside Vicki's car. But Sierra wasn't through making her point.

"It doesn't feel friendly to me. It feels uncomfortable, and I don't want you to do it. Okay? Just don't put your arm around me anymore. Got it?"

Warner shrugged his agreement. He folded his tall frame into the front seat of Vicki's car. Sierra climbed into the back with Margo. No one spoke as they drove the few blocks back to school.

Just before they pulled into the school parking lot, Warner turned around and said, "Do you have a boyfriend, Sierra?"

Without hesitating, she said, "Yes, as a matter of fact, I do."

Vicki stared at her with large eyes, as if she thought Sierra were telling a lie.

"He's in Scotland right now," Sierra filled in for Vicki's benefit as well as Margo's and Warner's. "His name is Paul. Why do you ask?"

Appearing satisfied with her answer, Warner said, "I thought something was going on this past month. You haven't come to watch us practice or hang out with Randy the way you used to. Since you weren't interested in Randy, I thought maybe the rest of us losers might have a chance getting you to notice us."

His comment produced a more sympathetic response from Margo than from Vicki or Sierra. "You're not a loser, Warner. Don't talk like that," Margo said.

Vicki parked the car and walked close to Sierra while Warner and Margo took their time.

"Would I be correct in assuming a few things are going on in your life that I haven't heard about?" Vicki said in a low voice.

"You mean about Paul?"

"Of course about Paul. Or did you just say that to get Warner to leave you alone? Because if you did, I wouldn't blame you. He kept following me around last year and drove me crazy."

Vicki and Sierra had to part ways to go to their separate

classes. They were already late, so Vicki added, "Wait for me here after class."

Sierra did wait afterward, but when Vicki didn't show up after a few minutes, Sierra hurried to her next class. One tardy a day was more than enough. The pair didn't catch up with each other until after school in the parking lot.

"Do you want to go shopping with me?" Sierra asked. "I need to run by Wrinkle in Time to look for something to wear for my picture for Paul."

"Is this the picture I'm supposed to take of you when the rain stops?" Vicki asked.

Sierra nodded.

Vicki looked up at the billowy clouds that seemed to herald clear skies. "We could take it today."

"I couldn't find anything to wear, so I thought if I could buy something at Wrinkle in Time, I'd feel a lot better about the picture."

"I have time," Vicki said. "Do you want to drive or should I? I have to be home by five."

"Let's take both cars."

"On one condition," Vicki said. "When we get there, you have to tell me absolutely everything about Paul. Every single detail that I somehow was not informed of, like, for instance, when you two actually became a couple."

Sierra nodded. She had a twenty-minute drive alone in which to find a way to explain her relationship with Paul to Vicki. That wouldn't be so hard if only she knew how to define it herself. Was he truly her boyfriend? What if he were still living in Portland? Yes, she was certain they would be dating. Wasn't it the same now even though the miles separated them?

376 ❦ Robin Jones Gunn

Sierra coaxed her unreliable car out of the school parking lot and into the three o'clock flow of traffic with Vicki right behind her.

Yes, she convinced herself, it was the same. Paul was her boyfriend.

ten

SIERRA AND VICKI ARRIVED at the small vintage clothing shop at the same time. As soon as Vicki exited her car, she began to pepper Sierra with questions about Paul.

Sierra heard herself say, "We're dating by mail. We write each other almost every day. I just sent him a four-page letter."

Vicki looked delighted. "I knew he sent you a picture for your birthday, but I had no idea you two were this far along in your relationship. It's great, Sierra. You know I think he's wonderful, handsome, and even a little mysterious."

Vicki had met Paul at the Highland House last spring. At that time, Sierra thought Vicki was interested in him. But as far as Sierra could tell, Paul had never showered Vicki with the kind of attention she was after. Sierra was surprised, since Vicki was the center of attention in most of the circles in which she orbited. Now Sierra was glad Vicki knew Paul and thought he was wonderful. Sierra felt it confirmed that she hadn't made all this up.

"Now can I tell you something?" Vicki said.

"Of course." Sierra felt a little shiver of concern that Vicki was going to say she had a secret crush on Paul and was jealous of Sierra. That's what had happened in the spring between Sierra and Amy, who had been Sierra's good friend at the time. Amy had a crush on Drake, and then, out of the blue, Drake had asked Sierra out. It caused a lot of tension even though Amy said at the time that she didn't mind. Now Amy and Sierra had little contact, since Amy was at a different school and was wrapped up in her boyfriend, Nathan. The strange thing was, Amy and Vicki had been good friends the year before and had a similar sort of rift in their friendship when they both liked the same guy. Sierra was enjoying Vicki's friendship and hoped that what Vicki was about to say would have nothing to do with guys.

"Remember?" Sierra joked. "I'm a certified hotline adviser. You can tell me anything."

As they opened the door to enter the quaint little shop, Vicki smiled and said, "I think Randy and I might be getting together finally."

Sierra hadn't expected this news. "Really?" In her mind, she went over the last few times she had seen Randy and Vicki together. She hadn't been aware of a dating relationship blossoming between them.

Vicki nodded and smiled. "You know I've liked him for over a year."

"You have?" Sierra was still trying to process all this. She knew Vicki had invited Randy to a formal dinner in the spring and that lately Vicki had been hanging out with the band, but Vicki hadn't said anything about her interest in Randy.

"Of course I have. I thought it was obvious. But all

along I thought Randy was interested in you, and only you, from here to eternity. So, not that I'm really humble or anything, but I was waiting to see what was going to happen with you and Randy. And now that you're going with Paul, I finally feel as though we can talk about Randy and me."

Sierra stood in the doorway, staring at Vicki. "This is all news to me."

"Good." Vicki slipped off her jacket in the warm shop and gave Sierra a contented smile. "I didn't want to get in the way if there was a chance of something happening between you and Randy."

Sierra assured Vicki, "Randy and I have been through this evaluation before. We're just buddies. I thought you knew that."

"Who knows anything for sure with relationships? All I know is that if it's time for something to happen between Randy and me, I'm ready for it. Your going with Paul makes things nice and uncomplicated."

The curtain to the changing room next to where Sierra and Vicki stood opened, and the customer, who couldn't have helped but hear their conversation, stepped out.

"Amy?" Sierra said. Sierra and Amy used to come to the Wrinkle in Time often, since they both loved vintage clothes, but they hadn't seen each other for several months. Amy's long, wavy, black hair was now cut short, with bangs that hung to the tips of her eyelashes and fluttered every time she blinked.

"Amy!" Vicki went up to her and offered a hug. "I've been hoping to see you. Did you get my phone messages about a month ago? I wanted to talk to you."

Amy didn't respond. Sierra had seen her this way

before. Amy would clam up in situations that would cause Sierra to be wildly vocal.

Vicki plunged on. "I've been trying to call you because I wanted to tell you something. I went to camp this summer and got my life back on track with the Lord. I've asked several people to forgive me for stuff I did, and I wanted to apologize to you for what happened last year. You know, that big fight we had. I was wrong. I'm sorry, Amy."

Amy looked shocked. For a moment she didn't move. Then she said, "I'm sorry, too. I'm sorry everything went the way it did with us."

Vicki offered Amy another hug, which Amy hesitantly returned. "Thanks, Amy. I hope we can start over."

"We can start over. If that's what you want."

"That's definitely what I want!"

Sierra felt as if she should step in and ask forgiveness for something or offer a hug, too. She and Amy had talked heart-to-heart a few months before, but they hadn't exactly become friends again.

"It's so good to see you," was all Sierra could think to say.

Amy gave Sierra a quizzical look. "So you and Paul are together?"

Sierra nodded.

"When did he come back from Scotland?"

"He's still there. We write each other every day almost."

Amy smiled. "That's great. I'm happy for you. He's writing you every day?"

Sierra nodded, feeling herself blush a little. "Just about every day. I write him every day. You can get to know a lot about a person through letters."

"And the distance solves the purity problem, doesn't

it?" Amy tilted her head and gave Sierra a knowing look.

The two of them had heatedly discussed physical intimacy when Amy confided how she and her boyfriend were getting involved. Sierra had come down hard on Amy, pushing Scripture verses at her and telling her how she needed to remain a virgin.

Vicki touched the ends of Amy's short hair. "I love this. When did you cut it?"

"A few weeks ago. Don't try it, either of you. You'll be sorry afterward."

"Are you going to buy that?" Vicki said, pointing at a blouse Amy had draped over her arm.

"No. It didn't fit. You want to try it on?"

"Yes, it's adorable," Vicki said. "Are you looking for blouses?"

Amy shook her head. "Just looking around. Killing some time."

"Then you can help us find the perfect outfit for Sierra. She's going to send Paul her picture for Christmas, and she needs something original."

Amy, who had always been enthusiastic on her shopping sprees with Sierra, took on a happier look. "Did you see those hats with the rolled brims over there?" She went over to a large wicker basket that sat on an old trunk and pulled out a soft black hat. "Try this on," she said, placing it on Sierra's head.

"That's so cute on you," Vicki said.

"It looks like a Sierra hat," Amy agreed.

Sierra gave her reflection in the oak cheval glass a quick glance. "I don't necessarily want to look like me in the picture. I mean, look the way I always look."

Amy and Vicki exchanged confused glances.

"I want to look like me, only better. Does that make sense?"

"Ah!" Amy said knowingly.

"I saw just the dress." Vicki dashed over to the display in the front window. Without asking the store clerk, she reached into the display and lifted an emerald green, crushed-velvet dress from the peg where it hung on the side of the display.

"Just picture yourself in this," Vicki said, holding the dress up with a dramatic flare, as if she were the keeper of a fine Parisian dress shop. "In this dress, you will most definitely be transformed into the Sierra you long to be."

Sierra laughed.

"Go ahead," Amy urged. "Try it on."

"Are you guys sure?" Sierra asked, eyeing the short green dress. It wasn't like anything she had ever worn before.

Vicki held it up to Sierra and said, "Look, it's going to be a perfect fit."

"Perfect," Amy echoed.

Sierra took the dress from Vicki with a tilt of her head and slipped into the dressing room. It felt strange yet natural that the three of them should be shopping like this. What felt good was that their long-standing disagreements and conflicts appeared to be cleared up. They could be friends and have fun together. But it was all so unexpected that Sierra felt surprised, too.

"Ta-da!" she announced, stepping out of the dressing room wearing the long-sleeved, scooped-neck dress. The dress was cut well. Sierra felt regal, elegant, and dressy as she smoothed her hands over the velvety curves of her frame.

"That's darling!" Vicki exclaimed.

"When did you get a figure?" Amy blurted out.

Sierra blushed. She had noticed her body making subtle changes over the summer, adding some gentle curves and rounding out in all the right places. It was embarrassing, though, to be seventeen and just beginning to have the kind of figure all her friends started to acquire when they were much younger. During most of high school, she had suffered the silent agony of a late bloomer.

"Sierra, you look five years older in that dress," Amy said. "I can't believe how different it makes you look. You're gorgeous!"

"You think?" Sierra stood with her shoulders straight, taking in a full view of herself in the mirror. She couldn't stop smiling. She liked the way this dress and the attention of her friends made her feel. She didn't think of herself as the freckle-faced little tomboy dressed in baggy jeans, or the free spirit who wore long, gauze skirts. She felt like, well, like a young woman worthy of the honor of being called Paul's girlfriend. If she sent Paul a picture of herself in this dress, he would definitely notice how much she had matured. And if he harbored any doubts about Sierra's being old enough and mature enough to enter into a serious relationship, the sight of her in this green velvet dress would dissolve any such thoughts.

"I don't even want to know how much it costs," Sierra said to her friends, turning slightly and examining her backside in the full-length mirror. "I have to have this dress."

eleven

THE THREE REUNITED FRIENDS each bought something at Wrinkle in Time. Sierra purchased the dress and had enough money for the black hat, which she thought would come in handy with all the rain they had been having lately. Amy bought a small leather purse and Vicki bought the blouse Amy had been trying on when they entered the shop.

They were enjoying their time together so much that Vicki suggested they troop down the street to Mama Bear's to celebrate becoming friends again. The welcoming fragrance of cinnamon invited them to enter the store and find a quiet table.

Sierra felt content. She and her friends were nestled in a cozy corner. She was enjoying a hot cup of tea, and the new emerald green dress was in a shopping bag in her car. All that was missing was Paul. She wished it were possible for him to step through the door and physically enter into her life. The best she could do was write another long letter tonight and tell him everything—everything, that is, except about the green dress. He would have to be surprised when he saw the picture of her wearing it. It was a delicious thought.

"What shoes are you going to wear with that dress?" Vicki asked. "It won't exactly go with your cowboy boots."

"Oh, you don't think so?" Sierra pretended her response was serious.

Amy chuckled. "You still have those disgusting boots? I thought they would have gotten up and walked away on their own by now."

"I love those boots," Sierra said with a pout.

"We know!" Amy and Vicki responded in unison.

They all laughed and picked at a shared cinnamon roll in the center of the table.

"So," Amy said, turning to Vicki, "you and Randy might be the latest couple around Royal?"

Vicki smiled. "Maybe. You never know. He cut his hair real short. Did you hear about that?"

Amy shook her head. "I don't hear much from anybody at Royal."

"He stopped a riot over the school dress code almost single-handedly," Vicki said. "He's my hero."

Sierra and Amy laughed.

"You and Randy," Amy said, shaking her head. "Is it 'senioritis' or what? Everyone is ending up with someone I'd never expect them to be interested in." Amy talked about some people Vicki knew who had gotten together, but Sierra didn't know them.

"How are you and Nathan doing?" Vicki asked. "How long have you guys been together, six months now or seven?"

Amy swished the last sip of latte around in her cup. Without looking up, she said, "We broke up."

Sierra felt a squeeze in her heart. She never had wanted Amy to become involved with Nathan, but that didn't matter now. What mattered was that her friend had had her heart broken, and Sierra ached for her.

"Oh, Amy, I'm so sorry," Sierra said.

"You are?" Amy looked up, surprised.

"Yes, of course. It hurts, I'm sure, to break up after being together so long."

Amy looked down. "Yes. It hurts."

"What happened?" Vicki looked at Sierra and then at Amy. "I mean, if you don't mind my asking. I'm not trying to pry or anything."

Amy was silent for a moment. Then she looked up at Vicki. "We were doing fine for a long time. He's a great guy. He was there for me when my parents started their divorce."

"I heard about that," Vicki said. "I'm sorry. I should have been there for you, too. All those stupid arguments we had that we never resolved. I look back now, and I think it was so immature and pointless. I hurt a valuable friendship by not coming to you and trying to clear things up."

Amy drank her last sip of latte. "Well, it doesn't matter now. We're all back to being friends, and I'm glad for that. When I really needed someone, Nathan was there for me, and I'll probably always love him for that." She looked off into the distance as if pulling back a memory that she had sent far away.

"You don't have to tell us anything if you don't want to," Sierra said.

"Yes, she does," Vicki said, flashing her bright smile at

Sierra and Amy. "We want to hear every gory detail."

Vicki's joking tone lightened the mood as all three of them chuckled. Then Sierra and Vicki sat silently, waiting for Amy to continue.

"I guess I was too demanding. That's what he said. I kind of lost my life and became wrapped up in his. We started to fight, which we never did the first few months. Then I found out he had lied to me about something. It wasn't a big thing. He told me he was going to stay home one night, but I found out he went to the movies with a bunch of other people, and I got mad. He said he just wanted a break from me. We didn't talk to each other for about a week, and then we got back together at work that weekend. We did okay for about another week and a half, and then it started all over again. We broke up for good about two weeks ago. He's already going out with someone else."

"That's awful," Sierra said.

"I thought you would say that that's what you had been praying for, that we would break up," Amy said. "Or at least I thought you would want to give me a good 'I told you so.'"

Sierra shook her head. "That's the last thing I want to give you, Amy. What I want to give you is my friendship. From my track record, I obviously don't know a lot about friendship, but one thing I do know is when a friend hurts, the other person hurts, too."

Amy turned misty-eyed and said, "Thanks, Sierra."

"Is there something wrong with me?" Vicki said. "I mean, I'm sorry, Amy, but I'm glad you broke up with Nathan. I'll admit it even if Sierra won't. I don't think he was the best guy in the world for you. Good riddance, I say."

"Vicki!" Sierra said.

Amy was quiet for a moment and then said, "So, Vicki, could you tell me how you really feel?"

The three of them laughed.

"I never have been one to hide my opinions," Vicki said.

"So I remember," Amy said. She quickly added, "I guess that's one of the things I always liked about both of you." She took in Sierra with her gaze before looking back at Vicki. "Both of you are strong, and I have to admit, I'm feeling pretty weak right now."

Sierra and Vicki gave Amy sympathetic looks.

"It's okay," Sierra said.

Amy shook her head. "You're both right, you know. He probably wasn't the best guy in the world for me. I guess it's a good thing we broke up when we did. And it's humbling for me to have to admit this, but I need you both to be my friends. I need you to hurt for me a little, like Sierra said. I think the worst part of the breakup was when I realized Nathan had friends to go to the movies with, and I didn't have anybody I could call. I had cut off all my friends from Royal Academy, and I hadn't even tried to make friends at my new school. I don't want to be lonely like that again."

Sierra reached over and gave Amy's wrist a squeeze. "You don't have to feel like that anymore. The three of us need to start doing stuff together again. I think God set it up for us to run into each other just so we could restart our friendship."

"Why don't we plan to meet here every Monday afternoon?" Vicki suggested.

"Agreed," Amy said. "As long as you'll both promise me one thing."

"What's that?" Sierra asked.

"Don't push the God stuff on me. I know what you guys believe, and I think it's great, Vicki, that you got your life back together with God this summer and everything, but don't put that stuff on me."

Neither Sierra nor Vicki answered.

"Promise me," Amy said.

"I can't promise I won't talk about God," Sierra said.

"Me either," Vicki said. "He's the biggest thing in my life."

"Okay," Amy said, holding up her hands. "You can talk about all that God stuff, but don't expect me to participate, okay?"

Sierra and Vicki nodded.

"So what time should we meet on Mondays?" Vicki asked. She glanced up at the bear-shaped clock on the wall; the clock face was in the bear's tummy. "Oh, no!" she cried. "I was supposed to be home at five o'clock, and it's already five-thirty. Is there a phone here?"

Sierra led Vicki to the phone in the back of the bakery and asked Mrs. Kraus, who was in the kitchen, if it was okay for Vicki to make a local call. Sierra left Vicki there and returned to the table, where Amy sat alone, folding the ends of her napkin in tidy triangles.

"I need to get going, too," Sierra said. "Before I forget, Randy's band is playing at The Beet this Friday. Do you want to go with us or meet us there? He would love to have as many friendly faces in the audience as possible."

"Sure. I'll just meet you guys there. Nathan and I used to go to The Beet when we were first dating, but I doubt he'll be there. If he shows up with his new girlfriend, you'll keep me from scratching her eyes out, won't you?"

Sierra knew Amy well enough to realize her hot-tempered friend was more serious than kidding. "I'll be there for you, Amy. I said that a couple of months ago, but now it looks as if I'll have a chance to prove it. Yes, I'll be there for you, even if I have to cut all your fingernails before we go inside."

"Already did that," Amy said, holding up both hands and showing her nibbled-off nails. "When Nathan and I broke up, I cut my hair, cut my nails, and cut up a picture of the two of us at the Portland Jazz Festival. Am I pathetic or what?"

"You're not pathetic."

Amy met Sierra's comforting gaze. "Thanks, Sierra. I only hope I can be as encouraging to you one day when Paul breaks your heart."

Sierra felt her lips part, but no words tumbled out. Vicki rushed up to the table and announced that she had to fly. The three of them went their separate ways with plans to meet at The Beet on Friday night.

Sierra hurried home, eager to try on her new dress again, but even more eager to check for a letter from Paul. The mailbox was empty, so she headed for the kitchen and asked her mom, who was busy admiring the new oven that had been installed that afternoon, whether they had gotten any mail. Mrs. Jensen told Sierra there had been none for her.

Retreating to her room, Sierra thought of Amy's final statement about Paul breaking Sierra's heart. She always felt a little insecure when she didn't hear from Paul for a few days, but then a letter or postcard would arrive, and her fears would dissolve. She wished she had said something to Amy about not needing to plan on comforting Sierra because Paul was not going to break her heart.

Was he?

She flopped onto her unmade bed and took Paul's picture from her nightstand. She visually retraced every detail of his face. This was not the face of a guy who was out to break her heart. But then Nathan certainly hadn't intended to break Amy's heart, had he? Nobody ever sets out with that as the goal of the relationship. It just happens. Things change. People change.

Sierra rolled onto her side and held Paul's picture close. She couldn't change her feelings for him—ever. She wouldn't. And he wouldn't change, either. They would only grow closer and closer. Then he would come back from Scotland, and... What if he didn't come back from Scotland? What if he stayed another year or three or fifty?

Sierra pursed her lips together and thought hard. Why did she have to go to a college in the States next fall? Why couldn't she go to the same university Paul was attending in Edinburgh?

She sat up, her mind flooding with plans. She could go over to Scotland as soon as school was out and find a job somewhere doing something. She could take a train down to Switzerland for a week and visit Christy so Paul wouldn't grow tired of her the way Nathan had gotten tired of Amy. She would have her own friends there, too, so she wouldn't smother Paul. But they would be close. They would study together, and on weekends he would take her hiking in the Highlands and out to his grandmother's cottage for tea on Sunday afternoons.

Sierra hopped up and began to pace the floor. She needed to find the address for admissions and send in an application right away. Should she tell Paul or wait until she heard back from the university? Her parents would need to know, of course. But if Tawni could announce she was going off to Reno, why couldn't Sierra announce she was going to Edinburgh?

Scooping up the new green dress, Sierra held it in front of her and waltzed around the clutter on her floor. Never before had her spirit soared to such dizzying heights. She laughed when she thought how she would show everyone what a magnificent free spirit she was. She could just picture herself, the minute she had her high school diploma in hand, taking the next plane to Scotland.

twelve

"NO," MR. JENSEN SAID FIRMLY. He sat in his desk chair, showing by his crossed arms that he wasn't going to budge.

"But, Dad, can we at least talk about it?"

"You're not thinking clearly right now, Sierra," her father said.

Sierra shifted uncomfortably in her favorite chair in the study. She had on her new green dress, which she had worn to dinner for effect. She got effect, all right. Her parents said more than once they were startled by her choice, that the dress was so unlike her other clothes. Their less-than-favorable response didn't dampen her spirits when it came to her plans for school in Scotland. She did decide to wait until after dinner when her mom was helping Dillon and Gavin with their homework before she talked to her dad in the study. When he closed the door behind them, Sierra had excitedly blurted out her plan.

That's when her father said no.

"I am too thinking clearly," Sierra protested. "This is something I'd love to do. My grades are good enough; you know that. I've been to Europe twice before. Why can't I go to school there?"

"Sierra," her dad said, unfolding his arms and leaning forward, "you know nothing about this university. Your only reasons for going there would be adventure and, if I can venture a guess, to be close to Paul. Those are not good reasons for selecting a college. Financially, we're depending on several scholarships to come through for you. I know nothing about how scholarships might transfer to Edinburgh."

"We can find out," Sierra said. "We can ask. I'll ask. I'll research it."

Her dad shook his head. "The answer will still be no."

"Why?" Sierra pleaded. "You let Tawni take off to California, where she lives near her boyfriend."

"That's different. Tawni started to date Jeremy after she moved to San Diego; she didn't move there to be near him. And Tawni is nineteen, almost twenty. You just turned seventeen a few weeks ago."

Sierra let out a frustrated sigh. She knew her parents had a thing about the magical age of eighteen. Her two older brothers and older sister had all stayed home until they were eighteen, and then they were given several options of how their mom and dad would help them get on their feet. Sierra knew that to leave home before she was eighteen would be the same as cutting herself off from the family blessing.

"Sierra, what I'm most concerned about is what's gotten into you."

"What do you mean?"

"This dress, for one thing. It's so unlike you. And

where did the idea you wanted to be near Paul come from?"

"We've been writing each other almost every day. It's just that I'm the one who brings in the mail, so nobody knows how often he writes me. I write him all the time."

"Is that why you kept disappearing during Thanksgiving?"

"What do you mean?"

"You weren't around much. Were you going off to write Paul?"

"Yes. What's wrong with that?"

"Did you spend any time with your relatives?" her dad asked.

"Yes, I did."

"Without being told?"

"Well…" Sierra was hard-pressed to come up with a yes. She knew Aunt Frieda had been upset that Sierra had avoided Nicole and Molly, the two cousins who were close to her age. Frieda's parting words to Sierra had been sharp, but Sierra had brushed them off. Many of Frieda's words had little stingers attached to them. Sierra always figured that the only sure way to keep them from penetrating her skin was to brush them off quickly.

"You haven't been yourself lately," Mr. Jensen said.

Sierra considered saying she was in love, but she knew that would not score points with her dad. "I'm growing up, Dad; that's all. This is me—the new, improved me. I know I'm a late bloomer, and I'm experiencing at seventeen what most girls experience much earlier." The words tumbled out before she had time to evaluate them. "But like it or not, I'm becoming a woman. No, I take that back. I am a woman. I'm not your little girl anymore."

Sierra had blurted out her opinions many times over

the past seventeen years. Sometimes she regretted being vocal. Sometimes she caught herself before she really blew it. Sometimes she thought about it later and was glad she had spoken up. Still other times she thought about it and wished she hadn't said anything.

Then there was this time. It was like no other. With her words, she had just cut an invisible string that had tied her heart to her father's for all these years. She was making it clear she wanted to take the end of that severed string and tie it to Paul's heart.

And her father was telling her no.

"We need to talk some more," Mr. Jensen said after a long moment of silence. "This isn't a good time. But we need to talk some more."

"Okay," Sierra said calmly. She set as her goal to prove to her dad she was composed and mature and could discuss whatever he felt was necessary to talk through. "Let me know when it's convenient for you."

"I will." Her dad left her alone in the study, sitting stiffly in her favorite chair with her short green dress and her pounding heart.

The next day Sierra raced home from school, certain a letter from Paul would be waiting for her, and there was. The letter was short, but every word tasted sweet as she stopped in her tracks on the front porch to read it:

A quick note, Sierra. I'm swamped with exams, and unlike you, I can't boast a 4.0. So I must torture my brain beyond its natural limits. I'm glad you liked the photo. It was taken in one of my favorite hiking areas. I hope to go there this weekend, if the storms let up. It's been nothing but rain here for days. You asked about my

birthday. It's December 10, and if I may be so bold as to make a
birthday wish, I'm hoping for a picture of you to put here on my
writing desk. Your breezy smile during the long hours of study will
ease my pain. Must fly.

With all good wishes to you,
Paul

Sierra quickly calculated backward from December 10. If she had the picture taken this afternoon, she could run it over to the one-hour photo lab, find a frame, wrap it, and mail it tomorrow. It was close, but the picture could be there by Paul's birthday. Sierra wished she had a digital camera the same way she often wished she had a cell phone. *Taking a picture should not be this difficult!*

"Mom?" Sierra called out as she entered the house. "Mom, where are you?" She searched until she found her mother stretched out on the couch with a blanket over her. "Oh, are you okay?"

"Just feeling tired. What is it?"

"I need a favor. Could you take some pictures of me? It's not raining for once, and I wanted some photos taken in the backyard. I have the film and everything."

"Do you need it done this instant?" Mrs. Jensen didn't look as if she wanted to move from her cozy spot.

"No, that's okay. Sorry I woke you up. We can do it later."

But Sierra didn't want to do it later. She wanted it done now. Heading for the kitchen, she tried Vicki's number. No answer. She called Randy, but his mom said he wasn't home yet. Going through the list, she called other people she knew. No one was available. She phoned Vicki again. Still no answer. Desperate, Sierra was about to wake her mom. After all, it had been a whole five minutes since their conversation. But then Granna Mae shuffled into the kitchen.

"Hello, Lovey. How was your day?"

"Great! Hey, Granna Mae, would you mind taking my picture in the backyard?"

Granna Mae's slowed reflexes caused her to give Sierra a funny stare before answering. "I suppose I could."

"Great. Wait here. I'll be right back."

Sierra blasted upstairs, changed into her green dress, applied a quick splash of makeup, and tried to corral her unruly hair.

"I'm coming," she called downstairs as she grabbed the camera and made sure the film she had loaded the other day was ready to roll.

"Okay, I'm all set," Sierra said, dashing into the kitchen.

But Granna Mae wasn't there. Not wanting to yell and wake up her mom, Sierra tried to skitter around quietly downstairs, searching for her grandmother. She went back upstairs and found Granna Mae in her room, silently looking out the window.

"Okay, I'm ready," Sierra said. "Can you take my picture now? In the backyard? I thought it would be pretty by the tree that hasn't lost all its leaves yet. The little bright yellow one."

"All right," Granna Mae agreed.

She followed Sierra with slow, steady steps. By the time they were down the stairs and out the back door, Granna

Mae was winded. It took her a few minutes before she was able to manage the camera.

"I'll be standing right here," Sierra said, going over to the tree with the yellow leaves. "And you take the shot from my knees up because I don't have any shoes to go with this dress." She stood there, barefooted, shivering slightly in the scoop-necked dress. "You know which button to push, don't you?"

"Say cheese!" Granna Mae said. She snapped the picture.

"Keep taking them," Sierra said. "We can use up the whole roll. Get some close-ups. I want this to be a nice picture."

She stood as straight as she could and smiled for the camera. As the shutter clicked again, Sierra thought of Paul's words, that her breezy smile would ease his study pains. He was such a poet. She smiled more broadly and hoped the glow in her eyes, the glow that burned there for Paul alone, would show up in the photos.

thirteen

SIERRA TOOK BACK THE CAMERA from her grandother. "It's cold out here." You'd better get warmed up inside."

"All right," Granna Mae agreed. "I hope your pictures come out nicely, Emma."

Granna Mae had confused Sierra with Emma more than once. As the youngest of Granna Mae's children, Emma in her younger days had looked like Sierra.

Did Emma ever come home with a short green dress? Sierra wondered. *If so, what did her father say to her about it?*

Brutus barked wildly from the end of his chain as Sierra helped Granna Mae up the leaf-covered back steps.

"Sorry, Brutus," Sierra called over her shoulder, "you can't come back in the house until you've had a bath, and I don't have time to give you one now."

"Maybe he's hungry," Granna Mae suggested. "Or thirsty. Has anyone checked his water bowl lately?"

"I'll take a look," Sierra promised. "Let's just get you back up to your room, where it's nice and toasty."

"I've enjoyed our little walk," Granna Mae said. "Let's do it again tomorrow."

"Okay," Sierra said. She held Granna Mae's elbow all the way up to her room, where the wearied woman sat down in her recliner.

"Thank you, dear. That was lovely."

Sierra gave Granna Mae a kiss on the cheek and then hurried to her own bedroom. She was cold, too, so she changed into her favorite pair of jeans and an old fisherman's knit sweater that used to be Wesley's. Her toes were icy. Pulling on a pair of socks, she shoved her feet into her cowboy boots. Then, because she remembered her dad's old saying about covering your head if you want to warm up fast, she reached for her new black hat with its rolled brim and popped it on her head. Her crazy blond curls poured out from under the hat like party streamers.

Oh well, Sierra thought, catching a glimpse of herself in her mirror. *What I look like won't matter to the people at the one-hour photo shop.*

She hurried downstairs. Brutus's persistent barking stopped her.

"Okay, you big lug. I'm coming." Sierra went out the back door to check on him. Just as Granna Mae had suggested, he had neither water nor food.

"You poor baby," Sierra said, turning on the garden hose and pulling it closer so he could lap up the water as she rinsed out his water dish and filled it. "Can you wait an hour for your dinner? I'll be back then. If Gavin hasn't fed you yet, I promise I will."

Brutus stuck out his long, moist tongue and panted appreciatively.

"See you later, buddy." Sierra returned the water hose

to the side of the yard and headed for the back steps. She smiled to herself, thinking how fun it was going to be to send her picture to Paul and wondering what his letter would say when he wrote to thank her for it.

She was on the second step when she heard her mother call her name. Sierra looked up, rosy-cheeked and smiling.

Click. Mrs. Jensen stood on the landing with the camera.

"I already have the pictures, Mom. There shouldn't be any film left."

Just then the camera began to automatically rewind.

"I guess there was one more," her mom said.

"I'm taking the film to the one-hour place. Is there anything you want me to pick up on the way home?"

"No, but thanks for asking. Are these pictures for a school project or something? Why the rush?"

"It's for Paul. I just found out his birthday is December 10, and I have to mail the photo off to him by tomorrow if it's going to arrive on time."

"I see," Mrs. Jensen said. She looked a little confused. Or was it concerned?

Sierra felt the need to explain. "He sent me a picture of himself for my birthday, remember? And now he's asked if I'd send him a picture of me for his birthday."

"I see," Mrs. Jensen said again.

But when Sierra looked more closely at her mother, she was afraid her mother didn't see at all. If her mom understood what it was like to have a blossoming relationship with the most amazing guy on the planet, then she would understand why this was all so important to Sierra. But her mom didn't seem to understand.

"I'll be home in a little over an hour," Sierra said, grabbing the camera and her backpack. "Love you. See you later. Bye-bye!" She flew out the front door and hopped into her car.

Only one clerk was working at the photo lab when Sierra dropped off her film, but he guaranteed her it would be ready in an hour. Deciding to use the time to find a card, a frame, and maybe the ingredients for the tea party for Paul's Christmas present, she hurried out of the shop. She could send the tea party for his birthday, instead, if she could find everything right away.

Her shopping spree took more than an hour, but she managed to buy everything she was after. The only bad part was that it cost more than she had figured, and she only had enough money left for the pictures. The quarter of a tank of gas in her car would have to last until the next paycheck.

"There you are. I have a question about one of your pictures," the photo clerk said when Sierra entered the shop.

"Yes?" She began to fan through the stack of pictures. One of them showed the tree in full length and only the very top of Sierra's head. The next one was of her arm and her torso. Another was just her face, but it was fuzzy. Sierra groaned.

I bet he's going to ask how anyone could fail so miserably with an entire roll of film. Why did I ask Granna Mae to do this, especially when I wasn't sure she was thinking clearly? He's probably astounded I would admit to owning them.

"We would like to buy one of your pictures," the clerk said.

"You're kidding."

"No. We occasionally buy some of the really good shots and put them up in the window to advertise."

"The really good shots?" Sierra repeated.

"This one," he said, pulling out a photo from the bottom of the stack.

It was the one her mom had taken. Sierra had to agree. Everything was just right. The background was a smear of gold and orange from the trees; Sierra was smiling expectantly, and her cheeks were blushed, which made her eyes sparkle. The picture was from her chest up, and the dark felt hat with the rolled brim contrasted with the fire-colored leaves behind her. But the best part was her hair. The blond curls fell in a gleeful cascade, lit by the late-afternoon sun and giving off a golden shine that overshadowed the autumn leaves.

"Do you have any more like this?" the clerk asked.

"Nope. That was just the last frame, and it was sort of taken by accident."

"It's a very good photo. May we buy it?"

"You can buy a copy, but I need this original, and I'll need the negative."

"Good deal," he said. "If you'll sign a release form, the company will mail you the check."

"Great. Thanks!"

Sierra felt kind of special as she told her news at the dinner table that night. She didn't show anyone the other pictures because she didn't want Granna Mae to know what a goofball job she had done.

"Did you find out how much they're going to pay you?" Mrs. Jensen asked.

"Only twenty dollars. Do you want me to split it with you since you were the photographer?"

"No, of course not. You probably need it for Christmas gifts."

Later that night, in her room, Sierra realized how true her mom's words were. She had depleted all her funds on the needlepoint kit, the film, the frame, and everything else for Paul. Now her money for gifts for her family was all gone. Sierra realized as she wrapped the picture that she didn't even have enough money to pay for the postage to mail the birthday box.

She didn't let that worry her, though. At least she had pulled together exactly what she wanted to give Paul. The card alone had cost three dollars, but it was a gorgeous illustration of a guy and a girl walking hand-in-hand through a meadow of wildflowers. Inside it said, "Thinking of you on your birthday and sending more wishes than your arms can hold." She liked that it was tender and a little bit mushy.

The tea-party items were what had depleted her account. She had bought a lot of little goodies, especially candies and treats she didn't remember being able to buy in England or Ireland when she was there almost a year ago. Paul was probably ready for some good ol' American candy by now. She also bought a small cake that came wrapped for school lunches and a package of birthday candles. She included a can of mixed nuts; a party-favor bag of horn blowers, noisemakers, and birthday hats; and a plastic pin-the-tail-on-the-donkey game. Sierra also bought a black ceramic mug to go with a little bag of gourmet coffee. The coffee fit inside the mug, and she wrapped it with bubble packaging before putting it in the birthday-party care package.

Several hours later, Sierra had prepared everything just

the way she wanted it. She had debated a long time before she wrapped the framed picture and laid it carefully in the box. It wasn't that she didn't like the photo her mom had taken. It looked exactly like Sierra. That was the problem. The girl in the green dress would have made much more of an impression. But she was out of money and had no time to find someone to take another roll of pictures.

Sierra lined up all the poor shots Granna Mae had taken of her. She decided if she cut them up—an arm out of this one, a leg here, her head from this one, she could form a puzzle of herself. It made her wonder if Granna Mae viewed the world in that fragmented way some days. Sierra decided it might make an interesting art project to try to fit all the picture pieces together. Not tonight, though. The wrapping had taken a long time, and she still had homework to do.

At ten minutes after midnight, when Sierra finished the letter that went with the surprise box, she was exhausted. Taping up the box and writing Paul's address on the front seemed to take a lot of effort. No way could she do any homework tonight. She would have to finish it tomorrow before class somehow.

The "somehow" didn't happen. The day zoomed by, and Sierra had to take a zero for one of her English assignments. She was mad. Now she would have to do extra-credit work so her grade wouldn't suffer. And the last thing she needed in her already busy schedule was more homework.

Sierra had borrowed ten dollars from her mom that morning so she could mail the gift. She drove to the post office right after school and then went to Mama Bear's Bakery to see if she could pick up some extra hours to earn more holiday money. Mrs. Kraus checked the schedule and offered Sierra two additional mornings during Christmas week, which Sierra agreed to take. It wouldn't help her current financial crisis, but if she had to borrow money, she needed to earn more to pay it back.

When she arrived at home, she immediately checked the mail. Nothing from Paul. She tried not to let it bother her. Still, a gloomy mist settled on her as she thought of how hard she had worked on his gift box the night before, even at the expense of taking a zero in English.

Sierra knew it would be difficult for her to finish her homework again tonight because she was so far behind on the needlepoint for Paul that she needed to put in several hours on it. Tomorrow she worked; Friday was the big night at The Beet; Saturday she worked again; Sunday was church; and Sunday night she volunteered at the Highland House. That didn't leave much time for putting tiny little stitches in a row.

Sierra hurried up to her room and went right to work on the needlepoint. Her thoughts were of Paul, and nothing but Paul.

As she carefully stitched the top flame on the mountain, she thought, *All I can say is, he had better appreciate everything I'm doing for him!*

fourteen

"OVER HERE!" Amy called to Sierra and Vicki. Amy waved her arm and indicated they should join her at the corner table in The Beet. Waves of loud music and louder voices crashed over Sierra and Vicki as they threaded their way through the crowd.

"This place is packed!" Vicki exclaimed, as she pulled off her jacket and hung it over the back of the chair next to Amy. "I've never seen it so full."

"Yeah, well, guess who the main group is tonight?" Amy had to shout over the piped-in music. "The L's."

"You're kidding!" Vicki shouted back. "Here? At our little place?"

Sierra had heard The L's before and really liked the energetic sound of their trumpets and saxophones combined with guitars.

"So, The LB's have to open for The L's?" Vicki asked.

"Yes," Amy said. "Only our guys aren't The LB's anymore. They thought it sounded too wannabe, performing just before The L's and everything."

"What are they calling themselves?" Sierra asked. The loud music was beginning to hurt her ears.

Amy shrugged. "I think they're trying to decide right now."

Sierra settled into the straight-backed chair and moved closer to Amy. The table wobbled. Each of the chairs was a different style and painted a different color. Sierra liked the bold, crazy decor. A long, green canoe with a big hole in the bottom was suspended from the ceiling with a light hanging from the opening. A moose head hung over the stage area. The moose wore an oxygen mask on its long snout and a red flower over its right ear.

The admission into The Beet was three dollars and a can of food, which was donated to the Salvation Army downtown. Sierra had a total of thirty-seven cents to her name and had to borrow the three dollars from Vicki to get in. Now a waitress dressed in green corduroy overalls stood by their table asking if they wanted to order something to drink. Sierra had to settle for water.

She pulled her needlepoint from her backpack, thinking she could add a few stitches while they waited for Randy's group to open the night's performance.

"What's that?" Amy asked.

"A gift I'm trying to finish for Christmas."

"Here?" Amy looked at Vicki and back at Sierra. "Hello, Sierra, this is not a quilting club. This is a nightclub. You're supposed to talk, laugh, and have fun. Not sit and knit."

Sufficiently chided, Sierra returned the needlepoint to her backpack. "How can we talk? It's so loud."

"This isn't loud," Amy said. "Wait until the bands come out."

Sierra suddenly felt like an old lady. Since when did noise like this bother her? And why had she thought it would be a good idea to bring along a stitchery project? If she wasn't going to enter into the wacky atmosphere of this place, she might as well have stayed home.

Vicki waved at some friends of hers, and Amy looked around. "You guys don't see him, do you?"

"Who? Nathan?" Sierra asked.

"Of course Nathan. Tell me if you see him. I've been worrying about this all day. If he's here, I'm warning you, it could get ugly."

"You wouldn't do anything stupid," Vicki said confidently. She pulled her long, sleek hair back and wrapped it up in a scrunchie. "You have us here to support you. Is anyone else hot, or is it me?"

"It's hot in here," Sierra agreed.

She was about to suggest they go outside to cool off when the canned music stopped and a guy in a black stovepipe hat stepped onto the stage. "Dig that crazy beat!" His voice ricocheted off the walls and was answered by a chorus of regulars at The Beet, who gave their "code" response of "Time to move your feet!" Sierra had never seen anything like it. It was fun—silly, good clean fun.

"Let's hear it for the Three-Two-Ones!"

"The Three-Two-Ones?" Sierra and Vicki echoed.

"They must have decided to try numbers instead of letters," Amy suggested, yelling over the roar of the applause.

Randy and the band hustled onto the stage, and the drummer immediately pounded out a steady rhythm. Sierra could tell Randy was nervous. Both sides of his mouth were turned up in a forced smile. When Randy normally smiled, it was a crooked half-grin. Tonight he looked a little like a kid at a spelling bee, standing tall and stiff with his feet pointed straight out and the guitar slung over his shoulder. He wore his black baseball cap with a ponytail attached to the back. At that moment, the moose in the oxygen mask over the stage appeared more natural than poor Randy.

The first song was one of Sierra's favorites. She thought the group played it flawlessly. The audience responded with wild applause, and Sierra began to breathe a little easier. At least the Three-Two-Ones were off to a good start, and they had the crowd with them. It would be hard not to have an enthusiastic response from this crowd, since everyone crammed into The Beet seemed to have come to have a good time.

Randy appeared to relax a bit on the second song and was smiling at Sierra with his usual crooked grin by the end of the third song. Unfortunately, that song was also their last—and right when they were starting to crank.

"They were great!" Vicki said excitedly. "Didn't Randy look adorable?"

"He looked nervous," Sierra stated.

"At first, but then he loosened up."

After a short break, The L's were to come on. The server returned with the drinks, and Sierra gladly swigged her water. The crowded room was heating up. She wished she had worn a T-shirt instead of a sweater.

"Hey, Megan!" Vicki yelled at a girl across the room, who waved back.

Just then Amy grabbed Sierra's arm and pressed tightly.

"There's Adam," Amy said. "He's Nathan's best friend. Is Nathan here? Have you seen him?"

Sierra looked over her shoulder. "No. He might not be here."

"If Adam's here, Nathan probably is. I don't want to see him."

"It's so crowded," Sierra said. "Even if he's here, you might not run into each other. I wouldn't worry about it if I were you."

"Well, you're not me," Amy snapped. "I'm going to leave. I'm not up to this."

"But The L's!" Sierra said.

Amy grabbed her purse and swung it over her shoulder. "I'll see you guys on Monday." She began to edge her way through the crowd.

Sierra and Vicki looked at each other.

"What is her deal?" Vicki said. "I don't get it."

"I'm going to go with her," Sierra heard herself say. She hadn't planned to make such a statement, but there it was. "Can you find a ride home?"

Vicki smiled. "Sure. I'll ask Randy."

Sierra grabbed her backpack and flashed a smile at Vicki, knowing that needing a ride from Randy was the best thing Vicki could think of happening to her tonight.

"I'll see you later," Sierra said.

Pushing her way through the thick crowd, Sierra tried to see which way Amy had gone. The L's stepped onto the stage, and a lively blast of trumpet and sax opened the act. "If you give a man a fish...," the lead singer began. Sierra wished she were staying. She liked this song; the music of the L's always had such a cheering effect on her. Instead, she was following her erratic friend, who had given no indication she wanted company.

Sierra stepped out into the cold night and spotted Amy along the side of the building. She was standing face-to-face with Nathan. In the glow of the large, red neon Beet sign over the entrance, Sierra could see the expression on Nathan's face. He did not look happy.

fifteen

SIERRA DIDN'T KNOW WHAT TO DO. She stood only four feet away from Nathan and Amy, but Amy's back was to her. Dozens of teens were milling around the front of The Beet, and Sierra tried to blend in so she wouldn't draw Nathan's attention. Would Amy be mad if Sierra interrupted them? Should she just go back inside? What if something bad happened? Amy had sounded almost frightened about seeing Nathan. Might he hurt her?

Sierra slung the backpack over her shoulder and shifted her weight from one foot to the other. The night air cooled her hot cheeks. She decided to move a little closer to hear what was going on so she could determine if everything was okay. Suddenly, Nathan reached over and took Amy by the arm. Sierra couldn't tell if he was being rough because she couldn't see Amy's face. All she knew was that Amy wasn't pulling away. But what if Amy couldn't free herself from his grasp?

Sierra decided she needed to jump in and defend her friend. Wesley had taught her some self-defense tactics, and

Sierra had an air horn in her backpack. She quickly pulled it out, prepared to use it if necessary. The loud blast of noise, Wes had told her when he gave her the horn, would startle an attacker and give her enough time to run for safety.

Holding the air horn, Sierra carefully watched Nathan's every move. Amy put her head down, and Nathan grabbed her by the shoulders, looking as if he might start to shake her. Then he put his arm around her and hurried her toward the parking lot in back.

With her heart pounding, Sierra rushed after them, her finger poised on the air horn's trigger. When she was right behind them, she could tell Amy was crying. A burst of adrenaline gave Sierra the confidence she needed to point the air horn at the back of Nathan's head and press the trigger.

"Run, Amy, run!" Sierra screamed over the deafening blast.

Nathan dropped his arm from around Amy, covered his ears with his hands, and spun around to face Sierra. Sierra backed away, but Amy didn't move.

"Run, Amy, run!"

"Sierra!" Amy's tear-streaked face reflected shock. "What are you doing?"

"You were crying," Sierra stammered in the silence that now followed the loud blast. "He was forcing you to go with him."

"He was not," Amy said, now looking furiously at Sierra. "We were just going to talk things out."

"What is with you?" Nathan said, grabbing the air horn

away from Sierra. "What are you doing with this thing? And why are you following us?" Nathan wasn't a big guy, but he could look fierce when he wanted to—like now.

"I—I'm sorry.... I thought..."

"You thought what?" Amy said.

Sierra couldn't answer.

"You of all people should understand how important it is for friends to work out their unresolved issues." Amy had stopped crying. "Nathan and I need to talk, Sierra. We would like a little privacy to try to work a few things out here, if you don't mind."

"I—I'm sorry...."

Nathan handed her the air horn. "Go rescue somebody who wants to be," he stated, giving Sierra a withering look. "Since that's apparently what you think your mission in life is."

Sierra apologized one more time and turned to go. Never had she felt so foolish. Here she thought she was helping her friend, but obviously Amy had a much stronger sense of loyalty to Nathan than she had let on. Swallowing hard, Sierra numbly stuffed the air horn into her backpack and made her way to the front door of The Beet.

"I already paid," she told the guy guarding the front door.

"I need to see your stub."

Sierra dug her hands into her pockets and then realized that Vicki had the stub, since she had paid for both of them. "My friend in there has it," she said.

The guy gave her a knowing nod. "Yeah, right. Sorry. No ticket, no laundry."

Sierra looked over his head into the crowded room. Vicki was nowhere to be seen. The L's were playing their hit song, "The King of Polyester." With all her heart, Sierra wished she could slip back into the happy crowd and forget what had just happened with Amy. But there was no way. She couldn't spot Vicki, and she had no money. Her only choice was to drive home. Either that or hang out with the other penniless fans who hovered around the door, eagerly snatching the scraps of music that the cranked-up speakers randomly flung in their direction.

"This is pathetic," Sierra muttered to herself. She considered going around to the backstage door and trying to convince someone there that she was with the band. Randy would vouch for her and get her back inside. And then what? How could she relax and have a good time knowing what a jerk she had just made of herself with Amy and Nathan?

Dejected, Sierra drove home and comforted herself by deciding she could spend the rest of the evening working on Paul's Christmas present. That's what she probably should have planned to do all along.

She couldn't decide if she would tell Paul what had happened tonight. Lately she had been writing everything that happened to her. But all she had heard from him was the poetic letter right before Thanksgiving and then that quick note earlier in the week when he told her his birthday was on the tenth. Even though she had written to him daily, giving him every detail of her life, he hadn't responded as often or with as much detail.

Still, there was always tomorrow's mail. Sierra told herself that often. Weekends seemed long since no mail came on Sundays. Yet every Monday she would check the mailbox with as much hope as she had felt on Saturday. If no letter from Paul appeared, she stored up that hope and kept it ready to pull out again on Tuesday.

Sierra parked her car in front of the house and glanced at the gas gauge. The arrow teetered on the red zone. She knew the next time she started up the car it had better be to drive straight to a gas station. But how much gas could she buy with thirty-seven cents?

The way Sierra felt at the moment, all she wanted to do was hide in her room, put on some sad music, and work on Paul's gift. She walked in the front door, intending to do just that.

Her father called to her from the living room. Her parents were sitting on the couch, watching a movie with Gavin and Dillon.

"You're home earlier than we expected," her mom said.

Deciding to skip the reasons for her early arrival, Sierra said, "Yes, well, it was fun, but I have stuff to do."

"Mind if we have a talk first?" her dad said.

Sierra did mind. She knew this would be the talk about her going to school in Scotland.

"It's a nice night," her dad said. "Why don't we go out on the porch swing?"

"I'll make some coffee," her mom said.

Sierra's heart sank. When her mother made coffee and brought it to her father on the porch swing, it meant a long talk. Some of the talks they had had on the front porch had been wonderful and sweet, such as the night she returned from her trip to England. Tonight Sierra imagined it would be a painful conversation in which she would have to defend herself and try to prove she was mature enough to make her own decisions. The week had been so busy that she hadn't done any of the research she had offered to do on the university or the loans. She didn't have any fuel to feed her fired-up desire to go to Edinburgh. The conversation could only go in favor of her dad at this point. And she had a pretty good idea he hadn't changed his opinion on the subject.

She followed her dad out to the porch, grabbing a throw blanket off the couch on the way. The night was clear, which meant it was cooler than when the clouds hovered low like a down comforter over the city, turning the sky a dull cream color.

"I thought we should talk about you and Paul," her dad began.

"Why?" Sierra heard herself say. She quickly added, "I mean, I thought the issue was about my going to school in Scotland, not about Paul."

"The two seem to be connected," her dad said. His voice was calm and welcoming.

Sierra knew she could talk to her father about anything. She always had been able to. However, now she felt she should distance herself from him to prove she was old enough and wise enough to make her own decisions. She was reluctant to let down her defenses.

"Tell me about your relationship with Paul," her dad said. "You mentioned the other day you've been writing to each other."

Sierra nodded, not volunteering any information.

"How often do you write to him?"

"Pretty often," Sierra said.

"Every day? Every week? Twice a day?"

"I don't know. About every day."

"And how often does he write to you?"

"About every day," Sierra said.

Her dad raised an eyebrow. "When did you last receive a letter from him?"

"A few days ago."

"And it was a long, detailed letter?"

"No, it was short. But the one before that was really long."

"When did that one come?"

"The Wednesday before Thanksgiving."

"What about before that letter?"

"I guess that was the package with his picture."

"Was there a letter with that package?"

"No." Sierra was beginning to do the math in her own head. A full week and a half had passed between the picture and the letter that followed it.

Mr. Jensen paused and was about to say something when Sierra said, "I guess he writes to me more like every week or every week and a half."

Her dad nodded.

"It just seems as though it's more often. I know he's thinking of me more than that, and I'm certainly thinking of him more than that."

Mrs. Jensen arrived with two mugs of dark, rich coffee and handed one to her husband. Then she sat down in a chair across from the two of them and pulled up the collar on her fleece sweatshirt.

"What kinds of things does Paul say in his letters?" Mr. Jensen said.

"What do you mean?" Sierra felt her defenses rising again.

"I mean, does he say he misses you? That he's looking forward to seeing you again?"

"Well, yes," Sierra said slowly. She couldn't think of an example of when he had actually used those words, but she knew the thought was there. She had certainly said those words to him.

No one spoke for a few moments. The coffee's rich fragrance floated to Sierra's nose.

Funny, Sierra thought. *My parents are right here, and yet we feel miles apart. Why are they questioning me like this? Don't they trust me?*

Across the great distance, she felt they were condemning her for letting herself become emotionally involved with this guy who, as the facts showed, didn't appear to be as emotionally involved with her. It wasn't that way, though. Sierra tried to think of a way to make her parents understand.

Paul writes me poems. Sierra stopped mid-thought. *Wait a minute! Did he actually write those poems to me? Or did he simply write them and then share them with me? Paul did send me his picture, and he asked for a picture back from me. He wouldn't have done those things if he didn't care about me and want a visual memory of me close to him.*

"I can't believe you guys don't remember what it's like to be romantically interested in someone and to read between the lines what that other person is saying." Sierra felt her voice quivering. "It seems so unfair that when, for the first time in my life, I'm really, truly, deeply interested in someone, you would try to break it up. Can't you just be happy for me? There is absolutely nothing wrong with Paul and me writing to each other. I don't appreciate your trying to make it seem as though I'm doing something wrong."

Sierra stopped. She mentally repeated the last few lines

she had said. Something was hauntingly familiar about them. And she knew what it was. Those were the words Amy had spouted when Sierra questioned Amy's relationship with Nathan after their first date.

"I..." Sierra paused. "I'm not feeling up to this conversation right now. Would you guys mind if I went to my room and did some thinking? I'd rather talk about all this later."

Mrs. Jensen looked at her husband, and he nodded.

"Okay," Mrs. Jensen said softly.

Sierra started to leave, her head pounding.

"We love you, Sierra," her mother said. "We only want what's best for you. Don't forget that, okay?"

Sierra couldn't think of anything to say. She gave her parents a sad look over her shoulder and disappeared inside the house.

sixteen

"THE THING IS, our relationship is nothing like Amy and Nathan's," Sierra said the next day to Randy.

He had shown up at Mama Bear's just as she was going on her lunch break, and he had decided to join her. Usually, Randy spent Saturdays mowing lawns, but the pouring rain today kept him out of the lawn-care business. And the Christmas sales at the mall seemed to have kept holiday shoppers in the stores and out of Mama Bear's.

As a reflection of her goodwill toward everyone this slow Saturday, Mrs. Kraus had offered Randy a free cinnamon roll, frosted and warmed the way he liked it. She suggested that Randy and Sierra sit at one of the corner tables and enjoy the afternoon lull.

Sierra pushed her empty carton of milk away and leaned closer to confide in Randy. "I mean, with Amy and Nathan it was physical right from the start. With Paul, it's a spiritual connection. We enjoy each other's company emotionally. I guess you could say we're kindred spirits."

Randy listened, offering no comment, judgment, or agreement.

Sierra continued. "I just don't understand why my parents are making such an issue out of this. I'm totally pure. They know that. You know that. Everyone knows that! If they are so convinced I'm blowing it, then what is the point of having this?" She stuck out her right hand to Randy, drawing attention to the gold band on her ring finger. It was the purity ring her dad had given her. "Answer me that? What good is it for my parents to say they trust me, or they're proud of my choices, if they can't understand why this relationship with Paul is so wonderful? Why would they want to ruin it for me?"

Randy didn't answer. He just slowly raised an eyebrow and reached for the cinnamon roll in front of him.

"What?" Sierra challenged.

Randy stuffed the last bite of roll into his mouth.

"You did that so you wouldn't have to answer me, didn't you?"

"No," Randy said, his mouth full. "I don't have a problem talking with my mouth full. I was trying to be polite."

Sierra looked away from the mush in Randy's mouth. He swallowed and smacked his lips loudly.

"Just answer me this," she said, turning back to her buddy. "Why would my parents act as if something were wrong with my relationship with Paul?"

"Is there?" Randy asked.

"Is there what?"

"Something wrong with it?"

"No! Everything is great. It's better than great. It's fantastic."

Randy didn't respond.

"Am I boring you here?" Sierra gave Randy a careful

look. "I seem to be doing all the talking about my problem."

"That's how you solve your problems," Randy said.
"You don't need to hear my answers. You always figure it
out when you hear yourself talk it through. Remember that
night on the backpacking trip when you were trying to figure out how you felt about Drake?"

Sierra remembered all right. It was a humiliating
memory. She had poured out her heart to Randy in his
dark tent, thinking he was her brother. Then the tent had
collapsed on the two of them, announcing to the whole
camp that Sierra was where she shouldn't be—in a guy's tent.
She wished Randy and she could both forget that night.

"Besides," Randy said, "I don't know what the answer is.
I don't even know what the problem is."

Sierra dropped her head in her hands. "Randy, the
problem is my parents are hinting I don't have the right
perspective on my relationship with Paul." She looked up to
make sure Randy was paying attention. "I know they want
me to stop writing to him. But why? Is it because they think
I'm too young for him? I'm seventeen! That's old enough
to be married in some states."

"It is?" Randy appeared shocked at the thought.

"I think. I don't know. The point is, I'm old enough to
know what I want and what's good for me."

"And what's that?"

"Paul!" Sierra stated emphatically. "Haven't you been
listening?"

"Of course I have. So tell me. Why is Paul good for
you?"

Sierra smiled. "He makes me feel good about myself,

and he brings out the creative side of me. I feel warm when I read his letters."

"And he brings you closer to the Lord," Randy added.

"What?"

"Wasn't that one of your criteria?" Randy asked. "One time you told me you had written out your standards for dating, and I remember one of your goals was that the guy you're dating would bring you closer to God, and you would do the same for him."

"Oh, right. Yes, of course Paul and I draw each other closer to the Lord." Sierra stated the words as if she were reciting the Pledge of Allegiance.

"Remember when we talked that night in the tent, and you said you were stuck on a steady diet of all your feelings and nothing else?" Randy asked.

Sierra gave him a look of vague recollection.

"I told you not to beat yourself up because you're a sensitive, emotional person," he continued.

She didn't remember.

"I still think you shouldn't beat yourself up because you're a sensitive, emotional person."

"And?"

"And watch your emotional diet."

Sierra leaned back. "That's the best you can do? You're not going to arm me with statements I can use on my parents?"

Randy shook his head. "The answer will come to you. On your own. Just keep talking about it. It'll become clear what you should do."

Randy's laid-back logic didn't settle with Sierra. What

did he mean, watch her emotional diet? The only thing she agreed with was that she usually did figure out solutions to her problems by talking them through.

Her challenge was to figure out whom she was going to talk to now that Randy had offered his insights but she was still stuck. Amy? Chances were Amy wasn't talking to Sierra anymore. Neither was Tawni—which was too bad, because on several occasions she had offered Sierra good advice. Plus Tawni would understand what it was like to be emotionally involved with a Mackenzie man, since she was so attached to Jeremy. How about Vicki? Sierra could talk to Vicki, not only about the Paul conflict with her parents, but also about Amy. Sierra decided to call her as soon as work ended.

Glancing at the clock, she realized her break would be over in three minutes. "I have to get back to work," she told Randy. "Thanks for your listening ear."

Randy grinned. "By the way, they paid us two hundred dollars for last night."

"Oh, Randy, I forgot to ask. That's great! You guys sounded so good. I was really excited about your big debut— opening for The L's, no less! The place was packed. I think it went perfectly."

"We had some trouble with the third song. You didn't notice?"

"Not at all."

"That's good." Randy appeared pleased. "How come I didn't see you afterward?"

Sierra drew in an exasperated breath. "I kind of got locked out. Vicki had my ticket, and when I went out to check on Amy, I couldn't get back in." She shook her head.

"I made such a fool of myself. I saw Amy walking to the parking lot with Nathan, and I thought he was forcing her to go with him, so I…"

Randy waited for her to finish.

"I can't believe I did this. I blew an air horn at Nathan and told Amy to run."

Randy's eyes grew wide. He seemed to be trying to stifle a grin. "Did Amy run?"

"No. It turned out they wanted to be together so they could talk. Now they're both furious with me."

"A little is good. A lot…"

"I know," Sierra said. "I went overboard again."

Randy slowly grinned. "There are melted marshmallows, and then there are kitchen fires."

"What is that supposed to mean?"

"You know, the Thanksgiving fire at your house. I just thought of it. Melting marshmallows is like a little warmth, and that's good. But too much of a good thing, and your whole kitchen goes up in flames."

Sierra ignored his logic. "What bothers me is that just last week it seemed everything had turned around with Amy. She, Vicki, and I had a great time talking, and the three of us planned to get together every Monday here at Mama Bear's. Now that's all gone up in smoke, to use your analogy."

"Maybe not."

Sierra glanced at the clock again. "My break is over. I'd better get behind the counter. Thanks again for listening to me, Randy."

"Any time." He reached over and gave her wrist a squeeze. "Don't let it get you down. It'll work out—Paul,

Amy, the whole thing. It always does. God rules."

"Thanks. I needed your encouragement today. And, hey, congratulations again on how everything went last night."

Just before Randy walked out the door, Sierra said, "Oh, and thanks for giving Vicki a ride home." A hint of curiosity touched her voice.

"Vicki? I didn't give her a ride," Randy said. "Warner did."

"Oh." Sierra turned and made an "uh-oh" face to herself. She couldn't wait to hear Vicki's side of this story.

As it turned out, she didn't get the scoop until Monday afternoon. Saturday night Vicki wasn't home when Sierra called. Then Sierra spent the evening furiously working on Paul's needlework and did the same thing again all Sunday afternoon. That evening the Highland House hotline was busy, and then she stayed up until after midnight to finish her homework. On Monday at lunch, Randy, Warner, and the other guys from the band sat with Vicki and Sierra at lunch, so Sierra couldn't gather any information from Vicki.

The talk around the lunch table and the whole school was about The Beet and whether Randy's group was going to keep the name "Three-Two-One." Randy said it just came to them at the last minute Friday night. Most of the group liked it. The others thought it was lame and promised to come up with something better for them.

After school, Sierra waited by Vicki's locker. When she finally showed up, Sierra said, "Okay, we need to talk. Where do you want to go?"

"To Mama Bear's," Vicki said. "Aren't we supposed to meet Amy there in fifteen minutes?"

430 🏃 Robin Jones Gunn

Sierra leaned her forehead against the locker. "I don't think Amy is speaking to me at the moment."

Vicki looked surprised.

Sierra gave Vicki a sideways glance. "I told you. There's a lot we have to talk about."

"Well, Amy's still talking to me. I think we should go to Mama Bear's as we planned. If there's a problem, we need to talk it through. That's what we all decided last week, isn't it? We missed out on our friendships this past year because none of us worked hard enough at talking things through when we had problems."

Sierra felt a knot in her stomach. She had experienced that same clenching sensation a lot the last few days. Something wasn't right. She was off track, but she couldn't figure out in what way.

Earlier that day, during one of her classes, Sierra pretended to take notes as her teacher lectured, but Sierra had really been writing a letter to Paul, telling him how much she wished he were here so she could talk these things through with him face-to-face. It had been good to talk to Randy on Saturday, for the sake of letting off steam. But Randy didn't have answers. Only vague quips about burning marshmallows and how she shouldn't beat herself up, since she was a sensitive, emotional person.

With Paul, she knew such a conversation would have turned out differently. Paul knew her heart. He would hear her words but still be able to read deeper, between the lines, the way they did with each other's letters. Paul would give her the right kind of encouragement and direction. He would know how she could convince her parents that her relationship with him was beneficial and how to move on with Amy.

As it was, Paul wasn't here. That was the downside of having an absent boyfriend. By the time he received the letter she wrote him today and answered it, Christmas would have arrived. By then, anything could have happened.

Suddenly, Sierra remembered what Uncle Mac had said about love being patient. She had thought she knew what that meant. Maybe she didn't understand yet. Maybe she needed to be more patient about Paul's being far away and more patient with herself and all her goof-ups. And maybe she needed to be more patient with Amy. She could follow through on that one right now.

Emerging from her reverie, Sierra adjusted the backpack on her shoulder, looked at Vicki, and said, "Okay, let's go to Mama Bear's to see if Amy shows up."

"She will," Vicki said confidently. "She needs our little circle of friendship as much as the two of us do."

seventeen

THE CHEERY BELL over Mama Bear's door sounded when Sierra and Vicki stepped into the bakery. The fragrance of gourmet coffee and freshly baked cinnamon rolls rushed to greet them.

"I love the way this place smells," Vicki said. "Do you ever get tired of it when you work here?"

"Not tired of it, but maybe a little immune." Sierra scanned the tables to see if Amy was waiting for them. She wasn't. And they were five minutes late.

"Do you want something?" Vicki asked, heading for the counter. "Some tea? It's my treat."

Sierra appreciated Vicki's generosity. After all, Sierra had borrowed five dollars from her dad on Sunday to buy enough gas to drive to the Highland House and to school. Tomorrow was payday, but by the time she paid back everyone she had borrowed money from, little would be left for Christmas presents.

"I'd like some peppermint tea," Sierra said. "Thanks, Vicki." Following Vicki over to the counter, Sierra greeted

Mrs. Kraus and then asked her, "Do you remember my friend Amy? Have you seen her in here?"

"I don't think so," Mrs. Kraus said. "It's been kind of busy, though."

She was wearing one of the Christmas aprons she had made for the staff. The red aprons had brown appliquéd teddy bears on the top portion. The teddy bears were wearing headbands with reindeer antlers, and they had red noses. The aprons were cute in a silly way. When Sierra wore hers on Saturday, it drew much more attention than any of Mrs. Kraus's other original apron creations.

"Did I tell you a customer on Saturday asked if she could buy my apron?" Sierra asked.

"No, you didn't. You told her yes, I hope?"

"I told her you made them, and she would have to ask you."

"That's a great idea. I could whip up a couple of extra aprons and hang them around the store. I think I'll do that this evening."

Sierra had a hard time imagining anything that required sewing being whipped up in an evening. Her needlepoint project was taking forever. And it wasn't turning out all that great. The more she worked on it, and the longer she stared at it, the more flaws she saw in it. The joy of the project was long gone.

Mrs. Kraus went to get the hot water for Sierra's tea while Vicki pulled out some money.

"Tell me what happened Friday night," Sierra said. "Randy told me he didn't take you home, but Warner did."

Vicki rolled her eyes and said, "Please, I'm trying to forget."

434 🦋 Robin Jones Gunn

"I would have called a cab rather than go anywhere alone with Warner."

"We weren't alone," Vicki said. "Four other people were crammed into his car. He dropped me off first. There's really nothing to tell."

"Yes, there is. Tell me why Randy didn't give you a ride."

"He already had Tre with him, and when it came time to leave, he didn't offer to squeeze me in."

"But Warner did," Sierra said, taking the small teapot and mug from Mrs. Kraus and thanking her.

"Yep. Good ol' Warner." Vicki smiled at Mrs. Kraus. "And I'd like a mocha latte with cinnamon."

"Our lives don't exactly seem to be working out the way we had planned, do they?" Sierra said.

Vicki paid for their beverages, and the two of them moved over to a table by the front window.

"Oh, I don't know," Vicki said. "I don't have too many complaints at the moment. I don't know why you should either."

"I've been a wreck," Sierra confessed. She slid her chair closer to Vicki so none of the other customers or employees could hear her. "I have this conflict with my parents that's hanging over my head. They're waiting for me to talk it through with them because when they tried to talk to me last Friday, I couldn't discuss it."

"Couldn't discuss what?"

"Paul. They don't like him."

"Excuse me? Would you like to try that one again? Since when did your parents stop liking Paul?"

"Since I started to write him, I guess. They have this way

of making their point without saying it outright, so we kids have to figure out the answer."

"That's better than how my parents handle it. They come right out and tell me everything I'm doing wrong."

"I think I'd rather my parents would do that with this whole Paul issue. I don't know what they have against him. Or against my being involved with him."

"Why don't you ask them?" Vicki suggested. "Your parents would tell you what was wrong if you asked them, wouldn't they?"

"I guess."

"Or is it that you don't want to know what they think?"

"I don't know. I just don't like living with this feeling that something is wrong all the time."

"I know what you mean. I felt that way when my relationship with the Lord was all messed up."

Sierra brushed away the thought that she might have a similar problem. She considered herself a strong Christian. She had been for years. What could be wrong with her relationship with God?

Then an afterthought floated past. How long had it been since she had spent time talking to God or reading her Bible? A long time—weeks. But she had been busy—very busy. Certainly God understood that. It didn't change anything. He still loved her unconditionally, and she was ready to defend her faith on a moment's notice. And she was working on the hotline. People who fall away from God don't volunteer to work on a hotline, do they?

The knot in Sierra's stomach tightened. She had ordered the peppermint tea because she knew it was good for stomachaches. Now she lifted the mug of steaming liquid to her lips and sipped eagerly yet cautiously. She wanted to be soothed, not burned.

The thought stuck with Sierra. That's all she wanted from so many of the things going on in her life. She yearned for a warm, comforting relationship with Paul. She didn't want to get burned or have her heart broken, as Amy had warned. Sierra wanted to have a calm, soothing talk with her parents without getting fired up and burning all the bridges she had built with them over the years. Her "soothe, not burn" thoughts even applied to Amy. She never wanted her actions to burn out of control the way they had Friday night.

"I don't think Amy is going to show up," Sierra said.

Vicki shrugged. "If she doesn't, I'll call her. I think it's important we don't all give up on what started between us last week. If Amy tells me she has a problem with you, you'll agree to talk it through, won't you?"

"Of course," Sierra said. She still felt foolish about what had happened at The Beet. What was it Paul had said to her when they first met? Something about her one day growing into her zeal. Obviously, that hadn't happened yet. She considered herself mature enough to leave home in June and move to Scotland; yet here she was, unable to keep her most important relationships in balance.

"And if you don't mind my saying this, Sierra, I think you should sit down and talk to your parents real soon so you can get this conflict about Paul settled."

"I know," Sierra said. She sipped her peppermint tea and found it brought little comfort.

Amy never showed up, which made Sierra feel even worse. She went home and crawled into bed. When her mother came up to check on her, Sierra said she felt as though she was coming down with something, and she didn't want any dinner. She slept fitfully for about an hour and then sat up, turned on the light, and finished her letter to Paul.

Is it that I'm too much of a perfectionist? I want everything to be just right. I want my friends to like me, I want my parents not to be mad at me, I want everything to work out and be peaceful. But right now it seems nothing is. Well, some things are okay, I guess. I don't want this letter to be a total downer for you. It's not like there's anything wrong. It's just that a lot of things don't feel completely right. Do you know what I mean?

Sierra stopped writing and sighed. She read the letter, beginning with what she had written in class. The whole letter was nothing but a bunch of words that rambled over the pages and went nowhere. Sierra crumpled it up and tossed the paper ball toward her trash can. That wasn't the kind of letter she wanted Paul to read on the train. Her crazy string of pathetic words was not what he needed for encouragement. Since that's what his letters brought her, Sierra knew her letters should bring him the same thing. She refused to let herself write to him when she was so distraught.

A tear pushed its way to the corner of Sierra's eye. "I can't do anything right," she accused herself. "What's wrong with me? I can't even write to Paul anymore. And my relationship with Paul is the most important thing in my life."

Hearing herself state her feelings aloud shocked Sierra. She repeated her words to make sure she had heard them correctly.

"Paul is the most important thing in my life."

That was a sobering revelation. Had Paul taken the place in her heart where God had always been? Years ago she had decided her relationship with Christ was the most important one and always would be. Sometimes, when she informed others that such was the case, her words carried a bragging tone, but she had confessed that and gone on. Her bragging hadn't changed God's place in the very center of the garden of her heart.

Now when she closed her eyes and tried to imagine her heart's garden, she couldn't see the Lord anywhere. Instead, she saw images of Paul. And it wasn't that Paul had forced himself into that place in her heart. She had put him there. She had also slowly but surely started to ignore God and had stopped spending time with Him. The hollow aching in her stomach began to make sense.

"Sierra?" Her mom called to her from the other side of the closed bedroom door and knocked softly. The door opened, and Mrs. Jensen stepped in, holding the remote phone in her hand. "It's Tawni. She wants to talk to you."

eighteen

"HELLO?" Sierra adjusted herself on the bed as her mother handed her the phone and left the room.

"Hi. Mom says you're not feeling well." Tawni's voice sounded sympathetic.

"I'm okay."

"I hope you don't have the flu. It's been going around here. They say it's pretty bad this year."

"I think I'll be okay." Sierra plunged in before Tawni had a chance to say any more. "Tawni, I still feel bad about saying the thing about Reno at the restaurant. I know it bothered you a lot. I'm sorry."

"It did bother me," Tawni said. "It bothered me more than it should have. I'm sorry, too."

Sierra felt that at least with this relationship she could begin to breathe a little easier. Maybe she should open up to Tawni and tell her about the revelation regarding how Sierra had made Paul too much the center of all her thoughts, feelings, and hopes.

But before Sierra could start, Tawni said, "I wanted to

tell you what happened today because I know you've been praying for me."

Sierra looked down. She couldn't tell her sister that she hadn't prayed for anyone or anything for many weeks.

"I received a phone call from Lina. Lina Rasmussen. My birth mother."

Sierra sat up straight, eager to hear all the details.

"She's a Christian, Sierra. She was so excited when she heard I was a Christian, too. And she's coming here in two weeks so we can meet."

"Oh, Tawni, that's amazing! And exactly what you've been wanting for so long."

"I know! I can't believe it all happened so fast. I was just telling Mom and Dad that she said my letter was shuffled to the bottom of her desk, and she opened it last Friday. She spent the whole weekend praying about how to respond, and then she called me. I just answered the phone, and there she was. It was a huge shock."

"For both of you, I'm sure. What does she sound like?"

"She sounds sweet, but with a little bit of an edge to her voice, if you know what I mean."

Sierra smiled to herself. She knew exactly what her sister meant, since that's the way Tawni came across.

"I told her I was modeling, and Lina said she modeled professionally for three years before she went back to school. Isn't that amazing?"

"Wow! This whole thing is amazing. You're going to love having a face to put with her voice now, aren't you? I mean, you found out her name and where she lived, then what she sounds like, and now you're going to get to see her face. I can't even imagine how excited you must be."

"Thanks, Sierra. I knew you would understand. You guys are the first ones I've told. As soon as I hung up with Lina, I called Mom and Dad. They're happy for me, I know, but they had all kinds of cautions and advice for me. I needed someone to be completely happy for me."

"I'm very happy for you," Sierra said. "This is a huge thing in your life."

"Thank you." Tawni sniffed quietly, apparently unable to speak for a moment.

Sierra filled in the silence by asking, "Do you still think you'll go to UNR in January? I mean, did you really want to take classes there, or was it like Wesley and the others suggested, that you were eager to meet Lina?"

Tawni sniffed again. "I don't know. A little of both, I suppose. I can't explain how important it is for me to see her. No one seemed to understand that. They all thought I was being psychotic to go there, knowing I'd be around her. But if she wasn't going to answer my letter, how else was I going to get what I needed? At least that was my thinking at the time. I know it wasn't real healthy. Everything has changed now that she's called."

"I'm sure she wants to see you as badly as you want to see her."

"I hope so."

"It's obvious she does," Sierra said. "Otherwise she wouldn't have called and made the plans."

"I hope you're right."

"I'll be honest. I haven't been right about a lot of stuff lately. But I think I'm right about this."

"Problems?" Tawni asked, inviting Sierra to open up.

She hesitated and then decided Tawni would be a good person to give Sierra her perspective.

"How can you tell if you're obsessed with something or someone?"

Tawni paused, then said defensively, "Are you trying to say you think I've been obsessed with finding my birth mother?"

"No, no. I'm saying...well, okay, I'll just come out and tell you. I'm asking about Paul. How do I know if I'm imagining the relationship is more than it is? And how do I know if I've weakened my commitment to the Lord by becoming too wrapped up in Paul?"

"If you're asking, then it means you've probably gone overboard."

"Great," Sierra muttered.

"Otherwise you wouldn't be feeling that there's a problem. It's the old theory of 'When in doubt, don't.'"

"How do you have a good relationship, then? I mean, if you really, really, really care about the other person, how do you not become wrapped up in him?"

"I've always been of the opinion that you shouldn't change what's important to you when you enter into a close relationship. You keep doing the things that make you strong and healthy, and then you have more to offer the other person. Otherwise, you slowly start to lose your life and your identity and become unbalanced trying to please the other person."

Sierra thought about Amy's saying she had given up all her friends and other interests when she began going out with Nathan.

"For instance," Tawni said, "I started to attend a Bible study on Thursday nights when I moved here. It's for college-age women, and I need it to keep me on track with the Lord. When I started to date Jeremy seriously, he kept asking me out on Thursday nights because he had that night open. It was one of the only nights he didn't have to work or go to class. But I kept my commitment to the Bible study because that time makes me stronger and provides me with more to offer in my relationship with Jeremy. Does that make sense?"

"Sort of. But Paul's not here. It's not the same thing."

"Yes, it is. Have you given up other important things in your life to spend time writing to Paul?"

Sierra knew the answer was yes. She just didn't want to admit to her sister that the main chunk of time she had given up was her time with the Lord. It was especially painful to realize that it had been the first thing to go. She still found time to shop, watch TV, and talk on the phone. But she never seemed to have any time left in her day to read her Bible.

Tawni continued before Sierra had to confess. "I guess what seems to be working so well with Jeremy and me is that both of us have other friends, activities, and commitments, and we stay involved with all of them. Then, when we get together, which is about once or twice a week, we have all kinds of stuff to talk about. We don't talk to each other every day. Have you been trying to write to Paul every day?"

"Not *every* day," Sierra said.

"Maybe you need to pull back and just give yourself one night a week that you spend a couple of hours writing to him. That's how it would be if you were dating. Or at least that's how it is with Jeremy and me."

Sierra knew her sister was probably right. Between the gifts she had worked on for Paul, the letter writing, and the daydreaming, not a day had gone by during the past few months that Sierra hadn't dedicated several hours to Paul.

"I know you're right," Sierra said to Tawni. "I'm just beginning to realize some pretty important facts about relationships. One is that I need to pull back and not write Paul so often."

"How often does he write you?"

"That's what's funny. I was sure he was writing to me every day. I really believed that. Then Dad started to quiz me, and I realized Paul writes only about once every week or once every two weeks. And his letters are never as long and detailed as mine are."

"That's a good measuring point for you," Tawni said. "It will be better if you respond to him at the same level that he's pursuing you. Believe me, I've seen far too many of my friends become lopsided in a new dating relationship and pretty soon the teeter-totter gets too heavy on their side. All of a sudden, Plop! There they are, crashed in the dirt and devastated because they had thought everything was going so well."

"I don't want this relationship to crash in the dirt," Sierra said quietly.

"I know exactly what you mean," Tawni said. "I can tell you from experience that the best way to nurture a relationship with a Mackenzie man is with patience."

"So I've heard," Sierra murmured. Sierra knew she

could do that. She could be patient. She could pull back and respond to Paul at the same level he was communicating with her. And she could definitely invest her time in developing other areas of her life.

"Tawni?"

"Yes?"

"Thanks."

A gentle pause enveloped them.

"I needed to hear everything you've told me," Sierra said.

"I should have made more of an effort for us to talk while I was there," Tawni said. "I could tell you were spending a lot of time writing to Paul and thinking about him even when you were with other people."

"I don't think I would have heard your advice. It's like Randy said, I have to talk my problems out, and when I hear myself explaining them, everything begins to make sense and I can accept advice. I know I wouldn't have been ready for advice at Thanksgiving."

"Randy said that, huh? I like Randy. Did he have any other advice for you?"

Sierra started to laugh. "He told me I was like the marshmallows on the sweet potatoes at Thanksgiving. A little fire makes them melt, a lot of fire and the whole kitchen burns down."

Tawni laughed softly. "That's pretty perceptive. What was that clan motto you showed me for 'Mackenzie' on the stitchery kit you bought?"

Sierra had the needlepoint right beside her, but she didn't need to read the Latin phrase. She had memorized it. *"Lucero non uro,"* she repeated.

"Yes, but what did you tell me it meant in English?"

Sierra stopped and stared at the square piece of needle-work. She finally understood the key to unlock the great mystery that had kept her stomach in knots. With her heart suddenly open to a new understanding of relationships, she repeated for her sister, "'I shine, not burn.'"

nineteen

SIERRA WROTE THOSE WORDS—*Lucero non uro*—in her journal that night after her phone conversation with Tawni. According to the last entered date, Sierra hadn't written out her thoughts and prayers in this private book for almost two months. Beneath the Latin words, she wrote a letter to the Lord as freely as she had been writing letters to Paul for so many weeks. She apologized for ignoring Him and invited Him to again take the center place in the garden of her heart.

> *I want to shine for You, Lord. I don't want that light to burn out. I want to have just the right amount of fire—light, warmth, and energy—in my relationship with Paul, but I don't want to overdo it and watch the whole thing go up in flames.*
>
> *From now on, I want to put You first and keep You first. Teach me how to do that, Father. My heart is Yours, and all the emotions You made that are stored there. I want You to protect my emotions and keep me from pouring them out too much at a time. Teach me to be patient with myself and with others.*

Sierra continued to write rapidly until her hand started to cramp. It felt so good to get everything out. The only ache she felt in her stomach now was from hunger.

After she finished her prayer-journaling, she went downstairs. It was almost nine, and the house was quiet. She found her dad working on the computer in the study.

"Feeling better?" he asked.

"Much. Pretty exciting news about Tawni."

"Yes, it is. We hope it works out and that she doesn't have unrealistic expectations."

"I think Tawni has realistic expectations of all her relationships. She'll be fine."

Mr. Jensen looked somewhat relieved at hearing Sierra's words. "You know what? You're right. Tawni has always displayed maturity and good insights. She makes wise choices."

Sierra felt like adding, "Not like your other daughter, who manages to make an emotional mess of nearly all of her relationships." But she didn't say that. She remembered Randy's admonition not to beat herself up for being a sensitive, emotional person. That's who she was. That's how she embraced life—with open arms and a vulnerable heart full of feelings. She could see how Tawni's self-discipline and sparing use of emotions had helped her to make wise choices over the years. Still, Sierra would rather be a bubbly bumbler than an aloof thinker like Tawni.

"If you and Mom have some time tomorrow, I think I'll be ready for our talk."

"Good," her dad said. "We'll talk after dinner. By the way, three e-mails are here for you."

"Really? Who are they from?"

"One from your friend in Switzerland, and two from

someone named Katie. Would you like me to print them out?"

"Yes. Thanks."

Sierra realized it had been weeks since she had written to either Christy or Katie. Those were two other friendships she didn't want to lose, but she sure hadn't made an effort to maintain them while she was going overboard with Paul. Sierra thought of the items she had bought at the gift shop that she had intended to use to create a tea party for herself. Since her funds were low for Christmas, she decided she would send the tea party to Christy just as she had sent the instant birthday party to Paul. She would have to think of something else creative to send to Katie.

Gathering the e-mail messages from the printer, Sierra went into the kitchen to fix her favorite snack. She called it "mush." It was a mug of smashed-up graham crackers mixed with just enough milk to make them wet and soft. For flair, Sierra added a handful of miniature marshmallows. Then she sat at the kitchen counter to enjoy her creation and to read her messages.

Christy's was short. She said she was learning a lot at the orphanage in Basel and that she and Todd had been keeping in touch through letters. Sierra remembered how concerned Christy had been that her relationship with Todd would suffer when she went to Switzerland for a year, since, in all the years she had known him, he had never written to her. Well, Sierra vaguely recalled something about a coconut Todd had sent Christy, but that couldn't have held much of a message. Sierra smiled to think that Todd was now writing letters to Christy.

Sierra also thought about how powerful letters could be.

Maybe that's why she had become involved with Paul so quickly. They both seemed to say in their letters what they probably would never say face-to-face.

She decided she wanted to reread all of Paul's letters with her new, clearer understanding of what their relationship should be about. She carried the e-mails and the little bit of mush left in the mug upstairs and went to the antique dresser in her bedroom. In the top drawer, she had placed all of Paul's letters, which were tied together with a ribbon. Flopping onto her bed, she untied the ribbon and read each letter in order. There were only eight letters and two postcards. She knew he had received at least twice that many from her. It made her wonder if he had saved her letters or tossed them once he had written back.

What surprised Sierra most as she read Paul's words with a less-expectant heart was that, though his letters were warm and personal, nothing in them indicated he was falling in love with her, as she had supposed. Clearly, he cared about her and was interested in her as a person, but nothing hinted at his being as emotionally wrapped up in her as she had become in him. Painful as that realization was, it was freeing, too. The truth was setting her free. She could continue to write to him, care about him, and even daydream a little.

Sierra turned over onto her back and stared at the ceiling. She had no way to judge the tone of the letters she had sent Paul. Had she smeared her emotions all over the pages in a fashion as messy as she had been processing her feelings? No, some of the letters, she knew, were calm. Some were newsy. Some were dotted with teasing and joking in response to experiences Paul had written about.

Again, Sierra remembered Randy's advice not to beat

herself up. She couldn't change the past. Maybe she had gone too far emotionally with this relationship. But now she knew that she could start over. She could trust God for this area of her life and be more responsible in how much of her emotional self she gave away. She had all kinds of hope for a fresh start.

As it turned out, Sierra didn't have an opportunity to talk to her parents on Tuesday. The chance for the three of them to sit down didn't materialize until Sunday afternoon. That additional time allowed Sierra to work through a lot for herself.

One night she reviewed her written goals for dating and her purity creed. She had some amendments to add now that she realized that saving herself for her future husband included saving herself emotionally as well as physically.

When Sierra and her parents finally sat down together in the living room Sunday afternoon, she brought her lists with her.

"I guess you both know I've kind of been going through a lot lately, and I guess the easiest way to explain things is to say God has been teaching me a bunch of important lessons. First let me say I'm sorry I've pulled away from you guys and claimed I was old enough to make my own decisions. I realize now I do best when I take advice and input from other people. I should have listened to what you were trying to say about Paul rather than being defensive."

"What was it you heard us trying to say about Paul?" her dad asked.

"I think you wanted me to see that I was getting too involved emotionally and that maybe the feeling wasn't mutual."

Her parents both nodded.

Sierra pulled out all her papers. She felt like a junior lawyer presenting her case. First she showed her parents two of Paul's letters, which was something she hadn't done before.

"You can see that he's interested in corresponding with me, which is what I felt I had to prove to you. But I also see more clearly now that he's not approaching our friendship on the same emotional level I've been operating on."

Sierra then handed her parents her revised list of dating goals and her purity creed. "The biggest thing I've learned is that purity and waiting in a relationship don't pertain only to the physical. The feeling happens first in the heart, I think. When I become emotionally involved, I'm giving away a part of my heart, just as physical involvement is giving away your body."

She felt a little embarrassed admitting these thoughts to her parents. Yet she knew it was the only way to make clear what God had been teaching her.

"I think I'm beginning to understand that the area of emotions might be a challenge for me, whereas the physical side, well, that's nonexistent. But I see now that I'm a pretty emotional person, and I seem to get way more into my feelings than other people do."

"That's part of your personality," her mom said. "Even when you were a little girl, you were more emotional than the other five kids. Don't be ashamed of that. God gave you that level of sensitivity as a gift."

Sierra nodded. She really felt as if she were beginning to understand that. "But like any other gift, I can misuse it, can't I?"

Her dad nodded quickly several times.

"So, being the free spirit that I am, I have to be more on my guard than Tawni or Wesley, because they approach relationships with more logic than feelings."

"That's a wise insight, Sierra." Her dad looked over the papers she placed in front of him. "But don't sell yourself short in the logic department. This is very well thought out. It shows maturity."

"Does it also show you that I have a better understanding of what's going on in my relationship with Paul and that I'm ready to continue the relationship at a lower level of intensity?"

"Yes," her mom said.

"Definitely," her dad said. "We trust you to take it from here. Thanks for being so open."

"Thanks for being so understanding."

Sierra picked up her pages and felt a sweet calm coming over her. This is how communication usually was between her and her parents, and this is how she wanted it to always be.

She returned her letters and other papers to her room and spent about twenty minutes halfheartedly picking up the endless clutter on her floor. She had homework to do and Christy's Christmas tea-party present to wrap and mail, and in an hour and a half she was supposed to report to the Highland House for her Sunday shift on the hotline. Tonight was going to be her last night until after Christmas vacation, so she didn't feel right about canceling on Uncle Mac.

Sierra made herself sit down and do her homework. When it came time to leave for the Highland House, she tucked her picture of Paul in her backpack. Last week she had mentioned it to Uncle Mac, and he had asked her to bring it so he could see it.

twenty

THE EVENING SKY HUNG LOW as Sierra drove to the Highland House. The dull gray hinted at rain, so Sierra had pulled on her black, rolled-brim hat. She had also stuck the needlework in her backpack, with the hope that she still might finish it before Christmas. Sierra had already decided that if she didn't, she would send Paul a homemade card rather than frantically try to find something else to buy him. The card would wish him well and promise that a little something would be in the mail soon. He would have to be patient.

Uncle Mac stood by the back entrance, holding open the door for Sierra as she arrived.

"Hi, how's it been going tonight?" Sierra asked, stepping into the warm room.

"Good. It's been real slow. I have you set up over here, on this phone tonight."

Uncle Mac led Sierra to a corner where a phone sat on a round, wooden table. He had been trying to fix up the phone areas to make them more private so that the counselors wouldn't feel distracted while they talked to callers. It was a challenge because the room wasn't very large, but it was clean and well lit.

"Here's the picture of Paul I told you about," Sierra said, laying her backpack on the table and unzipping the front pouch.

Uncle Mac took the picture and looked long and hard at his nephew. "How's he doing? Have you heard from him?"

"I received a letter right after Thanksgiving, but it was only half a page. I think he's still enjoying school, but he says his grandmother rations the heat in her house, and it's been cold."

Uncle Mac laughed. "That sounds like my mother. She has a heart of gold, but trust me, nothing is ever wasted when she's around. Everything is measured to the minute." Uncle Mac placed Paul's picture on the round table. It made the desk look as if it were Sierra's personal area.

"You know it's already Monday morning in Edinburgh," he said.

Sierra waited for Uncle Mac to make his point.

But all he said was, "You prefer tea, don't you?"

Sierra nodded, not following his logic.

"I'll be right back." He went out the side door that led to the kitchen of the homeless shelter. Sierra could hear the other hotline volunteer as he spoke on the phone at a table across the room. She recognized the points he was going through with the caller; they were from the blue section in the counseling notebook.

All the counseling topics were listed on the side tabs. In the weeks that she had been helping out, Sierra had grown more confident and had to refer only one of the calls to Uncle Mac because she didn't feel she could handle it. The rest were pretty much "by the book."

The front door opened, and Sierra looked up. Amy walked in with Vicki beside her.

"Hi," Vicki said cheerfully. "Will we get you in trouble if we talk to you?"

"I don't think so," Sierra said slowly. "I'll have to answer the phone if someone calls."

"That's okay," Vicki said.

"So, what's up?" Sierra asked.

"We went by your house." Vicki pulled up a chair and sat across from Sierra. Amy did the same. "Your parents said they thought it would be okay if we came by and bugged you."

Amy and Sierra still hadn't made eye contact. Sierra turned to Amy, determined to look at her until Amy looked back.

"Amy, I'd like to apologize about the air horn last week. I still can't believe I did that. I'm sorry."

Amy met Sierra's gaze. "It's okay. You thought you were helping me."

"I'm learning that sometimes I lunge ahead because of my feelings instead of thinking things through."

"We all do that," Amy said.

"Oh, not me," chimed in Vicki. "I'm completely calm...unless Randy happens to be around. Now, if only he would notice when *I'm* around."

The girls laughed.

Then with a sigh Sierra said, "It always seems to come back to patience, doesn't it? Uncle Mac tried to remind me of that a few weeks ago. You know, from I Corinthians 13: 'Love is patient.'"

Vicki and Amy both looked at Sierra, waiting for her to explain herself.

"I've realized," Sierra said, lowering her voice, "I need to take a few steps back in my feelings for Paul. I need to be patient."

"I guess it's my turn for a true confession," Amy said. "Nathan and I didn't get back together. But we did talk things through, and I think that was good for both of us. I just want to move on from here." Amy motioned to the sign above the bulletin board and read it aloud, "'A safe place for a fresh start.' That's what I want."

"Good," Vicki said, leaning forward and reaching for Paul's picture. "I'm all for moving on. Especially with the three of us. Everyone friends again?"

Sierra nodded. Amy nodded.

"This is such a good picture," Vicki said, examining Paul more closely. "Patient or not, he's going to love the picture of you in your green dress."

"Didn't I tell you? The pictures didn't come out. I ended up sending him one my mom snapped of me right after I gave the dog some water."

"Sounds glamorous," Vicki said with a laugh.

"I can't believe I didn't tell you. The guy at the one-hour photo place actually bought a copy to put up in their window."

"What did you look like?" Amy asked, taking the picture of Paul from Vicki and looking at it.

Sierra gazed down at her fisherman's knit sweater and

tilted her hat-topped head at her friends. "Just like this. I looked like me."

Uncle Mac came in with a mug of tea for Sierra. "Looks like I didn't make enough. Tea sound good to both of you ladies?"

"Sure. Thanks," Vicki answered for them.

Uncle Mac slipped back out, and the phone next to Sierra rang, causing her to jump. She reached for it on the second ring. Vicki and Amy motioned that they would be quiet.

"Highland House Teen Hotline, Sierra speaking."

After a fraction of a second delay, the male voice on the other end said, "Oh, is it now? I thought I was talking to the Daffodil Queen."

Sierra felt as though her heart had stopped. Both her friends noticed the sudden change in her expression and leaned forward.

When her voice finally found its way out of her mouth, Sierra whispered, "Paul?"

Vicki's and Amy's mouths dropped open.

"All I can afford is a three-minute call, so I'll talk fast. Thanks for your gift. I have your picture here in front of me. It looks just like you, Sierra."

"Th-that's funny," she stammered. "I have your picture right here, too. I brought it to show Uncle Mac." Sierra reached for the frame and looked into Paul's face as she listened to his words.

"And the party food you sent is going to be eaten tonight with great enjoyment. Very creative of you. Thanks."

"You're welcome. I'm glad you like it. I hope you have a happy birthday."

"Thanks. I think I will. Tell Uncle Mac hi for me."

"I will," Sierra said. "He just stepped out, but we were talking about you only a few minutes ago. Were your ears burning?"

Paul laughed. He sounded happy—content, yet slightly amused. "It's not quite dawn here at my grandmother's cottage, and believe me, nothing around here is burning."

Sierra laughed. "She's still rationing the heat, I take it."

"Let me just say I'm looking forward to my dash to the early train. It will make me warmer than I've been all weekend."

Sierra smiled but didn't fill the moment of silence with any words.

"Look," Paul continued, "my three minutes are about up, but I want to be sure to say what I called for. I want to ask a favor of you."

"Sure," Sierra said.

"Could you pray for me this week? I have exams, and I'm trying to make some decisions about the future. You're my prayer warrior, Sierra. Will you pray?"

"Of course," Sierra said.

"Great!" Paul sounded relieved. "I have to run. Thanks, Sierra. I'll write to you after exams. 'Bye."

With that, the line went dead.

Sierra felt a pinch in her heart. *You're my prayer warrior* echoed in her head. Paul hadn't said, "You're my long-distance girlfriend," "my kindred spirit," "my heart friend," or any of the descriptions she would have imagined even a few days ago. She was now, as she had been from the very beginning, Paul's prayer warrior.

And that was a good thing. That hadn't changed while she had been on her emotional spree, vividly imagining what she and Paul meant to each other. She realized now she hadn't had much time to pray for him while she was busy daydreaming about him.

"Sierra?" Vicki said cautiously, waving her hand in front of Sierra's dazed face. The phone, which Sierra still held in her hand, was emitting a sharp dial tone. "Was that really Paul? From Scotland?"

Sierra blinked. She hung up the phone and nodded.

"What did he say?" Amy asked, leaning forward.

"He received my picture. I think he liked it."

"That's good," Vicki said. "What else?"

"He asked me to pray for him."

Amy leaned back, looking disappointed in Sierra's report.

"He called me his prayer warrior."

At that moment something wonderful happened in Sierra's heart. She felt calm and warm. The wild emotional surges she had been experiencing quieted within her. Her prayers for Paul, offered from a clean heart, could cut through the thick fog of all her feelings and reach the very throne of God. And God answers prayers. She knew that to be true.

"Was that all?" Vicki asked. "Didn't he say anything else?"

"No," Sierra said, leaning back and enjoying the contentment that had settled on her. "That was all."

Then, with a gleam in her eyes, she smiled at Paul's photo and added, "And for now, that's enough."

Happenstance...
or God's Great Plan?

She's the bold, free-spirited type. She's cute, she's fun, and she's following God. She's Sierra Jensen, Christy Miller's good friend, ready for her junior year of high school! All twelve books in the popular Sierra Jensen series come together in four volumes to reveal the ups and downs of Sierra's incredible God-led journey!

Volume One: In *Only You, Sierra*, she's nervous to be the "new girl" after her family moves to Portland and wonders if meeting Paul in London was only by chance. Just when everything important seems to elude her, all it takes is one weekend *In Your Dreams* to prove otherwise. But even a vacation doesn't keep her troubles away in *Don't You Wish*.

Volume Two: Paul's voice lives in her memory, but now it's loud, clear, and right behind her in *Close Your Eyes*. With summer fast approaching, it is *Without a Doubt* bound to be Sierra's best yet. In *With This Ring,* she can't help but ponder the meaning of first kisses and lifetime commitments.

Volume Three: An exciting trip to Europe challenges Sierra to *Open Your Heart* to loving others without expectations. At the start of her senior year, only *Time Will Tell* the truth about Sierra's friendships. And in *Now Picture This*, she wonders if her relationship with Paul is as picture perfect as she thinks!

Volume Four: In this final volume, Sierra Jensen's only just beginning the roller coaster of adventures leading up to college. Join her in this exciting, challenging time of faith and fun!

Don't Miss the Next Chapter in Christy Miller's Unforgettable Life!

Follow Christy and Todd through the struggles, lessons, and changes that life in college will bring. Concentrating on her studies, Christy spends a year abroad in Europe and returns to campus at Rancho Corona University. Will Todd be waiting for her? CHRISTY AND TODD: THE COLLEGE YEARS follows Christy into her next chapter as she makes decisions about life and love.

CHRISTY AND TODD: THE COLLEGE YEARS by Robin Jones Gunn

Until Tomorrow • *As You Wish* • *I Promise*

SISTERCHICK® Adventures by
ROBIN JONES GUNN

SISTERCHICKS ON THE LOOSE!

Zany antics abound when best friends Sharon and Penny take off on a midlife adventure to Finland, returning home with a new view of God and a new zest for life.

SISTERCHICKS DO THE HULA!

It'll take more than an unexpected stowaway to keep two middle-aged sisterchicks from reliving their college years with a little Waikiki wackiness—and learning to hula for the first time.

SISTERCHICKS IN SOMBREROS!

Two Canadian sisters embark on a journey to claim their inheritance—beachfront property in Mexico—not expecting so many bizarre, wacky problems! But there's nothing a little coconut cake can't cure...

AVAILABLE NOW!

www.sisterchicks.com

More SISTERCHICK® Adventures
by
ROBIN JONES GUNN

SISTERCHICKS DOWN UNDER!

Kathleen meets Jill at the Chocolate Fish café in New Zealand, and they instantly forge a friendship. Together they fall head over heels into a deeper sense of God's love.

SISTERCHICKS SAY OOH LA LA!

Painting toenails and making promises under the canopy of a princess bed seals a friendship for life! Fifty years of ups and downs find Lisa and Amy still Best Friends Forever…and off on an unforgettable Paris rendezvous!

SISTERCHICKS IN GONDOLAS

At a fifteenth-century palace in Venice, best friends/sisters-in-law Jenna and Sue welcome the gondola-paced Italian lifestyle! And over boiling pots of pasta, they dare each other to dream again.

AVAILABLE NOW!

www.sisterchicks.com

About the Author

Robin Jones Gunn grew up in Orange County, California, where both her parents were teachers. She has one older sister and one younger brother. The three Jones kids graduated from Santa Ana High School and spent their summers on the beach with a bunch of "God-Lover" friends. Robin didn't meet her "Todd" until after she had gone to Biola University for two years and spent a summer traveling around Europe.

As her passion for ministering to teenagers grew, Robin assisted more with the youth group at her church. It was on a bike ride for middle schoolers that Robin met Ross. After they married, they spent the next two decades working together in youth ministry. God blessed them with a son and then a daughter.

When her children were young, Robin would rise at 3 a.m. when the house was quiet, make a pot of tea, and write pages and pages about Christy and Todd. She then read those pages to the girls in the youth group, and they gave her advice on what needed to be changed. The writing process took two years and ten rejections before her first novel, *Summer Promise*, was accepted for publication. Since its release in 1988, *Summer Promise* along with the rest of the Christy Miller and Sierra Jensen series have sold over 2.5 million copies and can be found in a dozen translations all over the world.

For the past twelve years, Robin has lived near Portland, Oregon, which has given her lots of insight into what Sierra's life might be like in the Great Northwest. Now that her children are grown and Robin's husband has a new career as a counselor, she continues to travel and tell stories about best friends and God-Lovers. Her popular Glenbrooke series tracks the love stories of some of Christy Miller's friends.

Robin's bestselling Sisterchick novels hatched a whole trend of lighthearted books about friendship and midlife adventures. Who knows what stories she'll write next?

You are warmly invited to visit Robin's websites at: www.robingunn.com, www.christymillerandfriends.com, and www.sisterchicks.com.

Excerpt from *Secrets,*

Book One in Robin Jones Gunn's Glenbrooke Series

JESSICA MORGAN GRIPPED her car's steering wheel and read the road sign aloud as she cruised past it. "Glenbrooke, three miles."

The summer breeze whipped through her open window and danced with the ends of her shoulder-length, honey-blond hair.

"This is it," Jessica murmured as the Oregon road brought her to the brink of her new life. For months she had planned this step into independence. Then yesterday, on the eve of her twenty-fifth birthday, she had hit the road with the back seat of her used station wagon full of boxes and her heart full of dreams.

She had driven ten hours yesterday before stopping at a hotel in Redding, California. After buying Chinese food, she ate it while sitting cross-legged on the bed watching the end of an old black-and-white movie. Jessica fell asleep dreaming of new beginnings and rose at 6:30, ready to drive another nine hours on her birthday.

I'm almost there, she thought. *I'm really doing this! Look at all these trees. This is beautiful. I'm going to love it here!*

The country road meandered through a grove of quivering willows. As she passed them, the trees appeared to wave at her, welcoming her to their corner of the world. The late afternoon sun shot between the trees like a strobe light, striking the side of her car at rapid intervals and creating stripes. Light appeared, then shadow, light, then shadow.

As Jessica drove out of the grouping of trees, the road twisted to the right. She veered the car to round the curve. Suddenly the bright sunlight struck her eyes, momentarily blinding her. Swerving to the right to avoid a truck, she felt her front tire catch the gravel on the side of the road. Before she realized what was happening, she had lost control of the car. In one terrifying instant, Jessica felt the car skid through the gravel and tilt over on its side. Her seat belt held her fast as Jessica screamed and clutched the steering wheel. The car tumbled over an embankment, then came to a jolting halt in a ditch about twenty feet below the road. The world seemed to stop.

Jessica tried to cry out, but no sound came from her lips. Stunned, she lay motionless on her side. She quickly blinked as if to dismiss a bizarre daydream that she could snap out of. Her hair covered half her face. She felt a hot, moist trickle coursing down her chin and an acidic taste filling her mouth. *I'm bleeding!*

Peering through her disheveled hair, Jessica tried to focus her eyes. When her vision began to clear, she could make out the image of the windshield, now shattered, and the mangled steering wheel bent down and pinning her left leg in place.

Suddenly her breath came back, and with her breath came the pain. Every part of her body ached, and a ring of white dots began to spin wildly before her eyes, whether she opened or closed them. Jessica was afraid to move, afraid to try any part of her body and find it unwilling to cooperate.

This didn't happen! It couldn't have. It was too fast. Wake up, Jess!

Through all the cotton that seemed to fill her head, Jessica heard a remote crackle of a walkie talkie and a male voice in the distance saying, "I've located the car. I'm checking now for survivors. Over."

I'm here! Down here! Help! Jessica called out in her head. The only sound that escaped her lips was a raspy, "Ahhgg!" That's when she realized her tongue was bleeding and her upper lip was beginning to swell.

"Hello in there," a male voice said calmly. The man leaned in through the open driver's window, which was now above Jessica on her left side. "Can you hear me?"

"Yeath," Jessica managed to say, her tongue swelling and her jaw beginning to quiver. She felt cold and shivered uncontrollably.

"Don't try to move," the deep voice said. "I've called for help. We'll get you out of there. It's going to take a few minutes, now, so don't move, okay?"

Jessica couldn't see the man's face, but his voice soothed her. She heard scraping metal above her, and then a large, steady hand touched her neck and felt for her pulse.

"You had your seat belt on. Good girl," he said. The walkie talkie crackled again, this time right above her.

"Yeah, Mary," the man said. "We have one female, mid-twenties, I'd say. Condition is stable. I'll wait for the ambulance before I move her. Over."

Jessica felt his hand once more, this time across her cheek as he brushed back her hair. "How ya' doin'? I'm Kyle. What's your name?"

"Jethica," she said, her tongue now throbbing. From

the corner of her eye she caught a glimpse of dark hair and a tanned face.

"I saw your car just as it began to roll. Must have been pretty scary for you."

Jessica responded with a nod and realized she could move her neck painlessly. She slowly turned her head and looked up into her rescuer's face. Jessica smiled with surprise and pleasure when she saw his green eyes, straight nose, windblown dark hair, and the hint of a five o'clock shadow across his no-nonsense jaw. With her smile came a stabbing throb in her top lip and the sensation of blood trickling down her chin.

"So, you can move a little, huh?" Kyle said. "Let's try your left arm. Good! That's great. How do your legs feel?"

Jessica tried to answer that the right one felt okay, but the left one was immobile. Her words came out slurred. She wasn't sure exactly what she said. Her jaw was really quivering now, and she felt helpless.

"Just relax," Kyle said. "As soon as the guys arrive with the ambulance, we'll get you all patched up. I'm going to put some pressure on your lip now. Try breathing slowly and evenly like this." Kyle leaned toward her. His face was about six inches from hers. He began to breathe in slowly through his nose and exhale slowly through his mouth. The distinct smell of cinnamon chewing gum was on his breath, which she found strangely comforting.

Jessica heard the distant wail of an approaching siren. Within minutes she was in the middle of a flurry of activity. Some of the men began to stabilize the car while several others cut off the door to have more room to reach her. Soon a team of steady hands undid Jessica's seat belt, removed the steering wheel, and eased her body onto a long board. They taped her forehead to the board so she couldn't move her head, and one of the men wrapped her in a blanket. They lifted the stretcher and with sure-footed steps walked up the embankment and carried her to the ambulance.

Jessica felt as if her eyelids weighed a hundred pounds. They clamped shut as her throbbing head filled with questions.

Why? Why me? Why now, right on the edge of my new beginning?

With a jolt, the men released the wheeled legs on the stretcher and slid Jessica into the back of the ambulance. One of them reached for her arm from underneath the blanket, and running a rough thumb over the back of her left hand, he asked her to make a fist.

Another paramedic spoke calmly, a few inches from her head, "Can you open your eyes for me? That's good. Now can you tell me where it hurts the most?"

"My leg," Jessica said.

"It's her left one." Jessica recognized Kyle's strong voice. His hand reached over and pressed against her upper lip once more.

The siren started up, and the ambulance lurched out onto the road and sped toward the Glenbrooke hospital.

As the stretcher jostled in the ambulance, the paramedic holding Jessica's left hand said, "Keep your fist. This is going to pinch a little bit." And with that an IV needle poked through the bulging vein on the top of her hand.

"Ouch," she said weakly.

She felt a soft cloth on her chin and lips and opened her eyes all the way. Kyle smiled at her. With one hand he pressed against her lip, and with the other he wiped the drying blood from her cheek and chin.

"Can you open your mouth a little? I need to put this against your tongue," he said, placing a swab of cotton between her tongue and cheek. "The bleeding looks like it's about to stop in there. Now if we can only get your lip to cooperate, you'll be in good shape. We'll be at the hospital in a few minutes. You doing okay?"

Jessica tried to nod her head, but the tape across her forehead held her firmly in place. She forced a crooked, puffy-cheeked smile beneath the pressure of his hand on her lip.

Jessica felt ridiculous, trying to flirt in her condition. Here was the most handsome, gentle man she had ever laid eyes on, and she was a helpless mess.

He's probably married and has six kids. These guys are trained to be nice to accident victims.

The full impact of her situation hit Jessica. She *was* a victim. None of this was supposed to happen. She was supposed to enter Glenbrooke quietly and begin her new life uneventfully. Yes, even secretly. Now how would she answer the prying questions she was sure to receive at the hospital?

As tears began to form in her eyes, she remembered that today was her birthday. Never in her life had she felt so completely and painfully alone.

THE GLENBROOKE SERIES

by Robin Jones Gunn

COME TO GLENBROOKE…

A QUIET PLACE WHERE SOULS ARE REFRESHED

Imagine a circle of friends who enter into each other's lives during that poignant season when love comes their way. Imagine the sweetness of having those friends to depend on as the journey into marriage and motherhood begins.

Meet the women of Glenbrooke: Jessica, Teri, Lauren, Alissa, Shelly, Meredith, Leah, and Genevieve. When their lives intersect in this small town, the door to friendship is opened and hearts come in to stay.

Perfectly crafted, heartwarming, and rich in truth, Robin's Glenbrooke novels have delighted half a million readers with their insights and charm. All souls looking to be refreshed are warmly invited to come to Glenbrooke.

SECRETS
Glenbrooke Series #1
Beginning her new life in a small Oregon town, high school English teacher Jessica Morgan tries desperately to hide the details of her past.

978-1-59052-240-0

WHISPERS
Glenbrooke Series #2
Teri went to Maui hoping to start a relationship with one special man. But romance becomes much more complicated when she finds herself pursued by three.

978-1-59052-192-2

ECHOES
Glenbrooke Series #3
Lauren Phillips "connects" on the Internet with a man known only as "K.C." Is she willing to risk everything...including another broken heart?

978-1-59052-193-9

SUNSETS
Glenbrooke Series #4
Alissa loves her new job as a Pasadena travel agent. Will an abrupt meeting with a stranger in an espresso shop leave her feeling that all men are like the one she's been hurt by recently?

978-1-59052-238-7

CLOUDS
Glenbrooke Series #5
After Shelly Graham and her old boyfriend cross paths in Germany, both must face the truth about their feelings.

978-1-59052-230-1

WATERFALLS
Glenbrooke Series #6
Meri thinks she's finally met the man of her dreams...until she finds out he's movie star Jacob Wilde, promptly puts her foot in her mouth, and ruins everything.

978-1-59052-231-8

WOODLANDS
Glenbrooke Series #7
Leah Hudson has the gift of giving, but questions her own motives, and God's purposes, when she meets a man she prays will love her just for herself.

978-1-59052-237-0

WILDFLOWERS
Glenbrooke Series #8
Genevieve Ahrens has invested lots of time and money in renovating the Wildflowers Café. Now her heart needs the same attention.

978-1-59052-239-4